STOLEN VOWS

Welcome to the

BLACK ROSE
AUCTION

In **STOLEN VOWS** by Sav R. Miller, a Rapunzel remix, a virgin is forced to marry a Mafia heir determined to kill anyone who touches her—only to flee from him the day after their wedding. But he's done waiting and has the perfect trap in mind to lure her back...

In **IRRESISTIBLE DEVIL** by Jenny Nordbak, a Rumpelstiltskin remix, a society darling is willing to make any bargain to benefit her family, but each deal draws her deeper into a dark and decadent world ruled by the dangerous man who's been pulling her strings from the start...

ALSO BY SAV R. MILLER

Be Still My Heart

KING'S TRACE ANTIHEROES SERIES
Sweet Surrender

Sweet Solitude

Sweet Sacrifice

MONSTERS & MUSES SERIES
Sweet Sin (novella)

Promises and Pomegranates

Vipers and Virtuosos

Oaths and Omissions

Arrows and Apologies

Souls and Sorrows

Liars and Liaisons

The

BLACK ROSE
AUCTION:

STOLEN
VOWS

STOLEN VOWS

SAV R. MILLER

sourcebooks
casablanca

Copyright © 2024, 2025 by Sav R. Miller
Cover and internal design © 2025 by Sourcebooks
Cover illustration and design © Elizabeth Turner Stokes
Internal design by Tara Jaggers/Sourcebooks
Rose frame art © Marek Trawczynski/Getty Images
Header illustration and design © Azura Arts

Published by Sourcebooks Casablanca, an imprint of Sourcebooks
P.O. Box 4410, Naperville, Illinois 60567-4410
(630) 961-3900
sourcebooks.com

Originally self-published in 2024 by Sav R. Miller.

Cataloging-in-Publication Data is on file with the Library of Congress.

Printed and bound in the United States of America.
LSC 10 9 8 7 6 5 4 3 2 1

*For the hyper-independent girls still waiting
for their villainous prince.*

FOREWORD

When we set out to create the Black Rose Auction series, we knew we wanted it to be luxe and dangerous and sexy! The premise is that there's an annual auction, presided over by the mysterious Reaper, where anything can be purchased for the right price. It's a place to make statements, to auction off the services of some of the world's most exclusive sex workers, to find priceless artifacts that the general public has only heard rumors of. Within these six books, you'll find dangerous men, powerful women, and a heist or two! Be sure to check out read.sourcebooks.com/blackroseauction or scan the QR code to get an introduction to all six authors and their work!

   Sav told us that she'd been dreaming up a story for the forgotten Ricci sister from her Monsters and Muses series, and we were instantly intrigued to see what she'd do with the unassuming, quiet sister. Naturally, the answer was to immediately throw Stella Ricci into *a forced marriage with a merciless Mafia don because it's a Sav R. Miller book, and we'd expect nothing less. But Stella isn't as quiet and unassuming as the rest of her family would have us believe, and she runs from her violent, possessive new husband who means* touch her and die *quite literally.*

He lets her go, allowing her to believe she's escaped, but he's really just biding his time, waiting for the perfect moment to lure her back. What better place to do it than at the Black Rose Auction? This Rapunzel remix has the most delightful threads of the fairy tale woven into Sav's gripping, sexy storytelling. You'll want to devour this book in one fulfilling sitting!

Jenny Nordbak and Katee Robert

CONTENT GUIDANCE

TROPES AND TAGS: Forced marriage, Mafia, virgin heroine, blackmail, boy obsessed, he falls first, billionaire.

CONTENT WARNINGS: Dubious consent, graphic violence, explicit sexual scenes, graphic vomiting, stalking, murder, depictions of domestic violence, sexual assault, child abuse, mentions of drug and alcohol abuse, choking, virgin sex, jealousy, light exhibitionism, and parental death.

NOTES: *Stolen Vows* is a complete standalone set in my Monsters & Muses world, so if you finish and are wondering about other characters, I suggest taking a trip to Aplana Island, starting with *Promises and Pomegranates*.

PLAYLIST

Throughout *Stolen Vows*, you'll find footnotes referring to songs that inspired a scene, might be playing in the background of a scene, or may otherwise enhance your reading experience. We encourage you to queue up these songs so they're ready to play whenever you see them referenced. For a handy Spotify playlist tailored to each book, go to read.sourcebooks.com /blackroseauction or scan the QR code and search for *Stolen Vows*.

ELEVEN—heylog

RAPUNZEL—John Michael Howell

MAYDAY—PmBata

CHOKEHOLD—Sleep Token

VENUS FLY TRAP—brakence

I LIKE IT WHEN YOU SLEEP, FOR YOU ARE SO BEAUTIFUL YET SO UNAWARE OF IT—The 1975

WE'LL NEVER HAVE SEX—Leith Ross

KEEP ME—Novo Amor

BEAUTIFUL THINGS—Benson Boone

SLOW DOWN—Chase Atlantic

Then Rapunzel lost her fear, and when he asked her if she would take him for her husband, and she saw that he was young and handsome, she thought: "He will love me more than old Dame Gothel does"; and she said yes, and laid her hand in his.

—*The Brothers Grimm*

STELLA

P apà thinks I'm nervous.

Given the gravity of the situation, I probably should be.

Unlike when my oldest sister, Elena, stood in a similar position just three years ago, there's no one waiting on the other side to steal me away from this life. No one stands in the shadows, ready to slit my betrothed's throat and whisk me to his private island, where we can live happily ever after.

My sisters don't even *know* this is happening. Not that they'd be able to save me if they did.

Any rescue from this situation rests solely in my hands. Or mouth, I suppose.

My tongue dips to the side, feeling for the small razor blade wrapped in athletic tape that's hidden between my lip and gums. It's the size of my thumbnail—not big enough to impede my speech if I'm careful, but still, a deterrent if utilized correctly.

Papà's grip tightens on my elbow. "Chin up, coniglia. If you ruin this for me, I'll have you shipped off to Sicily."

This isn't a new threat, but I still have no clue what the hell kind of atrocities await across the Atlantic Ocean. In the past twenty-four hours, I've had my plans to go to college and start a new life for myself completely uprooted, all in favor of fulfilling my father's twisted deals—what could possibly be worse than that?

I scan the front of the nave, past the rows of wooden pews, though the lights are dimmed and not much is visible. A few votive candles sit atop the altar, and a looming statue of our Blessed Mother is situated among the ornate wooden displays on the wall.

"Does my posture actually matter?" I mutter, careful to speak only from the unoccupied corner of my mouth. "He can't even see me."

"It's about *respect*. De Tore won't hesitate to kill someone he thinks is mocking him."

My blood runs cold at the thought. "He sounds so pleasant."

His fingers bite into my skin, as if trying to crush bone. "Shut it, or I'll save him the trouble and rip out your tongue now."

He moves forward, practically dragging me down the aisle.

It feels strangely appropriate to have Mother Mary watching this unfold. Given the sacrifices she made and the trust she had in the Father, surely *she* can understand my struggle.

Of course, she wasn't leaving one prison for another. Giving birth to the savior of the planet wasn't an instant death sentence—it was a freedom within itself, a gift she thought she was bestowing upon the world. The entire point of the religion is to be released from the shackles of sin and an eternity of hellfire, whereas I'm simply being given to another monster by the one on my arm.

Only damnation awaits me now.

Sweat pours down my spine, seeping into the fabric of my dress. Air scarcely makes its way to my lungs as we approach a tall, broad figure shrouded in shadows. Papà's fingers turn icy, continuing to hold me in a punishing grip even once we stop at the altar.

If I were naive, I'd think maybe his hesitation was laced with regret. That perhaps he was capable of feeling bad for forcing me into this.

But naivete is a luxury I've never been able to afford. Any regret of his comes from the knowledge that I'm his very last bargaining chip—the only daughter left at his disposal. Once he's given me over, the former don of Ricci Inc., Boston's once-premier crime syndicate, loses all remaining vestiges of his power.

My feet shuffle forward, my body eager to get on with things. Maybe if it happens quickly, the fear and anger coagulating in my gut like concrete won't feel so immobilizing.

Once we're alone, I'll strike. That way, my chances of escaping will increase.

I tug my arm, trying to remove it from Papà's grasp. His hand curls, his fingernails digging into my sleeve and the skin underneath.

His jaw clenches tightly as he stares over my head. I frown, shoving at him with my hip, but still, he doesn't budge.

"Let *go*," I snap under my breath, alarm bells chiming in my mind.

Suddenly, I'm the only thing standing between two made men, and if I've learned anything from being the youngest Mafia daughter, it's that being caught in the crossfire of any war means death.

These men are ruthless. It wouldn't surprise me if Papà went from trying to bargain with me to using me as a human shield, given what's gone on behind the scenes with me and my sisters. Elena got the emotional hits, while Ariana took the brunt of Mamma's physical and mental abuse.

Meanwhile, I was ignored by both parents—hidden away at events because my parents hated how boring and socially inept I seemed. Sometimes, they didn't acknowledge they had a third daughter at all.

For a long time, I convinced myself it was better that way, but now, I can't help feeling like I've made myself a sitting duck where my father is concerned. Perhaps if I'd not been so intent on getting out and going to college far away, I'd have been able to anticipate this. Maybe I'd have been able to escape.

"I've changed my mind," Papà says after a moment, still not looking at me. "I realize this isn't the money I told you I would bring, but I have a feeling you'll find my daughter a bit more interesting."

Fuck. It's too late. I should have run before we came inside.

A dark chuckle echoes from the altar's penumbra, followed by a stentorian voice that sends a shiver down my spine. "Where's the cash you owe?"

"Isn't a pound of flesh worth more to you?" Papà presses.

My bones grow hollow as I continue standing, struggling to break free from my father's hold. We've all heard the stories about the man in the shadows—how he possesses the brute strength of a feral animal and the patience of one recently caged. Though he's only a year older than me, the men in my father's ranks have feared him for ages, with rumors of his detachment and thirst for blood making him a terrifying threat to the tenuous hierarchy of the underground world.

They say he kills indiscriminately and has been known to feast on his enemies just to keep an edge over his opponents.

"I'm afraid you're overestimating your daughter's value."

Ouch. My head whips in the direction of that faceless voice, my brows drawing inward. "*Excuse—*"

"Stella's priceless," Papà cuts in, squeezing my arm so tightly that it tingles. "You have no idea how many offers for her I've fielded since she turned sixteen."

A long, drawn-out pause. Then: "What exactly are you presenting to me?"

He sounds much older than his nineteen years, and I wonder if the pressure from a life of crime does that to a person.

Do I seem older than eighteen to him?

Then, an immediate follow-up: *Why do I care how I appear to him? I'm not planning on sticking around anyway.*

Still, Papà doesn't let me go. A small sound of frustration blows past my lips, and I grapple with his fingers, trying to pry them off one by one.

He gives me a harsh shake. "The last daughter I have at

home. Take what every other man in the city wants, and we can discuss money later."

"How convenient for you."

"She's untouched."

At that, I recoil from Papà completely, releasing him and distancing myself as much as I can while he maintains a hold on me.

"My older two fucked up my plans before I could get them involved in their full duties for the family, but this one...I managed to keep her under lock and key. You want to be the first to ruin her? Be my guest."

The shadows ripple with dull laughter, and it almost feels like the sound is coming from the darkness with the way its owner is hidden. "What makes you think I'm interested in a virgin?"

"Oh, come on. You're young, De Tore, but you're a man." Papà's free hand comes up, reaching out before I have a chance to smack it away. He grabs my chin, curling his fingers into my cheeks so my mouth scrunches up. "Look at this face and tell me you don't want to know how red it'll get choking down your cock in an hour."

Bile burns the back of my throat; if he weren't pinching so hard, I think I'd puke right on the altar.

I wonder if this is the kind of thing my sisters endured in private. *How did they manage to get through it?* Five minutes into this show of humiliation, and I wish God would smite me right inside this place of worship.

"Coglione." The word—deadpanned in a language neither of my Italian American parents bothered to pass on to their children—is the first thing I hear outside of Papà's heavy breaths in my ear.

A second later, the silhouette steps out of the shadows. Slowly, as if savoring the anticipation of his audience.

Long, strong legs reveal themselves first, clad in tailored black dress pants. Then, a tapered waist and broad shoulders beneath the matching suit jacket and leather gloves pulled tight over big hands. Two tendrils of ink-colored hair brush against his tannish skin, and his sleek jaw is covered in a thin layer of stubble that looks coarse to the touch.

People call him *the Demon of Boston.*

In presence and stature, Leopoldo De Tore is massive. He practically takes up the air around us, vacuuming it from the altar space and leaving me gasping for breath as he stalks forward.

But it's the eyes I can't look away from—a smoky-gray color, like the clouds around a misty full moon. Outside of church functions, I've only seen him in passing at different occasions: funerals, weddings, holiday parties. As bad as his reputation may be, I've never been able to corral my interest.

I'm too busy admiring those eyes to notice when he raises his arm and nudges the barrel of a gun against my forehead.

LEO

didn't come here for sex.

I'm truly only here because my father convinced me to meet with Don Ricci. Given the elder mafioso's infamy, I can't fully fathom why, except that my father was convinced that I'd hand over any money after the meetup.

The only problem is that Flavio De Tore hasn't *really* been in charge since I was a kid, so I wouldn't give him shit. Complications with secret health issues stripped him of his ability to manage the De Tore family and its business interests, which ultimately led to duties being split between me and my uncle Gino.

My father's pride—and I suppose the nature of our world—keeps him from admitting his failing health, though. Deals are brokered from behind closed doors and big wooden desks or through a proxy who pretends Flavio is otherwise occupied.

Since I turned eighteen last year, I've been his most trusted soldier. The one he's grooming to take over when he can't hide anymore.

Ironic, considering the abuse I suffered until the day I became a legal adult, but still.

He gets the glory of leadership, and I'm in the trenches.

But the blood I've spilled on the family's behalf says I *earned* my title. I genuinely don't appreciate Rafael's assumption that I'm willing to renege on a contract now just because he's too chicken to hand over his financial assets.

Even if the girl before me is possibly the most stunning woman I've ever seen.

Like her two older sisters, Stella Ricci's beauty defies logic. Her cheekbones are soft, flushed even in the piss-poor cathedral lighting, as are the other angles of her face. Like they've been carved from clay instead of stone and shaped with the utmost care.

Rage courses through me as I watch his grubby paw mash her cheeks together.

Luscious dark-brown locks spill down her body, ending just below the gentle curve of her breasts in the hideous dress she's wearing. Its sleeves billow out above the ruched skirt, and I can't help wondering who the hell thought it was a good idea to use that as a seduction tactic.

I rake my gaze over her form slowly, then come back up to her head. *Christ*, her hair is magnificent. Soft and a little wavy. My fingers ache with the urge to reach out and run through the strands, maybe even count each one as they grace my pillow.

Two elegant brows border magnificent russet eyes, hooded as she stares at the gun pressed to her forehead.

She seems more annoyed than anything else. Not an ounce of fear shines in her gaze even though she's quite literally looking death in the face.

Perhaps she doesn't know any better. Rafael's daughters likely grew up sheltered, given his religious beliefs and the traditional tendencies of the Mafia, so I suppose her ignorance of who I am isn't out of the realm of possibility.

Or maybe she's already decided there are worse fates than death.

Attending the same church or community functions is the closest I've ever been to Stella. I was homeschooled from age nine, while the Ricci kids famously attended private all-girl academies. I've watched her, heard the rumors, and seen the things adult men write about her on the restroom stalls.

It's nothing like standing before the princess herself—like staring directly at the stars.

The closer you get, the clearer they become.

I focus my attention back on the matter at hand. "You want to fuck me, stellina?"

There's a split second of hesitation, and then she gives a short shake of her head.

The quiet, smart one. Headstrong and unsociable, whereas her sisters are bold and generous with their interactions. Accepted into some prestigious college on the West Coast, though attendance would be unlikely, given our world.

Perhaps that's why Rafael brought her to me instead: to keep her on this side of the country, where he can continue manipulating her for his gain.

"Hmm. You'd give me an unwilling lay?" The question is directed at her father, though I don't look away from her.

"I'm standing right here," she murmurs, pursing her lips to one side as she speaks, as if too nervous to open her mouth fully.

I smirk, amused that she'd say anything at all.

Something lights up in my chest, piquing my interest. The supposedly dull, studious girl is a stone-cold statue as Death whispers against her pale skin.

As if a wildcat exists beneath the surface of her skin, waiting for the chance to pounce.

"That you are." I wait for her gaze to lift to mine. "So, what exactly *do* you want?"

Her eyes narrow. "Right this second? I want to go home and sleep. In the long term, I'd like to attend Stanford, like I'm *supposed* to, and get my microbiology degree. Work in a lab for a few years, do some genetic mutation fellowships, and maybe cure cancer."

My brows hike up. I wasn't expecting an honest answer, especially not one so detailed. "I see. So, you're saying you have no intent to see this arrangement through?"

"I didn't say that."

"Are you always so honest?"

"I don't see the point in lying right now," she says with a shrug. "I can yearn all I like, but I can't change anything that's happening...right?"

Her eyes shimmer with that question, and it takes me a moment to formulate a reply.

"Tales of the Ricci sisters' backbones run rampant in the

Boston underworld. How unfortunate for me that I seem to have gotten the only one lacking in that regard."

"This is highly unorthodox," Rafael snaps, squeezing her harder. She winces, and I know it's not because of me. He glares in my direction, over her. "You shouldn't even be speaking until this arrangement has been carried out."

"The *arrangement* was you paying off what your greedy wife stole from my family."

"*Stole* is a bit of a harsh term—"

"Did she not trick her way into men's beds in exchange for favors and cash? *My* cash?"

I keep my gaze on Stella, waiting to see if the revelation changes anything for her. Either she's aware that her mother is a lowly vermin, thieving from the gardens of others, or she doesn't care.

"Anyone else would've already put a bullet between your teeth, Rafael. You should be grateful I have more patience than most."

"She did it because she *had* to," he rushes out. "Necessity drove Carmen to your finances; we were desperate, drowning in debts caused by our eldest turning informant. Surely, you can understand something like that. Have some fucking mercy, De Tore, for Christ's sake."

"How dare you beg me for mercy." I turn slightly, removing the gun from Stella's forehead to press it to her father's temple. "In the Lord's house. Don't you find that blasphemous? As if I'd ever grant you it anyway."

"I—I don't have the money," Rafael says finally, shaking

like a leaf. "Carmen has been…missing for the better part of the last few years, and there is no way to access anything without arousing suspicion. The goddamn Feds are still watching me, you know."

He blows out a breath, and Stella cringes again. I glance down, noting the vise grip he has on her arm, and irritation roars between my ears.

"So you lied to get me here. Then, instead of admitting you're a sniveling cazzo, you present me with your *youngest* daughter. She's not even your most valuable player." They both bristle at the proclamation, which fuels me further. My finger unlocks the gun's safety, and while fear registers immediately on his face, hers remains calm and collected. "Very disrespectful, Rafael. Someone needs to teach you some fucking manners."

"*Please*, I'll do anything, but…she's really all I have."

I'm not sure how much of his spiel is true, given the contacts he retains and business he still controls, even after the trial for his many crimes. If I hold it at face value, then taking his daughter will shift any of his remaining power to my hands.

But not for a simple one-time lay. That won't change anything except make her an open target for men in the city. If they don't already desire her for her looks, then they'll undoubtedly jump at the chance to mess with her father.

No, she needs to be something more than a fuck.

I glance at her dress, then back to Rafael, a thought unfolding in my mind. "Then let her go."

He sputters, beads of sweat pouring down the sides of his aged face. "What?"

"You're soiling my gift."

"Y-your gift? You're accepting my offer?" He exhales roughly, glancing between the two of us.

"No, but I'll counter." I wait, raising my brows pointedly at where he still holds her. After a moment, he releases her, and she stumbles out of the way with a grunt. "You want mercy, Rafael? Want me to pretend all this didn't happen? I'll need a bit more than a single night."

"Oh!" He brightens at that—the pig. "Yes, absolutely. You can have as many goes with her as you'd like."

My head turns, taking her in as she stands a few feet away with her arms crossed over her chest, watching silently. If she were as smart as they say, she'd be halfway out of the church by now while I'm otherwise occupied.

Not that it'd matter.

She wouldn't get far.

"I don't want *turns*," I tell her father, my pulse quickening as I lock eyes with Stella. "Your last-born *princess* will be my wife, and no one else will touch her."*

---

* RAPUNZEL—John Michael Howell

STELLA

glare at Papà as the priest rushes through our vows, barely stopping long enough for me to even utter, "I do."

Since Leopoldo's marriage offer, things have moved at lightning speed. A priest was called in, asked for our first names, and then jumped right into the ceremony.

I've hardly had a chance to process the fact that my father didn't drag me here solely to fulfill his end of a business arrangement but to absolve himself of apparent debts created by Mamma.

Marriage wasn't even where he wanted to start negotiations, despite what I'd naively come to this place believing. He used my inexperience as a selling point; while I've always known the people in this world to place emphasis on such patriarchal notions, for some reason, I believed the Riccis were above that.

I'm not sure why. Perhaps it was the ease with which they allowed my older sisters to continue their lives, uninterrupted. How they didn't care when I showed more interest in science and academia than the pageantry of being a Mafia princess and socialite.

Whatever the case, I'm in it now. My dreams of Papà coming to my aid are dashed as he continues to ignore me, bearing witness as the priest seals my union to Leopoldo De Tore.

"Y-you may kiss the...bride," the older man stutters, pressing his Bible to his chest.

Shit, shit, shit. I don't know why it didn't occur to me that we'd need to kiss to complete the transaction—perhaps because this is a farce, and I didn't think Leopoldo would care about such displays of affection.

Wishful thinking, I suppose.

I'm forcibly turned toward him as he steps slightly away from the priest. I don't know who moves me—whether it's Papà or one of the De Tore guards who revealed himself from the shadows—but in the next second, I go from wishing death upon my father to staring into the bleak gaze of the man I'm now legally tethered to.

I lick my lips, then curse myself when his gray eyes drop to track the motion.

He's handsome—in a lethal way. His cheekbones are severe, like two shards of glass, and his jaw is something you could sharpen a knife on.

When I was younger, I found him fascinating. He'd attend Sunday Mass like everyone else on our block despite spending the week indulging in every sin known to man. I'd watch him take a seat in the back, listen to the homily, and leave before the Eucharist. Almost as if he thought himself better than God.

Back then, I couldn't help but take note of his every move,

his every breath and attribute—like the leather gloves he seemed to wear at *all* times and the black hair he kept just a tad too long, which made him seem strangely boyish.

Something about him was intriguing. Maybe it was the way he didn't repeat or finish the Father's prayers, or how an aura of darkness seemed to follow in his wake despite the holy backdrop. It amazed me that evil like him could exist, even inside a blessed structure, and that his skin didn't seem to burn.

Maybe that was what killed my religious faith and made me store it in scientific thought instead—the realization that my parents' beliefs and stories held no weight in the real world. Evil would prevail whether God watched or not.

Sometimes, I'd catch him looking back and find myself unable to break away. As if he were a magnet and I were some precious metal drawn to him.

Mamma used to curse at me and say I shouldn't stare Death in the eye.

Now I can't seem to look anywhere else, though I do my best to ignore the tug in my stomach as he inches closer.

Death shouldn't be attractive to me.

Yet the razor blade in my mouth says maybe it always was.

My legs wobble, bringing me forward a step. Hints of amber and cedarwood drift casually around me, and I wonder if he donned cologne to mask something or if he smells like this all the time.

"Well?" he goads, cocking a dark brow.

Neither of us moves again. My feet feel like they're stuck in concrete.

I'm so fucked.

A smirk plays at one corner of his mouth, and he lifts a hand. The black leather glove is rough as he reaches to cup my cheek, sliding his thumb under my chin and angling my face upward.

"Just how far does your inexperience go?"

My pulse hammers inside my neck, and I think if he glanced down, he'd be able to see the vein trying to jump out of my skin. Luckily—or maybe unluckily—he keeps his stare on mine.

"Hello?" he prods, pursing his lips in amusement. "Have you ever been kissed, stellina?"

At my sides, my hands ball into fists. I can't seem to help myself. "Why is that any of your business? Afraid you won't compare?" The words come from my lips involuntarily, slicing through the tension between us. Only, instead of clearing the haze, it allows something heavier—*headier*—to fill in the gaps.

"*Stella*," Papà hisses from behind me.

Leopoldo just grins.

His grip on my jaw tightens, and something sinister flares in his irises. "Would you tell me if I was better?"

"Than the others?" I shrug one shoulder, feigning nonchalance. The razor blade slides up a little, and I press it back down with my tongue. I wonder if it looks as odd as it feels to talk with it there. "I'd tell you if you were worse."

"*Others*—plural?" Leopoldo *tsk-tsk*s, then glances at my father. "Does *untouched* mean something else to you, Ricci?"

I can practically hear Papà sweating. "I assure you, De Tore, I—"

With his free hand, Leopoldo cuts Papà off, and his eyes dart back to mine. They're cold, solid granite, yet a liquid heat bubbles at the edges, too. "No matter. I suppose the details are hardly important at this point."

His breath is minty as he leans in, pausing mere inches from my mouth. I can't seem to concentrate on one part of him: The gloved hand holding my head still and yet somehow burning me through the leather. The icy warmth in his gaze. The outline of his plush lips as they edge closer.

Everything blurs together in a cyclone of lust and resentment, causing me to remain immobile even after I realize he's waiting on me.

Still, I can't make myself move. I don't know if it's fear or embarrassment or just a deep-seated desire to do the opposite of what he wants, but as my body absolutely refuses to cooperate, I know it can't be self-preservation.

Leopoldo's likely planning where he'll dispose of my body with every agonizing second that creeps by.

He slides one hand back, threading his large fingers through my hair. For a moment, he focuses solely on the tresses, a faraway look in his eyes. "You're quite beautiful," he notes, finally bringing his dark stare back to mine. "Your hair is lovely. Complements you well."

My jaw slackens, and I try to ignore the furious blush crawling up my skin. I say nothing, unsure of what to do with that information.

"It's official, whether you kiss me or not," he says, gently tugging at my roots. "Might as well pretend you had some say in the matter."

Obedience is something ingrained in the women of this world. From birth, we're bound by tradition and violence, often born to men who care more about the business they conduct than the fact they're ruining their daughters.

Or maybe that's why they do it. Because to them, we're nothing but pawns in the game of life. We're valued, but not as sentient beings—as *property*.

The longer I stand here, staring at Leopoldo, the more I realize that coming here was a mistake. While I expected this outcome, I suppose a part of me was also hoping my father would try to stop it—or at the very least acknowledge the great sacrifice I was making by doing this for him.

Property doesn't make sacrifices, though. Its sole purpose on this planet is to increase the value of whoever owns it, and right now, these men own me in every way.

The only way for me to take back who I am is to force my own choices into the fray.

I can't necessarily change what's happening, but I can control how I react to it.

I can control how it affects me. What he gets from me.

So, even though I don't know what I'm doing, I reach up to grip Leopoldo's designer lapels and yank his face down to mine.*

---

* VENUS FLY TRAP—brakence

LEO

If I'd known Rafael Ricci's daughter was a witch, I'd have been a bit more hesitant before making her mine.

Sorcery is the only possible logic behind why her kiss leaves me breathless—that her lips hold a deep, sinister magic within, capable of beguiling even the most detached and heartless of men.

She's tentative at first, as if her bravado from moments before was a simple facade. Her lips don't open, though her fingers hold tight to my suit jacket and refuse to let me move back even an inch.

I don't try to pull away, shifting and sliding my dominant hand into the hair at the nape of her neck. That earns a tiny, almost-imperceptible grunt, which unlocks some bestial part of me. My other hand clutches at her waist, at her dress, as I desperately try to press closer.

A humming sound reverberates in the back of my throat as I discover she's just as soft and pliable as she looks. Her flesh, hidden beneath the hideous gown, molds under my fingers like it's been waiting all this time for my touch.

Even though I can't feel her skin, I know she must be the epitome of every wet dream I've ever had.

How many times have I imagined this very moment? I don't know if I can even admit to myself yet how long I've desired this woman.

Tugging on the roots of her hair, I angle her head and pry her lips open. She resists at first, her body twisting as she attempts to flee my grasp.

But I'm stronger and far more determined. One chaste taste isn't close to being enough, and I push through the seam of her mouth, stealing the gasp that puffs out of her.

She tastes like mint and a hint of blueberry.

My tongue flicks out, tracking and tracing, and my grip on her hip becomes ironclad with my sudden brutal desire. She trembles, fitting herself tightly against me as I commit her feels, flavors, and sounds to memory.

Something bumps against my lip; at first, I assume it's her teeth. Upon further inspection, I realize it's some sort of object, and for a moment, my mind snaps back to our situation. I don't break the kiss, but I do wait, seeing what happens—if she's losing herself the way I am or if she's intent on some other goal.

All she does is squirm closer, grinding into me, so I simply slide the object into my mouth and tuck it away before diving back in.

I'm spiraling fast, losing my hold on reality as our lips mash and teeth clash; we're somehow battling for dominance even though we both know there will be only one victor.

A strangled noise vibrates in her chest, and I swallow it, wishing I could feel it in mine. Then she's pushing, flattening her hands against my pecs, and shoving, trying to break this spell twining between us.

I release her hip and grab beneath her chin, not caring if it's the bite of my fingertips that makes her jolt or the way our kiss deepens exponentially. My dick aches in my slacks, and if we didn't have an audience, I'd be seeking immediate relief.

As if she can read my mind, she reaches between us with one hand and palms my length. I startle at the contact, then groan in my throat, nodding as if this entire situation is completely normal.

Her fingers are gentle at first, and it strikes me as odd how comfortable she seems groping me in front of her own father. But then she's curling those digits in, squeezing, and she doesn't stop.

She fists my cock as much as she can through the material of my pants, and a flash of pain shoots up the shaft. My nostrils flare, and I break our kiss with as much force as I put into prolonging it.

Our mouths are slick with saliva, our faces hot, and our breaths heavy. I keep my hands where they are, and she doesn't move hers. Inside my chest, my heart beats an irregular rhythm, and I take several deep breaths to steady it.

Shock pulses a sharp path through my central nervous system as my tongue re-situates in my mouth. Immediately, I let go of Stella, and she stumbles without the support.

"Well?" Rafael snaps from over my shoulder. He's standing with his arms crossed, glaring at his daughter. "Are we finished here then?"

I turn my head back toward Stella. She's holding her hand to her lips, and if I didn't know better, I'd think the glassy look in her russet gaze was from our apparent sizzling chemistry.

Everyone, the priest included, seems to be waiting for me to say something. Clearing my throat, I push my tongue to the corner of my mouth and then run my palms over my lapels, smoothing out the wrinkles made by my new wife.

My wife.

A surge of something bright and unfamiliar washes over me, though I quickly squash it.

"We're finished," I tell Rafael.

Hardly a minute passes before I hear him shuffle away, and then the front doors to Saint Paul's creak open. When they slam shut, it echoes through the nave, rattling the stained glass windows lining the walls.

Still, I keep my eyes on Stella. I'm not sure if I'm waiting for something or simply trying to put off the inevitable meeting with my father, but the reality of our situation slams into me like a broken brick.

I married the last Ricci daughter.

Now I just have to figure out what to do with her.

STELLA

Papà leaves us standing there with nothing more than a glare tossed in my direction.

He just...*leaves*. And even though it shouldn't hurt, at least not more than everything else he's done, I can't stop the sudden ache from lancing straight through my heart.

It's fucking ridiculous to give a shit when he never gave one about me, or my sisters, but the desire for a parent is intrinsic. I can't stop the wound from opening up and trying to swallow me whole.

They say a father's anger lingers forever. What about his absence?

Does that ever stop stinging?

Regardless, I don't have time to dwell on it. There are far more pressing matters at hand, like the fact my razor blade ended up in *Leopoldo's mouth*.

I tried to keep the kiss simple, thinking maybe he'd be satisfied with something superficial to give our witnesses. Clearly, I under-estimated the man.

As soon as I could no longer feel it tucked against my lip, I knew I was in deep shit.

When silence blankets the church, I wait for some acknowl-edgment or for him to take it out to inspect.

Instead, one of his guards—a tall, burly man with a buzz cut and bleak eyes—grabs my biceps and drags me away from the altar. I trip over my feet, trying to keep up with him as he rushes me out a side door and then down a narrow, poorly lit hall.

Only the sound of Leopoldo's distinct heavy footsteps alerts me to the fact he's following us.

We come to a fork in the path, and I'm shoved outside, through the door beneath a glowing **EXIT** sign. The guard's grip on me smarts, and I try to extract my arm before it loses all feeling.

"Plotting your escape already?" Leopoldo's voice bounces off the brick walls surrounding us, ominous with its echo.

We're sandwiched between three different buildings, the alleyways not big enough for a car to veer down, and it strikes me as an odd place to bring your new wife.

Unless you aren't planning on letting her leave.

The guard stops when we're a few feet from one wall, then yanks hard, turning me around to face my husband. As he strides closer, gloved hands shoved in his pockets, my mind flashes briefly back to our kiss.

Once he forced my lips open, it was all flames and no extin-guisher. Two angry mouths, each trying to push the other into submission, yet falling into oblivion instead.

For a moment, I lost myself in the heat of it all and forgot my plan entirely.

"Release her," Leopoldo tells his soldier, though he barks the order while staring at me. He's *always* staring at me.

The guard hesitates. "I don't think that's a good idea—"

"She won't run," Leopoldo cuts in, a slow smile spreading across his handsome face. "Will you?"

I quickly peek past both sides of him, noting the damp darkness we're in. Two paths open up on either side of the church, presumably heading toward the street, but there's no guarantee I'll be able to fit through them or that there aren't men waiting at the curb to grab me.

My eyes shift straight ahead, focusing on the slight knot in Leopoldo's nose. "Where would I even go?"

He waits, and finally, after what feels like a lifetime, the guard drops his hand. I rub at the area, certain that between Papà and him, the skin is already bruised.

"Why did you marry me?" I ask eventually, hoping to keep him talking long enough that maybe he forgets about the razor blade. Since he hasn't mentioned it yet, I'm not sure what his angle is. It wasn't *that* small, but perhaps he was too distracted to really notice. Or he's waiting for the chance to strike. "You could've easily told Papà no if what you wanted was money."

"Make no mistake, money is *always* my priority. But I didn't feel like traumatizing you further today."

"Don't pretend you did any of this for *me*. I'd probably be better off dead."

One of his brows rises. "How long have you been suicidal, stellina?"

"I'm not. It's a figure of speech," I say, shrugging one shoulder. "And my name is Stella."

"I know what your name is." He gives me an unreadable look, then comes closer. "I've been watching you, you know."

"Creepy."

He grins. "Every Sunday at church. You'd come in with your head down and sit between your mother and sisters, like a buffer between them. Eventually, you started to come alone, though you sat in the same pew like the dutiful little Catholic girl you are. Most people told me not to bother, because you were more interested in your books than anything else. But sometimes, I'd feel your gaze. You wouldn't look anywhere but at the priest or me, and it felt *good* when I had your attention. Like the Devil winning against God. I could never stop staring."

I roll my eyes, though something churns in my stomach at the idea of him watching me. Like a predator stalking its prey. "I don't know what you're talking about. I never noticed."

How could I have missed him looking back?

He moves forward again, standing so close that our clothes brush. "You wore these thick square-framed glasses that were almost too big for your face, but also made you look wise beyond your years. They once gave you a choir solo, and I remember questioning my faith because your voice was so perfect. You weren't given another after that, supposedly because they didn't want to highlight someone with your worldly curiosity. I've always wondered if that was why your participation seemed to become robotic. Is it possible you lost your way then, too?"

My eyes burn. "Science doesn't mix so well with creationism. I tend to have more faith in the former."

"As do I." He licks his lips. "What happened to the glasses?"

"Contacts." The word is barely a whisper, and I'm not sure he hears it.

Instead, I watch his gaze dip to where my hand still rests on my biceps, and I try not to get too caught up on the bombshell he just dropped on me.

Leopoldo De Tore noticed me? No one else ever has—or at least, they've never been bold enough to say so.

Even though it shouldn't, that knowledge makes my belly twist with some sort of perverse pleasure.

"Get her an ice pack," he snaps suddenly at the guard, who scurries away with his tail tucked.

I press my lips together, trying not to laugh at how pathetic I find the ranking system in the Mafia. How these grown men, capable of gruesome acts of violence, fall into line so easily depending on who has the most money or physical prowess—or the preferable bloodline.

"Something amusing?" Leopoldo asks, raising his hand to my face.

I flinch out of instinct, then freeze when he only tucks a strand of loose hair behind my ear. "No. I just find your trained rats vaguely entertaining."

The one *rat* still standing out here with us clears his throat, turning away.

"Funny that you, of all people, would call them *rats*, considering what the whole of Boston calls your family." Putting his back to the other guard, Leopoldo lowers his voice and tilts his head. "But I suppose that doesn't matter much now, does it? You're a De Tore as of five minutes ago."

A knot forms in my throat. This is the opposite of freedom—of everything I've worked so hard to get.

"*As* a De Tore," he continues, pulling away from me, "do you care to explain the grievous act of treason you committed by bringing a weapon to a business meeting?"

I watch in horror as he reaches up, slides two fingers into his mouth, and pulls out the blade. He holds it between us, and I notice that it's still wrapped in blue athletic tape.

My chest tightens, and I take a step back, bumping up against the brick wall. "*You* had a weapon."

"I wasn't hiding it, was I?"

"So, it would've been fine if I'd come to you with it in plain sight?"

He ignores the question, leaning back in. "Do you realize what would have happened if one of my *rats* knew you had this on you? If they thought, even for a second, that you were some kind of threat?"

I don't answer. I don't need to.

"It wouldn't stop with you either. Sure, I'd be forced to slit your throat with the damn thing—although it's so small, I'm not sure that would be very effective. But I'd send people after your family. Your papà. Your bitch of a mamma, wherever she is. Your sisters." His eyes almost seem to glow in the flickering overhead lighting, like talking about violence excites him. "Everyone you've ever loved would suffer, all because you were too stupid to wait and kill me with something you found at my home."

My thoughts are clouded. "Are you saying you wanted me to try?"

"I'm saying I thought you were supposed to be the smart Ricci daughter. Yet here I stand, disappointed again."

Closing my eyes, I suck in a deep breath and try to square my shoulders. "Just kill me then, Leopoldo."

"Leo," he corrects with a tsk. "And why on earth would I give you an easy out when punishment promises to be so much more fun?"

He pulls away, his breath no longer tickling my nose. I grit my teeth, bracing for the impact of whatever abuse he's planning to hurl, and he pries my mouth open again, pushing the blade inside. I don't have a chance to blink before he pounces, cupping my jaw and crushing me to the brick as he crashes his lips to mine.

His tongue flicks in, maneuvering the blade around, and his teeth scrape against mine. My head bounces off the wall, and he cups my skull with one palm, covering the spot as he continues the assault.

Mind swimming—drowning, rather—I press my hands to his chest to keep from falling completely into his embrace.

Heat stirs in my gut, sparking like a thousand little firecrackers. I jerk my head, trying to escape before the sensation can really take root.

Something coppery blooms inside my mouth, but I can't seem

to focus on the taste of anything but him. Bitter, like hard liquor and blood.

The hand in my hair flees, snaking a fiery path down the front of my dress. He bunches the long skirt in his fingers, inching it up until I feel a cool breeze brush my ankles. A sound of protest dies between us as he drags the fabric higher, exposing a sliver of my flesh to the moonlight.

"What are you—" I attempt to say around the kiss and blade, but suddenly, he's grazing the outside edge of my lacy pink panties while his tongue plays a wicked symphony inside my mouth.

When he finally yanks his head back, his breathing is ragged, and his eyes are wild. One finger skims over the seam of my pussy, above the lace, in a horizontal motion that makes my hips buck, immediately seeking more.

"Uh-uh." His voice grows as dark as the night air above us. "Be careful, stellina. Wouldn't want you to cut yourself."

My brows furrow as confusion weaves a tapestry in my chest—until a little scrap of blue fabric appears between his lips.

The athletic tape.

I swallow hard, and my tongue twitches inside my closed mouth, locating the uncovered metal blade sitting right in the middle.

My breaths grow short and staggered. God, I am an *idiot*.

"Stay very still," he says, even as his hand continues its exploration, dipping beneath my panties for a millisecond before sliding back out and drawing invisible circles over my pulse point. "Or would you like a mouthful of blood, wife?"

At that, my skin heats—and not just because he's tugging

aside the crotch of my underwear and stroking me. He does it lightly, as if testing the waters to see if I might protest.

I should. Oh my God, I should.

But I don't want to.

"Are you afraid of me?" he whispers, bringing his forehead to mine.

I shake my head.

"Interesting. Then you're wet because you *do* want to fuck me?"

When I don't reply, he releases a deep chuckle, swiping through my sensitive flesh once, twice, and a third time for good measure. His glove is rough, creating an extra layer of friction that I should find uncomfortable, but for some reason, it's kind of nice.

"Tell me to stop." His chest rises and falls rapidly. "If you don't want it. *This*. Otherwise, I'm going to take what your father offered me inside. Right here, while you do your damnedest not to cry out for mercy."

If I open my mouth to speak, the blade will almost certainly cut me. He knows it, I know it, and that knowledge makes the core of my being throb with heightened awareness.

Still, he said I could stop it. That he wouldn't continue if I didn't want it.

I could shake my head again or push at him. He's not restraining me, despite being plastered to my body. Dark, delicious tension coils tight in my stomach as he shifts, revealing the evidence of what I'm doing to him against my hip, and it's...powerful.

Surreal.

The Demon of Boston is unraveling because of me, and I find myself wanting to see his threads lying in a pile at my feet.

But before we can continue, a sharp voice cuts through the night air.

"Didn't I teach you better than to fuck your whores in public?"

Leo's hand falls away from my pussy, and it's alarming how much I miss the pressure.

He swallows audibly, but he keeps his forehead against mine as he answers. "Can't you wait in the car, like I asked?"

I can't see the intruder, but I hear his feet shuffle to a stop somewhere behind my husband's massive body.

"Forgive me for coming to see what the hell was taking my son so goddamn long. Collecting a debt and disposing of a body shouldn't take longer than an hour, max."

Leo's jaw clenches. He smooths his gloved thumb over my chin. "I've been occupied."

"Which leads me back to my original question: Do I need to step in because you're too incompetent to take care of shit?" There's a pause, and then the voice edges closer. "Who've you got back there anyway? You know I hate when you hide your pretty little toys from me."

My eyes widen at the nasty words, unease creasing my mouth, but Leo just shakes his head.

"Don't worry," he mutters, pressing one last kiss to my lips before pulling away completely.

He steps aside and turns to face the other man. Halfway between us and the church stands an older version of him with graying dark hair cut very short, wearing a loose-fitting designer suit. His right hand clutches a black cane.

Beside him is the pushy guard from before, though he lacks the ice pack he was instructed to retrieve.

I glare at him. *Tattletale rat.*

The man—presumably Leo's father—glances at me, and his eyebrows hike up to his hairline as he lets out a string of Italian. I don't know the language, but I can tell they're expletives.

"Leopoldo."

"Father."

"What the hell are you doing with Don Ricci's daughter?"

"Wife." Leo leans back against the brick wall and shoves his hands in his pants pockets.

His father blinks. "Excuse me?"

"Stella is not *his daughter*." A shiver runs down my arms at the finality in his tone. "She's my wife."

LEO

Normally, when a don takes a wife, she's been thoroughly vetted by his *consigliere* or the Commission." Uncle Gino sits on the arm of my father's chair and crosses a leg. "I don't recall you running the Riccis by anyone when you left this afternoon."

I lean back against the sofa in the center of my living room and throw my arms across the top. Through the condo's massive wall of windows, the Boston skyline glitters against the stars, and I can't help wondering where Stella is right now. After leaving the church, I sent her home with a guard to retrieve a bag of her things, and she still hasn't arrived.

Can't say I enjoy the waiting.

Shaking my head, I tear my gaze from the city and level my uncle with a look. "Well, I'm not the don, am I?"

"Ti sei rincoglionito?" my father demands, slamming his fist on his knee. He's seated on the edge of an armchair across the glass coffee table from me, anger sparking from him like invisible flames. "If I wanted to fraternize with the enemy, I'd take a trip to the goddamn Orsinis."

I cock my head at him. "You'd be dead before you even stepped foot in Corsica. Besides, Stella isn't the enemy. She's barely even a pawn."

"Your infatuation with her has always been a fucking problem," my father grumbles, leaning forward to stamp out the cigar he hasn't smoked since entering my home. "I should've known it wouldn't pair well with your impulsivity."

Ignoring that dig, I make a sweeping hand gesture, indicating to my house staff lurking close by that we're ready for drinks. Anna, a petite strawberry blond with a matching pinkish complexion, scrambles in quickly, setting a silver tray of cocktails before us.

Silence settles in the air while she's here, and she pauses, looking at me for direction. Despite being among us for a few years now, she's never been comfortable in the presence of De Tore men. Not that I blame her when they're sizing her up in the white polo and black dress pants she has on, as if she's their next meal.

The others hate cocktails, but I'm a fan of them, so I lean forward and snatch one up. Taking a sip, I bask in the raspberry flavor and give Anna a curt nod of dismissal.

I don't miss the sideways glance she tosses Frankie Galenti, who stands just behind the couch, his wrists crossed over the juncture of his legs. He doesn't return it or meet the gaze of the men here, choosing to remain close enough to react only if I need him to. He's my right-hand man, the only one I really trust in this room.

"We're worried about the way it looks." Ranolfo D'Avanzo, the oldest and most revered Elder, shakes his head, pointing his lit Cuban at me. "She's Italian, which is good, but we don't want to be seen as an ally of a known traitor. Not when we're trying to move in on former Ricci trade and protection sanctions, make them our own."

A few glances are cast in Frankie's general direction, at the blue diamond inked on the tanned skin beneath his left eye. The informant's diamond.

I smother a smirk at their discomfort. If his loyalty weren't enough to make them uneasy, the fact he's a former boyfriend of mine certainly would. Not that we were ever that serious; I've always been too involved with the family business to entertain deep commitments, and Frankie prefers a partner he doesn't have to answer to. Our relationship is better suited to the dynamic we have now.

"We can still do those things whether she's here or not," I tell them. "I fail to see the issue."

"It makes you look weak," my father notes. "Which makes *me* look weak. Like I don't have control over my own son. What else might I not have control over? How can I be trusted to organize deals with premium product, or to facilitate services that'll keep officials off our asses?"

I roll my eyes and get to my feet, strolling across the room to the connecting kitchen. A knife block rests on the breakfast bar, and I run my fingers over one of the larger black handles, removing it slowly. My back is to them when I speak again. "Please. Rafael didn't have the cash we wanted, and he said he didn't know where his wife was, so I made an executive decision and took what he valued. If anything, our *allies* will thank me for getting leverage on the bastard. Christ knows you were never able to."

They're barking up the wrong tree if they're looking for remorse over my taking of Stella. I won't apologize, and I won't give her back.

Not now that I know how terribly sweet she tastes. Like rainfall at night. A beautiful song in the midst of utter silence.

My father grumbles something to Ranolfo. I listen to them silently, the tip of the knife still lodged just inside the block, taunting me.

"You'll have to deal with your nonna then. Not to mention Aunt Regina and the cousins who'll look at a Ricci as a slap in the face," says Zeno Zorzi, a second or third cousin and the head of import oversight.

"They'll be mad that there was no wedding," my father adds. "Expect a formal ceremony soon, if your nonna gets her way. Lord knows she's been dying for the chance."

"Aurelio's gonna want bedsheets," Ranolfo points out.

My heart drums an unsteady rhythm in my chest.

Why hadn't I thought about all the bullshit I'd be dragging Stella through just to be with me? Aurelio's pushing one hundred, but since he's the former underboss to my great-grandfather, his desire to uphold tradition is generally respected by the rest of the De Tores.

There are rules in this world. Expectations.

But I didn't give a fuck about any of that when I had the woman of my dreams offered up on a silver platter.

I just...*wanted* her.

I would've put the De Tore family and business through hell to have her.

Uncle Gino, at least, sighs in resigned acquiescence. "My advice? Lock her up in this tower. Get her pregnant. If she spits out a brat for you, the other families will know you're serious and not just trying to pull something over on them. The De Tore lineage will live on, and you won't be risking our fucking necks because you wanted to show how big your dick was."

"I wanted a wife, not a broodmare." My dominant hand curls around the knife's handle, heat rushing to my face as rage simmers in my blood. "I will do with her as I see fit."

"Perhaps we should all do that," my father suggests, his voice cutting through the air with a screech. "Do with her as we see fit, that is. If she's just a business asset to you, I don't suppose you'd mind running her through more...rigorous tests to prove her loyalty?"

Zeno seems to slap someone on the back before he chimes in. "*Cristo*, of course! If you're not man enough to handle it, I'm sure any of us would be happy to break her in for ya. You're not the *only* one with De Tore blood."

Everything seems to freeze. A hush falls over the men, and my neck cracks as my head swivels slowly to the side. My shoulders come next, then my hips, and lastly my feet, until I'm once again facing my men.

A sinister smile graces my father's angular face—my face, though older and without the influence of the mother who abandoned us three weeks postpartum. Can't say I blame her, but she could've taken me along.

The chef's knife is heavy against my palm, and I touch the sharp tip with a gloved finger, twisting it slowly. "Is that a threat?"

My father lifts a shoulder, nonchalant. "Hardly, Son. Just a suggestion. There's no better way to ensure someone's obedience than to send them through our ranks. The men have a history of testing out new initiates, you know?"

One of them chuckles, and Stella's wide brown eyes and sharp smirk flash in my mind. I can still taste blueberry, mint, and a hint of blood on my tongue. I imagine that long dark hair of hers twined around my fist while I fuck her on every surface of this condo, then on others outside it.

Touching her pussy through my gloves was utter torture. I wanted to drop to my knees right then and figure out if losing my mind and marrying her was worth it.

Something in my gut says yes. If nothing else, I can tell the hellcat will at least be a great lay.

But she's *mine*. Not theirs to touch, or speak to, or even look at. I made the decision to marry her, to have her by my side, and no one will fuck that up. Not some random person, not Stella herself, and certainly not the arrogant bastard before me.

"What would you have her do first?" I ask, making my way back over to where my father sits. "Service you, then Ranolfo... maybe Gino too?"

Talking about her like she's a piece of garbage I happened to find on the street makes my brain scream, but I want to get a rise out of him. Want him to disrespect me in public so I can make him pay for it later.

I need this to be justified.

My father sits up straighter, snatching Ranolfo's cigar. "Well, Christ, I haven't thought about—"

"Or maybe you'd skip the foreplay and just take her all at once?" My blood sings a song of violent chaos between my ears, rushing so loudly that I can barely hear myself over it. "She's got three holes. I'd be willing to bet they're great for stuffing if she fucks anything like she kisses."

Unease ripples through the men. Ranolfo shifts away as I come to a stop in front of my father, crouching so we're at eye level. I drape both arms over my thighs, gripping the knife so tightly that my thumb goes numb.

"She's a hot piece of ass, isn't she? You wrinkly old fuckers are just *dying* to get your dicks up long enough to use her, aren't you? Show her what the De Tore family is all about?"

A half snort comes from Ranolfo, but my father remains stone-faced. He sucks on the cigar, then blows the smoke directly at me, unbothered by my taunting.

"You're getting awfully worked up over a girl you say you don't care about," my father says, his words laced with a tenor of disgust. "It's obvious you don't have the guts to run this business. Still too much of a petulant child."

He's an idiot. To Flavio, I'll always be a kid thrust into a role too big for him. Nothing more.

But perception is not always reality, and just because my father doesn't think I'm capable of doing something doesn't mean it's true. Even though he's *tried* to make it impossible for me, damaging my hands and affecting the mobility of one, I'm still better than him.

He flinches when my arm rises, and I flick my wrist so fast that the motion is a blur in my peripheral vision.

When the knife lodges into Ranolfo's thigh, inches above the knee, no one blinks. No one even breathes. The older man makes a garbled noise and sucks in a labored gasp when I pull the blade back out, warm blood pumping immediately from the wound onto his chair and the white rug beneath.

Frankie hovers near me, ready to spring into action if anyone decides to retaliate. He's got two Glocks at his sides, and I hear someone else release the safety on a gun, but I don't see where it comes from.

They don't shoot, though. I don't think any of them really know what to do, since they'd been expecting me to stab my father.

But that's why I went in the opposite direction.

Now they're afraid of what else I might do if I was willing to do *this*. Maim an Elder.

Fear shines in their eyes, and that's the way I like it.

I pinch the blade between two fingers, wiping off Ranolfo's blood. Then I pin my father with a look. "Come near my wife, and you die."

STELLA

Leo's goon drags me out of the skyscraper's private elevator, his nails biting into the skin above my elbow, which rests on my duffel bag. I'm not sure why I keep allowing men to manhandle me tonight, but I suppose the shock of the situation hasn't exactly worn off yet.

My fighting instincts are in hiding, and while I'd like to think they're saving their strength for later, it's getting to the point where I can't even lie to myself.

Not after letting Leopoldo De Tore defile my mouth behind Saint Paul's. I would have let him do more, too, had we not been interrupted.

The thought sours my stomach.

Perhaps a bout of temporary psychosis could be blamed if I hadn't seemed to enjoy his kiss so much, despite that razor blade cutting the inside of my cheek. Even now, my tongue slips to the side, gently roving over the pocket of skin it sliced through.

If I try hard enough, I can still taste the blood mixing with his saliva. I don't like the little thrill that races through me with the memory.

I'm shoved into a heavy metal door, and the force of my collision pushes it open, revealing an immaculate penthouse. Massive walls of glass frame the open area, highlighting the backdrop of the Charles River and the harbor beyond.

The numbing white interior screams emotionally distant luxury, which I suppose is fitting for someone like Leo. I can't help standing in place, afraid that moving around might taint the wide-planked hardwood floor with my presence.

In the living room, a woman dressed in a polo and black pants, with her reddish-blond hair pulled back and tucked under her collar, kneels on the corner of a white shag rug, scrubbing furiously. Across from her, a man lounges on a cream-colored leather sofa, one leg crossed over the other as he sips from a beer bottle, watching the woman.

His eyes cut to mine as soon as I'm past the door's threshold, and I try not to recoil from the depth of their coldness.

"Well, well." He glances behind me as the guard slips back into the hall, pulling the door shut behind him. "My son couldn't even be bothered to retrieve his bride, I see."

In my peripheral vision, I notice the staff member has frozen in place, her hands covering the dark red stain.

I gently roll my shoulders back and steel myself against Leo's father. "I assume he had more important things to do."

"Yes, I do believe I recall something about stopping by one of the clubs. Not sure what he could possibly be doing there, as we hardly ever conduct business in them these days. They're mostly kept around for our pleasure." A taunting grin tugs at his haggard face, and he takes another drink from his bottle. "Not to worry, though. If he comes home with lipstick on his collar, maybe he'll spare you tonight."

I know he's trying to get a rise out of me, but I'm not exactly sure why. Nor am I able to resist the bait. "Why should I need sparing?"

His eyebrows hitch. "What, a topolina like you? I highly doubt you're capable of keeping him satisfied, my dear. He'll eat you alive."

I'm not sure the wave of liquid heat that rushes through my limbs is the response he's expecting his words to elicit, so I ignore it. "You seem very interested in your son's bedroom habits. Is there something you're not telling me?"

A dark look passes over the senior De Tore's face. Slowly, he leans forward, setting his bottle down on the glass coffee table before him. He rises, still in the same suit as before, though I can't ignore the stain splashed against the lapel, as if rinsed but not thoroughly cleaned.

My gaze darts to the rug, where the strawberry blond resumes her furious scrubbing.

I've seen enough spilled blood in my life to recognize it easily, even from across a room.

For a moment, I'm stricken with panic—and not for myself, at least not immediately.

Where is *Leo?*

Given his possessiveness at Saint Paul's, I can't imagine he'd just take off without waiting to make sure I made it to his condo in one piece. Yet he appears nowhere to be found, and here his terrible father is instead, stalking across the room like he has only seconds to make it.

He's surprisingly quick, even while gripping a cane in his right hand. It doesn't seem to do anything but make him faster, and then he's standing before me, glaring down like he'd like to flay me alive before I can open my mouth again.

Hatred burns in his dark eyes, and something deep inside me knows it's not just me that fire roars for.

Maybe I'm not the only one stuck in this tower.

"If it'd been me at that church," the man says, his free hand whipping out to grab my throat and yank me closer, "I'd have carved out your lying, cheating father's tongue, then fucked you on that altar while he watched with blood pouring from his mouth. The last thing he'd have seen was me violating every virgin hole in your boring little body, and then I'd have fed him to you before ripping your heart out."

Fear rattles my rib cage, but I do my best to focus on his grip. It tightens with each word, constricting my airway, and I'm not sure how much longer I have before I pass out. My vision darkens at the corners, and out of reflex, my fingers claw at him, seeking a reprieve.

"But I suppose watching my son ruin you will be just as fun," he continues, leaning down so his face is a breath away from mine.

I watch as he comes even closer, thinking for sure that he'll stop eventually. That he's just trying to scare me.

His lips land on my mouth mere milliseconds later, dry and cracked as they attempt to mold themselves to me. I make a noise in the back of my throat, instantly jerking away, but he fists my neck even more and then shoves his tongue inside.

It's nothing at all like kissing Leo. That, even if driven by spite, lust, and a sense of doom, had at least been warm. Consuming. Like staring up at a night sky full of stars.

Kissing his father feels like falling into an abyss. It's a slow implosion, where you feel each molecule and atom in your body expand before nothingness swallows you whole.

I bite him the second I get a chance. He pulls back and slaps me, then runs his tongue over the seam of my lips, chuckling darkly as he finally lets go.

"Perhaps now I understand my son's keen interest in Rafael's youngest," he says, wiping his mouth with the back of his hand.

My stomach churns, and I stumble backward, ignoring the harsh sting in my cheek.

Clearing his throat, the older man smooths his hands down the front of his jacket and turns to the girl across the room. "Anna, tell Leopoldo I'll see him in the morning. Bright and early. We'll be waiting for the sheets at our unit on K Street." He looks back at me, dragging his gaze over my form, and tosses a sadistic smile my way. "Tradition is tradition. Arrivederci, topolina."

He leaves without saying anything else, though the film of disgust doesn't evaporate from my skin, even when he's gone. I rub my face, trying to erase the feel of him, and eventually, the other woman appears in front of me with an ice pack.

"Here," she says, pressing it into my palm. I didn't even

notice her leave the room to get it. "Sorry about him. He was waiting for Irene, the other housekeeper Mr. De Tore employs, but she was out getting groceries. I swear, it's like she has some sixth sense when it comes to that man, and I don't know if it's because they used to sleep together or what, but she's *always* leaving me alone with him."

I just stare at her. She spins on her heel, marching back to the stain. Gently lifting the ice pack to my cheek, I drop my duffel bag on the floor, watching as she tries with all her might to get the red out of the white fabric.

"What are you using?" I ask, the ice pack freezing against my heated skin.

She pauses, glancing up with big blue eyes. "Uh…club soda?"

I bend down and take the spray bottle, sniffing it. "You need a mixture of warm water and vinegar. *And* you shouldn't be scrubbing—you're just pushing the stain around. Blotting wicks up the liquid from the fabric without making the soiled part any bigger."

"Oh." She drops her hands into her lap, and her head falls.

"Also, you should probably be wearing gloves."

She doesn't respond for several moments. It takes a second for me to notice her shoulders shaking and that she's crying.

Eyes wide, I put the bottle down and hold my hands up. Mamma always hated when I told her how to clean things, and Papà hated if I corrected him when he got statistics and figures wrong. It's a wonder I haven't learned to keep my mouth shut, even now.

"Look, I wasn't trying to be a know-it-all—"

A sob breaks free from her, and she launches herself at me, throwing her arms around my shoulders. The force of her sudden hug throws me off-balance, and I reach behind me to keep from falling over.

"*Thank* you!" she squeals, her breath hot on my neck through her hair. "I'm new here, and the other guests Mr. De Tore brings by are *so mean*. If I mess anything up, they just laugh or spill something, making it even worse. One time, they broke a vase and blamed it on me, and Mr. De Tore threatened to dock my pay if it happened again. If I don't have this cleaned up by the time he gets home, I'm afraid of what he'll do to me."

She keeps sobbing, clinging to me so tightly that my neck starts to go a little numb. Awkwardly, I lift a hand and press it to her upper back, patting until she quiets down a bit.

I also try to ignore the fact she's touching me with bacteria-laced fingers. I don't know whose blood that is or what pathogens she's spreading, but clearly, she doesn't care.

After a few minutes, she finally hiccups to a halt, withdrawing herself from me. She wipes aggressively under her eyes, making them even redder as she sits back on her knees.

"Sorry," she mutters. "I'm just really excited that you're here, Mr. De Tore's wife! You seem really...good. Maybe you'll rub off on him, too."

I'm not sure how she can get a sense for my character when she's known me for all of three seconds, but I don't point that out.

"My name is Anna, by the way. I guess I should've introduced myself before I ruined your..." She glances down with a perplexed expression, as if she expected me to be in a wedding gown on my wedding night.

"Stella," I offer.

"Oh, I know who you are. Mr. De Tore's told us *a lot* about you. Mainly about how you're not supposed to leave the condo, but...other stuff too! Is it true you were accepted to Stanford? And that you got an almost-perfect score on the SATs? You must be, like, supersmart."

Only some of that is true. I bombed my SATs yet wound up with an acceptance letter anyway.

I don't admit that, though, because I want her to believe the rumor—that's what *I* want to believe still—and yet a smart person wouldn't be here right now.

Trapped in a tower, awaiting her villainous captor's return.

An intelligent person would have found a way out—or wouldn't have been in this situation in the first place.

So, maybe the years I spent with my nose in books, sneaking into the science labs after school, or studying above my grade level—maybe none of that matters.

At least not to fate.

It was foolish of me to believe my end would be anything other than tragic.

The front door of the condo swings open. "*Anna.*"

A tall, pale woman with black hair, dark eyes, and bright red lips juts her hip out to the side, glaring at the blond beside me as she appears in the doorway. She's got an armful of brown paper bags, and she's wearing the same uniform as Anna, though she fills hers out a bit differently.

I can't help admiring the striking beauty she emanates. Anna is innocent and young, whereas this stranger is...*alluring*. Fierce and unyielding.

Her presence feels much like Leo's, and I spend more time than I should staring at her.

Despite my situation, I feel a longing in my chest. One I haven't paid much attention to my whole life, aware that my parents would never have approved of an attraction to the same gender. To them, men were my only option, but I've always wanted more than that.

When this woman looks at me, though, that desire dries up. Like she's cutting it off with her own scissors.

"Help me bring up the rest of these bags and stop pestering the new resident." She directs the order at her colleague, who breaks into a wide grin and scrambles to her feet.

"Irene!" Anna runs over, pulling the new woman into a hug. A head of lettuce and a box of lasagna fall to the floor, and Irene grunts but allows the contact anyway. "You missed it. Flavio was here, and he was *awful* to Mrs. De Tore."

My nose scrunches up at that name.

"What a surprise. He doesn't have a decent bone in his disgusting body." The other woman gently peels Anna from her, bending down to scoop up the food. She glances at me, narrowing her eyes. "What? Are you planning to tell your new master that his staff uses premade pasta? It's a little early to be plotting ways to get us fired, don't you think?"

I frown. "Why would I do that?"

"Oh, please." She rolls her eyes, heading to the open attached kitchen, where she sets the bags on the marble island. "Every one of Leopoldo's paramours who steps foot in this place is the same: threatened by the existence of others, desperate to get him to change. Men, women, it doesn't matter—they always think throwing us under the bus will put them in his good graces, but it never does."

"Irene," Anna says, looking at me from the corner of her eyes. "Stella's not like that. Seriously. She's not like the others, and even though Mr. De Tore doesn't want her to leave the condo, I can already tell he's different with her. Maybe he's in *love*!"

Pausing, Irene seems to consider this. She stares down at the counter, her gaze so unyielding that she could probably strike a hole through it.

"Just think!" Anna bounces over, grabbing my arm and sighing wistfully. "Soon, you'll have a big ceremony with the whole family. Maybe you'll even honeymoon somewhere fun, like the Maldives! And then you'll come back and never have to lift a finger or worry about a single thing *again*. Mr. De Tore will take care of everything—forever. You can just relax and do whatever you want up here. I mean, you'll be expected to cook, probably, and make nice with the other wives of Mr. De Tore's business associates, but still. You'll be totally taken care of. Won't that be lovely?" Anna turns, beaming up at me.

God, she's young—possibly younger than my eighteen years—and I can't help wondering how she came to work for Leo's family. Inviting outsiders into the fold is generally frowned upon, yet it's clear that Anna has no real understanding of how terrible everything she just said sounds.

Suddenly, my chest feels unbearably tight, like a thousand-pound weight was thrown on me. My throat closes, cutting off my airway and stifling the oxygen from my lungs.

My entire future gone in the blink of an eye—the length of one brain-melting kiss.

Death would have been better than this, right?

Am I really giving up? Resigning myself to this fate?

This is all you will ever be good for. I can practically hear Mamma's mantra, beaten into us as kids about how we were meant to be wives and nothing more.

But this was never what I wanted for myself.

Never what I thought I deserved.

Eventually, Anna runs out of the condo to help bring up more groceries. I meet Irene's cold, calculated gaze through the columns separating the kitchen from the living room.

She gives a small half shake of her head. "There's no escaping now."

STELLA

t's late when Leo finally comes home. I can't tell exactly what time it is, but the moon is high in the sky, bathing my pale skin in its glow through the large window across from me.

I hear his footsteps, feel their vibrations against the floor. The mattress is soft beneath my body, which is *so heavy*. It feels as if I'm drowning in a vat of molasses, and right now, I don't think I'd mind.

The bedroom door opens, providing a sliver of warm light from the hall. It vanishes as quickly as it arrives, shrouding me in only the presence of the moon and city once again when the footsteps shuffle to one end of the bed.

His presence is overwhelming and cold, and I shiver under the plush throw draped over me, closing my eyes.

"I see Anna didn't bother dissuading you from raiding my liquor cabinet."

Cheeks burning, I squint against the harsh bravado of his

voice. "I picked the lock," I mutter, trying not to laugh at how slow my words sound. This molasses is *thick*.

Maybe it wasn't a good idea to steal his alcohol, but the girls left an hour or two ago, and I couldn't find anything better to do. At least some liquid courage would help me get through tonight.

"You're going to be a problem for me, aren't you?"

"Hope so." I turn my face into the mattress. It's so soft. "Where have you been all night?"

"Had a few fires to attend to. Believe it or not, some family members don't appreciate my getting married without their knowledge."

"Especially to a Ricci. Right? They all probably think I'm some traitor waiting for the right moment to turn you over to the Feds. Just like my sister did with Papà's assets."

"Your lineage might have come up, yes."

"So, are you going to send me back? Demand my father pay you some other way?"

Leo hums, and a second later, I feel him sliding the blanket off, baring my calves. Startled, I jackknife into a sitting position, pain shooting through my temples with the sudden motion.

He pushes my shoulders down gently, the way you might restrain a wild animal. My heart hammers inside my chest, so loud that I'm certain he can hear it in the quiet bedroom, though neither of us acknowledges it.

"Relax," he says, and my eyes close again on instinct. A second later, his fingers are on my ankle, lifting my foot off the bed. "I'm merely removing your shoes so your feet don't ache in the morning."

"And here I thought you were the evil sorcerer, locking me away in a tower for your own sick enjoyment."

"If you're already injured, torturing you is less fun." A soft thud echoes through the silence, followed by a second one.

I tense, although I'm pretty sure if he wanted to hurt me, he'd have done it by now.

"Don't worry." When his hands leave my body, an empty coldness is left behind. "I have no interest in drunken pussy. You're safe."

Safe. In my murderous, criminal husband's home. It's almost laughable.

"Even though it's our wedding night?"

He comes to my side, and the corner of the mattress dips with his weight. I peel an eye open, watching as he leans toward the nightstand, inspecting the bottle of scotch I smuggled out of his kitchen. Barely anything is gone, yet I can hardly see straight.

"Is that why you got drunk?" Leo asks. "Because you thought it would make tonight easier?"

Mamma's warnings from before she went MIA flash in my mind—how men only want one thing, and when you've given it up, your freedom is gone. Forever. There's no getting it back, no way to debase yourself lower than allowing someone like Leo— like Papà, I always assumed she really meant—to defile you.

But this is all my sisters and I were told we're good for. No number of trophies won at academic decathlons in school, or tests aced, or college interest would ever be enough to erase the fact that the Riccis sisters were brought into this world to serve our father's purpose.

Now I'm supposed to fulfill Leo's desires. My purpose is to be a wife and nothing else.

A wave of nausea washes over me with that thought. It bucks up out of nowhere, and I slap my palm over my mouth, heaving before I get my head over the bed.

Leo snatches a small metal trash can from the floor and holds it up just in time for me to retch directly into it. Dull brown acidic fluid spews from my mouth and nose, burning my throat on its expulsion. My fingers dig into the bed, clawing at the sheets as more vomit exits my body, and dizziness washes over me with it.

His gloved hand smooths over my hair, gathering its length at the base of my neck. It takes me several seconds of staring into the soiled trash can to realize he's holding the strands back so they don't get messy.

I can count on two fingers the number of times anyone's ever bothered to assist me when I was sick, and both instances were my sisters. Never a parent, and definitely never a man. No one like Leo.

My eyelashes tickle as I stare up at him. Sweat beads trail along my temples, tracking down the sides of my face, and I don't want to think about how unattractive I probably look to him right now.

"You have beautiful hair," he says after a moment, pushing some back behind my ear. "It's so long and soft."

Uh, okay then. "Thanks."

"It was the first thing I noticed about you."

"Tonight?"

He chuckles. "No."

My brain is too fuzzy to fully process the weight of that one word. Eventually, my nausea dies down a bit, and he leaves to bring me a bottle of water and a toothbrush. I try to sit up more, but everything spins as I do, so he takes the brush, squeezes a dollop of minty paste onto the bristles, and pries my mouth open.

I'm frozen in place, watching this brutal beast—the *Demon* of Boston—gently scrub my mouth clean. His dark eyes focus solely on the task and not the haphazard shape of my silky pajamas or the fact that I'm in his bed, of all places.

I'm grateful he doesn't ask why I came here and that I don't have to admit I wanted to be surrounded by his scent.

It's unnerving, his undivided attention. Up until now, it's presumably been concentrated on one goal—to get me naked and beneath him. Consummation, which is what's expected of us.

I'm not sure what to do with his kindness.

"So, why Stanford?" he asks, finally removing the toothbrush.

I blink, trying to grapple with the change in conversation. "What do you mean?"

"Well, there are plenty of prestigious colleges on the East Coast. Why pick one so far away?"

"Haven't you ever wondered what else is out there?" My question is spoken so softly, murmured between my partially open lips. "Not just outside of Boston, but *out there*. In space and beyond."

"Can't say the thought's ever crossed my mind, no."

"Of course not. Why would a king need to seek asylum elsewhere?"

It's a rhetorical question, and Leo doesn't bother answering it, but something shifts on his face nonetheless. "So, you're interested in space and beyond."

"I'm interested in anything that isn't *this*," I admit quietly. It's the first time I've said the words out loud, a confession that my interest in academia and intelligence is a front, because I'm afraid of what will happen to me if my mind is idle.

I seek facts and concrete data, or theorems on the principles of gravity and the makeup of the universe, because I don't want to be like my parents. Bound to their heritage and tradition, lacking any identity outside it.

With knowledge comes a certain level of responsibility, but there's also *freedom* innately attached. That's why I cling so tightly to my books, my peer-reviewed articles, and my scientific journals. Because of the possibilities within. The potential for expansion and experimentation that doesn't exist within the scope of the Mafia.

Not that I can tell Leo any of that. It's too pathetic. "In the past twenty years or so, demand for geneticists, specifically, has increased about forty-three percent. In the next decade, vacancies and positions are only expected to further increase. It's a steadily growing field, and I like the idea of helping to identify hereditary risks with the intent to benefit the masses. If I can do something like that, something that matters...I don't know. I guess that'd make everything else in my life worth it."

"How very practical of you. I'm impressed that you're able to spout statistics while inebriated." He folds his hands in his lap, seeming to consider my words. "And your father was willing to let you do this? Before he got the idea to sell you off, I mean. You did receive an acceptance letter, I've heard."

Heat scores my chest, and I don't reply. I *can't* reply—can't tell him that one of my only accomplishments in life was paid for by my oldest sister and her husband.

Without answering, I take the bottle of water Leo offers, ignoring the grittiness from the toothpaste as I guzzle it down. Breathing heavily, I wipe my mouth and look up at him, trying to see the angle—the reason he's asking. He's already taken my future away. *Is this the final nail in the coffin?*

"Why do you even care about any of this?" I probe after swallowing.

"I suppose morbid curiosity, stellina. I find that I can't help myself when it comes to you."

My pulse throbs against my neck. *What is that supposed to mean?*

He leans in, his face so close to mine that I can feel his breath fan across my mouth. I swallow hard, and my stomach flips over on itself as he brings his leather-clad hands to my shoulders again, rolling me.

When my back connects with the mattress, fear snakes down my spine.

"Obviously, college attendance now is out of the question."

Resentment boils in my chest. "I don't need the constant reminder that my life is over."

"The don's wife is always a target."

Tears prick my eyes. "You're not even don yet."

His dark gaze searches my face. If I lifted my head, I could probably kiss him. "That isn't the point. You're still mine, and being mine makes you a part of this."

"Then let me go," I whisper, a half-hearted plea I wasn't planning on voicing. Maybe desperation will sway him in a way nothing else has. "I—I won't tell anyone what happened. We can just pretend we never crossed paths at all."

"Pretend I don't know the exact shape of your mouth?" A gloved finger comes up, tracing the edge of my bottom lip. "That I haven't been on the receiving end of your absolute hatred, your violence? That I haven't had the divine pleasure of tasting you and calling you mine? I could never forget, stellina, and I could *never* pretend."

I open my mouth to respond, but nothing comes out.

After a moment, he leans in even more, and I feel his kiss before I can fully process what's happening. My limbs are sluggish, unmoving, but my lips return the gesture. It's soft, tender almost, and it sends a flurry of unfamiliar sensations through the length of my body—lust, warmth, and an undeniable shift in perspective.

Is this what it's like—being noticed?

Should it feel so good, coming from my captor?

"I've wanted to do that for too long," he murmurs against me.

My mouth chases his, seeking more. I can't tell if it's the alcohol or something deep within that I don't want to acknowledge, but I enjoy how his touch lights me up like a starry sky. I'd give almost anything to keep feeling that way forever.

"Rest," Leo says, pulling back and yanking the throw blanket to my chin. He tucks it in at my sides as if I'm a child, and I can't do anything but stare. "You don't need to worry about anything else."

A thought slides through my watery mind. "But we're supposed to...you know. Your father said something about tradition—"

"My father?" His voice is cold, and he freezes in place, still looming over me. "He was here?"

I nod.

"Did he touch you?"

Something hollows out inside my chest. A defense mechanism, though I know it's not to protect Flavio. Just myself.

Leo's jaw clenches, visible even in the moonlight. He reads past my silence, withdrawing his hands. "I see. So, that bruise on your face...that's not from stumbling in here drunkenly?"

My eyes widen, and I slide one hand out from the blanket, pressing my fingers to my face. It's sore to the touch, and I wince, not having realized until now that he hit me so hard.

For several moments, neither of us speaks. It's not until he repositions himself on the bed, stroking his fingers through my hair again, that I realize my eyes have closed. I open them, my vision blurring a bit, and see a flash of flesh as he moves away. When my gaze focuses, all I'm met with is empty air.

"Sleep," he commands from somewhere in the room. My body is all too eager to obey, shutting down as soon as the word leaves his mouth.

For the first time I can remember, I don't spend any time tossing and turning, dreading what's to come in the future. I don't lament over what I've lost or the terrifying monster who seems attached to the idea of keeping me.

I just *sleep.**

* I LIKE IT WHEN YOU SLEEP, FOR YOU ARE SO BEAUTIFUL YET SO UNAWARE OF IT—The 1975

LEO

Frankie glances at me and arches his brows. "This seems ill-advised."

"I don't remember asking for your opinion."

"As your right-hand man," he replies, folding his tattooed arms against the chest of his T-shirt, "I feel the need to warn you when you might be making a rash decision. Especially one that'll end in catastrophe."

Stepping around him, I walk into the office building on K Street, where the De Tores rent space to seem legitimate. Our counterfeiting and drug-running operations happen below the city, where fewer people are likely to stumble upon them, but this setup allows us to sail smoothly under federal regulations.

I'm not sure why we needed to meet here for this lousy tradition instead of my aunt Regina's or Nonna's, but after spending my night pacing outside the bedroom while Stella slept, I'm in no mood to argue.

You did this to her, Leo.

The guilt of bringing a helpless rabbit into a lion's den scrapes at my insides. It's not something I'm accustomed to, and I don't want to dwell on why I care so much about a practical stranger's well-being.

There's no time to read into it.

"Are you sure you want to go up there right now?" Frankie asks as we make a beeline for the stairs in the lobby's back corner. "Maybe we should hit the gym, do a few reps, and blow off some steam. Hell, there are probably half a dozen guys around the city you could rough up or fuck, even, instead of what you're about to do."

"I don't know what you're talking about."

He slides me a knowing glance. "You're three seconds from self-annihilation. Something tells me you're going to take it out on that group of men upstairs, and the lack of a bloody bedsheet indicates it has something to do with your wife."

The stairwell door slams shut, echoing around us as we ascend to the top floor. Despite Frankie being my closest associate and brief lover, it still grates how well he knows me.

"And if it does? You gonna tell me not to get worked up over someone hurting her?"

"She was hurt already? Jesus, she hasn't even stepped outside your condo."

"Monsters will find a way. Sometimes, they have keys to your place and nothing better to do than terrorize your guests."

He doesn't reply, likely catching on.

We've known each other for years, so I don't have to spell

everything out. I was the one who brought him in after he got into trouble with a member of the Commission, the overseers of Mafia activity in the States. They tried to frame him as an informant despite having no evidence to prove it. The diamond on his face was their doing, something to target him with, and now no one in Boston wants to come within three feet of Frankie.

So I keep him at my side. Where I can watch him closely, but also so others are less likely to approach me.

Besides, I've never been one to play by the rules of our family. Especially considering the majority of them are vile snakes, waiting to betray one another.

They're just usually better at hiding it.

Upstairs, the De Tore office is the last door at the end of the hallway. Freelance contractors, tax specialists, and occasionally mediators work on this floor, again giving us a film of legitimacy when investigators eventually come sniffing around.

Half of Boston's police force used to be on Ricci's payroll, and now no one knows who they can trust, so in general, we keep everything in this building aboveboard.

My father sits at the head of a long wooden conference table with a backdrop of windows behind him, like a false king overseeing a kingdom he doesn't deserve. Gino and Zeno flank him on either side while the rest of the chairs are filled with other relatives and associates, all here for the proof that I fucked my wife last night.

Proof they won't be getting—not now and not ever.

"Ah, Leopoldo, you're here. Wonderful. We can—"

The first shot leaves my pistol before my father can finish his sentence. Everyone watches the bullet whiz straight past his head, buzzing a path through the graying hair above his ear before it lodges into the wall. Blood trickles down the side of his face, dripping from his chin, and he reaches up with a stunned expression, pressing his index finger to the droplet.

Shock immobilizes the room.

"I warned you, didn't I?" My voice is hard as steel, unrecognizable as rage powers through my veins, reigniting when I think of a drunken Stella in my bed last night. How she didn't seem to notice the bruise until I pointed it out, which must mean she'd been caught off guard when it happened.

Leaning back in his chair, my father gives me a resigned look. "Don't you want to know if she deserved it?"

The second shot fires without me fully focusing, and it goes over his head, piercing the window behind him. A hole forms in the glass, and fissures crack around it, framing the sun in the sky.

"I told you not to touch her." My entire body is on fire as I edge closer to the table, noting in my peripheral vision the few chairs scooting back. I feel Frankie hovering close by, probably assessing the situation and trying to decide if he should intervene.

I'll kill him first if he does.

A sadistic chuckle comes from my father. "I knew she'd make you soft. You've had your eyes on her for years, and you've just been waiting for an opportunity to drag her into the fold. Did you honestly think it was going to be so easy, cazzo? That I'd let you bring Ricci filth into a world I've spent my entire life strengthening, just so she could fucking ruin it all?"

Gino rolls his eyes at my father's dramatics but says nothing.

My fingers flex, my nondominant hand aching with the effort it takes to curl inside my leather glove. A painful, unyielding reminder of just how my father "strengthened" the De Tore family—by abusing me, making me an agent of his chaos, and trying to keep his title anyway.

As if the things we've accomplished—the allies, the new business products and protection contracts, the contact points with premier dealers in the harbor—were *his* doing.

When I was young, he'd slice my hands open with whatever sharp object was within reach: a broken beer bottle, a butcher's knife, a box cutter—anything he could wield easily and use to carve me up. But only on the palm, where it'd be easiest to hide with bandages.

Sometimes, he'd just hold the fresh cuts in an open flame. I hated the fireplace in my childhood home for that reason.

Friends and family thought I was sick or clumsy since I always came around with my hands bandaged. The damage was worse on my left palm than the right, because my father didn't want me needing too much assistance for simple, everyday tasks. Nor did he want to arouse suspicion.

The problem was he started grooming me to be his muscle—the intimidator who'd convince people to do his bidding by sheer force. Even at a young age, with one hand's mobility compromised, my impulsivity and bloodlust were insatiable.

I was everything he'd never be, and that only drove me to do *more*.

I wanted his fear. I wanted *everyone's* fear so I'd never be in a position to suffer again.

But even when you gain the upper hand, you never lose the feeling of vulnerability. You don't forget what it was like when you were helpless.

You never forget who made you feel that way.

The third bullet leaves the gun before I answer my father, the popping sound deafening in the ensuing silence. Everything unfolds in slow motion after that: Crimson springs to stain the shoulder of his crisp white dress shirt, his hand moves to cover that spot, and blood seeps between his fingers. Delightful agony twists his face, heightening as I round the table.

A river roars between my ears, drowning out the others' shouts of disapproval. At least one Elder draws their own gun—though, once again, nobody shoots. I can't help wondering if they react out of a sense of duty and secretly want to see Flavio suffer as much as I do.

My father lets out a string of vulgar Italian phrases when I grab his shoulder, gently digging two fingers into the gaping, gushing wound there. Warm flesh and muscle give way with the pressure as more blood pumps from the hole, soaking his sleeve and the carpet beneath.

Maybe this wasn't the best idea, but it doesn't matter now. Sure, the eyes of our men are on me, judging, even if they don't have the balls to act. If I kill my father here, I'll have to kill all of them, too, just to keep up appearances with the De Tores who aren't here.

To pass this off to the rest of the family and business partners as someone else's doing, we'd need more than just Frankie and me as witnesses. We'd need an established alibi.

Time. If I want this organization to crash and burn, to pay for this grievance against me, I can't do it all right this second. Just because no one's made a move to stop me yet doesn't mean they'll let chaos reign forever; even made men have their limits, and bloodshed isn't typically what they opt for when there are other potential solutions.

So, even though every fiber of my being screams in protest, I reel myself in a bit, putting a forceful pause on the spiral my mind drifted into, thinking about my father's hands on my wife, touching her, *hurting* her.

This is only the beginning. Now that he knows what it'll do to me, he won't stop.

I thought keeping her locked away in a tower was the safest option, but I'm afraid it's only made her a sitting duck.

"Don't be stupid," my father grits out, his breathing labored. He glares up at me, a few strands of sweat-slicked hair falling into his eyes. "You keep on like this, and you'll lose every ounce of support you have. The Elders won't put up with someone who can't control himself. Think about what you're throwing away— and for an ugly, boring Ricci slut, no less."

My resistance wears thin. I push my fingers deeper until I feel bone beneath my glove. "Aw, what's the matter, old man? She didn't accept your slimy advances? Had to hit her to make yourself feel better?"

With my dominant hand, I press the mouth of the gun to the top of his thigh, pulling the trigger before he answers. A blood-curdling noise chokes out of his throat, and his eyes roll to the back of his head briefly; he refocuses as the conference room erupts into shouts and threats, the other associates now squabbling with one another or fleeing.

My father's sanguineous smile greets me as I lean down, smashing the pistol into the fresh wound, watching as blood pumps from the area.

He spits, painting my collar and face red. "Guess I should've fucked her right then and there. You always did learn lessons the hard way."

"Wonder where I got that from."

He snorts, and more bright red liquid spews from his nose. "Blame me all you want, Son, but killing me won't end this for you. There will always be someone ready to take my place. That little slut of yours will never be safe as long as the De Tore family lives and breathes in Boston. As long as you're a part of this."

I bring the gun beneath his chin, shoving the barrel so his head is forced back at an unforgiving angle. "Then I suppose I'll have to correct that for her."

This time, when I pull the trigger, my finger barely seems to move. Time itself suspends, as if putting distance between me and my actions.

Chaos descends around me. This wasn't what I meant to do, and yet, standing in the midst of it all while my father's brain matter splatters on the windows behind him, I don't feel an ounce of regret.

STELLA

Anna shifts nervously behind me on the glass balcony. "I *really* don't think Mr. De Tore will be happy about this…"

Irritation simmers in my chest, and I walk to the transparent railing, cradling the clothes that were dumped on the sofa while I was sleeping. Expensive designer brands in varying sizes, as if the things I brought weren't good enough for my new husband.

Anna tries again. "I-if you don't like the clothes, we can get you new ones. Copley Place is only a couple of blocks away."

I ignore her, too tangled up in my thoughts of the past twenty-four hours.

Never mind the fact that after my drunken mishap, I woke alone. There truly is nothing in the world that makes you feel more inferior than that, except maybe the silent suggestion that your wardrobe needs upgrading.

My hands shake with an unmitigated amount of angry

energy, and I try balling them into fists and taking deep breaths, but the emotion accumulates anyway.

I didn't ask for any of this. All I wanted was to get away from this life, not dig my grave deeper into it.

A strangled, frustrated noise tears out of me, and my body jerks almost reflexively, sending the stack of clothes over the balcony to the ground below. I lean over, ignoring the tears stinging my eyes as each item floats down to the sidewalk, occasionally getting caught on another level, until I can no longer see them at all.

It doesn't change anything, but the defiance makes me feel better nonetheless.

The door behind me slides open, and I assume Anna's going inside to tell Irene about my behavior. A part of me feels bad because I'm sure one of them—or both, perhaps—will be blamed for my actions, but at the moment, I can't bring myself to care.

Anna would be more than happy to swap places with me, so I'm sure this doesn't make any sense to her. Irene, on the other hand, seems to understand my plight on some level, and I wonder if that's because she's been in a similar situation before or if she's just wiser than her colleague.

Either way, it doesn't matter. Her understanding won't grant me freedom.

"You know..." A smooth, dark voice comes from directly over my shoulder. "Littering is bad for the environment."

I jump at the sound, immediately whirling to face the intruder. Before I can fully turn, though, he rushes up and plasters himself to me, trapping me. He grips the rail with both gloved hands, holding tight.

His hips crush mine to the glass barrier, and a startled gasp expels from my lungs with the impact. "I'd have expected a future scientist like you to know that."

The teasing makes me see red.

"*Jesus Christ*," I swear, struggling against his hold. "Let *go* of me."

"This is not the warm welcome a husband anticipates after being away from his wife all day." Leo chuckles, his mouth close to my ear. "And I thought good little Catholic girls weren't supposed to take their Lord's name in vain."

"I guess I'm not a good little Catholic girl then, am I?"

"Mmm. That's exactly what I'm hoping for." His moan caresses my cheek, and even as I continue jerking against him, trying to maneuver myself free, I can't deny that the sound stokes a fire low—*very low*—in my stomach. "Although your recent charitable contribution to the streets of Boston cannot be denied. Do you have any idea how much those clothes were worth?"

I attempt a shrug, but it catches on his body. "So go *fetch* them."

One hand retreats from my view, and in the next second, he shoves his gloved fingers through my hair, forcing my head to angle downward. An endless stream of windows marks the entire side of the skyscraper—some lights on, some not. I wonder how far up you can see—if any residents in the building might witness the battle for my freedom.

"Is it that easy?" he whispers, his lips pressing directly to my ear now. I bite the tip of my tongue to suppress a shiver. "You throw something, and I'm to retrieve it like some dog?"

Stop pouring kerosene on this fire. Don't answer him.

I do anyway. "They say it's never too late to learn new tricks."

"I'll need a good leash. Something metal that I won't be able to chew through. Maybe a muzzle, too. I've been known to bite when a pussy gets close." He shifts, and I feel *all* of him pressing against my bottom while his words echo between my legs. "Normally, I'd drag your wicked little ass inside for privacy's sake; however, I relish the idea of Boston watching me lay claim to my wife for the first time."

Fear courses through my veins, pumping wildly. At least, I think it's fear. "Far be it from me to shatter the fantasy."

Cool air strikes the backs of my thighs as he begins slowly dragging my skirt up. My elbows hang on top of the rail, and I can't move otherwise with how he's leaning, so I just hiss as more of me becomes exposed.

"What's your fantasy, stellina? How do you want this to go down?"

"I don't have one."

"Everyone has fantasies. Even sweet virgins like yourself." A pause, and I feel leather scrape against me, sliding inward and upward. One sweep over my panties makes my knees tremble. "What is it you get off to?"

Gritting my teeth, I shake my head. "That's none of your business."

"No?" While he continues exploring, his other hand glides up my throat, collaring me. "Whose business would it be, aside from your husband's?"

I don't respond. Already, I'm starting to recognize this little game he wants to play—cat and mouse—where he wins every time.

Well, *almost* every time.

"Fine. If you don't want to share with the class, I'll just use my own."

"Your own what—"

Pressure blossoms on my pussy as he curls his fingers under me from the back, swirling lightly. I suck in a gasp of air, the sudden friction making me dizzy. Aside from outside the church yesterday, no one's ever touched me there before; my stolen groping sessions in the Fontbonne Academy bathrooms and the confessional at confirmation were strictly above the waist, because the older girls said it wasn't a sin if you did it that way.

But this feels like sin. Delicious, deadly sin. The kind that gets you kicked out of heaven for good.

His hand leaves my throat to thread in my hair, and he buries his nose in my scalp, inhaling deeply. "God, your hair is fucking magical. I wish I knew why I want it wrapped around my dick so badly."

My eyes widen, and for a second, I'm afraid he'll do just that. I cringe, imagining the mess, but then another image takes over—his complete and utter desperation, driving him to such miserable heights that he finds arousal from my hair alone.

Neither of my sisters can say they've driven a man *that* mad before. Just me, the boring one.

It fills me with a surge of pleasure, but then Leo's speaking again, strumming that thread and making it coil tighter within me.

"We can save the depravity for later, I suppose. My cum in

your hair might not be the best decision right now, so I'm just going to finger fuck you right out here. You're going to ride my hand to oblivion, and you're going to come all fucking over me. *All* over me, got it? I want to be dripping wet. I want to smell you before I taste you, and then I'm gonna get on my knees and eat your pussy until you forget your name."

I feel leather on my bare flesh, parting me and finding that sensitive spot again. He rubs slowly, breathing in tandem with me as I try to steady myself. Each stroke feels better than the last, like he's learning how to play my body.

People could be watching right now from the comfort of their residences across the street or maybe even from the sidewalk down below. We'd never be able to know for sure, and for some reason, that implication is alluring.

I shift, falling into the moment a little more as he continues to tease euphoria from me.

"How's that?" he whispers, gently biting my earlobe. "Feels good, doesn't it? My hands on you after leaving you needy all day? Don't you wish I'd taken advantage of your state last night and not waited to satisfy you?"

My mouth dries up as tension coils in my gut. "Take them off."

"Take what off?"

"T—" I swallow again, my brain short-circuiting as he pauses and starts moving in the opposite direction. A little pressure to the right, and my toes curl inside my shoes. "The gloves. I—I want to feel you on me."

He freezes, and I sense a shift in the air around us. His hand retreats from my clit, quickly removing itself from my body, and the one in my hair follows a second later. Deflated, I adjust my clothes and spin around to face him as he moves back, putting a considerable amount of distance between us.

What the hell just happened?

One minute, he's hot, dragging me to the edge of oblivion, and the next, he's leaving me out to dry with no satisfaction.

Shame bubbles up in my chest at the sudden unexplained rejection, even though I shouldn't care. If anything, I should be *glad* he stopped. The less he touches me, the more capable I am of keeping my wits about me.

Clearly, I need them.

"You should go inside." His throat bobs on a swallow, and he shoves his hands in his pants pockets. "It's late, and you'll catch a cold out here."

Confusion pulls at my nerve endings. My eyes slowly drag down his form, noting the torn suit jacket and the red splashed across the chest of his shirt, stretching into a splatter on the side of his neck and beneath his chin.

"Is that blood?" I ask, my hands moving of their own accord, seeking a solution of some sort. Immediately, the desire to correct and erase fills me, and I step toward him, wondering what's going on.

"Don't worry." His lips twitch. "It isn't mine."

With that, Leo turns on his heel and makes his way back inside. Anger boils in my veins, hot like a volcano on the verge of eruption. Before I can think better of it and stop myself, I chase after him.

He goes to the kitchen and pours himself some scotch, and I watch him pop a little white pill from an orange prescription bottle. As I stalk toward him, he turns and leans against the white cabinetry, sipping slowly. His eyes don't leave mine as I approach, fueling something strange inside me.

My whole life has been so focused on getting away that I haven't spent much time looking within, figuring out what I might enjoy beyond pure escapism.

What I'd desire if I let myself *want*, even for just a moment. One night, with someone who actually seems to want me back.

Even if that man is a nightmare, hell-bent on keeping me prisoner. At the very least, I can get something out of the arrangement—until I've found an out, that is. While I'm stuck here, I'll let myself give in. Temporarily.

It's a split-second decision, but I seem to keep making those around him anyway. *Surely, one more won't ruin me for good.*

My chest heaves as I try to catch my breath, and I glance down at his shirt again. "What happened to you?"

"Nothing, Stella." His jaw tics, and he looks past me. "I told you not to worry about it."

"How can I not? You don't touch me on our wedding night, and then you disappear all day today and leave me to rot up here with your housekeepers. When you do finally show up, you look like you've been elbow-deep in someone's chest cavity, and I'm supposed to just ignore that?"

"Aw, how quickly you've come to care for your terrible, monstrous husband's well-being."

He doesn't even flinch when I knock the tumbler from his hand or when it shatters on the floor, spraying the cabinets and our feet with alcohol.

"That wasn't very nice."

"I care about *my* well-being," I snap, shoving at his shoulders. "You being stupid and reckless puts my life at risk now, too."

Two fingers curl around the ends of my hair. "And if I said I also care about your well-being?" Those smoky eyes rise to mine, half-lidded and smoldering. "Would you believe me if I said this blood was spilled in your honor?"

There's a flash in my mind of last night—me lying in his bed, tipsy enough that the room was spinning, but not enough that I couldn't register the hard anger in his body when I mentioned his father.

Is it possible he's telling the truth? I suppose, and I can't deny how that possibility warms my insides with something deliciously insidious.

But the *why* makes no sense. Not when he's just as responsible for my suffering.

Still, I decide that it doesn't necessarily matter either way. If I stay here, this is a scene I'll likely just have to deal with, so my hands lurch out, grabbing the lapels of his jacket. "Shut up," I tell him, dragging his face to mine and sealing our mouths together again.

Immediately, his tongue sweeps in, as if trying to savor every foreign inch of me. His hands twist in my hair, and he crushes me as close as he can. I let out a little sound of desperation when he swivels, pinning me to the counter and shoving his thigh between mine.

"Shit," I mutter, pulling away slightly.

Leo grins. "No razor blade this time?"

"You sound disappointed."

"Well, I'd be lying if I said I didn't enjoy the taste of a threat on your lips." Instead of letting me respond, he dives back in, plundering my mouth with his until my mind spins.

His kiss is heady and wrong. While I might lack experience, it doesn't take a genius to realize that each scrape of his teeth and flick of his tongue has a carefully executed flourish. It's dirty, sinful, and I fall too far into it to notice what he's doing in other places.

The sound of a zipper unlatching cuts through the air, but when I jerk against him, he doesn't let me pull away again. Air sweeps across my lower back, exposed as he undoes my skirt, and then he uses both hands to tear off my shirt and yank the skirt down my hips.

I move to cover myself, but he grabs my wrists and shakes his head.

"Absolutely not," he breathes. "I want to see you."

My heart stutters a beat as I give a short nod, abandoning logic and reason for the tempting fire in his gray eyes. They remain on my face, slowly tracking the skirt as it continues its descent down the length of me, joining the pile of clothing on the floor.

Next to go is my bra, unhooked with ease from the front.

"What *were* you planning to do with that blade yesterday?" he asks quietly, almost reverently. His hand skims the curve of my side, brushing the outside of one breast before moving up and along my collarbone. "You didn't think that would be enough to kill me. I know you're smarter than that."

"It wouldn't have killed you, but it'd have given me a head start."

He pauses, his eyes flicking to mine. "You were going to run?"

"I was going to try."

The staring continues as if he's working through some mathematical equation in his head. "What a waste of time that would have been," he says, his jaw clenching. "I'm beginning to doubt your intelligence, stellina."

Chuckling, he inches his hand down, covering my entire breast. The leather is rough against my skin, and I bite my bottom lip to keep from making a sound.

He clamps down, squeezing my flesh until I cry out in pain.

"Would it truly have been a better alternative than this?" He steps closer, his eyes blazing. "I haven't forced you into anything, haven't shredded your virginity against your will just for the sake of doing it. What makes me such a terrible match?"

My eyebrows knit together, and I shove against him. "I didn't want to marry you in the first place! I had goals. Things I wanted to do, places I wanted to see. None of which involved another selfish, egotistical man who cares more about power and money than anything else in the world. Perhaps you haven't forced yourself on me fully, but you did take my father up on his offer. You're keeping me *here*."

"In this luxury condo, where you'll be taken care of and never want for anything? Where you'll be safe and protected against your enemies? What a miserable life I'm offering."

"A tower is a tower, Leo." My voice softens. "I'm a prisoner whether I'm safe or not. It should've been my call to make."

"So, what would you rather do? Run off to the other side of the country? Get your degree, bury yourself in research, maybe fall in love with a man who reads *Popular Mechanics* for fun and names a star after you?" His free hand comes up, wrapping around my throat, and he swipes over my nipple with the other, causing it to pebble. The touch is at odds with his angry tone, and I don't know what to focus on. "Do you think someone else will be able to make you feel like this?"

"You don't know how I'm feeling."

"Don't I?" He's getting more riled up with every response I give. The tendons in his neck tighten, bulging against his skin.

With little effort, he yanks back and spins me around so I'm facing away. He stops touching me briefly, and my hands fly out, smacking against the countertop. In the next second, I feel him pushing my hips forward and spreading my ass.

With no gloves.

I'm not sure when he got rid of them, but the feel of his warm skin on mine is distinct. His palms are a bit rougher than I imagined, although I suppose living a violent life doesn't allow for smooth, soft anything.

I don't mind how they feel, though. Not as much as I thought I would.

"You're *angry*," he says, gripping my cheeks with his fingers. He takes one digit and slides it forward. It brushes my clit, just barely, but I gasp anyway.

"I just told you I am."

"You're wet." When his finger starts to move back, it pauses, pushing between my slick flesh to rub against that sweet spot. "*Throbbing*, my wife."

Heat scalds my cheeks. "It's an involuntary reaction to being assaulted. The hypothalamus releases chemicals from the sympathetic nervous system and adrenal medulla, and the body gives an instantaneous response. I have nothing to do with it."

"Yes, fight or flight. I'm familiar with the basic concept." He draws slow circles on me, coiling tension low in my belly and up my thighs with each deliberate stroke. "Although, if you wanted me to stop, you wouldn't have followed me inside and mauled me yourself."

"Stop talking about me like you know me."

"Would you rather I eat instead?"

My heart skips a beat. "What—"

Unsurprisingly, in true Leo fashion, he doesn't give me time to finish the question. I feel his hot, moist mouth on me in the next second, and the sudden invasion of opposing sensations sends my hips into the cabinet.

"Am I correct to assume this is a first for you?" he whispers, his breath warm on my skin.

My fingers flex as his lips work against me, gently massaging without fully tasting.

I nod and keep my gaze on the white tile backsplash.

Two bare digits pinch one ass cheek, and I jump in surprise. "When my head is between your legs, wife, I expect a verbal answer to my questions. Do not make me ask twice."

"What happens if I do?"

Leo's tongue is on me before the sentence is finished. He spears into me, maneuvering his body so I have to stand on my tiptoes to allow him access. I'm spread out on the counter, my hands grazing the wall as my entire being shakes to the core with the feeling of him eating happily below me.

Him licking at my most private place is downright lewd, and despite everything, I let out a low moan. "Oh *God*," I mutter into the marble counter, pinching my eyes shut as electricity shoots up my legs.

"Louder," Leo says. "I want *Him* to hear me defile you."

My body obeys as if struck by some spell. I moan louder, arching my hips as he chases my pussy. When he plunges a finger in without preamble, a mangled sound rumbles from deep in my chest.

"Aw, look at that. She likes being filled."

I can't even focus on his mocking tone because, God, he's fucking huge. As he saws in and out in tandem with the lashing of his tongue, I begin to feel dizzy.*

"How much more do you think you can take?"

I shake my head, unable to answer.

An unbelievable stretching sensation ricochets between my thighs as he adds a second finger. "How much more, wife? Do you think you can handle all of me?"

"N-no," I say, even as the uncomfortable expansion morphs into blinding pleasure.

He curls upward, and molten lava sears across my body, sheer bliss threatening to engulf me.

I'm vibrating, biting my lip so hard that I taste blood. The invasion is foreign, so utterly abnormal to me, and I don't know what to do as my pussy tries caving in on itself, desperate for the high he promises.

"I can't take more," I admit, my voice breaking as tears spring to my eyes.

* SLOW DOWN—Chase Atlantic

It feels so fucking good, him working me over, and when he presses the flat of his tongue to my clit and then sucks hard, I realize I'm a goner.

"I'm—I think I'm close."

"You think?" The suction of his lips grows more intense, and I squeal. "I believe you're right there, baby. Just need you to let go for a moment. Enjoy the feel of my mouth devouring your sweet, untouched cunt. You love it, don't you? You wish I'd give you more."

Fuck. The idea sends me over the proverbial cliff of ecstasy.

My fingernails scrape against the countertop as my pussy spasms, pulsing around him like a tide trying to pull in a victim. He continues lapping at my sopping flesh, the strokes against my inner muscles not slowing as I catapult into paradise with him as my guide.

But then he withdraws as abruptly as this all began, and it's just…over.

He kisses slowly up one side of my ass while he stands, dragging his lips across my hip and then up my spine, until he's at my ear. With one bare hand, still slick with my arousal, he grips my chin and hoists my backside against him, angling my head forcefully.

The kiss is an explosion of unfamiliar tang and that slight minty taste of Leo. I open my mouth, welcoming his affection for the first time, but then he releases me and steps back.

Dazed, I brace myself on the counter and slowly turn to face him. When I do, he's already wearing those gloves again, and I feel strangely empty inside.

Stupidly, I reach for him, rife with vulnerability in the aftermath of the intimacy we just shared. A dark shadow crosses over his face, and he moves farther away. He shoves those gloved fingers into his pockets and gives me a once-over.

I frown. "What are you doing? I thought…"

"That I'd want your virginity like this?" He barks out a cruel laugh, and I recoil, tucking my arms against my breasts. "Come back to me when you've taught yourself a thing or two."

Seconds later, he turns and disappears down the hall. I stand there, my mouth agape, wondering what the fuck just happened—how this man who was all over me *minutes* ago has managed to reject me in the next breath, as if none of this mattered at all.

As if he didn't want me.

Maybe that's the inexperience talking or the weight of what's occurred tonight finally catching up with me.

Annoyed with *everything*, I yank on the ends of my hair until stars burst behind my eyes from the pain. Mamma's voice screams in my head, and I can practically see Papà's disgust on his face as she looms over me.

Stupid, Stella! You are so stupid. Why would a man like that want someone like you? Why would you matter to someone who sees you as a piece of property?

Even his earlier admission that he cares for me feels silly when I think about it now. Completely implausible, given we just met yesterday.

I guess I was holding out hope that it was more for him too. That things felt… *different*.

I'm beginning to doubt your intelligence.

Then again, we're all puppets to men like Leo. And I just played right into his large talented hands.

I need to get out of here. Somehow.

No more mourning the fact I didn't stay at my sister Elena's house three summers ago, returning to Boston instead because I wanted to finish my education in one place.

It mattered to the schools I was applying to. They wanted the cohesion, the dedication, and the references from esteemed faculty at the Fontbonne.

It mattered to *me*—at least back then. Now what's important is that my hard work doesn't go to waste. Staying here isn't an option if I want to make my decisions worthwhile.

My eyes flicker to the orange prescription bottle on the counter. I wonder if he even realizes he left drugs in plain sight or if he thinks he's big enough to overpower me if I try to use them.

Maybe...

Silently, I retrieve a tall glass from a cabinet and fill it with water and ice from the fridge.

Then I unscrew the bottle cap and drop one tablet in the liquid. Just to see what happens.

It dissolves in thirty seconds. Then, for a full minute after, I just stare at the drink while a plan formulates in my head.

Maybe this is stupid. It's likely he'll come after me either way, but perhaps his rejection tonight was only the start of a bigger plot to edge me out of his life. I mean, it's not like he *really* wanted to marry me, right? He wanted my father's money.

If I found a way to get that to him, maybe this would be over.

My parents are no help, so if he kills them anyway, I don't think I'll mind.

A part of me considers asking Elena or Ariana for help, especially since he practically threatened them already, but I don't want to drag them into this. It's too embarrassing to admit that I'm in it at all. Besides, they can fend for themselves; the main thing here is figuring out how to extract *myself*.

At the very least, maybe the fact we haven't consummated will prompt him to erase me from his memory altogether. If I'm gone, maybe that's what will matter.

Either way, I have to *try*.

I dump nine pills into the glass.

Wait for them to dissolve, too. Find a lemon in the fridge, slice it up, and add a few wedges to mask the taste.

And despite his rejection still stinging in the back of my mind, I bring him the glass and my naked form, hoping one distracts from the other.

LEO

wake with a start, immediately noting the bitter dryness in my mouth.

Not quite the taste I got into bed with. However, as I stare up at the tray ceiling in my room, I realize I don't remember getting into bed at all.

The last thing I recall is making Stella come on my face and then storming off before I could do something we'd both *really* regret.

Perhaps it wasn't my most tactful move, but I wanted the memory regardless.

Rolling over in bed, I reach for my phone on the nightstand and open my unit's security app, pulling up footage from last night. My dick pulses painfully as the image begins playing out— her standing naked before me, then me dropping to my knees to eat her like my life depended on it.

In the moment, it certainly felt that way.

I am such a dumbass.

There's no reason for me to feel so strongly about a woman I barely know, yet I can't seem to fucking help myself. It's as if a single meeting with her altered the stretch of time, and suddenly, the landscape of my future included her. I wanted it to be different for her—for us.

Like a dumbass.

The insult plays on a loop in my brain, assaulting me each time I play back what transpired between me and the youngest Ricci. How badly I fumbled this marriage, even if I made sure to give her something from it—something she'll likely never recognize as the gift it was.

Rejecting her was the very least I could do. That decision will have many repercussions, though none that mattered in the moment.

I sit up and shove my legs off the mattress, scrubbing at my face with both palms. Given last night's events, the condo feels unnaturally quiet, and the fluffed pillows on the opposite side of the bed indicate I was not joined in my slumber.

My gaze lifts toward the closed door, scanning the space underneath for signs of life. Irene or Anna should be here by now, yet the usual sounds of cleaning are absent.

After a quick shower in the adjoining bathroom suite, I wrap a thick white towel around my waist, slide my gloves over the scarred topography of my palms, and make my way to the kitchen. Irene and Anna are huddled together by one corner of the island, whispering in panicked voices.

"Ladies." I nod in their direction and grab a glass, going to fill it with orange juice.

"Mr. De Tore," Anna says, practically weeping as she clings to her colleague. "Y-you're awake!"

"Was there some sort of debate going? It isn't *that* late."

"Well, we thought...maybe something had happened with Mrs. De Tore—"

My hands freeze midpour, until the juice is overflowing.

Liquid splashes against my bare feet, and I calmly set the carton on the counter. My gaze darts to the overturned prescription bottle in the corner—the lid is off, and the contents are gone.

It's empty.

There'd only been a handful of pills left anyway, but, goddamn, I hadn't thought she'd use the entire thing.

I suppose that explains the haze I woke up in and the missing memories of the night before.

Apparently, my little wife was out for blood. Perhaps more than she even realized.

Turning slowly, I cross my arms over my chest and level both women with a look. "Mrs. De Tore is gone."

It isn't a question, but Anna nods in confirmation anyway. "I know you gave her strict instructions not to leave, and we were supposed to make sure she stayed in the condo, but when I arrived an hour ago for my shift, she was already missing. I'm not sure who was stationed at the door—"

No one was.

I drag my tongue over the front of my teeth. "The security cameras?"

The app on my phone is from a different company than the building's official cameras, so I only have immediate access to the indoor specs. Therefore, even if I could watch her leave the condo itself, I wouldn't be able to see where she went after that.

Anna chews on a pinkie nail, pulling away from Irene. "We don't have access to them."

"Find Frankie, tell him I want the footage—whatever he finds—but I don't want him looking at it first. He's to bring it directly to me, untouched."

"Can't you just tell him?" Irene mutters.

I glance at her, but she doesn't look up from the floor.

Anna nods, her eyes welling up with tears. "Sir, I am *so* sorry. Please, *please* don't fire me over this. I'll do anything. I'll help you look for her! I just can't afford to—"

"No one is getting fired." After reaching for my glass, I down my drink in a couple of gulps and set the cup in the sink. "My wife's sudden leave of absence is of her own doing. I won't punish someone else for her insolence."

"Okay, okay, thank you!" She breezes past me, and a few seconds later, the front door opens and slams shut, rattling the glassware in the cabinet next to my head.

I stare at Irene for a beat, then cock an eyebrow. "Mrs. De Tore's abrupt, unexplained departure *was* her own doing. Right?"

Her dark gaze swings to mine, narrowing. "Of course it was. Why in the world would I help a woman I barely know?"

That's the official party line. The one we settled on when she picked me up from downtown yesterday, covered in the blood of my superiors. The blood of my father.

I massacred nearly each and every one of the Elders after all. It seemed fitting. A message, of sorts.

Frankie was busy disposing of evidence, along with Gino, who didn't quite pledge his allegiance to me as the new official don but didn't want to see his hard work suffer either. I spared him with the assumption that he'd pass the news of the deceased along to Ranolfo and the Commission, likely putting a bounty on my head.

They wouldn't believe it was a rival ambush, but it would distract them from the bigger offense later—a Ricci getting access to a De Tore and then disappearing.

Treason, they'd call it when they realized Stella left. Grounds for immediate execution, based on the assumption that she'd immediately go to the authorities and turn us over to them—the way her sister had done to their father years ago.

There was no time to waste, so I asked Irene for assistance with getting her out.

She didn't ask questions—I suppose when you've worked for our family as long as she has, there aren't many you want the answers to. Where Anna is young and eager to please, Irene is an intelligent, shrewd woman. Once upon a time, she played the role of my father's mistress, and when he tossed her aside, she stayed on the payroll just to keep a close eye on him, waiting for the day she could get her revenge.

With him now dead, this felt like the next best thing I could grant her: a giant middle finger to the De Tores, who are no doubt scouring the city as we stand here, aware that I'm brideless. I'm certain Anna's leaked it by now, though not on purpose.

"So," I say, hooking my thumbs in my pants pockets, "she's gone. Do you know—"

Irene holds up a hand and gives a sharp jut of her chin. "The bird is in the nest no longer, Mr. De Tore. I'd suggest not worrying too much about it."

"I'll arrange a search party—"

"Do you honestly think she's even in the state anymore? We don't know when she left, where she was headed, or what contacts she has in Boston to help her escape. And I'm assuming, since you're still standing here, that you failed to bug her phone?"

I don't respond, and Irene tsk-tsks with glittering eyes, like she's the disappointed one.

"Face it, Leopoldo. Stella Ricci is lost to you, and that's that. I could have told you a simple tower wouldn't keep her, but your greed was too loud."

I stare at her silently for a full sixty seconds, wondering if I should reprimand her for speaking to me like this, even though I know it's for the cameras. For the spectators we likely already have—all a part of my plan here.

Still, even though I know it's an act, I can't deny the kernel of agony that pops up in my abdomen. The loneliness I feel already, as if a ghost passed through my condo and slipped through my fingers.

It's like I've been disconnected from an integral part of myself, which is nonsense, given that nothing really transpired between us. A simple want does not a connection make, and Stella certainly didn't seem to reciprocate any feelings.

At least not until I rejected her. Then her true self showed through, which only heightened my desire. The girl I spent years admiring from across the church turned out to be a fierce opponent.

Only, I don't want her opposition.

Just her affection.

Still, for the sake of appearances, I act like Irene's words are law. My hope is that they'll assume Stella's father had something to do with all this and go after him instead.

I'm sure I won't remain inconspicuous for long; it's probably only a matter of time before the Elders head over to get rid of me—or at least send some lower-level soldiers to do the work for them.

But that's no matter, so long as Stella's safe. Irene's script tells me she's made it. She's okay. Even if I can't know where she is just yet.

Despite everything, she's still *mine*.

And she might be gone now, but my wife will one day be found.*

STELLA

SEVEN YEARS LATER

'm hating this."

My roommate, Valerie, pins the final piece of my hair up and snorts. "You hate every work function."

"Not true. I had a good time at the Jeans for Genes walkathon last month." Leaning forward, I curl the mascara wand upward against my lashes, coating them in nighttime black. When I blink at myself in the vanity mirror, I hardly recognize the reflection staring back at me.

The dress I borrowed from Val for the occasion is a skin-tight, one-sleeved lavender mermaid gown that I can't help feeling naked in. It's a far cry from the usual lab coat and personal protective equipment I'm in during the week, but as I stand and do a little twirl, I have to admit I don't look half bad.

In fact, I look every bit the socialite that my older sisters have perfected being over the years. Maybe tonight won't be so terrible after all.

Two tendrils of hair frame my face, while the rest is twisted into a bun and pinned with matching diamond barrettes. Val spritzes me with perfume from a pink glass bottle and gives me a thorough once-over.

"Well, what do you think?" I ask, folding my fingers together in front of me. "Will I pass as the great Valerie Van der Vorm at this party tonight?"

She groans, dragging her hands through her warm-brown hair. "We may look alike, but you're not passing *as* me, and it's not a party. It's an auction. You're expected to spend money and network, Stelz."

"Okay." I shrug. "I can do that."

"Are you sure? Because I can barely get you to buy basic groceries every week. The stuff lined up at the Black Rose Auction is gonna be expensive."

"Then why don't *you* just go with me?"

"Because if I miss another grand opening at one of my father's hotels, my mother said he's writing me out of the will." She waves a manicured hand dismissively. "Besides, it's one invite per attendee, and *you* have a reason to go."

I roll my eyes and walk over to the small living room in our apartment before flopping down on the red suede love seat. The entire unit is less than twelve hundred square feet and on the ground floor of a building that we're pretty certain doubles as a money-laundering site, but it's cozy and close to both our offices, so we stay.

We met during the onboarding process for a molecular biology fellowship two years ago and instantly bonded over the fact that we came from wealthy families, but had set off on our own paths in life.

I don't know if her family consists mainly of criminals like mine, but I suppose it doesn't necessarily matter.

Not now that I'm an orphan anyway.

"Just because I don't enjoy spending the money I work sixty hours a week, hunched over a microscope or filling out paperwork, to earn doesn't mean I don't know how to spend it." Bending slightly, I tighten the straps on the Versace stiletto sandals Ariana sent me for my birthday last year. "Besides, it's Rampion Core's escrow account I'm using, not mine. And I can *definitely* spend someone else's money."

Moreover, you get used to spending someone else's money when you're too busy with school to earn your own. My admittance to Stanford had already been manufactured, so I didn't want my attendance to be something someone else could claim either. Which meant throwing myself into the biomedicine program and any extracurriculars to beef up my résumé, so there was no time for a paying job.

Elena and her husband have been sending weekly stipends, and I've always pretended it isn't hush money meant to keep me away from the East Coast. Since the deaths of both our parents a few years back, it's felt as if neither of my sisters wants me to return—they'd probably have a fit if they knew I've been in New York for so long without telling them.

But I've tried to keep my trail small and untraceable. Not to keep them out, but to keep them safe.

In seven years, I haven't had any trouble from my past life

or the man waiting in it. I'd like to believe that if he hasn't come at this point, he probably isn't going to, but there's a smidge of doubt that sits perpetually in the back of my mind.

Leopoldo De Tore wouldn't give up easily.

Perhaps the problem is that he's no longer interested, so there's nothing to chase. Even dead, my mother's critical voice pricks at the inside of my brain, though I usually try to stuff her down where I can't hear. Old habits die hard, I guess.

"Whatever you say." Val shrugs, tossing me an embossed white envelope. "That's your key in. Literally. Guard it with your life."

"What are your rules again? Be seen and not heard?"

"No." She gives me an exasperated look and flops down on the couch beside me, stretching her long legs up on the glass coffee table. "Be seen *and* heard. Network with the other attendees. It makes the evening go much faster, and by the time the actual auction rolls around tomorrow, you'll know what kind of competition you're up against. Plus, that way, you can tell me all about it since I have to miss out."

"Don't you think they'll be expecting you? Since you got the invitation, I mean."

"There are no names on the invite, so I doubt it'll be a problem as long as you fit in. It's all about how you speak and what you can offer. That's how these people operate. If you say you come from money and show up in designer digs, they won't question it."

She seems confident in the plan, and I really want to go for Rampion Core, so I don't refute her claims. Fifteen minutes later,

I'm being escorted by Val's personal driver to the massive estate where this elite auction is being held.

As the vehicle approaches the property, I try to concentrate on the why behind my attendance—a damn *flower*. It's genetically engineered, and only two of its kind exist. Scientists and pharmaceutical companies across the world have been trying to get their hands on it; one group wants it for supposedly altruistic reasons, while the other wants to extort it.

Someone purchased the clone at auction a year ago for half a billion dollars. Rampion Core—the genetic research lab I work at—doesn't have the funds to compete with *that*, so I'm hoping this crowd is less interested in this particular item and that I'll have a chance to get it for us. Especially since there are royal jewels and socialites rumored to be up for bid as well.

My options for getting promoted at the lab are either securing this ultrarare orchid or sleeping with my boss, Barry, and hoping he makes me a tech someday.

A couple of the other assistants are already trying their hand at the latter and have been unsuccessful so far. And I'm not interested in him anyway. In fact, I haven't really been interested in anyone these past seven years, and it's taken me a long time to come to terms with the fact that a forced marriage broke my libido.

Well, sort of. I've explored by myself, of course.

But unfortunately, there's only ever been one image I can get off to, no matter the porn I watch or the nights spent listening to Val get railed by various individuals in the room beside mine.

Only the memories of one man's tongue, fingers, and dirty mouth really do the trick.

The car approaches the mansion slowly, and my nerves fire on all cylinders. I stuff my hands into my lap, trying to keep the anticipation from boiling over.

I don't want to seem too eager.

Eventually, the driver rolls to a stop behind a long string of vehicles lining the curved, paved entrance.

The main house itself is ostentatious, its looming stone walls composed of expansive windows and multiple floors, complete with balconies and warm, inviting lighting. People spill out like fish spit from the sea from every conceivable doorway, and I tighten my grip on my overnight bag.

Anxiety lances my gut the longer I stare up at the mansion. Every atom of my being is frazzled, screaming at me to lean forward and ask the driver to turn around.

But I *can't*. I'm not willing to give up on my chance to climb Rampion Core's ranks so easily. Not when I've worked this hard.

Plus, Val might kill me if I waste her invitation.

The car door flies open, and a gust of wind rushes into the back seat with the motion, rustling my hair.

I didn't even realize we stopped.

Outside the vehicle, a valet attendant—wearing a red silk vest with a black rose corsage pinned to the left lapel—stands with his hand outstretched.

"Ms. Ricci," he says cordially, his blue eyes crinkling at the corners. They're almost soft enough to disarm me, but that fact only puts me more on edge—along with his immediate knowledge of my identity. "Welcome to the Black Rose Auction."

13

LEO

As I study my reflection, my fingers tug at the silk knot beneath my chin. For a brief moment, I'm tempted to pull at the fabric until oxygen becomes scarce. Not that it would do me any good—Frankie would waste no time in rushing to aid me, even as my face turned a familiar shade of purple.

I didn't consider how nervous I'd be after all this time.*

For seven years, I've let her do her own thing despite the backlash that ensued. I wonder if she realizes the lengths I've gone to in order for her to have her own life. The lives I've ended, the secrets I've kept, the deals put into place. All for the protection of the woman who fled my condo before the ink on our marriage license dried.

Forged ink, but still. What are the chances she'll remember that she didn't *technically* sign?

The floor creaks as Frankie shifts in the doorway, shuffling

* ELEVEN—heylog

inside and closing us in together. He's in dark jeans and a sports jacket, the gold chain he stole off some Fed a few years ago bright against his black T-shirt.

"Where is she?" I ask, careful to keep emotion from my voice. I prefer he thinks my interest is simply transactional and nothing more. That Stella and I have a deal she hasn't fulfilled and my presence in New York is merely to see her follow through with it.

When men in this world know you have a weakness, they'll use it. I'm not stupid enough to fully trust even those in my own circle.

Not when I would exploit the same thing, given the chance.

There's a pause as he hesitates. "She's arrived at the Black Rose Auction. They admitted her immediately, as she showed up with an invitation and key in hand."

My brows twitch in the mirror but don't fully lift. I keep my expression neutral. "I see."

She's early, that wicked girl. As if she thinks she'll be able to get in and out with no trouble.

Adjusting my tie, I don't say anything more, even as my molars grind against one another while I think about her being there, getting lost in the crowd or felt up by the perverts in attendance.

The idea of someone else touching what belongs to me doesn't sit well. All this time, I've ignored the possibility that she might have, at some point, escaped my detection and gone off with someone. That she might have allowed them to sully her innocence in ways I didn't.

"What exactly are you hoping to accomplish tonight?" Frankie asks, squinting at me.

"The Orchidée Sans Nom," I reply. "Are you familiar with it?"

"Uh…no."

"It's a genetically engineered plant. Only the second of its kind, and there are multiple guests attending this auction who are interested in obtaining it, all for varying reasons. Some are nefarious, some are just collectors, and others want the plant to do some good out in the world. Our target falls into the last category. According to several online forums, Stella's boss wants the flower for research—and likely to lord over the other scientists in his field. Wouldn't surprise me if he tried to extort some pharmaceutical companies for profit."

Turning away from the mirror, I smooth down the lapels of my suit jacket, then reach for the gloves resting on the back of a brown velvet bucket seat. My hands are steady as I slide the black leather over them, hiding the gnarled skin on my palms.

My father's death was long overdue. Even though the slaughter of Flavio and the half dozen men in that office seven years ago complicated my life considerably, I'll never feel bad about doing it.

The death of the De Tore boss opened a gap in a fervent market for control in the Boston underground. When I took over, no one seemed terribly convinced of my abilities or my innocence. So I've spent a long time proving myself among my men by securing new deals and bringing in prime shipments of product we couldn't get our hands on before. Even attending this auction took years of stealthy planning and a hint of luck.

Only a couple of Elders from the De Tore family remain. With the Riccis defunct and the Commission having washed their hands of us—after they were unsuccessful in linking my father's death to me, and I assured them I had things under control—the Boston underground is a fucking nightmare. Because of that, the remaining De Tore associates have set their sights on Stella once again. As a sort of payment, I suppose, for the reaping they could never prove.

The De Tores never were good at following protocol. That's probably why they were so easy to ruin.

Nonetheless, I have no intention of letting them have Stella. Or me.

That's my official reason for coming anyway. The other is that I'm just...tired of not being near her.

Seven years is a long fucking time to be stuck on the outside, only ever wishing on the stars instead of touching them like I once did.

"So, what does all that have to do with the girl?" Frankie asks. "You think she came here for a flower?"

"If there was a promise of a promotion upon securing the plant, yes."

Over the years, I've learned that Stella is an incredibly driven, focused person. That she's capable of accomplishing anything she sets her mind to.

It's part of why I want her by my side so badly; that kind of dedication to improvement and success is attractive, and I want to bask in her glow.

"Why would her boss offer a promotion? Couldn't he just... come himself?"

"It's a prestigious event, Frankie. Invite only. Barry Ashcroft wouldn't have gotten in."

Frankie exhales, watching as I flex each finger, ensuring my scars are hidden from public view. With my father gone, there's no shame attached to them anymore, but still. Better they stay obscured, where no one will know to prey on the vulnerability they provide.

"What if they don't even have the orchid? What if you've based all this on some big rumor and Stella realizes it and leaves before you can grab her?"

"It's no rumor." My arm falls to my side, and I lift my chin, pinning him with a bored stare. "I sent the flower."

STELLA

The ballroom buzzes with quiet excitement. Shadows dance across the polished floor, bathing throngs of people in half darkness as they mingle. Normally, I'd sink into the recesses of the crowd, avoiding all human contact until I could go home, but my refusal to leave empty-handed drives me deeper into the belly of the beast.

Every patron is dressed elegantly, their expensive silks and cashmere soft against my bare arms as I sweep past. Catering staff cut through the party with silver trays of champagne and hors d'oeuvres, occasionally pausing in offering.

Idle chatter continues around me, and I force myself into a few small conversations—mainly about the weather and how a storm is moving in quickly. Still, I catch snippets about some royals in attendance and the name *Reaper* a handful of times.

Other than that, I'm mostly a ghost. It wouldn't bother me, really, if Val's words from earlier weren't blaring like a siren in my head.

Be seen and heard. Network with the other attendees.

That's not a role I'm used to playing, though. Stella Ricci was hidden away at these kinds of events. My parents didn't think I was capable of contributing, so they'd often shut me in a room until the gathering was finished.

Back then, I didn't mind so much because it meant I wasn't party to the expectations of abusive criminals. My parents' shame mostly felt like a favor. Now I'm wondering if I didn't claim some of it subconsciously, as I find inserting myself into these conversations incredibly daunting.

My mind flickers back to my roommate. Valerie Van der Vorm demands attention. She gets what she wants.

If I'm ever going to obtain that promotion and make a real example of myself, that's who I need to emulate.

But first, I need alcohol.

I make a beeline for the bar on the opposite side of the ballroom, noting a few vaguely familiar faces among the lingering crowd. Wealthy socialites like Juliet Bryson—a beautiful brunette, and someone who definitely overlaps in the Van der Vorm circle—crowd the balcony overlooking the room. I steer clear of her and the two men she's speaking to, just in case.

At the bar, I order a lemon-drop shot and down it quickly, letting the liquid heat my insides. The bartender quirks a brow, and I nod toward them, taking the second glass they slide in my direction.

Just as I press the rim to my lips, a voice startles me, and the alcohol dribbles down my chin instead.

"Oh, quelle pauvre petite chiot. Are you nervous?"

My gaze swivels toward a tall woman with striking brown eyes, pale skin, and jet-black hair. Her deep-red gown does nothing to hide her lithe form and curves, and she gives me a feline smile over a martini glass as she openly ogles me.

Her assessment is warm, and I feel it somewhere in my chest.

As people pass by, they can't seem to help staring at us—at *her*. She oozes sensuality, and a low heat simmers in my abdomen as she slides closer, her grin widening as she seems to tower over me.

I will a response past my lips, wiping them with the back of my hand. "What makes you think I'm nervous?"

She cocks a brow. "Aside from how quickly you just took that shot?"

My chin lifts slightly. "Okay, maybe I needed a little liquid courage."

"Ah." My new companion nods as if she's already come to the same conclusion. "Let me guess: You're a scorned lover who thought coming to an A-list party might make you feel better about your shitty love life, but you've quickly realized how out of your element you are. That even if your former paramour *is* here, they might not even care that you are when there are so many other options."

As if to punctuate the accusation, a couple several feet away from us twists into a corner, their hands disappearing beneath their clothing as class and elegance devolve into something heady and dark. The air shifts in puffy clouds around us, growing thick as I rip my gaze from the sudden display.

At my side, the woman gives a low chuckle. "Now you're

wondering how long you have to stay before you can slip out unnoticed."

"Something like that."

"Well, I hate to break it to you," she continues, her voice like pure honey, "but *unnoticed* won't be possible. Not with this crowd and not with someone like you."

"Is that so?" I purr, leaning in. I'm not adept at flirting, but she seems to be eating it up as she moves closer. "I haven't seen any double takes, and no one is lining up to buy me a drink."

Our hands rest next to each other on the bar top.

"They wouldn't dare try to deny *me* an opportunity." A pause as she once again sizes me up. I wonder if my cheeks are as bright as they feel. "If you know any of the people here, rest assured they know who you are, too. Even if everyone is pretending not to notice, you're an impossible sight to look away from."

My eyes narrow slightly as I return her sultry gaze. That almost sounds like a threat.

"You're very forward," I note.

Her grin widens. "*Forward* is synonymous with progress. How would anyone ever get what they want by standing still?"

"Ever heard of the long game?" With each word that comes from my mouth, my nerves tangle together like a cluster of fine rope.

There's no doubt she's out of my league.

"Are you suggesting you need to be courted?" she asks.

"It might be a nice change of pace."

She watches me silently for several beats. Distantly, music floats toward us, winding around our bodies until it feels like it's pushing us closer. My toes curl against the tips of my heels.

Finally, she reaches out, dragging two fingers up my forearm. Compared to the length of the rest of her nails, these two are cut short, and a delicious shiver works down my spine at the clear message.

"Look," she says, edging closer. Spicy perfume wafts in my direction, seizing my senses. "You can stand around, waiting for someone to sweep you off your feet here. Eventually, one of these wealthy fuckers is bound to pay attention to you. Maybe they'll opt for a marriage proposal instead of something they can purchase tomorrow."

My brows furrow as she plucks the drink from my hand.

The woman pauses again, and then I feel those same two fingers graze my side, my hip, the curve of my waist. My gaze flies to hers, and I swallow over the sudden flare of nerves bursting low in my abdomen.

"Or..." she continues, her eyes hooding as she leans over and into me. She's warm, hot even, and I wish I had another drink so I could quench the thirst now claiming me. "We could slink off to one of the little outbuildings on the property, and I could spend the night devouring you."

Oh my God. My pulse skips a beat, hammering in my neck. I can barely hear over the cacophony of drumming and chatter around us.

I swallow again, every muscle in my body drawing taut. Sweat beads along the expanse of my skin.

It's been so long since I felt an inkling of anything sexual or romantic for anyone that I'm not entirely sure what to say.

She lifts a brow, beckoning an answer.

It's clear this is not a woman used to waiting.

"I don't even know your name," I tell her. I don't know what I'm saying or why I'm saying it. It's not like I'd really do anything with this stranger—*right*?

You're married, Stella.

Which is true, in reality, but my husband has kept his distance for seven years. I'm not stupid enough to think he can't find me, so maybe the problem is he honestly doesn't want me.

For some reason, that almost deflates the balloon of warmth bubbling up inside me. As if I find that prospect disappointing even though it's what I've always claimed to want.

"Genevieve Deveraux," she answers immediately. Eagerly. "But if you want, for the night, you can call me 'Mommy.'"

Jesus.

Head spinning, I steal a glance around the room. Other attendees mingle, oblivious to the seductress in their midst—or biding their time, just like me.

My options are limited: make small talk with strangers until the auction, or stow away into a dark room with this woman who promises a night of grandeur and passion. Maybe if I go with her, I can get a look at the orchid up close.

Excitement thrums through my veins at the image of being in the same room as such a powerful little prize.

"Fine," I say after a moment. "But I want you to take me to the viewing room."

Genevieve's dark brows arch. "What makes you think I have that sort of access?"

The bartender shoves a third shot in my direction and then gives her one as well.

I hold the glass up, gesturing at her with it. "You look like an important woman. I'd venture a guess that even if you don't *have* access, you can probably get it."

"I suppose showing you won't hurt. You'll see it all tomorrow anyway." She takes her shot, brings it to her mouth, and runs her tongue along the rim once before swallowing in one gulp. When she slams the glass back on the counter, she snatches my drink from me and finishes it off, then grabs my hand and yanks me from the bar.

Seconds later, she's dragging me out of the ballroom through an arched doorway and into a narrow, dimly lit hall. To our right is a foyer with a massive split staircase, and guests continue to enter past the primly dressed concierge stationed at the front door.

We veer left, down the hall and through a connecting corridor, take a couple of steps, and then she shoves me toward a dark room. Several Black Rose Auction guards stand outside, stone-faced, even as she approaches. Flipping her hair off one shoulder, Genevieve flashes a card at them, and one of them nods, reaching for the handle and pulling the door open.

Inside, a few glass cases make a circle in the middle of the room, each object housed within illuminated by soft white lighting.

My eyes find the orchid immediately. It's a large specimen with an eight-inch diameter and bright white petals that appear to glow purple, depending on how the light hits it.

It's like nothing I've ever seen. There's this magical quality, like it might actually possess the power to aid in more arduous cancer treatments as some sort of super drug, like the reports all say.

A hand curls around my biceps, halting my progression. Genevieve steps up, turning me to face her.

Our chests brush as I right my footing, and she loops one of the accent pieces of hair framing my face around her index finger. My breasts feel heavy and tight.

"You're in the viewing room. Now, what's in this for me?" Her eyes seem to glow, deep brown burning red as she looks down into mine.

"What do you want?"

"Well, we've already established that much." She plucks at my bottom lip with her thumb and then slides her palm along my jaw. "I'm just curious if you taste as sweet as you look."

Sweat slicks my palms, and I press them to the sides of my thighs as she leans in, tilting my head so it spins and spins and—

"Do you often make a habit of kissing other people's wives, Mrs. Deveraux?"

LEO

My dick gets incredibly hard the moment shock and fear register in Stella's posture.

The beautiful brunette goes from nearly colliding with Genevieve one second to swerving her head so fast that it knocks her off-balance. She stumbles slightly, those doe eyes going wide and glassy as soon as she spots me by the door leading into the viewing room.

Her jaw drops, and I take a quick moment to rake my gaze down the length of her body.

She looks almost exactly the same as she did seven years ago, yet there are subtle differences. The slender curve of her cheeks hollowed out as she aged, and the soft flare of her hips are wider now than before, and obnoxious beneath her light-purple gown.

Back then, her hair was down. It spilled over her shoulders and rained in silken strands across her back, and I've dreamed every night of having it wrapped around my fist, tugging until she begged me to stop.

It's up in some kind of bun now, but I wonder if it's gotten longer or if she keeps it shorter to spite my fantasies. Maybe to spite her own.

"*Wife?*" Genevieve's brows furrow, and then she snorts as she looks between us. "Wow, Leo, you've been holding out on me."

"We operate on a need-to-know basis." I keep my gaze on Stella. She doesn't move a muscle.

"And you didn't think I'd need to know you're *married* to the woman you told me to lure here?"

My jaw tics. "I didn't think it necessary, considering I asked you to do a *job*, not seduce the target."

Then again, the North American liaison to the Battestis—a Corsican crime family—has a reputation for being a massive flirt. I'm not sure why I didn't specify, other than perhaps the fact that I was hoping to keep my little wife a secret for a bit longer.

"Look, your target was into it." Genevieve shrugs, shifting away from Stella. "And it's not like *my* husband gives a shit what I do or who I do it with."

Rocking back on my heels, I still don't look in her direction. "Sounds like a conversation you should have with him then."

"What the hell is happening right now?" Stella glances between us, settling on Genevieve. "You work for him?"

A smirk tugs at the corners of my mouth when Stella finally speaks up. "Both fair questions. Perhaps we should delve into them without an audience?"

When I look at Genevieve, it's only for long enough to silently communicate the request for her departure.

Stella huffs. "I see no reason why I should be trapped in here, alone with you—"

"Mrs. Deveraux," I snap at Genevieve, irritation simmering in my gut with her continued presence, "see yourself out before I have you forcibly removed."

She bristles. "No violence on estate property, De Tore, remember?"

My annoyance spikes further. Fucking socialites and their house rules. "Fine. I'll wait to slit your throat until we're outside the house gates."

Genevieve rolls her eyes and moves to slide past Stella. But then she pauses, and I watch her gaze dart to the side, sizing me up, before she quickly dives in. Fisting the back of Stella's head, she drags my wife's face to her own, and their lips collide in a brief open-mouthed kiss that sets my skin aflame in the worst way possible.

Stella blinks, hard, when Genevieve yanks back. She lifts her hand to my wife's chin, dabbing at some saliva pooling on her bottom lip, and then flips her hair over one shoulder and saunters to the door.

"What was the point of that?" I ask through clenched teeth.

Pausing at the exit, Genevieve lifts a shoulder. "She wanted it. I figured she should have a little fun before you go and ruin everything."

The door swings shut as she exits, leaving just Stella and me. She watches as I cross the room in several slow, purposeful strides. I stop just before the orchid's case, pinning my hands behind my back, and stare down at the abomination, trying to understand its appeal. It's not a particularly attractive thing, yet it's rumored to have medicinal properties that could advance science for decades.

My wife wants it *badly*, the little humanitarian.

The question is, *how* badly?

How much will she break for me in order to get it?

"What are you...?" She trails off, then tries again. "Why are you *here*, Leo?"

"What, disappointed that I ruined your rendezvous?"

"I came here to see—"

"Is it true?"

Stella frowns, pausing. "What?"

"Did you want it?" I turn and step closer to her, my blood thrumming at our proximity after so long of only watching from afar. "Genevieve's kiss, I mean."

She doesn't reply.

As I inhale, I note that she still smells like blueberries and mint, though with a hint of something new and citrusy. "It's okay if you did."

It isn't. Not really. But the *principle* of the matter—if she thinks I care that she kissed a woman—that part makes no difference. She's mine regardless of who she desires.

"Are you asking because you think I'm here to cheat on you?" she mutters.

"*Are* you?"

"What difference does it make? You didn't come after me

anyway. After all this time, shouldn't I be allowed to kiss whoever I want and explore my options? Maybe I'm here tonight to
embrace the fact that I'm bisexual, and you're ruining everything
like you always do."

Her words are defensive, like she thinks I'm going to use
that information against her. And like she thinks I was abandoning her. It makes my chest ache. "I'm not here to crucify
you for liking more than just men. I couldn't care less about
that, and you shouldn't either. This was just my poor attempt
at gauging what all we have in common, stellina. Pardon me
for trying to get to know my wife a little better after our time
apart."

She goes quiet again, leaving me to wonder where her head's
at. If she thinks I've been with anyone since or if she's considering
her own missed opportunities.

"You're bisexual," she says softly. It isn't a question, but she
still seems unsure. Like she needs verbal confirmation to prove
something.

I wonder if this is the first time she's admitted her own sexuality out loud to another. If that's why she hesitates.

"You don't have to whisper. It isn't a secret, not that anyone's
listening now anyway."

"Have you—" She cuts herself off this time, those elegant
brows knitting together in a frown above her nose.

Sighing, I stop just shy of half a foot away, reveling in the
sensation of being in her orbit again. Back then, I failed to see
how much I had grown to crave her in such a short time, until it
was already too late.

Finally, she refocuses, shaking her head. "Why. Are. You. Here?" Frustration laces her tone, and my dick pulses madly.

"I've thought about this moment for years. How you might react to seeing me again. Though I always imagined your hair would be down so I could run my fingers through it, like I did the night we married."

Stella just stares up at me, her expression hard and guarded.

My hand lifts, aching to touch her. It drops at the last second, my fingers flicking a piece of lint from my jacket. "I heard your parents are dead."

"Did you come here to gloat?"

I cock my head to the side, studying the lack of emotion in her gaze. Other than annoyance, that is. "You don't seem too torn up about it."

"Were you sad when your dad died?"

One of my brows lifts. "Keeping tabs on the husband you hate, stellina?"

"My sisters talk."

"I see. And how are they enjoying their happily ever afters?"

"They talk. I don't."

My smirk grows, and I inch even closer. Warmth wafts from her body into mine in soft, cascading waves that buzz along my nerve endings. "That's what I like about you. Everything that comes from those beautiful lips is so brutally honest. Like you simply can't help yourself."

"Yeah, well, growing up in a household that doesn't let you speak your mind will sometimes do that to a person."

"Indeed." I lift my arm, my fingers tingling beneath the

leather glove as I force myself to cradle her jaw. She flinches, and pain scorches my body, but she doesn't pull away. "Now, for some more honesty. Did you *enjoy* Genevieve's kiss?"

Jealousy licks up and down my spine at the still-fresh memory of their passion. How, despite the kiss being sudden and unexpected, Stella gave herself over to it so easily, unlike the memories I have of our own shared moments—kisses soaked in violence and power struggles.

A part of me is curious how different they felt and which she prefers: passion or aggression.

I'm not sure which I'm able to offer or if I'm capable of anything outside the latter.

Her eyes flip back and forth between mine, and I wonder what she's looking for—or if she's able to find it.

"Can you please just tell me what you're doing here? I don't... I should probably get to my room before someone realizes I'm not out mingling."

The redirection is purposeful, and it only fuels the envy spiraling into a web in my chest. How can she possibly not realize I've come for her?

So, rather than answer, I decide to fix both my problems at once, bending down to press my lips to hers.

STELLA

forgot what it felt like.

Kissing Leo De Tore.

Where Genevieve's kiss was warm and languid, Leo's is all-consuming, like walking directly into a raging wildfire. Even after I spent years trying to ignore his memory, the effect remains the same.[*]

When his tongue flicks against mine, I forget all about the other woman. As if driven by some primal instinct, my hands slide up the lapels of his suit jacket, and my fingers claw at his chest. I shift closer, deepening the kiss, and he lets out a low groan that vibrates between my legs.

That's when I snap out of it.

Yanking my head back, I disconnect our lips and try to shove him away. Unfortunately, he doesn't seem to have changed one bit since I last saw him. His skin is a little tanner, his black hair a bit longer, and his sharp jaw is clean-shaven.

[*] MAYDAY—PmBata

Otherwise, he's the same bastard as always. His hands are encased in those damn leather gloves, and he loops them around my waist, keeping me pressed tightly to him. Rage seeps into my vision.

I beat at his pecs with my fists, trying to ignore how rock-solid he feels. It might be doing more harm to me than him.

His dark chuckle skates over my skin. He shifts, his right leg coming to the outside of mine so my thigh is stuck between his.

"Feel that?" he rasps, and it takes me a second to notice the pressure from his pelvis. "You should know your violence makes me really fucking hard, stellina."

"Maybe you should get your brain checked. Delusions like that are sometimes signs of a stroke."

"It's sweet that you care."

My breaths come in harsh bursts from my chest, the weight of reality crashing down like a boulder smashing into the earth. For seven years, he's left me alone. Years I've spent getting my bachelor's degree, fighting to be heard and respected in biomed forums, doing scut work for Rampion Core, and volunteering at local conferences and fundraisers. Being my own person and making a name for myself outside of the Ricci brand.

Still, at some point, I tricked myself into thinking he had no interest, because I can't help feeling pure, unadulterated panic now that he's here.

How long will it be before he takes everything from me?

I *thought* I was free, but freedom is just an illusion in this world. You don't really get to leave.

Finally, he releases me. I'm not expecting it, so I stumble a bit when he hastily steps back, making his way over to the auction items lined up in the center of the room.

"God, there's a lot of expensive bullshit in here."

I don't think he's looking for a response, so I don't say anything. He passes a diamond necklace and scoffs at a silvery-gold, ruby-studded chalice.

"These items pale in comparison to the people putting themselves on the block tomorrow. Inanimate objects tend to be more complicated to wield for personal benefit, whereas humans... well." He glances at me, his eyes growing somehow darker than ever. "Humans strike deals. Solicit favors. If you play your cards right, you can manipulate anyone into doing your bidding."

I lift my chin. "Too bad for you, I'm not for sale."

Another chuckle. "Are you forgetting the fact you already belong to me? If I wanted you up on a pedestal tomorrow, you'd be up there."

"No, I wouldn't."

"You would if you wanted the Orchidée Sans Nom that badly."

Surprise arches my eyebrows, and my jaw drops slightly at the mention of the flower. I suppose it's not difficult to determine which of the items I'd be most interested in, but there's something almost violating about hearing him say it.

His index finger slides along the flower's glass case, screeching loudly. "You know, there are only two of these in existence. The first was being held by some Japanese botany facility for preservation, and it sold at auction for half a billion. Didn't even go to a band of scientists or someone who wants to try and use it for good. It was just sitting at someone's home, gathering dust on its petals for the sake of vanity."

My eyes narrow. *How does he know all that?* The last auction was private, and the recipients' names were sealed to keep poachers away.

"I wonder what would happen if this got into the wrong hands," he says, squinting at the flower. "Someone with ulterior motives might use it as leverage."

"Well, that isn't going to happen."

He glances up at me, rounding the case so it's between us. "No?"

"I'm winning the orchid tomorrow, then taking it back to my lab so they can research it and see if it actually has medicinal qualities."

"Such an altruist." He taps the glass with one gloved finger. "Would be a shame if someone were to outbid you."

Anger courses through my fingertips, and I wish I had a weapon right now. Even if it got me escorted off the property, assaulting this man would be worth it.

"Are you threatening me?" I ask, growing weary of the back and forth.

"I don't like that term. I'd prefer if we called it 'blackmailing.'"

"Does that make you feel better about doing it?"

"Considerably, yes." Exhaling slowly, Leo rounds the glass case before stopping just in front of it. He leans back, extending his legs and crossing one ankle over the other.

The picture of complete ease. I wonder if this is a window into how simple it was for him to let me go back then and not even bother to come after me.

Not that I *wanted* him to. It's just the principle of the matter.

His eyes darken as they drag down my form, leaving a path of hot carnage in their wake. "Take down your hair."

"What?"

"Your hair. I'd like to see it down when I take your virginity."

"That's presumptuous." I tilt my chin. "Besides, who says I'm still a virgin?"

Something dangerous flashes in his gaze. "How about we test my theory?"

My hand immediately goes to the side of my head, feeling the soft strands held back by Valerie's pins. Every nerve in my body tightens, like wire coiling around a spring. "I... No. I'm not going to do that. *We* aren't doing that."

"I'm happy to see your spine is still intact after all these years. I won't feel so bad about coming to collect what I'm owed."

"I don't owe you shit."

He grins, big and toothy. It's unsettling—predatory. Like I'm prey, and I just walked into his trap.

"Your father is dead, cara mia. Normally, that'd make the deal we struck up null and void." His long legs carry him to me in a few strides, and I back up, trying to keep as much distance between us as possible. "Problem is, we're still very much married. So the deal transfers to you...and is currently unfulfilled, I'm afraid, as you left my condo without consummation."

"I don't remember signing anything legal—"

Within seconds, he slams me into a wall, and I'm thrust back in time to when he pinned me in the alley behind the church and kissed me. How it felt like my world shifted on its axis with that kiss. I've been secretly yearning for that same high ever since.

The only difference is that now I've tasted freedom. I won't give it up so easily—and certainly not for some measly kiss.

Leo's hips brush mine. My chest heaves, each breath a struggle as my brain begins short-circuiting from his presence and scent alone. I don't know why he has this effect on me—I can't even make sense of it biologically, though I know the technical evidence is there.

He's attractive, and my body remembers how good he is with his tongue and hands. But all that should be moot, given everything he represents.

Yet I ache for him to touch me. After all this time, the sting of his rejection still reverberates in the back of my mind, and I wish he'd prove it was a fluke.

After reaching into his interior jacket pocket, Leo pulls out a folded slip of paper. He presses it to my chest, his grin turning sinister.

"You signed. Or at least, *someone* signed your name."

"Forgery? Seriously?"

A shrug. "All I have to do is show a judge the security footage of you naked in my kitchen, letting me put my filthy mouth between your luscious thighs. It wouldn't take much more to convince them that we consummated, and in that case, why wouldn't you have signed? These factors are all very easy to manipulate, I'm afraid, Stella. And you *did* commit to being my wife in your vows. Before you left me."

Exasperation heats my body. My fingertips itch to scratch his eyes out. "I didn't leave *you*. I left *everything*. Do you think that was easy, abandoning my life? My sisters? I didn't even get to attend my parents' funerals, and you have the audacity to come in here and demand things from me, push me around, and try to drag me back? I'm not going."

His face remains impassive, as if he's unaffected by the raw emotion dripping from my words. It makes me angrier.

"Why do you even care all of a sudden? You rejected me, and then for seven years, I didn't hear a fucking peep. Why come back now when I've actually got things going for me? Do you just enjoy seeing me suffer? Is that why you showed up? Have you just been stalking me, waiting to ruin a perfect moment?"

"I suppose you could say that."

"Fine. You want me so badly?"

I shove him backward, then scramble toward him, reaching to undo the belt hidden beneath his jacket. His brows furrow, and he moves to stop me, but I smack him away and crouch.

Getting on my knees in this dress is probably not a good idea, but I'm so filled with rage and fear that I don't care.

"This isn't exactly what I had in mind—"

"Shut *up*. You want to come, right? That's why you want to fuck me. New deal—if I make you come, we're even. Tit for tat. You can leave me and the orchid alone. Sound good? Good." I undo his zipper, ignoring the tremor in my fingers, and peer up at him for some sort of confirmation.

His gray eyes are impossible to read. Sweat slicks my palms at the thought of him rejecting me once again, but he just tucks the folded marriage license back in his jacket and says, "I want to come *inside* you."

For some reason, the image causes goose bumps to sprout along my arms and my nipples to tighten. "Then you'll leave me be?"

"Let's not overestimate the quality of your services, stellina. You were a virgin when I met you, after all." He pauses as I yank his pants down. "I'm assuming your little tryst with Genevieve was an isolated incident."

"Not for lack of trying."

A muscle in his jaw thumps. "Fortunately for you, I know that's not true. You've been too busy studying and working to let anyone touch you. Not that they'd compare anyway."

"You're an asshole."

"An asshole whose dick you're about to put in your mouth."

The band of his black boxers slides lower, and suddenly, his dick springs free, dark pink and already hard as granite. A large vein twists up the side, and even though it's my first time seeing one this close, I can't help feeling a tinge of something intoxicatingly wicked in my stomach.

I've watched enough porn to know he's on the larger side and thicker than most. Frankly, even as I curl my fingers around his shaft, just above where he holds it, I'm having a hard time believing I'll be able to take him in my mouth.

Vaginas can stretch to accommodate dicks and babies. Mouths are a different story.

His smirk tells me he knows what I'm thinking, too. "Don't worry," he says, reaching down to grab the base, stroking once so it grows somehow bigger. "I'll fit as long as you're wet enough."

I roll my eyes. "I know how sex works."

"Is that right?" Something profoundly possessive flashes in his expression. "Prove it. Suck my dick like you know what you're doing, and maybe you'll come away from all this unscathed."

Shifting forward, I spread my ankles apart a bit to better distribute my weight, which is being held up solely by these skinny heels.

"Spit on it first," he says. "It'll make it easier for me to glide in and out."

"Aren't you afraid I'll bite?"

"Just afraid I'll like it."

His grin strokes a fire deep in my belly, fanning flames I've long left dormant. It feels so odd to have such perfect banter with a man I haven't seen in years, even if we have been married all this time.

Pursing my lips, I collect some saliva on the tip of my tongue and let it pool over the slit in his crown. He doesn't react, even as I slide my hand up to spread the spit around, awkwardly trying to mimic what I've seen online.

My sisters say porn isn't realistic in that aspect, but right now, I don't really care. I just want to get all this over with so I can bid on the orchid tomorrow, unimpeded.

Penises have four thousand nerve endings in the head alone, according to the biology lab I took my freshman year of college. It shouldn't take much effort to achieve an orgasm.

Plus, I'm an excellent student when I want to be.

Leo's hips flex, and his cock seems to twitch beneath my touch. I watch closely, looking for the spots where he seems to be most sensitive and using my thumb to apply extra pressure. It's mesmerizing, seeing his muscles and veins strain against his soft flesh and hearing the way his breaths hitch with each stroke.

"Tighter. You're not going to hurt me."

I glance up, startled by the choked command. His hand comes down over mine, forcing it to fist him in an ironclad grip. He guides me slowly, turning my wrist and dragging me from base to tip each time.

"Fuck. Put your mouth on me."

"Jesus, you could say please."

"*Please*, Stella. I need to feel you."

My eyes widen at how quickly he caves and the hint of desperation lacing his words. I stare at him as our hands continue moving and finally inch forward, letting my lips close over his tip. He's silky smooth on my tongue, and a slightly salty taste takes over my senses.

His head tilts back instantly, his hips bucking toward me in an attempt to fill more space.

Pressing my free hand to his pelvis, I halt his forward motion and pull back, removing him from my mouth and using the new saliva to coat his length.

He watches every movement of mine like a hawk. "Take off your dress."

"No."

"Put your hair down."

I squeeze tightly at the base of his crown, then drag my teeth lightly over the crown. He shudders.

"Stop telling me what to do," I tell him.

"Hey, I was just trying to help it go quicker. If you want more time with my cock, stellina, just say so."

Rolling my eyes again, I open my mouth and take him in it, this time a little deeper than before. He slides past my lips easily, and I chase the motion of my fist, testing to see how far I can go without gagging.

Leo releases a grunt when I pull off this time. One of his hands finds the back of my head, though he doesn't try to shove me down. It just rests there, as if grounding him in the moment.

His eyes are turbulent storm clouds, his breathing labored, and I can't deny the satisfaction creeping up my thighs at the realization that so little from effort me is unraveling him.

I move in again, bobbing my head in shorter, faster movements. My jaw starts to ache, and I go too deep at one point; the tip prods the back of my throat, and I immediately gag with him lodged there, cutting off my own air supply.

My toes tingle, and my pussy throbs like it's being directly stimulated by his actions.

He emits a low groan. "That's good, baby. *Really* fucking good."

I ignore the shiver his praise sends over my clammy skin and move away, drool pooling out when I free my mouth. "You like me choking?"

"I love the desperation. *Your* desperation. Knowing you're hot enough for me to gag on my dick makes me *very* happy." He cups my cheek with his free hand, and I'm in enough of a haze from everything going on that I don't reject the touch. "Open your mouth."

"Why—"

Grabbing his cock, he bats me away. I settle both hands in my lap and bounce slightly, trying to regain feeling in my legs from my crouched position. Leo tugs at himself in brutal, rapid strokes, moving so fast that his fingers are almost a blur, even right before my eyes.

"Open, Stella."

At the sound of my name, uttered with a broken whimper as crimson floods his cheeks, my lips part. I feel like one of Pavlov's dogs, but I refuse to consider the implication of what that means for me and my hyper-independency.

Slut. I can almost hear Mamma uttering the word from wherever she's being tortured in the afterlife.

But only the sounds of his harsh, stuttered breathing, a roaring noise between my ears, and his palm shuffling in slick thrusts fill the room. His noises drown out the maternal judgment, replacing it with something delicious.

I shift, rubbing my thighs together. If I could just reach under my dress, maybe I could—

My heart beats a staccato rhythm in my chest, almost in time with his panting, and I'm so focused on the pure pleasure stretching across his handsome face that I barely notice when he starts to come.

The first thick, warm spurt hits my chin, and then he angles differently, aiming directly inside my mouth. Ropes of semen land on my tongue, and I cringe at the still-unfamiliar sensation. But I don't close my lips and bar him access.

If anything, I lean into it, my face growing hot at the awe-struck look in his eyes and the slack in his jaw.

Having his complete attention, his touch, feels too good to ignore.

LEO

It makes no fucking sense what this woman does to me.

She shouldn't have such a visceral effect on my being, yet when my cum hits her tongue and she huffs out a startled noise, I nearly black out from the pleasure.

Stella moves to wipe her chin, but I grab her wrist and yank her up to me. She keeps her mouth open, as if aware on some intrinsic level that I want to see—that I *need* to see it. The evidence of me on her, in her.

I tug her close, and she stumbles, bracing against my chest. I take my gloved index and middle fingers, scoop the warm spend off her skin, and press both into her mouth.

"There we go," I say, my voice low and tight. "Can't have you wasting that when I've spent seven years saving it for you."

She slowly closes her lips around the leather and licks it clean, swallowing audibly. As if stuck in some haze. Finished, she blinks, and I remove myself so she can speak. "What does that mean? You haven't—"

"Been with anyone else?" I finish, deviant sensations spinning around my sternum. "How could I, knowing you were out here all by your lonesome, waiting for me?"

That seems to catch her off guard, and she spends several seconds just looking at my throat.

"Beautiful," I mutter, mesmerized by her mouth, her stare— every-fucking-thing about her.

Those brown eyes are wide and lust-filled, and I grit my teeth to keep from bending her over right here, right now. My cock stirs, likely ready to go again, but I need to play my cards right.

Otherwise, I'll leave empty-handed, and I refuse to do that.

Pinching her cheeks with my free hand, I push my fingers back in until she gags, then pull them all the way out. Before she has a chance to escape, I tilt my head down and plant a smothering kiss to her lips, swirling my tongue and tasting myself on her.

The mix of musk and her minty blueberry breath sends delectable tension spiraling through my chest. Our teeth clash, and she uses her tongue to push the remnants of my cum into my mouth, sharing like the good little wife she is.

With a frustrated groan, I disconnect. She looks so goddamn ethereal standing there, her red lipstick smudged from me, that I turn away immediately to avoid taking more than she's ready to give.

"Are we even then?" she asks, dabbing saliva from the corners of her mouth. Her mask of discontent slips back into place. "You got me off seven years ago, and now I've gotten you off. Our deal is done."

She's putting words in my mouth, but I don't feel like correcting her yet.

I do have to wonder if she's purposely misremembering our arrangement and the *marriage* it promised. Consummation was just an excuse—*extra*.

Then again, perhaps she's hoping I forgot or changed my mind. That her sucking me dry would sate me.

Or she thinks I've grown tired of her in our time apart. That my interest waned.

Unfortunately for her, it's never been stronger.

"I don't remember agreeing to a new deal." I toss her a grin that has the tips of her ears turning pink—or maybe it's from me finally bothering to pull up my pants and put my cock away.

It doesn't matter, I suppose, so long as I know I can affect her. That's my in here.

I'll keep her safe, driving her back into my waiting arms.

Before she can blink and try to stop me, and before I can make an even greater fool of myself, I stalk toward the exit and grip the doorknob in one fist, twisting violently. More so than necessary.

"You *said*—"

"I'll see you tomorrow," I interrupt over my shoulder, slipping out of the room and into the shadows.

She scrambles after me, her breathing frenzied as she screeches to a halt, her head swiveling left and right as she searches the darkness. Fury radiates from her figure when she turns the wrong way and stomps off to find me.

I smirk at the plain-colored wall as music from the ballroom trickles into the corridor like rainwater.

Tomorrow, my wife.

———

Frankie hands me a red silk tie, then flops down on the sofa across from the wall-mounted mirror. The guest rooms at the auction site are straight out of an *Architectural Digest* spread, complete with massive beds, luxurious satin sheets, and remote-controlled blackout curtains.

It's the picture of ultimate comfort, yet I barely slept at all last night.

A part of me is simply unhappy with being away from home, as I've never had much luck sleeping anywhere but my own bed. The other part is filled with an inordinate amount of adrenaline from thinking about my wife sleeping somewhere else in the mansion, all alone for the last time.

"Are you sure this is a good idea?" Frankie asks, kicking his feet up over the sofa arm and reclining with his hands behind his head. "Your uncle isn't exactly scouring the earth to find her. Maybe we should just leave her be."

"Gino might say he's not looking," I respond, knotting the tie at my throat, "but I don't believe him. Since the Elders haven't been able to make me pay for my crimes fully, I have no doubt they'll be closing in on her soon. There's no way her presence is going unnoticed. Not when they know I'm also here."

My uncle might have been undecided at first with an expectation to rat, but he turned completely after learning that Stella had simply walked out of our lives. Though forced to work under me after my father's death, the man's been waiting for an opportunity to correct what he views as treason, but not by Stella—by *me*.

Because I let her go.

"Why *did* you let her go?" Frankie asks.

I freeze, meeting his gaze in the reflection of the mirror. "Excuse me?"

He stares up at the vaulted ceiling. "You didn't think I bought the story about her just *walking out* of one of the most guarded towers in Boston, did you? Give me a little credit."

"I...wanted her to have more." My jaw shifts, clenching tight. "A real life."

"In exchange for your own?" He cocks a brow. "I mean, I'm sure you predicted they'd go after her."

I had, but there was never a version of that image that ended with them actually getting her.

I'll do whatever necessary, manufacture whatever meeting or rendezvous, to make sure of it.

A knock sounds at the door, and Frankie gets up to answer, one hand on the gun he smuggled in at his waist. Because of the auction's strict no-violence policy, we had to get a little creative in retrieving our weapons, enlisting the assistance of one of the royals in attendance.

I slide my gloves onto my hands, stretching my fingers.

Genevieve's smiling face appears in the doorway, and Frankie lets out an irritated noise, stepping back to let her in. She sweeps right past him in a bold, shimmering black evening gown, her toned biceps and deep cleavage on display in the strapless piece.

Without greeting me, she makes a beeline for the minibar

in the far corner of the room, then immediately uncaps a small bottle of water. She tosses Frankie a Diet Coke, which he catches and pops open before taking a seat on the chaise at the foot of the bed.

Genevieve struts over before draping herself on my shoulder. She's several inches taller than Stella, even without heels, so our eyes are almost level in the reflection.

An image of her yesterday with my wife flashes through my mind, and I shake her off. She chuckles, the sound dark and sensual, and every fiber of my being regrets roping her into this convoluted plan.

"Ready to get your bid on?" she quips, unbothered by the change in atmosphere in the room.

"I'm ready for you to be out of my life."

Genevieve pouts, leaning forward to adjust her bloodred lipstick. "Ugh, are you still mad about yesterday? I was *playing*, Leopoldo. Just like you asked me to."

I cut her a measured look. "I didn't ask you to seduce my wife."

"You didn't even tell me she was your wife! And she didn't mention anything either. How was I supposed to know?"

Frankie clicks his tongue. "She makes a good point. You can't respect boundaries you don't know about."

"Ah, but she *did* know when she kissed her." Shrugging into my suit jacket, I smooth down the collar and button it in the middle. "If not for the fact I already paid for your services, I'd have killed you for touching her."

"You know," she says, "most men would *die* for the chance

to watch me entertain their partners. My own husband's begged me to bring others into our bedroom."

"Probably so he doesn't have to touch you himself," Frankie mutters against his can.

There's a story there, only I don't care enough to ask about it.

I glare at her. "Unfortunately, I have no interest in seeing you in any state of undress. Ever."

She smiles, turning away from the mirror. "Not even if I were riding your wife's face? Or making her come with my mouth on her pretty pussy?"

"Not even if you sucked the cum from her cunt after I finished with her." Heading for the door, I glance over my shoulder, ignoring the mischievous glint in her dark eyes. "Touch Stella again, and it'll be the last thing you do."

I leave the room without another word, slamming the door shut behind me. The sound echoes down the hall, and a couple coming out of a different room across from mine pauses to stare inquisitively. I nod at them, tugging at my lapels, and make my way to the ballroom.

Like the rest of the mansion, the ballroom is ostentatious with its almost-reflective polished floor and furniture plated with twenty-two-karat gold finishings. Luckily, the obnoxious wealth is hushed by the dim lighting, kept low to promote anonymity in the crowd.

Most people are here purely for the spectacle of an auction. The only thing rich people love more than throwing their money around is watching others do the same.

A handful will bid on whatever items are put up onstage.

Typically, because viewing opens up earlier in the afternoon, attendees will know what they want and what they're willing to pay for it, so bidding wars aren't terribly likely.

But I foresee one happening, and satisfaction wraps around my ribs at the thought.

I find Stella immediately in the room, despite her being directly in the middle and engulfed in shadows. She stands beside a pub-style table, nursing an umbrella drink, with her hair in that same updo from last night.

She looks positively unsettled.

It's delicious.

Her outfit is different, though, which is likely the cause of the discomfort. A spotlight washes over the crowd for a moment, giving me a plain view of her before it lands onstage. The dress she wears is white lace and partially see-through, revealing skin I've only had the pleasure of seeing once.

Tight, perfect tits. Diamond-hard, dusky-pink nipples. Her tender cunt covered only by a nude thong.

A few people are standing far too close, stealing glances at her from the corners of their eyes. For some reason, it makes my cock twitch behind the zipper of my slacks to know they want her.

For no one other than me will have her.

Bracing my palms on the table, I bracket Stella in from behind, pressing my front into her backside. "You look good enough to eat," I mutter against her ear, my desire for her unwilling to take a back seat to reason.

"And you sound like the villain in a corny fairy tale." She doesn't try to get away, nor does she turn her head to look at me.

Instead, she just takes a sip of her drink, keeping her gaze trained on the stage.

"Does that make you the damsel in distress?"

"Only because you're here."

I shift, relishing in the feel of her ass cradled against my dick. "I never quite understood why everyone said you were nothing more than a quiet, boring carbon copy of your sisters. Dull, they told me back then. No one in my family could fathom why I'd married such a dud."

One of my hands leaves the table's surface, dropping to her hip and slipping lower. I flatten my palm to the outside of her thigh, squeezing her soft flesh.

"But from the moment I met you, you've been nothing short of bewitching. I think people have somehow mistaken your ire for monotony."

She doesn't say anything. The auctioneer—a tall, pale man named Reaper with long white hair, dark eyes that seem to penetrate everyone he looks at, and several piercings on his face and nipples—takes the stage, introducing himself to the audience before moving on to the first item.

"Maybe they think that because it's what I show them," Stella says quietly, spinning her drink in her hands.

"Why should I be any different?"

Stella clenches her jaw. "You're not."

"No? You've been lying to me then?"

"*No*, I just—" She halts, sucking in a breath. "Don't go getting any ideas, okay? Telling you the truth doesn't mean anything, just like you being here all of a sudden doesn't."

"Is that what you think, stellina? That us being here, it's a coincidence?"

"Of course not. I don't believe in coincidences. I'm sure you have some convoluted explanation for showing up out of the blue, but I'm not interested in hearing it."

Amusement toys with the corners of my mouth as I study her profile. She keeps her mesmerizing face forward, as if hiding her eyes from me might keep her truth within. But I didn't spend seven years watching her from afar without learning everything about this woman, and I can tell she's still sour over how things ended between us.

"Everything happens for a reason, right? That's the kind of research you do, trying to identify potential genetic abnormalities that might cause health issues in people. A *reason* behind a problem so you can one day develop a solution."

Her spine stiffens. Clearly, she didn't expect me to know much about what she does for a living. "Do you honestly think being a creepy stalker means you know me? News flash, it's actually pathetic."

"Most men in my position would have killed you the first time you talked to them like that," I tell her, pushing my cock more firmly against her ass. "You're lucky I happen to like being hurt by you."

"I don't think *lucky* is the word I'd use."

"No?" I slide my hand forward, my throat thick with desire. My fingers skim her thong, though the fact I can't feel her because of my gloves makes me irrationally irritated. Keeping my hand beneath her dress, I slowly work one off, then resume my exploration.

"Would you stop? I have no clue when they're announcing the orchid, and I don't want to miss it because you think you're entitled to my body."

"Everyone in this place thinks they're entitled to your body. They'd pay millions of dollars just to see it up close." My teeth graze the shell of her ear, and she shivers as my fingers dip beneath the elastic of her underwear and spread her soaked flesh. "The difference is, I'm the only one who *actually* has a claim here."

"I'm not a piece of land. You can't—"

She's fucking dripping, so my index finger slides right into her, stealing the rest of her sentence. Her muscles contract, warm and so goddamn wet that it takes me a moment to steady my own breathing.

"You talk too much. Try enjoying yourself for an evening, baby."*

A small, almost-inaudible gasp slips through her lips, and she frowns. "I cannot enjoy myself in your presence."

"Mmm, that's not how I remember it. In fact, I distinctly recall you *enjoying yourself* all over my face. Right in the middle of my kitchen." My finger pumps deeper, curling. "Perhaps you need a reminder? It has been quite some time."

"Whose fault is that?" she says through gritted teeth, gripping the table and abandoning the placard with her guest number on it.

"Not mine, if that's what you're implying." My movements in and out of her are agonizingly slow. Electric heat rushes through my veins, and I grunt in her ear as her hips seek friction, her cunt squeezing me so hard that my fingers start to go numb. "If it'd

* WE'LL NEVER HAVE SEX—Leith Ross

been solely up to me, I'd have tracked you down the second you asked Irene for help escaping, then tied you to my bed until you apologized for trying to rescind our deal."

Even if it was my idea for you to leave in the first place.

Someone next to us shoves their hand in the air, bidding on an auction item. Stella's spine straightens as if she just remembered that we're in public. Granted, I'm angled in a way that blocks her from onlookers at our sides, but there's nothing stopping the crowd in front of us from twisting and getting an eyeful.

I watch her throat bob as she swallows, and then her cunt gets even tighter.

Smirking against her bare shoulder, I move my thumb up and strum at her clit. Stella jolts, apparently not expecting the contact, and her mouth falls open as she glares at the stage.

"You didn't honestly think I'd be satisfied with last night, did you?" I ask, stroking her flesh languidly. My eyes are glued to her profile, tracking every twitch, every sharp inhale, every tiny noise she makes so I can get her pleasure exactly right.

Onstage, a diamond necklace goes for an amount I don't care to pay attention to, and they sweep it away swiftly. From the corner of my eye, I see the illusion of bright, glowing petals, and every muscle in my body tenses.

With my free hand, I grip Stella's chin and angle it toward me, capturing her mouth with mine. She jerks back, then seems to sink into the act, as if everything else melts away at the mere meeting of our lips.

Delight swirls in my stomach, a massive fireball of emotion I'm not used to. My fingers work harder, faster, attempting to wring the euphoria directly from Stella's soul so maybe I can keep bits of it for myself.

She closes her eyes, slumping back against me. Even when she grips my wrist, it's not to bat me away but to guide me better—to show me *precisely* where she needs me. I add a third finger, swallowing down my own desire.

"Fuck me, you're so goddamn tight. I actually don't know if I'll fit in you later." My words are barely more than harsh whispers against her skin. "I'll have to stretch you nice and wide so it doesn't hurt too much."

A soft moan drifts toward me. "Stop *talking*."

"But don't you feel what it's doing? You're practically milking me, baby. You're ready to come, aren't you?"

If I stop talking, it's possible she'll be able to listen to the auction in real time. My hand leaves her face, slamming down on the table where hers was moments ago.

"Come," I tell her in a rough, choked voice as my dick throbs and begs for release. I clench my teeth, balling my fist on the table in resistance. "While we're surrounded by dozens of people who wouldn't care if you lived or died, come on my fucking fingers. Like it's the last thing you'll ever do or give me and you can't think of anything else. Come while these fuckers stand here, none the wiser."

It takes a second, but she gasps a moment later, squeezing her eyes shut as my hand on the table lifts into the air. Her cunt grips me, sucking and soaking me where I'm lodged as deep as I can get three fingers. She spasms, her inner muscles throbbing, and drags my face to hers for a kiss while she crests that blissful wave.

There isn't enough time for her to stop it all from happening.

The second she opens her eyes, those beautiful brown irises like molten lava with the aftershocks of her orgasm, Reaper's voice calls out over the crowd. "*Sold!* The Orchidée Sans Nom to guest number seventeen hundred."

STELLA

The blood freezes in my veins when the auctioneer's words reach my ears.

Sold? How is that possible when I didn't even see it onstage?

It takes a second for my brain to fully catch up and even longer for my body. Leo doesn't withdraw, and the longer he remains lodged inside me, the worse I feel.

"Get *off* me." The words are a deadly venom, spewed from my barely open lips.

Leo chuckles. "But I'm so comfortable."

Grinding my teeth, I snake one leg away from him and use the momentum to drive my heel into the toe of his loafer. He removes his fingers while the rest of him stays in place, pinning me to the table.

I wrench my head to the right, finding the placard he's holding and my discarded one beneath it. Until now, it didn't fully cross my mind that I'd dropped the damn thing. I was too caught up in how good it felt to have him touching me.

Frustrated and flustered, I dip my chin forward and rear back quickly, slamming my skull into my husband's jaw.

Leo curses, pulling away from me in an instant. I *hate* how empty he leaves me feeling—I'm cold and vacant inside now, consuming any warmth left by his embrace and the residual elation of a much-needed orgasm.

He touches his thumb to his bleeding bottom lip as I whirl around, ready to dig my nails into his deceitful eyes.

"I'd think twice before lashing out again," he says in a low voice, glancing at the crowd. "There are rules here, stellina. You wouldn't want to get in trouble for being a bloodthirsty siren, would you?"

A few bystanders have turned in our direction, and an auction staff member makes their way over, clasping Leo on the shoulder.

"Everything okay here, folks?" the uniformed redhead asks.

Leo nods, rubbing at the underside of his chin. "Oh, yes, that was merely an accident. My wife has very limited spatial awareness."

The staff member doesn't seem entirely convinced, but when Leo turns away from them, it effectively ends the conversation. Still, I can feel dozens of eyes on us, and the knowledge makes my skin crawl.

Leaning against the table, I glare at Leo. "How fucking dare you."

"You're complaining about getting off?"

"You basically *stole* my bid. I wanted that goddamn flower, and you *knew* it. Why would you keep me from buying it like that?"

"I didn't—"

Spinning on my heels, I veer through the crowd, leaving him behind. Seconds pass, and he's hot on my trail, even as I weave through the throng of auction attendees. Red-hot anger burns in my skull, and I realize the last time I felt this way was probably seven years ago—first when Papà used me to broker a deal with a vicious man, and again when that man rejected my advances.

Stepping out of the ballroom is like waking from a deep slumber. Bright lights shine down, and I squint at the empty hallway, my brain working overtime to formulate a plan—or at least a single coherent thought. One that isn't about Leopoldo De Tore.

The odds of me getting a promotion are very low if I don't get that fucking orchid. For a moment, I glare at the wall, wondering if it's even worth it.

If any of this is truly worth it.

Maybe I should've just stayed in Boston. I'm sure someone would have killed me by now out of spite or suspicion. At least I wouldn't have to keep facing how fucking *worthless* I am.

Sure, I've worked my ass off these past few years to make up for everything else that was bought or handed to me because of my family. But I can't shake the thought that maybe Papà was right in marrying me off. Maybe Mamma was right that all I'm good for is being someone's imprisoned wife.

I couldn't even get this orchid for my boss because I was too busy allowing a man to distract me. Because this life I want isn't one I'm cut out for.

Maybe *I'm* not good enough.

"Look, Stella, I don't know what you think I did, but—"

Holding up my hands, I turn to Leo with an exasperated sigh. "Please, leave me alone."

"I don't want to do that."

"Well, it doesn't matter what you want." Anguish rushes through me like a river, and I groan so loudly that the chandelier dangling above us seems to tremble. "Why couldn't you just leave me be?"

He doesn't respond.

Throwing myself at him, I beat at his chest with the sides of my fists. I'm not a confrontational person, and the irony is not lost on me that every instance of violence I've mustered in my life has been in his presence. Almost as if he brings it out in me.

I hit solid muscle, and my wrists ache with the pummeling, but he doesn't even fight back. He just stands there, taking it, even when I put all my weight into the punches and shove him against the wall.

It's not until he grips my wrists and pulls me into an embrace that I realize we aren't alone. A few auction staff members have ambled outside the ballroom, and they've gathered down the hall, murmuring among themselves, interrupting my outburst.

It takes even longer for me to realize I'm crying.

You're pathetic, Stella. You should just give up and go home with him. Stop trying to be something more than what you are.

Eventually, I wear myself out. The grief of failure presses down on the center of my chest, and my arms drop to my sides in defeat. Leo releases me, and I step out of his reach, wanting distance between us. Especially when he steps forward, seeming to seek something else from me.

"Please don't." The words are barely audible, and I think he might ignore me, as usual.

Except this time, he stays put and leans his back against the wall. "Stella, I—"

"I need to use the bathroom."

Leo's brows rise, and he nods, pushing toward me. "Okay, we can—"

"*Alone.*" I turn, crossing my arms over my chest, shielding my breasts. With everything else that's happened, I almost forgot the risqué number Valerie packed in my overnight bag, and I regret putting it on now. It feels wildly inappropriate. "Please, Leo. I just need a minute."

His jaw tenses, emotion clouding his gray eyes. "One minute. Then you come back to me."

I press my mouth into a thin line of compliance, then shuffle down the hall before he can change his mind. Once I'm past the corner across from the main grand staircase of the mansion, I take a sharp right turn and disappear down a shorter corridor, looping around and coming to a door marked as off-limits to the general public.

Running right into Genevieve.

She's in a gorgeous black gown, her dark hair pulled back from her striking slender face. A simmering smile lifts her mouth as her glittering eyes meet mine, but then she pauses, taking in my state of disarray.

"Mon Dieu! What did that horrible man do to you?"

Sniffling, I just shake my head. "Nothing. I'm just pissed because I didn't get the item I wanted."

"Aw, my poor little puppy. Do you need Mommy to comfort you?"

My face contorts. "I wish you wouldn't call yourself that."

"Well, I wish you *would*." Sighing, she cools herself with a dark orange paper fan. "Still, I understand your loyalty to your husband, even if I disagree with you needing to be."

I squint at her. "Why?"

"Because it's a terrible shame that a woman as soft and beautiful as you is stuck with a brute like him. Especially one who makes you cry." My mouth opens to protest, but she waves the fan at me. "Don't lie to me a second time, please. I'm not stupid."

She steps forward, pressing a palm to my cheek and lifting my face. For a moment, I think she's going to kiss me again, and I don't mind one bit. A part of me even wants it, seeing as I know it'd make Leo mad. But I don't want to get her into trouble, and it wouldn't solve anything.

Instead of kissing me, however, she swipes her thumb beneath my eye, wiping away a tear. "The real question is, how are you going to make him regret hurting you?"

My eyes widen. "What?"

"Unfortunately, I don't mean with me. Though I'd love to help, I'm afraid my services have already been purchased for the evening." She grins again, squeezing my cheeks slightly. "Maybe yours should be up for grabs as well."

———

This is likely a terrible decision—not my worst, but definitely the most impulsive. I don't even give myself time to think it all the way through, revenge clouding my judgment as I push open the private door and slip inside.

It's almost pitch-black in the room, and a haze fills the air, although I'm not sure if it's from smoking paraphernalia or if the auction runners added it for dramatic effect. The connecting hall is short, and I come to a complete stop at the edge of the stage, where the auctioneer seems to be bringing the night to a close.

My hands tremble as I place one heel onto the stage. I inhale slowly, letting the events of the past twenty-four hours filter through my veins. I think about my wedding night and the one after that ended in shame.

This will not be a repeat.

Tonight, I'll be the one rejecting Leo.

It's exactly what he deserves for ruining my evening and making me miss the flower.

And maybe there's still a chance for me to secure the item, even if that means tracking down the winner and bargaining my life for it. In the meantime, my husband will pay for being an ass—tonight, seven years ago, and all the alone time in between.

Even if he's the one who manages to buy me, I'll make him pay before he's able to get me naked.

I press my hands to my thighs and scramble out as quickly as possible, rushing to Reaper before he can finish his sentence. He's shirtless, and as he turns toward me, his tongue darting to the piercing in his lip, his dark eyes rove over my form with a lazy heat I feel in my bones.

"I'm afraid all rides must wait until after the show."

My jaw falls open. "Oh, n-no. That's not... I'm not here to service you, Mr. Reaper."

Amusement dances across his handsome face. "It's just 'Reaper,' sweetheart. And if that's not what you're up here after, I hope you have a good reason for interrupting my show."

I steal a glance at the crowd, which is completely hidden by the stage lighting. They're specks of dust out in a sea of black, and I feel a little relief at the thought that maybe no one saw Leo with his hand between my legs ten minutes ago.

Not that it would've stopped either of us, I don't think.

"Weren't you about to end things?" I ask.

Reaper scans my face, then lifts his brows. Waiting.

I blow out a breath and rock forward, shifting my weight to my toes. "Right, well, I was hoping you could extend it for a few extra minutes?"

"Do you have an announcement?"

"No." My face burns, embarrassment scorching my cheeks. "I'd like to, um, enter the auction."

"I'm afraid we don't have anything else to bid on—"

"*I* want to be auctioned off," I rush out. My fingers tingle. "You know, like those other girls I saw earlier."

He stares at me silently for several beats. Someone calls out for him offstage, and he holds up two fingers in their direction without removing his gaze from mine. I squirm slightly, feeling undone by the intensity of his eyes.

"A little unorthodox to add items after the last one has gone up, but I suppose stranger things have happened. You'll need to sign a contract. House rules."

"Okay." I take the stack of papers and pen he hands over, scanning the legalese and signing quickly.

Reaper takes the contract back when I'm finished. "Might want to sweeten the pot a bit."

"I...I didn't bring anything valuable with me." A thought occurs to me, though I'm not sure how viable it is. "I've never, um...been with someone. Like this. Or, like...you know." Shame stains my entire body, and I know without looking that I've probably broken out in hives. "Maybe that could work?"

Now he smiles. Takes a step toward me, his clean scent taking over my senses. His long fingers come up, sweeping a stray piece of lint from my bare shoulder and making me shiver. "Stella Ricci's virginity. What a fucking treasure."

My jaw drops. "I'm not—I mean, I didn't think... How—"

Reaper laughs, stepping away again. He slides his hand over my lower back and shoves me forward into a bright spotlight with a wink. "I know everything. Now put your chin up and shoulders back. You want to be somebody's toy for a night or two? You'd better make them believe it."

LEO

My fist raps against the restroom door, the sound echoing down the mostly empty hallway.

Nothing happens, and I knock again, harder this time. Every muscle in my body tenses and strains, like I'm on the verge of a panic attack. "Stella, it's been several minutes now. If you don't exit by the time I count to ten, I'm coming in."

A hand grabs my shoulder when my foot connects with the door, pushing it open. "I'd suggest calming the fuck down before they haul your ass out of here."

The bathroom is empty, and the light isn't even on. I scan the immediate area, searching for a window or trapdoor she could have slipped out through, but there's nothing at all.

She didn't come here.

She *left*.

A chill skates down my spine at the realization. I was evidently too fucking distracted by her scent and those little sounds of plea-sure to notice that she was scheming.

Shoving Frankie away, I take in his flushed cheeks and the partially untucked shirt beneath his navy suit jacket. "Where the hell have you been? You're supposed to be keeping an eye on my wife. There are actual dangerous variables surrounding this situation, you know."

Yet I've been solely interested in playing house. Or at least getting her back to mine. Perhaps if I'd been better at planning and communicating, we wouldn't be in this fucking mess. If I'd told her about Gino and my men—

Frankie bristles. "I *thought* you could handle her one-on-one. Isn't that what you told me yesterday?"

"She's smarter than both of us. That's why I wanted two sets of eyes on her at all times."

"Well, I thought you'd want some alone time."

"That doesn't fucking matter when I'm paying you to..." I watch his face grow taut with unease. Narrowing my eyes, I take a step toward him. "What is it? Where were you?"

He swallows, yanking at the knot in his tie. As I crowd closer to him, I note the red lipstick on his collar and the smudge at one corner of his mouth. When Genevieve approaches a few seconds later, I'm not even a little shocked to see her lips match the shade.

"Leopoldo." She greets me with a coy smile. "I think you should get back in that auction room."

When I walk into the ballroom, I'm half expecting an ambush. It isn't like Genevieve is entirely loyal to me, so it wouldn't be surprising to find that she's working with the remaining De Tore Elders or even her own clan. Part of the issue with the criminal underground is that everyone is always looking for an opportunity to off a rival boss and take over their business.

I'm *not* anticipating the rage that zaps me like a lightning bolt when I glance at the front of the room and see my wife onstage with Reaper's fucking hand on her ass. It glides up, around, and over her hip. Then he's grazing the underside of her breast— almost bare, except for that sheer lace.

My teeth clench so hard that my vision blurs at the edges. I suppose this is what she thinks I deserve. To Stella Ricci, Leopoldo De Tore is the villain who wanted to keep her captive in a tower, not the prince who attempted to save her seven years ago.

I stalk back to the table we abandoned just minutes ago and snatch my placard. Frankie slumps on the tabletop at my side, seemingly out of breath now.

My hand curls tightly around the placard's wooden handle as the bid for Stella increases. Multiple arms fly up as Reaper highlights her virginity.

Blood roars between my ears, drowning out the white-haired auctioneer's taunts. He moves to stand directly behind her, fitting himself against her backside, and lifts a hand to toy with her slender throat.

She looks like a deer caught in headlights when his fingers gently cup the column of her neck, and I can't help wondering if she even knows what the hell she's getting into. If I don't get her—if another one of the guests places a winning bid—she's fucked. They'll expect their prize, and she'll have no other choice but to spread her pretty thighs and let the winner between them.

Before the night is over, she'll be an accomplice to murder. There's no goddamn way anyone else is putting their hands on her and leaving here in one piece.

"Well?" Frankie snaps, gesturing toward the stage. "Are you going to bid or not?"

I exhale slowly through my nose. "I can't."

He frowns. "Why the fuck not? We didn't come all the way here to watch your wife go to someone else."

"The escrow account's already been drained getting that goddamn orchid. I didn't think I'd *need* more." The point of the accounts is to verify the money before it's exchanged and simplify the purchase, but there's a finite amount loaded upon our arrival. I can't add more now.

She was supposed to be in my bed tonight, in my arms, ready to rejoin my life. Sure, I knew she'd need a little cajoling, but that's what the proposed sex was for.

I gave the woman seven years to herself. You'd think she'd be willing to accept fate's intervention by now.

Tapping my fingers on the table, I watch as someone else across the audience darts a hand into the air. Reaper grins, and Stella's mouth slackens to the point where I wonder if he's applying the slightest pressure to her throat. Showing the crowd how she reacts to his touch so they know what they're purchasing.

I can't kill such an important Black Rose Auction centerpiece like Reaper, but whoever wins my wife will likely be less consequential than him.

"Going once..." Reaper says, pressing his nose to the crown of Stella's head. "Going twice..."

Genevieve appears beside Frankie, her dark eyes wide. "What are you *doing*? You're letting someone else buy her virginity when you didn't even want me kissing her last night?"

Ignoring her, I lay my placard down on the table, fold my hands over my lap, and take several deep breaths.

When Reaper announces that she's been sold, panic seizes my lungs. I force myself to remain in place.

Even as he guides the brunette offstage, somewhere farther away from me where I can no longer see, I stay still. The attendees begin dispersing as the end of the auction is announced, and we're directed to the various areas where we can collect our prizes.

I stare at a warped circle on the table as the overhead lights flicker on one by one. Genevieve says something, but it's light-years away, traveling through muddy space and time.

I fucked up. That's all there is to it.

There were probably a million ways I could've gone about retrieving Stella, but giving her this much freedom was a mistake.

One I need to rectify immediately.

Turning to Frankie, I slide my placard beneath his fingers. "Fetch me that orchid, would you? Bring it to the suite, and do *not* leave it unattended. If you take your eyes off it for one second, I'll remove both from your skull."

He nods once. "Where will you be?"

"I'll be staying in the Glass Tower."

"The Glass Tower?" he asks. "No one ever gets that room. It's almost impossible to get out of."

"Because the elevator barely works," Genevieve adds. "You're liable to be crushed in it before you even reach the top."

"I'm not concerned with that. I happen to know there's a locked stairwell inside, and the Concierge can grant me access."

Genevieve shakes her head. "Are you not attending the play party tomorrow?"

I cut her a scathing glance. "Try not to sound so disappointed, Mrs. Deveraux. You're lucky you're still alive after everything you pulled."

She holds up her hands. "I wasn't *implying* anything. God. I was just saying…whoever just bid on your wife might drag her to that. I hear it's hunter-and-prey themed, so maybe—"

"Stella will not be in attendance. You don't need to worry." Tension spins a deadly web in my gut at the thought of my wife traipsing through these unfamiliar grounds, trying to escape someone other than me.

"What are you going to do, kidnap her?" Genevieve quips.

Frankie and I share a look.

She drops her head back with a groan. "*Men.* Why don't you just try *talking* to her?"

"Stella's past the point of listening to reason."

Plus, what would I even say? How do you explain complex feelings for a woman you barely know when you aren't even sure what exactly those emotions are in the first place?

Maybe I didn't think this through enough. I should just give her an annulment and cut my losses while I can. Lead Gino and whoever he brings along away from her and end them, once and for all.

The Commission would definitely have my ass for their deaths, but meeting my own demise would be preferable to existing any longer without my wife at my side.

Yet the idea of leaving the auction without her is completely unappealing.

———

An hour and a half later, I've managed to successfully convince the Concierge to switch my room and give me the second key card for the stairs. They didn't seem particularly averse to the idea since no one else wanted to stay in the old thing anyway.

Frankie transfers my luggage to the tower, begrudgingly using the elevator when I don't accompany him. He's not happy about it, but since I've yet to find Stella on the premises, I don't give a fuck. If I want him to be my bag boy for the rest of our lives, then so be it.

He'll do whatever I say, or I'll put a bullet in his head. I'm past the point of caring about anything beyond my wife.

Inside my pants pocket, my phone buzzes, and I immediately take it out, pressing it to my ear. "Speak."

"You could stand to be a little nicer," Genevieve says, though her voice is little more than white noise as I scan the crowd, searching every face for Stella. "Especially since I'm trying to help you."

"Where's Frankie?"

"Off to serve as proxy for the flower you bought. It's kind of disgusting how much money you spent on that thing, by the way."

I grunt. "What do you want, Deveraux?"

"I found your girl. She's with Damiano Candreva from the Gambini extension in the city."

Shit. Damiano is notorious for fucking fast and hard, leaving a trail of trouble and heartbreak in his wake. In the last year, he's stolen the virginities and identities of at least thirteen women, then framed them for various racketeering crimes.

I can only imagine what he wants with a Ricci, considering Rafael's notoriety remains despite his death.

Irritation knots my muscles. None of this would've happened if she'd *just let me explain.*

Then again, if I'd explained everything to her seven years ago, maybe we wouldn't have spent such a long time apart. Maybe we wouldn't be here at all.

I can't blame her for doing what she thought was best for herself, especially when I placed the opportunity right in her hands.

"Where?" I snap to Genevieve, rage pounding in my chest.

"Southern courtyard. Hedge maze? I'm not exactly sure, but Reaper said you'd—"

I don't bother asking what she did to the auctioneer to get him to talk, hanging up before she can finish her sentence.

Outside, partygoers mill about, sipping from their champagne flutes and engaging in idle chatter. Occasionally, I pass a couple or more tangled up, half hidden in the shadows, their bare skin exposed in the fading sunlight. This place, packed with the country's elite, is a safe space for their explorations.

What happens at the Black Rose Auction stays at the Black Rose Auction. Usually.

I don't intend to let that sentiment extend to Stella unless I'm attached to it. Our time together won't stay at the auction—I intend for it to continue past the event itself. It's only a matter of convincing her that a life with me wouldn't be as miserable as she thinks.

I'd be good to her.

I'm not the monster I used to be, and perhaps kidnapping isn't the way to prove that to her, but my options are limited. I'm running out of time.

A flash of dark hair catches my eye just before disappearing beneath the massive conservatory attached to the mansion. I notice the white lace of her dress, then the hand resting on the elbow of that Candreva prick. He leans down, angling his head, and leads her toward the hedge maze.

If I didn't know better, I'd think they were a legitimate couple. She even *smiles* as he says something, her short laugh carrying across the wind and slicing right through me.

I wonder what I've missed—if they've already had their fun somehow since they left the ballroom. She didn't seem to mind Reaper's hands on her, so maybe my belief that she's been waiting for me all this time has been wishful thinking. Maybe she eluded my security detail at some point over the years and let someone else have her.

Sliding my hands into my pockets, I stroll casually after them, whistling in the hopes of not drawing suspicion since I'm the only unpartnered guest outside.

The pair heads for the start of the maze, though Damiano walks in front of her now as if checking to make sure the coast is clear. My chest tightens, smugness rooting in the cavity at the fact he's so incapable of keeping her safe.

How can you miss the danger lurking right behind you?

I follow them inside, still far enough away that neither seems to have noticed they're not alone. They speak in hushed tones, too quiet for me to hear, though it's clear she's comfortable with him. Her hostility, it seems, is reserved for me.

The maze is stifling, with walls of green shrubbery caging us in an impossible path. It forks off at one point, splitting into four different directions, and I slip down one while they take another. Only a single row separates us, and I walk slowly, tracking the sounds of their footsteps.

"You're really quite beautiful," Damiano says, seduction dripping from his voice. "I couldn't believe my eyes when you stepped onstage tonight. Never mind my luck when my bid won."

"I suppose greed can be useful," Stella replies.

A silent snort puffs out of me. *God, I lo—*

That thought freezes me in my tracks. I *what?*

Surely, the end of that sentence was *loathe*. Or *long for*. Or something considerably less embarrassing than what I thought it would be.

But it seems my denial has been the problem all along.

Maybe my affection for Stella existed long before I was able to make her mine, and the culmination of those feelings is what led to seven years of isolation from her.

Or, more likely, I'm just a dumbass. That would be my father's explanation.

"Yes, well, greed and determination, I'd say. Everyone probably thinks I'm crazy for going up against a De Tore, but do you want to know what I think?"

"What?" she coos, and my entire body charges with white-hot electricity at the foreign sound of her voice lowering and taking on a sultry quality.

"*I* don't think you were ever married to Leopoldo in the first place." He laughs, so content with himself.

Most people in the outside world are unaware of our marital status, but I suppose it makes sense that the truth bled to other organizations.

"I mean, *you* with the Demon of Boston? You know he's slaughtered entire branches of his family tree? Imagine a pretty little virgin like yourself up against that. He'd eat you alive."

How little you know of her, I think, coming upon a clearing that, again, splits into multiple different paths. *That's exactly what she wants. Even if she'd rather die than admit it.*

They're facing away, headed for another opening, as I step out, gaining on their trail quickly. It has to be fast, or else I risk this fucker getting a look at me and reporting me to the auction organizers. I'm sure they would revoke the orchid at the least, and then all this would have been for nothing.

Stella stiffens, and satisfaction weaves through me at how easily she recognizes my presence. There's a nanosecond of hesitation as Damiano walks past her, but she doesn't have time to dodge me or cry out.

She struggles immediately as I slap my palm over her mouth, dragging her back the way I came before her companion can think to look behind him.

Cazzo. He should eat shit for not keeping an eye on her, although I'll settle for merely stealing his prize.

"Stella?" he calls out after a full minute. "Hello? I wasn't being serious, you know. God, it was a fucking joke. Quit being stupid and come out."

I continue retreating, ignoring the way my wife stumbles over her heels, barely able to keep up with our exit.

Stopping once we've put a reasonable distance between us, I wait, listening for the sudden pounding of feet on the ground. Not that it will matter much at this point. He won't know which path to start down, and by the time he finds this spot, we'll be gone.

One of Stella's elbows gets me in a tender spot above my hip, and I grunt, shoving her into the hedge wall.

"Stop fucking fighting," I snap, growing more and more annoyed with her by the second. "You knew exactly what would happen when you got on that stage tonight. This is what you wanted, isn't it, stellina? Your husband's wrath?"

My fingers buzz as she mumbles something into my hand. I pull away slightly, noting the smudged lip gloss and the excess saliva around her mouth.

"It's what you get, asshole," she spits, as if the insult will do anything to me except make my cock harder.

Rolling my eyes, I bend and turn her, looping my arm around her waist and hauling her over my shoulder. She squeals as her front flops forward, now facing my backside.

"Let go of me!" she demands, drilling her fists into my ass. "There are rules here, Leo. You can't just *take* something that doesn't belong to you. I was having a perfectly nice time with Mr. Candreva."

The Glass Tower enters my view when I retrace my steps out of the maze, and I grin to myself as I start toward it. "*Mr. Candreva,* is it? Strange that you can't even utter the first name of the man who paid such a large sum for your virginity. Are you sure that's what you had in mind for your evening?"

"Maybe I have an honorific fetish."

"Yeah?" I adjust her roughly, reveling in the huff of air that presses from her stomach. "Good. I'll be sure to have you call me 'Master' when I've got my cock in you later."

"That is *not* happening."

"Happened last night," I point out, swatting her ass. "I'd be willing to bet a very expensive and very rare orchid that it will happen again."

"I didn't call you...*that.*"

"True. Maybe that's not the right word then." My feet crunch against the grass, carrying us away from the auction. "*Sir,* maybe? *Commander? Your Esteemed Keeper?*"

She pinches me, hard. "How about *Poisonous Wretch?*"

"We're not discussing *your* nickname," I reply easily. "Besides, I don't want to degrade you like that when I'm making you come. I'd prefer something like *Mistress Darling.*"

"*Mistress*—" she groans. "What the hell is wrong with you? Why can't you just leave me alone? Was ruining my career not good enough, so you had to spoil any potential fun I could have, too?"

Gritting my teeth against the weight of her words and lack of understanding, I shift so she's not sliding off my back and stop at the entrance to the Glass Tower. "The night's young, stellina. Perhaps I've not spoiled anything."

With my free hand, I fish the key from my jacket pocket, unlock the door, and push her inside.

STELLA

Leo drops me in the elevator—or rather, he waits for the doors to trap us inside before letting me fall back to my feet. I have half a mind to take my heel off and stab him in one of his gorgeous eyes, but the elevator starts moving, and I'm catapulted against the far wall.

My hands grapple with the unsteady rail, gripping so tightly that my knuckles blanch a bright white. The car we're in creaks as tremors rattle it from side to side, and my eyes grow so wide that it feels like they might fall out of my head.

The elevator shifts violently, and I let out an involuntary squeak. Seconds later, Leo wraps himself around me, so the only thing I can see is a sliver of light between his chest and the elevator wall.

"Didn't realize you'd scare so easily."

"More than seventeen thousand elevator-related injuries are reported each year in the United States," I murmur into his shirt, craving his comfort even though I'm so fucking angry with him. "This one doesn't even *sound* like it works. When's the last time it was serviced?"

"That college education is really paying off, huh?"

I clench my jaw and shove at him. "You could've just killed me down there."

He tightens his arms around my waist. "Not trying to kill you, stellina. You've got to get this idea out of your head that I'm some monster."

"Demon," I mutter. "The Demon of Boston."

The car rocks, seeming to hit the shaft wall, and my fingers instinctively dig into Leo's chest when we're partially thrown off-kilter. He braces a shoulder against the corner of the elevator, staring down at me with an unreadable expression on his face. Then he tucks a strand of hair behind my ear.

"A demon no longer." His voice is unspeakably soft. "Not to you anyway."

My heart hammers against the inside of my rib cage. The same way it did the first time we stood this close.

I kissed him first back then. To gain some semblance of control over everything that was happening. It spiraled quickly, too fast for me to even comprehend, as Leo took charge—the way he seems to prefer things.

Uncertainly, I drop my gaze to his lips. They look as soft as I remember, such a stark contrast to how rigid the rest of him feels. Every night since we married, I lie awake and try to recreate the moment our mouths met for the first time, but I always come up empty.

Depending on where you're at in the world, a total solar eclipse happens once every 375 years. Kissing Leopoldo De Tore was my solar eclipse, and even standing here with him right in front of me, I'm not sure that initial sensation is possible to recapture.

Not when so much has happened since.

Shaking myself out of the memory, I push out of his grasp, flattening myself against the wall away from him. "Don't say stuff like that to me."

"Like what?"

"Like this means something to you. Like...*I* mean something." I maintain eye contact with him as the last words leave my mouth even though every atom of my being screams in agonizing protest. Panic sews itself into my DNA, leaving me a quivering mess of emotion, but I force myself to stay in place and not be the one who breaks.

Leo doesn't move either, save for the muscle above his jaw. It jumps once, then twice, and I wonder briefly how hard he has to refrain from snatching me up again.

It wouldn't be difficult, if the maze downstairs was any indication. Maybe I should've spent less time over the years researching how intravenous vaccines can prevent immunodeficiency viruses or reading about the life histories of soil bacteria in different biomes, and more time preparing myself for a fight.

But you like that he came for you. A tiny voice calls out in the recesses of my mind. *You want him to put in the effort. You want him to choose you.*

Some part of me has always liked that he seemed to *care*. Especially when everyone else around me didn't.

But for seven years, he didn't care. Not at all.

And I was alone.

The elevator chimes, jerking to a rocky halt, and a second later, the doors slide open. I dart to the exit and cross the threshold quickly, avoiding his gaze and hands when they reach for me again. My chest heaves, each breath evidence of my survival in that death trap.

My relief is short-lived, however, when Leo reaches behind him and slams his fist into the elevator buttons, cracking three and causing the lights to go out.

My shoulders tense, and I back away from him, belatedly noticing the anger radiating off his body in hot waves. He said he didn't want to kill me, but he clearly has something villainous planned.

But that's okay. I'm not the same naive girl he married. I won't be locked away in a tower and left to rot. If he wants something from me, he's going to have to give me what I desire first.

The three exterior walls around us are entirely made of glass. The building we're in is tall, displaying gorgeous panoramic views of the estate where the Black Rose Auction is being held. Outside, dark clouds hang low in the sky, setting pretty grays against the rising moon. Up here, it's almost possible to imagine I'm someplace else.

Across the room, a four-poster canopy bed is pushed into a corner. Candles line the white dresser and the nightstand, casting a soft glow against the satin sheets and fluffy pillows. Red rose petals line the white comforter and lead a trail from the bed to the elevator.

My stomach drops as I take it all in.

"Leo…" I don't dare turn around and look at him.

"Yes, wife?"

A teapot screeches between my ears. "What is this? What are you doing?"

"I *told* you."

His footsteps vibrate on the floor as he comes closer. He swarms me like an army of wasps, shoving me forward until I'm trapped against the glass wall, where a small balcony outside overlooks the in-ground pool across from the conservatory.

Leo takes both my hands in his gloved ones, splaying them out so my fingers make webs against the window. The glass is cool on my palms, compared to the heat coursing through the rest of me.

It's always been like this with him, as much as I hate to admit it.

"I didn't come here to watch you sell yourself to someone else," he mutters, lacing his fingers over mine. "If you hadn't done that, maybe I would've played nice."

Snorting, I ignore the way his words make my abs tense. "You don't like nice. Especially not with me."

"You pretend I've been cruel because it's easier to hate me that way." He nuzzles my neck. "But what have I done that was so terrible? When I gave you an escape from your shitty father? Maybe when I didn't have you executed for that goddamn razor blade you were smuggling? Or perhaps when I respected your wishes for boundaries—"

A sound that is half laugh, half disbelief comes from my throat.

"I never forced you to do anything. I made it clear that it was all up to you."

And you rejected me. I don't say that out loud, though, seeing as I can't let him know it affected me so deeply. I *won't* let him know that.

"Ooh, the bare minimum. You realize that doesn't really matter in the long run when you're standing here, forcing me to do whatever you want now?"

He remains quiet for several moments, his body barely relaxing against mine.

Then, as suddenly as he stopped speaking, I feel his lips against my ear, his nose in my hair. He shifts, pressing his pelvis *just so*, and mine has nowhere to go except flush with the wall. I swallow, my pulse throbbing in my neck and between my thighs.

"Tell me you want me to stop then." He squeezes the tops of my hands. "Say you wish for me to bring you back to the party and give you over to the sack of shit who bought you tonight."

He rips himself away, but only long enough to spin me around. I don't have time to blink before I'm facing him and he's pinning me against the wall again, his forearms bracketing me in.

Minty, slightly whiskey-laden breath fans my face as he leans down. "Tell me you haven't thought about this moment every day since I turned you away seven years ago."

"I haven't." My head lifts in defiance. "You don't cross my mind—ever."

"Sei solo una bugiarda del cazzo." After a pause, he reaches up with one hand, capturing my chin in two fingers. "Such a dirty fucking liar. You know, you're practically in a wedding dress right now. Granted, this one is much nicer on the eyes than the gown you married me in, so why don't we recreate the night we could've had?"

Molten desire liquifies inside my chest at the request, despite my reservations. It's impossible to ignore the feral desperation in his voice or the way his eyes glaze over the longer he looks at me.

"We can't do this," I breathe, holding on to the vestiges of my resistance. "Someone else *paid* for my time. After you fucked with me getting the orchid, it's only fair that I return the favor. So let me fulfill my auction duties."

"And if I don't?" His brows arch. "If I keep you locked in this tower until you've lost the will to spite me? What then?"

My nostrils flare. "They'll *fine* me for not appearing before the winner."

"Let them. I have enough money to cover it."

When he crashes his lips to mine, my mouth is partially open, ready to deliver a fiery retort. Instead, I catch him on my teeth, and he jerks my head forward to fuse our faces together properly. He shoves his tongue in, sweeping deep enough to lave over my molars, and I can't stop the tiny groan that rumbles in my chest at his utter abandon.

His hand leaves my chin to cup the back of my head. The padding of his glove is a nice shift from the unforgiving wall behind me, yet at odds with the brutality of his kiss. It sucks the protest out of me, like a vacuum leaving no crumbs behind.

Plastering himself to the length of my body, he wedges a meaty thigh between my legs. His knee angles up, and I lose my breath for a brief moment when he makes contact with my clit.

My palms find his chest, my fingers gripping his lapels as he moves against me, his rough nature making me dizzy.

One hand falls to my hip. Slowly, Leo bunches the lace fabric in his fist, keeping his eyes on mine, as if challenging me to put an end to this.

Right now, every card is in his repertoire. Just like when I was forced to marry him in the first place. Any feelings or sensations were overshadowed by that fact, and it's never fully felt like I've gotten a say in our interactions.

My desire was overshadowed by *duty*, but it was still there.

It's official, whether you kiss me or not. Might as well pretend you had some say in the matter.

His words from that night echo like church bells in the back of my mind, and I blink up at him several times, trying to see through the haze of anger, lust, and resentment. Staring back at me is the beautiful, brutal man I've spent the last seven years thinking about—and something feels different.

The rejection from before feels eons away, as if it happened to someone in another universe. The Leo pressing against me now wouldn't dare repeat that mistake, and that undoes something profound within me.

I grew up priding myself on my intelligence and not caring when people weren't interested in me because I wasn't as exciting as my sisters. In a world where free thought and quiet tenacity were interpreted poorly, I thought disinterest was a good thing.

It kept me safe for a while.

I never realized how much it would hurt to find someone

who seemed curious, even intrigued, and then to have that ripped away by indifference.

So, again, just like I did seven years ago when we stood in a similar state of limbo, I wrangle my arms out from his hold and reach for the hem of my dress. It's barely enough to constitute an actual outfit anyway, and I would be embarrassed about everyone who saw me in it tonight if not for the way their heated stares spurred me on.

I watch the tendons in his neck shift beneath his skin as I start dragging the skirt up. His knee is still wedged against my pussy, providing effortless friction where my pulse skyrockets with each exposed inch of skin.

My throat constricts when the fabric rises past my hips, then my belly button. Leo's eyes seem to darken as more and more of my body is displayed.

"Where did you even get this outfit?" he breathes, enraptured. "The one you wore last night was devastating, but this is... You look..."

"My roommate packed it. In case of...emergency, I guess."

"Remind me to ask what she planned for you to be doing at this auction when we meet."

Heat flares across my cheeks when the edge of the fabric reveals the undersides of my breasts. They feel heavy as his gaze dips just long enough for a single inhale, and then they're bare. *I'm* bare as I rip the dress off the rest of the way, impatience and adrenaline barreling through me like a rocket.

I drop the dress to the floor, standing before him in just my nude thong and heels.

Discomfort twists in my gut, but it's not the bad kind.

It's the kind that pushes you to do bad things. Things you'll undoubtedly regret in the morning.

But right now, I don't care.

"This is what you want?" I ask, dropping my voice to an octave I've never heard come out of me before. I move my hips, writhing slowly against his knee, and my body jolts with the hypnotic sensation the movement creates. "Our wedding night done right?"

I don't fully expect him to answer, but after a moment, he nods.

"You'll help me get the flower if I do this for you?"

His stormy eyes narrow slightly. "Talk about cruelty."

"That's my condition. Me for the flower. Take it or leave it."

It takes several more seconds. Eventually, he relents with a dip of his chin.

This is all I have in my arsenal. I might not be experienced, but I'm not sure it'll matter one way or the other to this man. I slide my hands up his chest and lock them around his neck before yanking him down to me.

It's a better plan than nothing at all.

STELLA

Leo presses me against the glass, and my immediate thought is of the auction attendees.

Can they see up here?

What would they do if they could?

Would people stop to watch as my husband kicked my legs farther apart, then dropped to his knees in front of me? Would they gasp when he lifted me, hooking my legs over his shoulders, and buried his face in my pussy?

What would they *say* if they knew his tongue was diving deep, parting me and plunging in while they stared?

What would they *do*?

I'm embarrassingly wet as the ideas race through my mind—so much so that when he pulls back, Leo's chin is drenched. My palms are splayed against the window, slipping as I attempt to wiggle away from him, but he just clamps down on my ass with those big gloved hands and pins me harder.

"Don't be shy," he commands, trailing open-mouthed kisses up the inside of my thigh. "I love seeing what I do to you. I'd fucking walk downstairs with you staining me right now if I didn't think you'd bolt at the first opportunity."

It's hard to breathe when he talks like that. "You're so vulgar."

"And *you're* fucking delectable."

One lick up my seam makes me tremble, and when he flicks the tip of his tongue against my clit, my back arches in pleasurable agony.

"I'm not shutting up about the way my bratty wife tastes. Not ever."

"Because you're vulgar. And difficult."

"You love it."

I don't—at least, I don't *want* to love it. Still, there's no denying the little thrill that zips through my abdomen at how much he wants me.

Pathetic? Maybe. But right now, I'm taking any victory over him I can get.

Leo's fingers slide around and dig into the soft tops of my thighs, indenting the skin, and I reach down to tug at his gloves. He glances up, arching his eyebrows.

"Off."

"Do you enjoy ordering me around, wife?"

I nod, hopeful that my honesty might sway him. "As much as you apparently enjoy calling me that."

He ignores my request, diving back between my legs with renewed fervor. My head tilts as his mouth covers me, spearing into my entrance and making my body quake.

Swallowing against the myriad emotions swimming through me, I let my eyes fall closed and focus on my senses: His clean scent, mixed with a hint of hard liquor. The musk of my sweat and arousal cloying to the air around us. The feel of soft leather as he continues to hold me in place, sliding one hand up to grasp firmly at my hip when I start to squirm.

His kisses are loud and lewd in the quiet of the tower's bedroom, echoing off the ceiling.

I'm dizzy, trembling with acute awareness of every little thing. Each breath I take draws a certain amount of my focus, as if I'm specifically categorizing the moments so I'm able to recount them later.

My toes curl as a bolt of satisfaction shoots through my pussy, ebbing upward and outward, like jelly working its way through my limbs. Just as I start for the cliff he's so good at pushing me over, I note the pointed absence of one of his hands.

Seconds later, just as I peel my eyes open, it's *there*—a bare, ungloved thumb brushes against my clit as Leo's tongue flattens against my soaked flesh. He circles lightly, teasingly, and I find myself unable to look away from his gaze, even when the pressure increases.

He pulls back a little, but his thumb keeps the pressure on me. "How's that?"

I nod again, unsure if I can do anything else. Before I've finished the movement, I feel the tip of a finger slipping inside, going as deep as possible. I inhale sharply, still not used to the invasion, even though this isn't exactly new territory.

It was only a few hours ago that he made me climax in the

ballroom while all those auction attendees sat, oblivious to the debauchery going on among them.

Or maybe they did know. Maybe they were watching, just like he said. Given the nature of the auction itself and the items up for bid, I wouldn't put it past them.

Stella Ricci's virginity. Jesus, why did I think auctioning that off was a good idea? Even though Leo has me holed up here right now, I'm sure there will still be expectations once I've returned to the party. He'll be fined for delaying the process, and the winning bidder will likely still want to collect.

My stomach churns at the thought of being stuck underneath some other man for any amount of time or sum of money.

"Shh," he murmurs, adding another finger as I cry out. He meets my gaze, and my stomach tenses violently. "Just listen to how wet you are, baby. That's all for me, isn't it?"

"L-Leo..." I exhale, my body feeling like it's being stretched in a million different ways.

He curls those fingers, stroking my inner muscles as he sucks my clit between his lips.

Shit. My face breaks out in pockets of excruciating heat, and I shift, trying to increase the friction, trying to get more, more, *more...*

"God damn it. Look at your cheeks, stellina. They're bright fucking red, like you're embarrassed to hear how soaked I make you." He moans into me, and I think I might pass out. "That's good, baby, I promise. Gonna feel *so good* when I slide my cock into your tight little hole in a minute."

He swears again and again, switching to Italian and back,

and then he's moving faster, harder, his tongue flicking and tasting until I'm shoved over the edge into oblivion.

I come with a hoarse shout, my hands diving into his dark hair and pulling tight like the reins of a horse. I'm riding him, our eyes locked as I grind on his mouth. His frenzied gaze reflects the way my soul feels, and it's several moments before I can even remember my name or what we're doing here.

Slowly, he withdraws from me once I've relaxed my hold on him. He drags his lips against the inside of my thigh and then gently disentangles himself, placing both of my heels back on the floor as he pushes to his feet.

Panic seizes the logical parts of my brain as he begins to disrobe, shrugging out of his jacket and then undoing each button on his shirt without breaking eye contact. With my arousal and his saliva coating my pussy and thighs, I shouldn't feel so completely out of my element, yet I can't keep the sinking feeling from settling in as reality dawns.

I talk a good game, I guess, but I still don't know what the hell I'm doing.

My thighs clench hard when he yanks at his tie, loosening it. I glance at his hands, trying to get a good look at the uncovered one, but he keeps his fist turned away, as if he knows exactly what I want to see.

Soon, he's shirtless, that tie still knotted and hanging limp around his neck. He reaches for his belt buckle, and my arms shoot out, halting his movements.

Surprise riddles his handsome face. "Changing your mind?"

"No," I rush out, my face on fire. "I'm just…"

Words fail me, and I deflate a little, letting my arms fall to my sides. Leo watches me silently for a beat, then works his jaw and steps forward, into me. He pulls off the remaining leather glove, and it falls to the floor with a dull *whoosh* before he grabs my wrist and presses my fingers to his belt.

"It's okay to want this," he says in a smooth voice. "To want *me*. I can keep a secret, stellina."

My chin lifts. I take several deep breaths and then swallow. Hard. Distantly, I can almost hear my parents berating me for indulging my carnal desires, but I ignore them and concentrate solely on the man before me.

The one I've yearned for longer than seven years, if I'm honest with myself.

"Okay," I acquiesce.*

"Say it."

"I want this." My fingers flex, curling over the waistband of his pants.

"Be specific when asking for blessings."

Huffing, I undo his belt quickly and yank him closer. "I want you to fuck me."

"Good." Shoving my hands away, he opens his fly and pushes his pants down his hips, kicking out of them before I can even blink. I got a good look at his dick last night, but seeing it again and knowing where it's headed fills me with equal parts dread and exhilaration. I'm not exactly sure which to focus on as he grabs himself, pumping once with his big fist.

Then he's gripping the backs of my thighs once more and

* CHOKEHOLD—Sleep Token

hoisting me up, fitting me against the wall. "You think they can see up here?"

I shrug. *God, I hope so.*

For once, Leo seems as agitated and fraught as me, and he glides his tip through my sensitive flesh, parting my lips and spending extra time rubbing my clit. When I'm on the verge of another climax, he drags it down and positions himself. "There is a request before I fill you, I'm afraid."

My grunt makes him smirk. "*What?*"

"Let down your hair."

"What is this obsession you have with my hair?"

"It's not the hair exactly. I mean, not *just* that." Crimson paints his cheeks, highlighting the vulnerability in his hooded gaze. It's only there for a second, but I notice. "I just want this to be the wedding night we didn't get and for the details to match."

I stare at him, trying to find a crack in his armor. Something that points to even a modicum of insincerity, but all I'm met with is blazing passion in his irises. Swallowing, I lift my arm above my head and pull one of the pins out, letting my hair fall in silky wisps down my shoulder.

The strands unfold and dangle by my hip, and Leo watches them, enraptured. I've let it grow longer than ever before, too swamped with school and work to find time to stop at a salon. Normally, I just throw it up in a bun or braid and forget about it, but the way he's awestruck by just half of it right now makes me want to keep it down forever.

He notches his tip against me, and I jolt, startled.

His grin is a flame serrating my chest. "Let the rest down so I can put my cock in you."

My hand tugs at the remaining pin, and the rest of my hair spills out in waves. It covers my breast, tickling the top of my thigh, and Leo hisses as he pushes forward, splitting me wide open.

I tense on instinct at the intrusion. My lungs expand but don't compress, stunning me with their immobility.

Pain, pain, pain. It radiates up my core, slicing through my abdomen. My sisters said it wouldn't be pleasant, but I didn't know it would feel like being *stabbed.*

Leo's fingers flex on my thighs. "Relax, Stella. There's still more of me to take."

"Oh *God.* You're not in yet?"

"Not all the way." He slides his thumb over my clit, and the muscles in my ass start to unclench. "You've gotta let me in."

"I'm *trying.*"

I peel one shaky, sweaty hand from the wall and grab his neck. The other follows suit, and they lock behind him, digging into his equally damp skin. *Is he nervous, too?*

"Relax. I'm going to make you feel so good." He pushes in another inch, and I can actually feel my body loosening, opening up like the petals of a blossoming flower. The sting is still there, but it's replaced by a fullness unlike anything I've known. "This cunt was made for me to slide right into."

Again, my body moves of its own accord, driven by some basal biological response. My legs press out, spreading wider; he adjusts, allowing me the extra room, and manages to slip all the way in so his pelvis is flush with mine.

I inhale through my teeth, my chest light.

"Fuck. There we go." Butterflies erupt in my stomach with his praising assessment. "I'm in, baby."

A lightning bolt of discomfort strikes through me, dissipating quickly. Now I just feel stuffed—impossibly so, like I'm being stretched to my limit. One of my hands curls up, tangling in the hair at the base of his skull.

He slides a rough palm over my side, squeezing my breast before wrapping his long fingers in my tresses. I half expect him to pull or grip as tightly as I am, but his touch is strangely gentle despite the bold heat lighting his eyes.

"Shit. Così dannatamente stretta."

I gulp down a breath. "Huh?"

"You're *tight*, wife. I can't fucking see straight." He somehow keeps me up with his hips, shoving the hand on my thigh between us to toy with me. "If you don't loosen up, I'm going to come before I've even fucked you."

For some reason, that makes my lungs constrict. "In me?"

"What?"

My breaths grow shallow, and I dip my chin, looking up at him through my lashes. "Are you going to come in me?"

He lifts his head, and I feel him slide out slowly. His fingers continue strumming my clit, making delicious tension coil in my stomach. Our eyes stay locked as he retreats, and then his hips snap forward, filling me instantly with every hard inch of him.

I see stars.

"Be careful with requests of that nature," he says, grinding each word. "Your father didn't give me his firstborn, so I'm liable to ensure I get yours."

Oh my God. It feels like a threat...or a promise.

Either way, his words send a fresh spray of goose bumps down the length of my arms. My pussy spasms, arousal spinning like a broken record in my veins, building and building. The idea of being shackled to him in such a permanent way should have me pushing him off and running for the hills, but instead, I'm pulling him closer and fusing his lips to mine.

As if startled by the kiss, he flinches into it. A moment later, though, he's tugging at my roots and angling my head so he can delve deeper. With each sloppy tangling of our tongues, he fucks me slowly, sawing his cock in and out as if actually trying to cut me in half.

When he grabs beneath my knees, using the leverage to push them to the wall and spread me as wide as I can go, an anguished moan works its way from my chest. My eyes flutter closed as waves of spiked euphoria rush through me.

"No," he snaps, and I gaze up at him immediately. "*Look* at what I'm doing to you. Watch my cock make a mess of your pretty cunt."

The filthy words and the lewd sounds are too enticing. I exhale shakily, forcing myself to stare at where we're connected. Inch after luscious inch of him disappears inside me with each flex forward, then reappears like magic when he moves back.

I'm enthralled at the sight of my juices coating him. So much so that I can't help but reach down, sliding two fingers over his shaft in a V shape, *feeling* him on top of just watching. Almost as if I need the touch to truly be grounded in this moment.

"*Jesus*. That's... *Fuck*, baby. So fucking hot."

My brows rise, and my heart stutters in my chest. "Really?"

Sweat tracks down his face, and he adjusts his hold on my legs, wrapping them around his waist. We're flush, our bodies lined up, and he pushes all the way in with a nod. My fingers brush my slick, swollen skin and come away saturated.

"I'm gonna go fast," he says, speeding up even before he's gotten the words out.

Every thrust makes my ass squeak on the glass, and I can't help wondering what the people outside think again. If they're looking up here, watching Stella Ricci's deflowering.

My synapses hum with excitement.

I focus on Leo's cock as it slides in and out of me, between my fingers, its silky, smooth shape reaching spots inside me that I didn't know existed. He hoists me higher, moving deeper, until I'm clawing at his chest with my free hand, half-mad with the desire to climb him.

My fingers catch on the tie, which is still around his neck, and I slip, trying to keep myself afloat. Instinctually, I hook my thumb on the fabric and draw tight, cinching it at the base of Leo's neck.

Shock shadows his features for the briefest moment. I go to remove my hand, fear combining with lust, just like it did seven years ago.

I expect him to shove me away and withdraw. I expect some kind of punishment.

But just like he did the night we married, Leo De Tore surprises me by leaning into the threat. He covers my fist with his own before I can pull away and forces it closer to his throat.

"Tighter," he huffs—no, not quite a huff. It's more like a whimper, something born from despair. He moves faster, fucking me in earnest, his hips bruising mine each time he plunges back in. "Make me come, baby. I need it bad."

My eyes widen at the heavy plea in his voice, and my tongue is thick in my mouth. "I don't know what I'm doing... It could *kill* you."

His grin stokes a fire deep in my belly. "What a way to go."

He makes my limbs feel wobbly, and I pull at the tie, watching it constrict around him until his skin blooms a dark pink. His nostrils flare, and I release the pressure, watching him for signs of distress or retaliation.

All he does is drive a hand into my hair and move faster.

I grip the tie again, my back arching with delight when he groans, half agony and half pleasure.

Licking my lips, I loosen the knot a little more. I move my hand from between us, sliding slowly up my sternum, and then run my thumb over my nipple. He watches the movement, his eyes wild.

"This feels good," I say in a soft voice, not really sure of how to do dirty talk, though willing to try anyway.

"Yeah?"

I bite my lip, tightening the tie once again. My hips slowly undulate, attempting to meet him thrust for thrust, even as I'm still trapped against the window.

"It's not enough, though, is it?" He grunts. "You feel full, but not *filled*, right?"

"I...I don't—"

"You need my cum. Say it."

Saliva pools in my mouth.

I shouldn't say it or want it.

But God help me, I do.

I'm powerless against it.

"Please come in me."

"God-fucking-damn. *Fuck*, Stella, what are you doing to me?" He sounds angry, though I'm not sure at who. "Whatever you say, baby. I'll dump my cum in you as many times as you want."

The image alone has me spiraling, and I wish I could explain it to myself, at least long enough to redirect the feeling or put a name to it, but I can't. It's wholly carnal and crazed, and I just let it happen.

As I yank at the tie, his movements grow more brutal. While at the same time, I wrap my legs as tightly around his waist as I can, pulling him closer. *Closer* still—it doesn't feel like it'll ever be enough.

I pinch my nipple, then scrape my nails against his chest, curling each finger back around his neck as I hang on. Leo fucks me with such primal power that the glass behind us trembles, and I tremble with excitement, too distracted by how good all this feels to fully notice when he seats himself inside me for the last time.

He moans—*miserably*, torturously—through his climax, and it echoes in my bones, pushing me off the edge into complete ecstasy. I wish I could soak up the sounds he makes and live forever within them.

My arms fall limp to my sides, Leo's body the only thing holding me up as electric shocks rattle me to the core.

When he's finished, he drops his forehead to mine and says something under his breath in Italian. I'm too spent to move, but then everything else about the night comes rushing back like water through a broken dam. I push at his chest, trying to gain distance between us, but he just shakes his head.

"Not yet. I'm nowhere near done with you, and before you try to escape me and head back to that fucking auction, I'm staying right here. Gonna let my cock sit in you, keeping you plugged up till your cunt's drunk her fill. Then I'm gonna start moving. Let you get me good and ready for another round, and do this all over again."

My throat is dry, so I don't say anything, even as emotions war for dominance in my mind. Alarm bells ring in the back of my head, but contentment seems to edge everything else out.

Right now, I realize, I'm too elated to care.

LEO

F uck. You look so beautiful. I should just parade you around the property. *Really* get my money's worth."

Stella's gasp enters my mouth as her cunt clamps down, suffocating my dick. We've finally made it to the bed, though it took two more rounds to get to this point. She's on her stomach, grasping the disheveled sheets, with her ass angled in the air.

A distinct bite mark reddens one cheek, and I trace my thumb over it. Payback for the ring around my neck that she created during our first session—not that I'm complaining either way.

Under normal circumstances, I'd never have let anyone do that to me. With other lovers, I've always had to be particular and careful when it came to any sort of pain inflicted, because it could easily go south with my position in the De Tore family. I've never thought someone might get close to me for any reason other than to ignite my downfall.

Stella, on the other hand, has always been different. From

our first kiss, or maybe even when her father offered her virginity, I could see that she wasn't trying to outmaneuver me. She didn't want to overthrow me and steal what I'd sacrificed a childhood to create.

She only wanted out.

I've been letting her hurt me ever since.

"You didn't pay for me," she mutters, turning her face away from mine. "Technically, this is a free fuck."

"Oh, it'll cost. That I'm sure of."

Clasping my hands on her hips, I use them for leverage, pulling her up as I drive into her. She buries her face into the bedding, each moan and grunt expelling from her lungs as if forced directly from them.

I smooth my palm down her spine, counting each groove, then wrap her soft hair around my fist and tug. If I could wrench my cock from her for a moment, I'd put the strands around my shaft, but right now I'm content to just touch them. "That's it, baby. Give me all your noises. Let me know how good it feels to finally have me in you."

"God, Leo—"

"Which is it?" I ask, gritting my teeth in a pathetic attempt to hold off a little longer. Pressure rushes up my back, spiraling out of control as it heads for my dick. "God *or* Leo? I'll bet Mass never made you scream like this."

She's soaked in a heavy sheen of sweat, her pretty cunt coated in several layers of my spend—it's too much for me to handle.

Stella squeals, and her body starts to arch away from the mattress as her orgasm approaches. I shift my weight, pinning her hips as I thrust in once, twice, and a third rough time. My own release chases the milking of her inner muscles; my groan is long and low, and I rock back, pulling out.

Keeping the crown of my dick against her, I watch as thick ropes of cum leak from her succulent hole, spurting still from my tip. Then I shove right back in, collapsing on top of her when the aftershocks have subsided.

We stay like that for a while. My heart thrashes inside my chest, against her shoulder blade, and I wait to see if she'll try to buck me off and get away. She's deflated, flattened out like a pancake on the bed, and still doesn't move even when I roll off.

Gathering what strength I have left, I get up on shaky legs and trudge into the small connecting bathroom. It consists of just a porcelain sink, a broken mirror, a toilet, and a tiny shower stall, but I don't need all that right now.

I turn on the faucet and fetch a washcloth from a little basket beside the sink, then let it warm in the spray. When I reenter the bedroom, Stella still hasn't moved an inch. If not for the steady rise and fall of her back, I'd think I killed her.

She gasps when I press the washcloth to her swollen cunt, swatting half-heartedly as I clean her up.

"Thank you," she says, rolling her head to the side. "I didn't realize how sticky I'd be after."

"Yes, I did make quite a mess of you." *And would like to continue doing that for the rest of our lives.* I don't say that part out loud, though, unwilling to break the quiet calm in the air around us.

Outside, the moon is high in the sky, illuminating parts of

the room that the candles don't reach. The property seems to be mostly empty now, as patrons have likely retreated to their rooms for the night.

She gets up to use the bathroom before quickly returning to the exact same position on the bed.

I toss the cloth to the floor and run my fingers over the curve of her ass, the dimples above it, and the ridges of her spine. There's something magical about having her in this bed, surrounded by candlelight and flower petals, her skin red and swollen all over from my hands, mouth, and cock.

The way her hair spills in dark waves, like the endless ocean— and just as dangerously enticing.

I'm committing everything to memory this time. Just in case.

She peeks up at me. "Although this was my first time, I just want you to know that Rampion Core requires physicals every six months because of the hazardous work conditions. So..."

When she trails off, I nod my concurrence. "I would not have taken you bare if there were any cause for concern on my end either. Because of my father's history of poor health, I get exams routinely. If you like, I can have the most recent one emailed over."

She scans my face, silently contemplating. "Earlier, you said you'd been waiting seven years for this. Did you really mean that?"

My brows lift. "I scarcely even touched myself, stellina. There certainly wasn't anyone else warming my bed."

No one else would have ever measured up, just with the one taste I had of her. They'd never be able to reach the depths of my soul like she had in such a short time, even if I begged them to try.

She's the only one I'd beg for anything.

"Okay," she concedes, bending her arm and propping her head on her wrist. "I'm on the pill, by the way."

My heart drops to my stomach. "Oh?"

How did that escape mine and Frankie's detection?

Somehow during the countless hours we spent watching her on security feeds and making note of everything she did, every award won, every article written and doctor's visit—we missed that.

"Yeah. I've never skipped one either, so you don't need to like...worry or anything."

As my hand continues its exploration of her lithe form, it slides beneath her hair, the silken strands soft against my scarred skin.

A distant part of me wonders what might have changed if we'd done this seven years ago. If I hadn't let my personal issues take precedence and allowed her to waltz out of my life. If I'd been more like the man I killed for speaking ill about her.

I'm certain the birth control is a new addition, so would we have children by now? Would our arguments be over how I'd ruined her body, her life, and her future instead of—

My hand freezes, the tips of my fingers twisting in the ends of her hair. *That is what the arguments have been about, isn't it?* I suppose no amount of time can make up for the actual loss of autonomy that comes from marrying someone like me.

I thought I was different. I went out of my way to try to be, for her, and wound up in the same fucking boat anyway.

Exhaling, I move up the bed. I'm not sure if it's the postorgasmic haze she's in or something else, but she seems to gravitate in the same direction as I rest my back against the iron headboard.

She doesn't touch me, her head on the pillow being as close to me as she's voluntarily gotten to me since our reconnection.

I don't want to read into it, but my stupid chest swells a little anyway. Like I'm some lovesick, touch-starved puppy whose owner let it sleep in the bed with her.

"Why would I worry about any of that?" I eventually ask, stroking her temple.

"Why *wouldn't* you?" Her brown eyes swivel to mine, narrowing slightly. "I know we're...married, but still. Do you really want to be saddled with the kid of a woman you didn't actually choose?"

"A strong, beautiful Stanford graduate? I'm sure I could do much worse."

She stays silent, and after a moment, she rolls onto her back. I keep my hand on her hair, toying with it aimlessly, unable to stop.

For a while, she stares up at the ceiling, which is also made of glass, like three-fourths of the tower walls. The stars are out, their visibility impeded slightly by thick clouds. I wonder which ones she's looking at and if she knows the names of the constellations.

I wonder if the night sky is as stunning to her as she is to me.

When she grabs my wrist, I'm not expecting it at all. She pulls me over, inspecting my palm, and a wave of stubbornness crashes through me. I try to retract out of habit, but she ignores me, her grip strong as her eyes soak up my scars in the dim lighting.

"Who did this to you?"

I'm not sure what I expected her to say, but it wasn't that. "Don't worry yourself, stellina. They're long gone at this point."

She glances at me over my fingertips. "The gloves? This is why you wear them, right?"

I nod, and she smooths her thumb over the mess of skin, gliding over a particularly rough pocket.

"Does it hurt?"

"No." I flex, curling my fingers beneath hers until they freeze midway. "This hand is worse than the other as far as mobility is concerned. Sometimes certain motions can be difficult, but the scars themselves are not painful. Not anymore."

My pulse skyrockets the longer she stares, and I tug at my limb, trying to close this part of me off to her. Paired with everything else, even the shit she has no clue about, it feels *too* vulnerable. Like I'm playing all my cards before knowing if I have a chance of winning.

I'm not insecure about the scars, but I don't display them either. That would be a death sentence; the second someone in this world knows you can be harmed, you're in trouble.

"It was a fluke, you know." She releases me and drags the white comforter up to her chin. "Me getting into Stanford. I mean, that was always my goal, but I didn't get there on merit."

"What do you mean?"

"My sister—er, well, I guess her husband, since we didn't really have any money after she got married..." Stella is seemingly lost in thought, and I wonder how much she really knows about her late parents' financial situation.

They *had* money, but since the eldest Ricci daughter ratted her parents out, assets were seized, and business went completely underground. Totally off-grid from where any Feds might notice.

That was why Rafael brought her to Saint Paul's that night, aware that even if he had cash to repay me with, doing so would put a target on his and his wife's backs, as they owed more than just me.

Of course, accepting his farcical deal put a target on mine instead. But I knew the risk when I accepted. I just didn't give a shit back then.

Even though I'm older now, I'd do it all over again if it meant getting *her*.

"Anyway, Elena's husband is this hotshot doctor who used to work for Papà. Before I was sold to you, I went and lived with them for a few months, and I told him at some point about what I wanted to do with my future. How I wanted out of Boston and Papà's life, so I could see the world and get an education. Try to make the world a little better."

Scoffing to herself, she continues, "When I got my acceptance letter to Stanford, I thought it was a fake. I bombed the SATs because Mamma kept making me stay up late the night before, so I hadn't expected anything from the schools I applied to. Really, I gave up on the idea of escaping altogether, but after calling the admissions office at Stanford, I learned the letter was real. Deep down, I think I always knew they'd bought it somehow, but at that point, I didn't really care how I got out. Just that I was going to."

My stomach tenses, my nerves tangling in knots.

"When I left you, I didn't...I didn't know how long I had before you came to drag me back home, so I didn't question any-thing once I got to school. I threw myself into coursework and refused to come up for air." A brief pause ensues, and she fists the sheets beneath her chin. "But as it turns out, there's a different kind of pressure that comes from not earning something you really, *really* wanted. The desire to eventually accomplish *something*, even if it kills you, because someone else is invested in it."

"So? What did you accomplish, stellina?" I brush some hair back from her face.

She shakes her head. "Nothing. I almost flunked out. My sisters called to tell me Papà had passed, and even though I didn't really feel bad about it, I wasn't allowed to attend his funeral. They wouldn't tell me where it was and wouldn't let me book a flight—anytime I tried, they'd call the airline to cancel. And even though I knew they were just trying to look out for me, it took a toll on me mentally. My grades dipped; my attendance was poor. Anyone else would've been put on academic probation."

My hand pauses at the crown of her skull. "But you weren't."

"Nope. I kept waiting for the hammer to be thrown down on my time at Stanford, but no one ever said anything. Finally, I went to my adviser, and all they said was that the academic parameters didn't apply." She scoffs. "I could fill in the blanks as to why. Money talks, no matter where you are in a capitalist society. Money will *always* mean more than anything else."

We fall silent, and I withdraw my hand, dropping it in my lap. Apprehension unspools slowly in my gut because of the despair in her voice. The hopelessness.

I fucked up big time. No way can I tell her I was the one paying the school off and threatening them when her performance suffered. Her sister may have started, but once Stella was enrolled, it became my mission to keep her there.

"Anyway, I took the job at Rampion Core right out of school because I thought it might give me that sense of accomplishment I was lacking. The freedom from my name and background—or at least my sister's influence. I don't know. It's a shitty job, but if I can move up in the ranks, I think I could really make a difference in the scientific realm. Maybe I won't cure cancer, but...maybe I'll do *something* on my own, you know?" She sighs, deflating. "That's why I wanted the orchid. My boss said he'd promote me if I could get it, and now..."

She looks at me from the corner of her eyes. I open my mouth to say something—to try to explain *again* that I didn't *steal* anything from her—but she cuts me off.

"I don't know why I'm telling you all this. Are orgasms some kind of word-vomit inducer?"

Forcing memories from my mind, I paste on a grin and slide my palm over her hip. "Should we fuck again and find out?"

She smirks, rolling so she faces away from me. "Sleep first. I think if we do it again right now, I might break in half."

Silence blankets the room, and for several moments, I just watch the slow rise and fall of her body, assuming she's fast asleep. When she speaks again, my heart feels like it ceases beating inside my chest.

"I just wanted you to know why I left back then. It wasn't *you*. Not really."

Unsure of what to say to that, I simply blink my desire away and get up from the bed to discard the washcloth. In the bathroom, I spray some cold water on my face to try and get a fucking hold of myself.

All I have to do is tell her my plan—tell her what I've done. My own confession for her hand.

Maybe it will be enough to come clean about everything.

To tell her that what was one moment in time for her was *seven years* for me. It didn't end when she escaped or when I found her not even a day later and chose not to pursue her. Whatever we started continued on all along as I spent each day watching her from afar, admiring the steps she was taking to become her own woman.

A buzzing noise draws my attention back to the bedroom. I scan the darkness for my pants, kicked off near the window, and yank my phone from the pocket. There's a text from Frankie telling me there's been some issue with the orchid, but they're dealing with it, and another from an unknown number.

Unknown: Bring the whore to us, or there will be consequences.

I ignore both messages, tossing the phone back onto my clothes and walking over to the bed.

When I slide in beside her, listening to her tiny snores fill the quiet, I can't find it in me to wake her. Instead, I wrap an arm around her waist and pull her close, silently cursing myself for being a fucking bastard.

"Penso di essere innamorata di te."

She doesn't stir, so I whisper it again into the stillness of the bedroom, where each word drifts into the air and disappears, leaving Stella none the wiser.

The Demon of Boston no more.

Demons don't fall in love. They don't have hearts.

Although maybe that makes me one after all, since the woman tucked into my side stole mine.

She turns in her sleep, nuzzling against me. My dick aches to be in her again, but when those beautiful brown eyes pop open, shining up at me in the moonlight, I'm frozen in place. Completely ensnared by her.

A total goner.

"Are you going to keep me in this tower forever?" Her voice is small, almost sweet, and thick from slumber.

"I'm the evil villain in this story, right? It wouldn't make sense for me to let you go." Her eyes widen, and I laugh, smoothing my thumb over her cheek. "I'm kidding, Stella. There is nothing I want less than to stifle your freedom and individuality. Those are some of the many things I've enjoyed watching you cultivate over the years."

The admission slips out too fast for me to stop.

She blinks slowly, as if processing each word. I wait for more questions, or maybe even accusations, but they never come.

"I used to watch you in church, you know."

Yes, I don't say. *I know.* We've had this conversation, sort of, but I suppose she doesn't remember.

"You were so handsome and terrifying. My mother hated when I stared, and my sisters would tell me you ate people."

I smother a snicker. "Cannibalism does not appeal to me, I'm afraid."

"But you let people think that anyway, right? It made you seem scarier, and you wanted their fear."

"I *needed* their fear," I correct softly, cupping her jaw. "Anything less would have meant my death."

"Did you want mine?"

Leaning down, I angle her head and gently press a kiss to her swollen lips. "Never."

In truth, I wanted something far different from her, even if I didn't realize it at the time. Even if I can't admit it now, out loud.

A part of me thinks she knows anyway. It's in the way her pupils dilate, shimmering like glass in the gentle glow of the candlelight. No matter my reasons for coming here, or for staying, or for harassing her, I think she knows.

Or I hope she does.

Fuck, De Tore, who the hell even are you anymore?

I expect more questions. Instead, Stella leans her forehead against my biceps and drifts back off to sleep.

STELLA

wake with a start, heat seeping into my body like a steady faucet leak. It's still dark, and most of the candles in the room have blown out. Only two on the nightstand remain burning, casting an ethereal glimmer across the bed.

My cheek is plastered to a naked pectoral, while my arm is thrown over a wall of hard muscle.

Slowly, my eyes still half-lidded with sleep, I take in the relaxed slant of Leo's mouth and realize it's the first time I've ever seen him look…peaceful.

If his anger and arrogance are seductive, this side of him is entirely disarming.

Something aches deep in my chest, like a bruise that never quite healed. I exhale, trying to write the feeling off as simple soreness from last night and nothing more. His breaths come in even puffs, and his heart beats a steady rhythm under my ear, so I carefully lay my palm on the patch of hair on his abdomen—just above where the comforter covers him.

When his stomach flexes, I freeze.

"If you go any lower," he rasps, "you'll create a problem you might not be able to fix."

I move my chin, looking up at him. His eyes are still closed, but his face has lost that passive quality. A vein in his forehead strains.

"Did I not prove last night that I'm very capable of a solution to this particular problem?" I purr.

He grunts, and then in the next second, he's sliding his arms around me and yanking me up, twisting my body so I'm straddling his waist. I squeak, immediately covering my breasts with my forearms and desperately attempting to ignore the erection pressing below me.

"Should we make sure it wasn't a fluke?"

My face heats, a mix of arousal and shame scorching my skin. "I...I wouldn't know what to do."

One of his brows arches. "Suddenly, you're above learning?"

"Don't you think we should get back to the auction? People are going to wonder where I went, and I don't want you to get in trouble."

"My, how we've changed our tune so quickly. A few orgasms, and you're finally concerned with my well-being?"

I narrow my eyes at him. "If you cause problems, they'll inevitably trickle down to me. That's all I meant."

"Don't worry about it. I'm a big boy; I can handle trouble." He yanks my arms away from my chest, drinking in the sight of my bare breasts. The liquid fire in his gaze kindles something dark and twisted in my gut, making me tremble. "Now let me handle *you*. Crawl up here and sit that pretty cunt on my face."

Horror zaps through me. "*What?*"

He grins. "You heard me."

My limbs lock up as I continue staring at him, but a flood of warmth spreads down my spine like drizzled honey. Still, I feel stuck, torn by the knowledge of the pleasure he's able to wring from me and the haphazard belief that I don't want anything to do with him.

How many times do you have to repeat something before it becomes true? Am I protesting because I genuinely can't see this marriage working, given the shoddy deal it was built on and the distance between us since? Or am I clinging to that because it feels like there's nothing else that makes sense?

Maybe I reject Leo because it feels right to. It feels like *me*.

And maybe I don't want to admit that I haven't felt like *me* since I left Boston seven years ago.

Not really.

Something has always been missing. Something that feels less out of reach here, in his embrace.

Leaning forward, I awkwardly move my knees, crawling up his torso like he asked. My heart is a kick drum beating against my ribs, and he shifts under me, sliding lower on the bed. Once I'm halfway up his stomach, he grabs my hips and manhandles me; I have to catch myself on the headboard to keep from hitting it and then to steady my quaking arms.

His lips and nose line up directly with my pussy, and I cover my mouth to avoid revealing how vulnerable I feel.

"Sit, baby." It's unnerving how gentle his voice is compared to the roughness of his grip. "You're not gonna hurt me. Not like this anyway."

My fingers scrape against the headboard, and I lower myself inch by inch. Apparently growing impatient, Leo squeezes and yanks me down, sealing his mouth to me so thoroughly that I cry out with the unexpected heat of him.

"Oh my *God*."

He lifts my hips for a moment, his eyebrows drawing in. "Are you asking for forgiveness?"

"I haven't done anything wrong."

"Keeping your cunt from me all this time qualifies as a deadly sin, I'm afraid." Another lick, just the tip of his tongue against me, and my thighs quiver. "So go ahead and pray, stellina. I'm the only one who can grant you mercy."

My chin almost touches my chest as I peer down at him, my heart thrashing inside against my ribs. "You're not my god."

A long pause ensues as he seems to contemplate this. His eyes darken, hot sparks ebbing within his irises. "No, but you're mine. You're right in that you don't need forgiveness—*I* do. Let me repent."

I can't breathe when he looks at me like this or when he says these things. Instead, I just nod, and he moves back in, devouring me slowly, like we have all the time in the world.

In the moment, it doesn't occur to me how quickly that time can come to an end.

LEO

When the sun finally comes up, my dick feels like it's going to fall off.

I haven't had a night with so much sex in—well, *ever*.

Christ, is that right? Before Stella, dating was too risky, so most rendezvous were limited to one-time things. A quick tryst in a dark room before a meeting or stolen when my father was out of town. Regardless of if I was with a man or woman, there was never an opportunity to prolong the pleasure.

Moreover, I never found myself wanting to. I was satisfied with fleeting moments, and yet from the second Stella Ricci was offered to me in that church seven years ago, the idea of her being a temporary fixture has never sat right with me.

Even when I was accepting the offer on the premise of taking something from Rafael, I knew I wouldn't be happy with having her once. I hadn't spent half my adolescence watching her, admiring her, only to be blessed with a few pressurized minutes of forced affection.

With Stella, I wanted it *all*. Despite knowing she didn't feel the same and that she was looking for an escape before she even came to Saint Paul's. My desire to keep her, to make her mine, was intrinsic.

My eyes find the rising sun past the mansion outside, and I tuck Stella's sleeping form closer into me. Her eyelashes brush the tops of her cheeks, pinkened from the long night we've had, and there's still a sheen of sweat gleaming against her skin.

Studies say it takes a man eighty-eight days to fall in love.

I believe it took me eighty-eight seconds, one single kiss, and the transfer of a razor blade from her mouth to mine.

A single verse sung during church choir—the perfect melody—heard when I was just a boy sitting in the back row of the nave and hating that I had to be there. Yet, when she opened her mouth to sing, it was impossible to focus on anything else. Her voice captivated me from that moment, like a spell weaved around my soul.

I've been careening off the cliff ever since.

Stella's body tenses, and her brown eyes squint up at me from where her head rests on my chest. "Are you watching me sleep?"

"Depends." I squeeze her hip, then wrap a fistful of her hair around my fingers. "Does it make me a pervert stalker if I say yes?"

"Well, it doesn't make you *not* one." Using her hand to push herself into a sitting position, she lets the comforter fall off us, then lifts onto her knees.

I swallow over a lump in my throat as her hair curtains her body, her nipples peeking through the silken waves. When she hooks a leg over my waist, straddling me without any prompting, my heart grows heavy in my chest.

"Stella," I warn, my cock springing to life at the mere brush of her cunt against it.

"What?" She bats her eyelashes, sliding her slit over my shaft. "I'm just trying to get closer to you. That's what you wanted, wasn't it?"

"This isn't the *only* thing I wanted."

Still, it's no use. I've created a little monster, and she isn't listening to me; her cunt is fully intent on getting its fill, and I can't help the dread that laces my insides, wondering if that's all she plans on doing with me. If this is as close as she'll let herself get.

I suppose I don't exactly deserve more, but that doesn't stop my soul from craving it.

The tip of my dick slips in as she shimmies her ass backward, and we gasp collectively.

"*Fuck*," I grind out, fisting the sheets. "How is it possible that I haven't ruined this yet?"

"You can't ruin fate."

My eyebrows shoot up. "Is that so?"

Her mouth parts as she slowly—*so goddamn slow*—pushes down on me, letting my cock split her open. She's so wet and perfect that my vision blurs, and my back bows off the mattress with the sensation of being fully seated in her.

"That's what this feels like, right?" she whispers, leaning with her palms on my shoulders. Her tits swing in my face as she starts to tentatively ride me. "Years have passed, and it's like we're picking up right where we left off. Almost as if time stood still in the distance between us, waiting for our reunion."

She flushes a deep fuchsia, and my nerves draw taut.

Fuck, she feels it, too?

"I can't explain why I'm here with you right now, doing this." Her nails lightly burrow into my skin, and I release the sheets to grab her hips, urging her to ride me harder. "The nerdy part of my brain wants to say biology is, obviously, winning out, and I'm just horny. But I could've said no to you last night, or the night before, or even back when we got married and I was afraid being your wife was going to be my only identity."

"Yet you didn't. You stayed, stellina, and now you're using my cock to get off."

Her cunt tightens around me, and she lets out a soft moan. "Yeah, exactly. That has to be fate, right? No matter where I've gone or what I've done over the last seven years, you've been a constant thought in my mind. Something I knew all along I wouldn't be able to fight if it came down to that. I could never deny this, and you could never mess it up, because it was an inevitability. Statistically, I don't know what the odds are, but even if the data doesn't necessarily support my theory, that's my educated guess."

I groan, clawing at her, guiding her movements on top of me. Each undulation of her hips is met by an upward thrust of my own, and I drag her face to mine. She keeps grinding, her cunt squelching lewdly in the silent room, even as I press a brutal kiss to her mouth, wishing there were a way for me to capture her intelligence, her faith, and fuse it into my being.

"You learn fast," I mutter against her mouth, recognizing the signs of climax as she bears down, then shoves a hand between us to play with her clit.

"I have an okay teacher," she says, and when we come, I black out a little from the rush of blinding pleasure.

Moments later, my cock softens inside her, warm and snug, and I do nothing to alter the situation. She heaves a stuttered breath as her high wanes, though she doesn't make a move to get off me.

Eventually, she slumps, resting her head on my shoulder.

My fingers shake slightly as I stroke her back, exhaustion finally catching up with me. Or maybe it's my nerves, frayed from all the overthinking I've been doing.

"So," I venture, brushing the hair from her back and reveling in its length, "what does Stella Ricci's future look like now?"

"Oh." I feel her blink, but she remains still. "What do you mean?"

"Well, you've done everything you told me you wanted to seven years ago. Save for curing cancer, but I'll give you a pass on that one, since you're far from the first person to not achieve that particular feat in their lifetime. But everything else—you've managed to check off an impressive list, you know? You graduated with honors despite your circumstances, you were president of at least two student organizations, and you published several *official* papers on stem cells and the future of genetics in esteemed journals. Now you work as an assistant at a lab, and you're spending your *current* free time with me."

"It's kind of creepy how you know all that."

I smirk, listening to her heart beating, feeling it pump steadily against my chest. "What comes next for you?"

"I..." Her fingers curl in, and she tucks her face into me as if hiding something. "Well, I guess I don't really know. I came here to get that orchid, but now..."

Now, I wouldn't mind staying with you.

The flower doesn't matter, Leo. I just want to be here, in this moment, for as long as possible.

Those words don't come, though, and I do my best not to take it personally. It's never been about me anyway; my question wasn't either, and that's what I remind myself as I gently push her onto the bed beside me, sitting up with a heavy sigh.

"You fulfilled your end of the deal," I tell her. "I'll help you get the flower."

STELLA

How do you know you're in love?

I watch Leo as he crouches, shoving his hand beneath the bed to look for my discarded high heels. Since neither of us bothered to grab anything from our rooms after the auction, we're dressed in our clothes from last night, preparing to go back downstairs to find the orchid.

He hasn't said how he plans on securing it for me, but I have no doubt he'll be able to either way. If I've learned anything about this man, it's that there's nothing he can't achieve once he sets his mind to it.

I can't help wondering if that's *all* I need to know. Do you have to be aware of a person's deepest secrets, their childhood backgrounds, and all their future plans before you can fall in love with them?

Or do you just have to be open to learning all that?

Maybe love isn't *knowing* but *feeling*.

Maybe that's what's been here all along, as completely impractical as that sounds, and that's why I ran. Because how do you keep a hold of yourself, your identity, and at the same time hand it over to someone else?

Maybe you're just naive, Stella.

Leo sits back, pulling himself from under the bed, and places my bare foot on his knee. Carefully, like I'm made of glass, he slides the heel beneath it, securing the strap at my ankle. He's been quiet since we got up from the bed and showered, and I can't help wondering if he's thinking about his earlier question.

I didn't answer fully before because I wasn't sure how to admit that now that he's here, there's a part of me wishing he'd stay. And maybe I wouldn't hate that as much as my previous self—my virginal self who thought she loathed him—wanted me to.

"So," I say as he switches feet, "what's the plan?"

"The plan?"

"Yeah, you know, to get me this orchid. Are you gonna offer them money? Threaten them?" Leaning back on my palms, I cock my head and rack my brain for more options. "De Tores are big on intimidation, right? Since violence is out of the question while the auction is going on, I guess you could lean heavier on the *implication*—"

"The De Tores no longer exist, stellina. You're aware that my father is dead, yes?"

Snapping my mouth shut, I nod.

"Good. So you understand that his death left us without a don."

My eyebrows draw together. "Wouldn't you have been his successor?"

"I was, but I'm also the one who killed him."

Reflexively, I draw my hands closer to my lap. He continues with his task, clasping the buckle on my heel, and gently sets that foot on the floor. Wholly unbothered by his admission.

I don't know why I'm surprised, really. You don't get called the Demon of Boston because you have a reputation for being kind and anti-violence.

Hell, the first time he went down on me, he was covered in someone else's blood.

Still, there was a little distance between me and his victims. A cognitive dissonance erected by the belief that he hadn't killed anyone I knew.

An icy chill skates down my spine. *But I knew his father.* I remember the way he spoke and the kiss he forced upon me.

When I meet Leo's gaze, I expect disgust or fear to take precedence in my bones. I brace for the impact of discomfort in my gut, but it never comes.

He isn't sorry. I can tell that much from the hard, even set of his brows and his unyielding expression.

I'm not either.

"The problem with me as the boss is that the remaining Elders never wanted me in that position, so the system has unequivocally broken down. It was barely hanging on by a thread anyway, with my father at the helm, but my subordinates have spent most of their energy recently on finding a way to get me out. The whole map of crime back home is a shit show these days, with everyone turning informant or siphoning off decent men for their own gain. Some have just been slaughtering anyone who questions them."

A tiny gleam in his eye tells me which category he falls into.

"So they won't be any help in this case." He walks over, then grips my chin with two fingers. "But that's all right, because I don't need them to get you the flower."

I arch my back, leaning into his touch. *"Tell me."*

"It's already mine." His hold tightens when my head jerks. "I bought it at the auction last night."

"You—" Confusion worms its way through the wrinkles of my brain, filling my skull with muddy conclusions. "What are you talking about? You had the orchid the entire time, even when I *cried* over missing out on it? When I said I didn't think I'd get a promotion now?"

Nausea roils in my stomach, and I grab his wrist, wrenching out of his grasp. My body aches as I move back on the bed, a painful reminder of what I've given up.

He moves, reaching for me, but I scramble away from his touch. Wrapping my arms around myself, I slide from the mattress and put it between us, standing on the opposite side.

"How could you do that?" My eyes burn, and I claw at my elbows, trying to focus on the physical pain. "Why didn't you say something when I bargained my body for your help?"

Leo's face remains impassive. I guess my rejection doesn't sting quite as badly as his did. "You would have ended up in my bed either way, *wife*. I came here to pick up where we left off seven years ago, not to play silly games. Whether I gave you the fucking flower before or after we fucked, it wouldn't have mattered. I bought it *for* you."

I blink. "Why?"

"Do you know how much that thing cost? Rampion Core didn't send you with enough money in their escrow account. You were out of the running by the time the second hand went up."

As I process his words, my stomach drops. Is it possible Barry deliberately sent me with limited funds, or did he honestly not know what a rare plant would go for?

Defeat hits my chest, weighing it down. My effort was wasted before any of this even began.

"How do you know all this?" I ask. "And why couldn't you have just said that last night instead of—"

"Instead of making you come in front of an audience?"

He grins, stepping around the bed and stalking toward me. I move back, trapping myself against the glass wall, and he plants a palm on one side of my head while his other dives into my hair. He lifts it, bringing a handful to his nose and inhaling deeply.

"When faced with a choice between your pleasure and anything else, I'm afraid I'm always going to choose the former."

My face heats. "That doesn't answer my other question."

"But I already have, Stella. Did you think this was all a coincidence? That you left my condo back then on a *whim*, with the help of my employee, and it just worked out?" He drops my hair, leaning to press his forehead to mine. "I let you leave once. I wasn't going to waste this opportunity a second time."

"That's a shitty excuse—"

"It isn't one. I'm not asking you to forgive *this* behavior. I'd be upset if you did, in fact."

His free hand glides against my jaw, and he kisses me slowly until my head feels dizzy. When he pulls back, looking into his eyes feels like standing at the center of a hurricane.

Anxiety pours through my veins, immobilizing me.

When I don't make a move to run, he continues. "I'm just giving you an explanation because you deserve one. Rationale has no home in my mind when it comes to you, so most of my decisions are not well thought out or even particularly good. I act because that is what you move in me. So be angry. Hate me for marrying you, for rejecting you, and for tricking you. Hate me for spending all my time watching instead of joining. As long as you do it *with* me. I prefer your wrath over your absence."

It sounds *a lot* like a confession, or an admission, or even a silent plea. My pulse throbs in my neck, and for a second, I focus solely on that because I'm not quite sure what to make of everything he's said.

I'm not given any time to either, because the elevator chimes before I can speak, signaling someone's sudden arrival at the top of the tower.

LEO

Stella tenses against me, her head veering toward the elevator as it reaches our floor. "Are you expecting someone?"

"Frankie." It takes every ounce of willpower in my being to pull away from her, but I don't want to keep her trapped when another person is in the room. It'd make her look weak, and that isn't something I desire. "I texted him earlier and asked him to bring the orchid here."

Her deep brown eyes narrow, and she crosses her arms, studying me. "You just don't want me near the play party."

I smirk, rubbing the back of my neck. "That is true. Though I think you should be the one worried about joining."

"Why? I could handle it. I walk three miles every morning. I'm in excellent shape."

"Oh, I'm well acquainted with your *shape*, wife." I toss her a wink, which she rolls her eyes at, pushing past me on her way to the elevator. I follow, letting my gaze drop, memorizing the outline of her glorious ass in that white lace dress. "However, the theme is hunter and prey. Are you sure that's something you'd like to navigate with me around?"

She pauses, twisting around as I approach. Wicked amusement pulls at her features, drawing the corner of her mouth up. When she reaches for me, she grabs the tail of my tie with both hands, yanking me close—tightening the knot at my throat.

I'm getting whiplash from her ever-changing emotions, and I don't even care. I suppose it's the very least I deserve after reinserting myself into her life with no warning.

"Maybe you can be the prey," she says, her voice low and unbelievably sexy.

My cock twitches. "You want to hunt me down?"

Her grip on the knot sharpens, interrupting my air supply a bit. "At this point, I think it's only fair if I get to do some stalking as well."

Across from us, the elevator chimes again, and the doors automatically slide open. No one comes out, though, and my eyebrows immediately draw inward. Stella makes a move to turn, but I grab her shoulders, directing her behind me.

"What's going on?" she asks, hooking a finger through one of my belt loops.

"I'm not sure." Moving forward, I slowly take in the empty car, scanning for a note or other sign of distress. "Frankie's supposed to be bringing the—"

My shoes cross over the threshold, and I instantly regret breaking the buttons last night. I can't close the doors now. So, when I spot my right-hand man slumped unconscious in the elevator's corner, beneath the electric panel, Stella follows me.

I try to shield her from the view, but she peers around, a small gasp escaping when she sees Frankie.

"Oh my God! What the hell happened?"

With my foot, I press against his leg, inspecting for any evidence of wounds or other trauma. I crouch, noting a distinct lack of blood surrounding him, and fit two fingers to his neck. "I don't know, but I don't like this. He's alive, although his pulse is pretty weak."

Getting back up, I fish my phone from my pants pocket and step back out of the elevator. When I dial Genevieve, she doesn't answer, and an uneasy sensation settles deep in my gut.

"Cyanosis," Stella says.

I whip around, glaring at where she's now kneeling by Frankie's side, squinting. "Get out of there, Stella. It isn't safe."

She scoffs. "Please, he's unconscious. What's he going to do?" With one hand, she gestures toward his face, drawing a circle in the air around his mouth. "Look at the blue ring around his lips and his fingers... He's definitely experiencing methemoglobinemia."

My grip on the phone tightens. "What the hell is that?"

"It's a condition that develops from changes in hemoglobin. Basically, his blood isn't getting enough oxygen, and he probably passed out from that." Pursing her lips, she glances over her shoulder at me. "Does he have any health conditions? Something he hasn't treated maybe since you came to the auction?"

"No. As far as I'm aware, he's completely healthy." It wouldn't do to keep him around otherwise. I suppose there's a possibility that he's been lying to me, but I have to believe for my own sanity that he wouldn't jeopardize our entire operation like that.

"Okay, well...you're probably not going to like this." Stella cringes. "I'd say someone's poisoned him."

I blink at her, then look at his form again. The tips of his fingers are a light purple, the same color as the outside of his lips, and the color seems to be spreading.

Shit.

There are only a few people who could have been at this party and would be willing to risk the event organizers' wrath by poisoning another attendee. I had Frankie extensively review the invite list before we arrived to ensure Ranolfo and Gino weren't on it, but I suppose they could've taken someone else's invitation and slipped in unnoticed.

After all, I did the same when I asked Valerie Van der Vorm to give her invite to Stella. The workers were aware, but the patrons had no clue who was really among them.

Which means we're probably in deep fucking shit.

"Stella"—I keep my voice steady so as not to alarm her, but every fiber of my being is suddenly pulled tight, primed for action—"exit the elevator."

She makes a face, getting up and walking to the doors. Only, she doesn't come out. Instead, she just crosses her arms over her chest and narrows those beautiful brown eyes.

"This is never going to work if all you plan on doing is ordering me around all the time," she says. "I will not be some silent, docile puppet that you keep on retainer to warm your cock whenever you're bored."

"That is *not* my intention with you." I redial Genevieve's number, trying to rein in the anger boiling just under the surface of my skin when it once again goes to voicemail.

"Well, you'd better be prepared to—"

A sudden whirring sound cuts off her sentence, and then there is a deafening mechanical *click*. Before either of us blinks, the elevator doors start to slide closed. I dive toward the entrance, and at the same time, she tries to wedge her body in the way to keep them open.

"*Stella, move!*"

My arm extends, and for a split second, I consider yanking her through to me, but there isn't enough time. The doors aren't stopping, and she's not close enough for me to grab. I shove her backward to keep her from getting caught and pull my arm out just before the doors slam shut.

Phone in hand, I move to slam the Open button on the panel, but it's broken.

Fuck.

My chest heaves, and I brace my arms against the doors. Anxiety races through my limbs, constricting airflow as I choke out, "Stella? Can you hear me?"

It takes a moment for her to respond, but finally her voice comes through. "Yes."

"Are you okay? We need to get you out of there, but first, I have to know you're okay."

"A little winded from where you *pushed* me, but otherwise…"

My heart drums against my rib cage.

"Otherwise?"

"I don't love that I'm in here. I told you this was a death trap waiting to happen."

Exhaling roughly, I lower my head. "I know, baby. I know."

More silence. Then: "Did you mean what you said about not wanting me to be your puppet?"

"What?"

"Just answer the question, Leo."

Christ, I love the sound of my name when she says it. Almost as if it's got some real meaning, like she enjoys the way it feels coming from her lips.

She continues. "When you came to this auction, when you stole the orchid from me...what were you hoping to get from all of it?"

"Why are you asking me this right now?" I push off the doors, balling my hands into fists as I refocus on a way to get her out. "Quit distracting me—"

"I'm trying to distract *myself*, because I think there's a good chance I'll die in here if you can't open the doors soon."

My heart ceases beating entirely. I stare at the metal, acute horror working its way up my sternum.

"When you pushed me back, I turned my head, and I guess... my hair got caught."

I glance down as she speaks, noting a handful of her hair sticking out from the seam of the doors. Blinking, I use my fingers to try and push it through, but the limp strands don't budge.

"Pull yourself free," I snap, the tightening in my chest growing to unbearable heights.

"I *can't*." She pauses, and the soft sounds of her straining trickle through our barrier, enraging me further. "There's too much in there. I can't get a good grip on it."

Shit.

Pocketing my phone, I try to slip my fingers into the cracks, wondering if I can force them apart if I get enough of my hand in between. But I can't. My fingers are too large, and the seam is too narrow.

Nausea rolls in my stomach like an angry ocean wave. I've never felt so entirely helpless.

Still, I can't let myself dwell on the fear. I need to get her out of there, especially if Ranolfo or Gino are the reason Frankie was poisoned.

I draw a deep breath and step away from the elevator. "Can you reach Frankie?"

"Um...yes. With my foot."

"Good. There should be a utility knife in his front right pocket. Try to get it."

There's some distant shuffling, and then her voice returns. "Okay, I've got it."

"Now cut it."

"Cut my hair?"

"Do you see a better solution right now?"

"But..." I hear her sigh, and it sounds like she's pouting. "You love my hair."

My fascination with those dark-brown locks is something that could undoubtedly be studied, though time isn't exactly on our side at the moment. If someone came into the tower and decided to take the elevator up, the shaft would receive their call and start its descent, scalping her instantly.

I open my mouth and immediately close it as a confession rolls from the tip of my tongue. Now is not the time.

"It will grow back. Cut yourself free, and I'll meet you at the bottom."

"You're going to leave me?" Panic laces her words, and I recall the way she trembled against me when we came up here last night.

Unfortunately, there's nothing I can do for her standing outside the door. "Baby, if you want out of there, I have to go down. This panel is broken."

"I knew your ridiculous ways would be my downfall." She laughs, but the sound is forced, and my heart seizes. "Fine, hurry up. Give me five minutes once you've reached the bottom to make sure I'm out."

Goddamn, I don't want to leave her here, but there isn't anything I can do to help. Every muscle in my body screams in agony as I jog to the bathroom, pausing to grab the Glock hidden beneath the sink, and push through to the door on the far wall. The stairwell is narrow and damp and, like the elevator, housed in the only solid wall of the tower, so a person's comings and goings are entirely obscured from the outside world.

It's probably the perfect place to carry out an attack, and I'm pissed as fuck that I didn't consider that when I brought her here. If my ridiculous ways are supposed to be *her* downfall, I don't want to imagine the bleak future awaiting me.

When I reach the bottom, my foot slips on the last step, and my hand lashes out, grabbing hold of the railing before I lose my balance. Gritting my teeth, I glance at the glass doors down the hall, trying to get a sense for any sort of tampering.

The alcove is totally empty and looks the same as it did last night. If not for seeing Frankie with my own eyes, I wouldn't have thought he'd made it to the building yet.

Suspicious.

There aren't even footprints on the ground, which is odd, considering that the outside looks freshly drizzled upon. As I head toward the elevator, a loud creaking fills the air, and then a snapping noise echoes down the tower.

I glance at the panel of buttons and notice they're all blinking. As if in some sort of error.

For a moment, I wonder if my breaking the one upstairs could have caused problems, but then Frankie wouldn't have been able to come up at all.

An earsplitting boom explodes around me like the shattering of metal and glass, and with it, my resolve.

With my hands shaking and mind racing, I whirl around and sprint back to the stairs. I'm not sure what exactly I think I can do, but my nerves are calling the shots, and my brain seems to short-circuit as it realizes that the elevator is fully malfunctioning and likely plummeting.

Just as I reach the steps, a brutal force impacts the side of my face, and my vision goes blank.

Liquid drips down my forehead directly into my eyes, and opening them becomes impossible.

My fingers curl around the handle of the gun, and I move

forward, trying to get my back to a wall, but another blow knocks me down. I fall to my knees as my jaw cracks, lifting my free arm to shield myself from another attack.

"*Careful*, Ranolfo." My uncle's voice drifts close, chilling my spine. Despite everything, I suppose there was something deep within me that hoped it wouldn't be him. "We don't want to make a mess."

Ranolfo's laugh whizzes past my ear, and pain explodes in my stomach and groin when the heel of his foot drives into my abdomen. Coughing, I buckle, hunching over my knees as stars dance behind my eyes.

"After what he did to me and his own father? I don't give a shit if we smear his remains all over this fucking property."

"We don't want to make a scene," Gino says. "It's bad etiquette to ruin a party you weren't invited to."

"If this cazzo had cooperated in the first place, we wouldn't have had to come to this godforsaken state to begin with."

Another kick to my gut, and blood floods my mouth, splattering past my clenched teeth.

"Now, where's that slut wife of yours? I was looking forward to stealing her from Candreva last night, but this will be good, too. Even if I suspect you broke her in for the men already, I'm sure she'll have fun getting all her holes plugged before we slit her throat."

"Pity it doesn't seem he'll be able to watch," Gino notes, his voice next to my ear. "The boy can't even open his eyes."

"Bet he'll be able to hear her scream, though."

Another crash splits the air, crunching and splintering

sounds reverberating off the walls. My body aches, agony rippling up to my temples and down my sternum, and still my eyes remain shut.

I'm going to die here, and then they're going to grab Stella. If the elevator hasn't fallen and killed her, that is.

That's my first thought.

The second is that I'm a coward. If I'd just told Stella everything about why I was sending her away back then or why I showed up now of all times, maybe...maybe I could've avoided this.

We could've left the auction and run away from the people after us. Instead, I wanted immediate gratification, and now, I've cost both of us our lives.

Coglione. My father's voice peeks up from where I've shoved it deep in the recesses of my mind, and I think he was right.

I'm not fit to be a figurehead, and I'm certainly not fit to be a husband. Not Stella's anyway.

Fuck that. My heart wars with my brain, telling it to shut the fuck up.

If I'm not worthy of Stella, then who the hell is?

Who else would have sent her away to make sure she got to live her life? I only came here in the hopes of joining her in some way—not to make her serve at my side as some puppet.

What were you hoping to get from all of it?

Her. That's all I ever wanted. Why the hell didn't I tell her that?

When I was a boy, listening to her in church and watching her every time after that.

When money was what sent me to Saint Paul's, and I had no intention at first of leaving without it, and then without her.

When I showed up after seven years of watching her accomplish her dreams from afar without me, falling head over heels with each secret smile of satisfaction.

All I've ever wanted was her.

And as I raise the gun, the sound of footsteps echoing around me very distantly, that desire is what I latch on to. Even if it's futile in the end, I'll go out loving her.*

* BEAUTIFUL THINGS—Benson Boone

STELLA

E yes wide, I stare at the fistful of long dark-brown hair my fingers are wrapped around. Cool air brushes across my neck, now exposed from the sudden change in length. The blunt, uneven ends are picked up by a light breeze drifting down from the vent in the ceiling, some spilling past my shoulders, some not quite reaching my collarbone.

I think I might be dead.

My left arm is extended behind my head, cushioning it. Each finger throbs, and I wonder if any bones are broken from the impact. The length of my spine screams in horrific agony as I lift a leg, trying to assess the damage to my body.

Frankie's form is now entirely slumped onto his side, his head bleeding from where it collided with the elevator floor.

His lips are still blue.

I don't know if he's alive.

Blinking, I attempt to orient myself, replaying the events that led up to my supine position on the ground. One second, Leo was telling me to cut my hair out of the closed doors and that he'd meet me at the bottom, and the next, we were free-falling and crash-landing.

I moved to my back instantly, using the rail on the wall to push myself into the position. Everything after is kind of a blur.

Most elevators have several safety features that kick in if one mechanism fails, but this one malfunctioning seems pretty on track with the decrepit state of the tower in general. I just didn't imagine *every feature* would stall and lump me in with the statistic I gave Leo last night.

Longing stirs in my stomach. *Leo.* Slowly, I turn my head toward the elevator doors, which split wide open upon crashing. He isn't standing outside of them or shoving his way in, however, so that tells me something very, very bad has happened.

Either I am dead or...

I glance at Frankie again, forcing a swallow despite the dryness in my mouth. A metallic tang works its way down my throat, and it takes me a moment to realize I must have bitten my tongue during the fall.

If Frankie was poisoned, does that mean someone's after him? After Leo?

What if that's why the elevator collapsed?

Dread swirls in my chest, aching worse than the physical pain in my bones. Breathing deeply, I start to peel myself off the floor, wincing when a stinging sensation rips through my shoulder, shimmying down my elbow to my hand.

My mouth falls open in a silent scream as I manage to force

myself up the wall, getting back to my feet. With trembling fingers, I undo my heels and kick them off, ignoring how my ankle spasms in protest.

Opening my hand, I let the severed strands of hair drift to the ground. It's the first time I've cut it in years, and there's a twinge of sadness as I watch the hair fall, but there's no time to soak in it.

I don't know where Leo is, and I don't know how much time Frankie has. Or if he has any left at all. I can't allow myself to linger here.

Dizziness floods my body, throwing me off-kilter as I move toward the doors. Twisted, puckered metal creates a massive gap in the seam and an exit for me.

Slowly, I haul my body up, hissing when I try to use my right arm as leverage. Moving it at all is a massive feat that makes me break out into a cold sweat. I glance down, one leg out of the shaft, and note the sagging and swelling of my shoulder.

"Fuck," I whisper, clenching my jaw. *Dislocated.*

I guess I should be grateful to be standing at all right now.

Somewhere down the hall, what sounds like a gunshot rings out into the damp wasteland that is the bottom of this tower, and I shake myself out of the idea to put my shoulder back into its socket. That will have to wait.

Bruised and battered, and likely unaware of more injuries due to shock, I climb out of the broken car. Each staggered breath I pull in feels like inhaling a bag of thumbtacks, but I push through anyway, worry striking my heart.

I don't know what to do, really. Textbooks and lab work haven't prepared me for any kind of altercations, and if it's someone

Leo knows, the odds of me coming out of this unscathed are low. My only weapon is the short utility knife I used to sawed through my hair, which I fish out from where I stuffed it into my bra.

Curling my hand around the folded object, I start down the hall as the noise cracks out a second time. The alcove where the entrance is opens into a slightly wider area, curving so that the front doors to the tower are obscured once you go a certain distance.

When I spot a set of wooden stairs, I stop in my tracks. My stomach hollows out, fear racing through my veins.

Less than a hundred feet away, Leo crouches on the bottom steps before a tall man in a brown suit who's using a baseball bat as a prop. Leo's handsome face, which I was riding less than two hours ago, is coated in bright red blood. His dark hair is matted to his forehead, which is split open in multiple places.

He's holding a gun, pointing it directly at the man in front of him, but his eyes aren't even open. My body tenses. When he pulls the trigger, an odd clicking sound puffs out of the device, but nothing else happens.

The stranger, who has slicked-back gray hair and a dimpled chin, yanks the gun from him and whips it across Leo's jaw; his head juts back suddenly, his neck hitting a terrible angle, and then he slumps silently onto the ground.

Without looking, the other man discards the gun by tossing it behind him. It slides across the floor, skidding to a halt a few feet from me.

I take a step in its direction, my pulse roaring between my ears.

I've never held a gun in my entire life. Never had the desire to. It felt like all Papà and his men were good at was wielding weapons to intimidate or eliminate one another, and I wanted something more than that.

Standing here now, staring at the weapon, my moral argument feels like bullshit.

Sometimes, a gun is all you've got.

Quickly, I dive for it and aim with my uninjured arm, not caring about anything other than getting that man away from Leo.

I don't think about the auction outside or how I could have probably gone out and found help if I'd been thinking straight. I don't consider the trouble this will likely get us into or even that I should focus and devise some sort of actual game plan.

Instead, my body launches into action, impulse weighing heavier than my usual desire for rational thought—just like it did seven years ago with that razor blade and then when I let Leo go down on me the first time in his kitchen.

Because when it comes to my husband, I've never had to put much thought into anything. It's all been gut feelings and internal knowledge pushing me, driving me into his arms and life. Even the seven years we spent apart, I spent so much of my time keeping busy to avoid thinking about him and running back to where I knew he'd take care of me.

He came for me. After all this time, after waiting seven years for me to figure out my life, he came. And he was willing to step back and continue letting me live, so despite all his selfishness and ridiculous antics, I can't help focusing on the growth. The effort.

I don't know if it's wrong or if it even matters. Maybe love is less of a concrete consideration and more of a sensation—one you feel in your toes first and your heart second.

But it *doesn't matter*, because I feel it regardless.

I'm unsteady on my feet as I wave the gun at the stranger's back. "Get *away* from him."

The man freezes, spinning around and raising the metal bat. He rakes his gaze over me, shock etching into his aged face, and then his mouth spreads into a sinister smile. "So, you survived that fall, huh?"

I lift a brow. *That was him?* "You sound disappointed."

He scoffs, lifting the bat with one arm. "Not at all, little girl. In fact, I'm glad your husband will get to witness what the De Tores do to you."

In the next second, he swings downward, the blunt end of the bat landing directly on Leo's uncovered hand. Crying out, Leo lurches forward, kicking the man in his kneecap with the heel of his shoe.

Something cracks, and the older man buckles with a grunt, bringing his weapon down onto Leo's hand once more. The sickening snap of bone breaking bounces off the walls, and I cringe, my finger pulling the trigger before I have a second to think it through.

It clicks, popping without releasing anything, and fear snakes its way up my throat, constricting airflow. I pull again and then another time, and still, nothing happens.

The man laughs, tipping his head back as he turns fully toward me. "A Ricci strapped with an empty chamber. How fucking embarrassing. Your father is probably rolling in his grave."

A hand clamps down over my mouth, and the gun falls from my fingers. I see a black shoe move forward and kick the weapon away, back toward Leo and the stranger. My body jerks in protest as I'm partially restrained, and pain explodes in my shoulder as my assailant grabs it.

I scream, shredding my throat from the anguish.

Leo, bloodied and sightless, starts crawling toward the sound. "*Fuck, stellina—*"

The stranger steps on what I suspect are already-fractured fingers, halting Leo's movements. "Please, Leopoldo. Did you honestly think this was going to end happily for you? Don't forget that this is *all* your doing. If you hadn't married this bitch in the first place or killed half the fucking family, there would've been no reason for any of it. You'd be don with no resistance, and Stella Ricci would probably be dead in a mass grave somewhere with the rest of her family."

Leo spits, watery blood dribbling past his lips. His breathing is labored, his eyes unopened as he tilts his head up. "*Fuck* you."

The man laughs, and whoever is holding me laughs, too. The sound is chilling, wrapping its billowy arms around me.

I think I might pass out, my vision softening at the corners.

"Okay, enough, Ranolfo," the person—man?—behind me snaps, shaking me a little. "We've got the fucking whore, so let's just get out of here before security comes. This is what we wanted anyway."

With that, I start thrashing, thrusting my head backward to try and catch the captor's chin or face. My shoulder aches so much that I'm close to passing out, but I keep on, digging my heel into the man's toes and pushing down the mounting panic rising within my chest.

I can hardly fucking breathe, but there's no way in hell I'm leaving here with them.

"Jesus Christ, stop fighting. We don't want to fuck a broken doll, and you're already in rough shape."

The other man snickers. "Whose idea was it to tamper with the elevator?"

"Speaking of, we should probably send someone to check on Frankie. Make sure he's dead and all." The man behind me starts pulling, dragging me backward. "We don't want to be chasing him down in a few years like this. No fucking repeats, capisce?"

Rage flares in my soul, sparking like an untamed wildfire. I grit my teeth against the agony tearing up my body and steel myself in place as a small plan formulates in my head. It's not much, but it will hopefully at least buy me enough time to dart outside and find help.

My hand curls around the utility knife in my free arm, unlatching it from where I've been cradling it in my dress.

"Do you have it?" I ask quietly.

The man by Leo narrows his eyes at me. "Have what, puttana?"

I work my jaw from side to side, resisting the urge to spit at him. "The Orchidée Sans Nom. Frankie was bringing it to us, and since you clearly intervened with that, I'm asking if you took it."

"So what if we did?" the man behind me quips.

"I want it."

They exchange a contemplative glance, and then the focus

is back on me. I slide a finger against the blade, testing its sharp edge, and feel a drop of blood bead along the path.

"I don't give a shit about Leo, or your family, or the party outside. I just want to know if you have the flower."

Silence. They don't answer at first.

Then the man restraining me chuckles low and deep, his arm slipping to give him access to my breast. He squeezes, pinching my nipple between two fingers, and sighs. "No, we don't fucking have it. Would've pawned it already if we did, but some bitch took off with it before we had a chance. So we just used Frankie as the gopher to get you both into compromising positions here."

Nodding, I move the knife down, gripping the handle tightly in my fist. "Okay then. That's all I needed to know."

The pervert's too busy pawing at me to notice when I knock free from his hold. I spin quickly, using the momentum from my fear and shock and my hope for the future, swinging the knife up and lodging the blade as deep into the side of his neck as I can get it.

Right in his carotid artery.

Blood spurts from the wound immediately, splattering across my face. I blink and yank the knife out, before driving it into the same spot, harder this time.

Surprise knots his features, and it stuns me how much he looks like Leo—the same sculpted cheekbones and hair the color of the night sky. Even their eyes are similar, though this man's gaze appears to lack any sort of passion or excitement. The dark irises are just empty as he reaches up, gasping as he tries to withdraw the knife.

A cramp forms in my stomach when I realize this must be a relative. But when he falls to his knees, paling within seconds, I turn and look at my husband, and the pain stops.

Relative or not, he deserves what he got.

"What the—" The remaining assailant, fuming, darts in my direction, wielding that baseball bat over his head.

I scramble backward, tripping over the corpse-to-be, and land on my shoulder. Excruciating agony splits me in half, and I let out a little sob, curling onto my side as I mentally prepare for a blow.

It doesn't come.

Instead, a third and final gunshot whips against the otherwise silent air, and the stranger crumples right before my eyes. I have no clue where it came from, as the world around me grows fuzzy.

I roll onto my back as Leo drags himself to me, his face still smeared with blood and only one eye swollen. He's dry heaving as he reaches for me with one of those beautiful hands.

"Fuck me, Stella. Baby, I am so sorry. This is all my fault. I never should've come here."

I shake my head, and he wipes my face with several noticeably broken fingers. "You're hurt—"

"So are you." His words have a bite to them, and I wonder if it's from the pain or from everything else. "Christ, I thought I was gonna fucking lose you."

My eyes drift closed. "I saved your ass."

"That you did." A pause, and my head feels like it's floating. Leo's voice gets farther away. "Stella, baby, you've got to stay with me. You're likely concussed."

"I'll stay with you." I hear myself speaking, but my mouth isn't moving. My eyes aren't opening.

He squeezes my hip. "Holding you to that."

And then darkness overtakes me.

STELLA

wake up to an irritating beeping noise right next to my head.

It's steady, or maybe that's the pulse rattling in my skull as I focus on my surroundings. Bright white light filters past my eyelids first, and I notice the scratchy blanket I'm tucked beneath, then the oxygen monitor on my right hand and the IV hooked to my forearm, leading up to the beeping machine.

My entire body feels like it was stretched to its limits and thrown from the very top of a mountain.

Or a tower, I suppose.

Flexing my fingers, I encounter something soft and shift to see Leo's head resting on the bed next to my leg. His eyes are closed, one purple and badly swollen, twitching in REM. I slowly run my hand through his black hair, admiring the luxurious feel of it under my fingertips.

There's a large bandage over his right eyebrow, and the index and middle fingers on his dominant hand are held together in a splint, confirming my previous suspicions.

I don't care about that right now, though. My heart is full as I look at him, noting the casual rise and fall of his chest, reminding me that he's alive.

Fuck. I had no idea it would feel this good to acknowledge life. That something as simple as touching my husband's hair would light me up inside.

My husband.

The longer I stare at him, mesmerized by his mere presence, the more I consider his question about my future.

Our future.

My touch rouses him, and he looks up at me with sleepy, smoky eyes.

"You're awake."

"You're here."

He smiles, and my stomach somersaults.

Leo says, "Where else would I be?"

I try to shrug, but one arm is trapped against me, the slight movement making me grimace. Glancing down, I notice the blue sling it's wrapped in and lift my brows in surprise.

"Dislocated," Leo offers, sitting up. He cracks his neck, revealing more purple-and-black skin down the side of his face. I'm afraid to see how the rest of him looks. "When the elevator crashed, the impact must have caused it to pop out of the socket. We're lucky that's all that happened, frankly."

Frankly. My eyes widen, and I rush forward, reaching for him. "What happened to Frankie?"

Leo grunts. "He's fine. Recovering down the hall actually, if you want to go see him later. You deserve a thanks for saving his ass, too. Since you suggested he was poisoned, the auction organizers were able to find and administer an antidote. He'll be on oxygen for a while because of the damage it did, but...I suppose it's better than the alternative."

Exhaling, I give him a look. "You *suppose?*"

"Would've hated for him to die before I could kill him myself. He was supposed to help me keep an eye on you, and instead, he almost got all of us killed."

"What were those guys even doing there? Why did they want me?"

Leo hesitates, leaning back in his chair. "I killed my father and a bunch of other De Tore men during a meeting the day after we married. The reason I rejected you that night was because I couldn't afford to take things any further. I needed you to leave before my superiors came after me, so I asked Irene to be your guide and to help you get as far away from Boston as possible."

A shiver skates down my spine, and I settle back against my pillow. "Why'd you kill him?"

"He deserved it." Leo shrugs and places his palm on my knee. "The man refused to see you as anything but some kind of pawn, and even back then, I knew I... Well, it might have started out that way, but I knew almost immediately after making you mine that I wouldn't let him use you. And so, if he couldn't have you, and none of the De Tores could have you and get vengeance against your family, then neither could I."

I glance down at my lap, toying with the oximeter on my

index finger. "I thought you said you'd keep me safe. That in your luxury condo, I'd live a great protected life."

"That was my belief at the time. But after your altercation with my father, I quickly realized that keeping you locked away up there made you a target. Plus...I don't know. You had this deep effect on my psyche, Stella. I told you I'd been watching you for a long time before we married in that church, and every second I spent with you, even though there weren't many, just dug my grave deeper. I couldn't believe how I'd lucked out, though I also didn't...I didn't want to be like your father, stifling you. Making you miserable. So I sent you away."

Irene's sudden vested interest in my escape back then makes sense now. I approached her after drugging Leo, certain that if anyone was going to help, it'd be her—even as she seemed to despise me. She didn't ask any questions, and I was on a flight across the country before the sun was up, trusting her promise that nothing would happen to me.

She said she'd keep my secret so long as I fulfilled my dreams to the best of my ability.

And it'd been Leo's sentiment all along.

Shaking my head, I ask, "So, what happened with the auction? Valerie's never going to be invited again, is she?"

"It's very doubtful. I made a hefty donation in order to keep the details of what happened in the tower on the down-low. Still, I think it's safe to say the Black Rose Auction organizers aren't going to be chomping at the bit anytime soon to invite a Ricci, a De Tore, or a Van der Vorm to another function." He pauses, squeezing my knee. "Not that it matters, seeing as I got the best prize there anyway."

"You didn't even pay," I point out, snorting.

He stands, then leans a knee on the hospital bed beside my thigh. Gently, so very gently, he presses a kiss to my lips, and my head swims for entirely different reasons.

"I paid," he says when he pulls back. "Something tells me I'll be paying for the rest of my life as well."

"Nah, that sounds like my sister Ariana. She's super high-maintenance." I slide my free hand over his jaw, reveling in the feel of him. My body heats as I remember all the ways I've felt him before, and suddenly, I want more. I swallow down my desire. "I'd be content just going back to Boston with you."

Leo freezes, every muscle in his shoulders seeming to tense. He draws back. "What?"

"Well, yeah." A blush crawls up my face. "It's kind of hard to be married and live in different states. Do...?" My breathing grows ragged as panic threads through my insides. "Do you not want to be married anymore?"

"No."

My eyebrows arch, offense stabbing me in the gut.

I blink, tears springing to my eyes immediately, and then blink again to keep them at bay. It doesn't work, and they spill down my cheeks anyway. I shove at his chest. "Then why are you even here, Leo? All this effort, and you're just giving up—"

He cuts me off with another kiss, and I let out a small "*tch!*" of surprise. This time, his tongue delves past my lips, warming me in places I forgot about.

When we break apart, he smiles. It's big and wide and *freeing*.

"You can't get rid of me that easily. I just don't want to go back to Boston."

"Oh." I frown, considering this. "How come?"

"There's nothing tying me to that city anymore. I've resigned my position within what's left of the family, and I have no desire to go back. I'd much rather spend my time going where you go and watching you flourish."

I scoff. "Yeah, well, that's gonna be kind of hard to do without the orchid. I don't think my boss will promote me without it."

"Fuck that guy," Leo says. "I'll buy you a lab, and you can run it yourself. Hire your own employees and do your own research without time constraints or authoritarian oversight. You don't need the flower, and you never did, stellina. You are a star in your own right, and...well, that's why I fell in love with you. What was maybe just one night for you back then was seven years for me, and I hope you'll let me stay by your side for the foreseeable future so that I can prove it to you."

"What will you do? If you're not a don?"

"I don't know. Leaving the Mafia isn't exactly a thing people do, but...I'll figure it out." He kisses my fingertips. "From here on, I won't live a life that endangers you in any way. No matter what I have to do, I will keep you safe for as long as you'll have me."

My heart does somersaults in my chest, but I'm not really sure what to say. I open my mouth, and nothing comes out.

Not waiting for an answer, he climbs on the bed, kicks off his shoes, and wraps an arm around my waist.

When he takes a piece of my hair between two fingers, I gasp. "It's so short!"

He twirls it, then brushes it against the tip of my nose. "I like it. Suits you."

"I don't think you'll be able to wrap it around your cock for a long time."

His deep belly laugh catches me off guard, and I stare up at him, awestruck, as his chest rumbles with the sound. Those smoky eyes cool off, as if being this close to me, being *here*, removes some of the pressure he's been feeling.

Slowly, I lift my hand, turn his face down, and kiss him thoroughly.

Deeply.

Maddeningly.

We're breathing hard when we pull away this time, and I return his toothy smile. "I think I love you back."

"You think?" He snorts. "Not exactly inspiring confidence, wife."

"Yeah, well." I poke him in his side, earning a wince. "You've got a lot to prove to me. Luckily, going where I go should give you plenty of time to do that."

"Oh my *God*, are you two done fucking yet?"

Genevieve stands in the doorway in a sleek pencil skirt and deep-red blouse, startling us. Her black hair is pinned back, and while she looks as devastating as she did at the auction, there's a slightly different air to her here. Something more formal and reserved, even as she looks us over with a hint of playful disgust.

"You wish we were fucking," Leo mutters, kissing my forehead.

"That's true. I'm a little offended I wasn't invited to the show, given everything I've done for you."

Leo rolls his eyes, but she ignores him as she struts into the room, giving me a once-over.

"You look like hell, puppy."

I smirk. "Thanks, *Mommy*."

Leo stiffens at my side.

Genevieve comes to my side, perching on the opposite edge of the bed, and pulls out a medium-sized purple box. She pushes it toward me, undoing the ribbon at the top. "That being said, I'm glad you're alive. Otherwise, this would've been completely useless."

The box's sides fall open as she removes the ribbon, revealing a smaller glass case and bright, almost-amethyst petals. My mouth drops in a gasp, and I reach for it, excitement thrumming inside me.

"Oh my God! How did you get this?"

"Grabbed it from Frankie when I realized he wasn't acting like himself. Figured he'd drank too much and didn't want to risk him losing it... I did *not* think he'd been poisoned. Although that's just another day in the life, huh?"

Neither of us says anything. I grab for the box, but she pulls it back, just out of my reach.

"Whoa, not so fast." She points a manicured finger at me. "I have one condition if you want this flower."

"Of course you do." Leo sighs.

She gives us both a seductive, wicked grin and places the orchid directly in my lap. Then she turns to him and sucks in a deep breath before releasing it slowly. Like she's building up the confidence for her request.

"I want you to kill my husband."

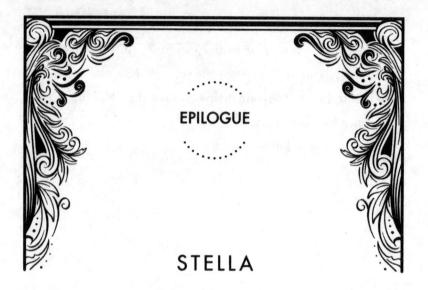

STELLA

L eo. We should *not* be doing this here."

My husband's scarred hand fists the soft cotton fabric of my dress as he slowly guides my hips atop him. The friction from my panties and the thickness of his erection has me salivating, desperate to let him have his way.

Despite being in the back of a rented town car, where the driver up front sits oblivious to Leo's deviant ways, parked outside my sister and brother-in-law's condominium. In the few short months since Leo fulfilled Genevieve's demand, he's permanently rejoined my world, fitting himself into my life more seamlessly than I'd imagined, and I've learned that location doesn't matter to this man.

He'll fuck me in the back of a packed movie theater or in the restroom at the Glass Tower—the nightclub he bought and is working on reopening, now that we're settled in an apartment without Valerie.

I know Val's happy to have the place to herself now, considering how insatiable Leo's proven to be.

Most of the time, I don't mind his passion—it helps chip away at the pesky insecurities I'm still working on, and I *really* like fucking him. But most of the time, we aren't about to enter a lion's den.

His fingers slip between my slick flesh, parting me and finding my clit. I tense, grabbing his arm and the door as sparks of pleasure ignite within me.

"You want it, though, don't you, baby?" he whispers in my ear, his breath warm on my skin.

"*Yes*, but my sisters are waiting—"

"We'll be quick." His middle finger travels lower, curling and then pushing inside me, and he catches my gasp with his mouth. "Need something to take the edge off from meeting your in-laws."

I roll my eyes but reach under me to undo his fly anyway. "Liar. You're not scared of my sisters' husbands."

He speeds up his pace, adding another finger, and the sounds of my arousal are loud in the vehicle. I blush fiercely.

"What if they don't like me? Or the fact I married you without telling them?"

"Both my sisters got married without asking my approval." I pant, fishing his cock out and grinding along its length. "They'll be fine."

"Better get in a last fuck anyway. Just in case." With that, he withdraws his fingers and lines himself up, filling me slowly.

I let go of his arm and plant my palm against the divider, hoping that our driver isn't paying any attention.

Leo moans into the back of my neck as my ass sinks all the way down on his lap. We're flush, damp skin to damp skin, and my brain feels like it's melting. The sensation of being so full is one I'm still not used to, even a few months after our first time in that tower.

I shudder as he fucks me harder, pushing me down slightly, hitting a new angle that makes spots dance at the corners of my eyes. My lips part, and I grab my ankles, trying to keep from coming too soon.

"Hey," Leo says through gritted teeth, squeezing my hip and sliding one hand into my hair. It hasn't grown much, now just past my collarbone, yet he's as obsessed with it as he was the first time we met. "Don't hold out on me. I can feel you resisting."

I whimper as the drive of his hips kicks up, hitting me *just right*. "I can't go inside with cum dripping down my thighs."

"But you're going to. Whether it's just mine or ours is up to you, stellina." His pace becomes erratic, and he tugs on my hair, looping it around my neck to gently rob me of air.

Pushing up, I reach behind me to yank at his pink tie. The color matches my dress, a detail he thought was incredibly cute and insisted on. My fist crawls to the knot, cinching, and a low groan spills from his chest.

"Shit," he huffs, his free hand coming to toy with my clit. "Harder, baby."

I obey, pulling tighter as my breathing scatters, caught up in the excitement of our mutual mercy. His thrusts turn punishing, bouncing me in his lap, and every nerve in my body begins to unspool as soon as he chokes out that he's coming.

There's no denial once he reaches climax. My own barrels through me like a bolt of lightning, exploding like a night sky of fireworks while my muscles suction in around his cock.

We sit there, unmoving and panting, for several moments. I feel him leak out of me and wince when I slide off, settling onto the seat beside him.

He hands me a baby wipe from the pocket inside the door, and I clean up as he does the same, adjusting my underwear. With a harsh sigh, I slump back and watch him fix his pants, then drag both hands through his hair, focusing those gray eyes on mine.

My heart skips a beat in my chest, the same way it always does when we make eye contact. After so long of being apart and then not knowing what was going to happen to us at the Black Rose Auction, such a simple gesture feels monumental.

Things aren't perfect—we're basically newlyweds, so living together and learning to be a couple has been an adjustment all on its own. With him leaving Boston and attempting to make a legitimate living by restoring run-down clubs in town, plus my takeover of Rampion Core—after he bought the lab and I presented a sister neuroscience company with the orchid—things have been busy and stressful.

But every night we come home to each other, and that's what matters.

I can't fathom a reality where he isn't there, nor do I ever want to experience one again.

Once we're presentable, Leo opens the door, and sunlight rushes into the vehicle. He starts to get out, but I lean over and put a hand over his, reveling in the warmth. He hasn't worn his gloves since the summer, having gotten used to being without them while his fingers were healing.

"I love you," I tell him in a soft voice.

Those are his three favorite words. I only sort of said them that day I woke up in the hospital, and it took me a while to reach a point where I could admit it without feeling like I was compromising a part of myself, but nowadays, the words flow freely.

Because being with Leo isn't a compromise at all. In everything, he's a partner to me—not a handler, or a guardian, or a captor. He accepts me for me and doesn't try to squash my hopes and dreams. Instead, he does what he can to help fulfill them.

That's love, I think. For me anyway.

He grins back, tugging me from the car and into his arms. Boston's just as busy as I remember, the scent of the harbor prominent, since Ariana and her husband live on the waterfront.

As Leo tucks a piece of hair behind my ear, his eyes crinkle at the corners. "I love you, too." He releases me, reaching for my hand, and we start up the walk to my sister's building. "Don't think I'll forgive you so easily if this goes south, though. If one of your brothers-in-law tries to shoot me, it'll take a *lot* more than just orgasms to make it up to me."

I laugh, squeezing his palm. "Don't worry. I promised to always save your ass when I agreed to keep being your wife."

"Good thing." He sucks in a deep breath. "Okay, let's go meet the family."

ACKNOWLEDGMENTS

After I published *Promises and Pomegranates*, one of the most asked questions I got from readers was whether Stella Ricci would get a story. My answer was always the same: if she had something she wanted to say, I would never get in the way of that.

A big part of her character was that she'd spent her whole life being overshadowed by her older sisters, and I felt like anything included in the Monsters & Muses realm wouldn't be enough for the strong, misunderstood character that she was. If she got a book, I wanted to make sure I gave her every opportunity to shine outside of the penumbra of the Ricci family.

Imagine my surprise when I finished the Monsters & Muses series and the opportunity for a Stella-centric book just dropped right in my lap (or, rather, my email inbox).

Thus, Stella took center stage in my brain and dragged Leo De Tore out of the depths along with her—and I knew immediately that their dynamic was going to be so much fun to write. Stella needed someone who saw her as an equal and wouldn't ask her to compromise anything about the vision she had for her life, and Leo just needed her.

Still, none of this would have been possible without the amazing team I've somehow managed to rope into my life, and I would be remiss if I didn't thank them profusely for helping make this book what it is.

Katee Robert and Jenny Nordbak, thank you for reaching out and asking me to be involved in this delightful world you created. I cannot tell you how loudly I squealed when I first read Katee's DM asking if they could pitch something to me, nor how excited I was to do a fairy-tale-inspired story. Also, thank you for your endless patience and understanding and for answering my rambling emails.

Emily McIntire, my best friend. Thank you for your constant support, being there to talk me off ledges, and making me laugh. I couldn't do this without you.

Becca, you truly are the Fairy Plotmother. I literally would not have finished this book without every message and email and virtual meeting. Thank you for helping me flesh out this story and its characters, for being there to bounce around ideas, and for reading through the first ten thousand words and talking me out of another complete redo. I cannot wait to squeeze you the next time I see you in person.

Manu, your insight in the developmental stage was crucial to me finishing this book as well. I must have read that editorial letter a thousand times, and even though it was humbling, I am forever grateful to you for taking the time to help make *Stolen Vows* the best love story.

Jovana, as always, thank you for being an absolute rock star and taking my deadline extensions in stride.

Angie, thank you for being a wonderful friend in addition to editor and for volunteering to listen to me ramble anytime. I know you love hearing my three-minute-long voice messages as much as I love sending them.

Sourcebooks Casablanca, the dream team. Thank you for championing me and taking risks and all the support to make sure these releases are phenomenal.

Jackie, thank you for keeping my head on straight and running things behind the scenes so I stay on track and we are able to at least pretend Team Sav is a well-oiled machine.

Savannah Greenwell, thank you for everything you do for me.

Mia, thank you for letting me bother you to make sure my translations are coming across correctly. I appreciate the heck out of you.

Lord Byron, Poe, and Arrow, thank you for existing.

And last but not least, to the readers—your enthusiasm keeps me going. All these words are for you.

ABOUT THE AUTHOR

Sav R. Miller is a *USA Today* bestselling author of adult romance with varying levels of darkness and steam.

In 2018, Sav put her lifelong love of reading and writing to use and graduated with a BA in creative writing and a minor in cultural anthropology. Nowadays, she spends her time giving morally gray characters their happily ever afters.

Currently, Sav lives in Kentucky with her dogs Lord Byron, Poe, and Arrow. She loves sitcoms, silence, and sardonic humor.

Website: savrmiller.com
Facebook: srmauthor
Instagram: @srmauthor
TikTok: @authorsavrmiller

The End of

STOLEN VOWS

and The Beginning of

IRRESISTIBLE DEVIL

Every book in the Black Rose Auction is meant to be read as a duology. Now that you've reached the end of *Stolen Vows*, simply close the book, flip it over, and start *Irresistible Devil* from the beginning. Happy reading!

The End of

IRRESISTIBLE DEVIL

and The Beginning of

STOLEN VOWS

Every book in the Black Rose Auction is meant to be read as a duology. Now that you've reached the end of *Irresistible Devil*, simply close the book, flip it over, and start *Stolen Vows* from the beginning. Happy reading!

ABOUT THE AUTHOR

Jenny Nordbak is an author, retired dominatrix, and former archaeologist. When she isn't writing romance novels, she delights in narrating the steamiest of audiobooks. Jenny lives in Southern California with her handsome Viking husband and two adorably feral children. She can pretty much always be found doing something outdoors.

Website: jennynordbak.com
Instagram: @jennynordbak
X: @JennyNordbak

Welcome to the

BLACK ROSE AUCTION

In **STOLEN VOWS** by Sav R. Miller, a Rapunzel remix, a virgin is forced to marry a mafia heir determined to kill anyone who touches her—only to flee from him the day after their wedding. But he's done waiting and has the perfect trap in mind to lure her back...

In **IRRESISTIBLE DEVIL** by Jenny Nordbak, a Rumpelstiltskin remix, a society darling is willing to make any bargain to benefit her family, but each deal draws her deeper into a dark and decadent world ruled by the dangerous man who's been pulling her strings from the start...

ALSO BY JENNY NORDBAK

BLADES AND BETRAYAL

To Seduce a Siren

To Wed a Warrior Queen

KEY CLUB

His Leading Lady

Her Filthy Rockstar

The Scarlett Letters

The Death God's Sacrifice

The

BLACK ROSE
AUCTION:

IRRESISTIBLE
DEVIL

IRRESISTIBLE DEVIL

JENNY NORDBAK

sourcebooks casablanca

Published by Sourcebooks Casablanca, an imprint of Sourcebooks
P.O. Box 4410, Naperville, Illinois 60567-4410
(630) 961-3900
sourcebooks.com

Originally self-published in 2024 by Jenny Nordbak.

Cataloging-in-Publication Data is on file with the Library of Congress.

Printed and bound in the United States of America.
LSC 10 9 8 7 6 5 4 3 2 1

For anyone who had confusing pants feelings for
Mr. Gold/Rumple in Once Upon a Time...

FOREWORD

When we set out to create the Black Rose Auction series, we knew we wanted it to be lux and dangerous and sexy! The premise is that there's an annual auction, presided over by the mysterious Reaper, where anything can be purchased for the right price. It's a place to make statements, to auction off the services of some of the world's most exclusive sex workers, to find priceless artifacts that the general public has only heard rumors of. Within these six books, you'll find dangerous men, powerful women, and a heist or two! Be sure to check out read. sourcebooks.com/blackroseauction or scan the QR code to get an introduction to all six authors and their work!

There was no question that Jenny was going to finally–FINALLY–write Reaper for this book. Reaper is a character who's been haunting her for as long as I've known her, a chaotic, mysterious, dangerous, aggressively pansexual man who gives similar vibes to Jareth

from The Labyrinth *and has the face of Thranduil from* The Hobbit. *Is it any wonder I'm a fan? THEN she told me it was going to be a Rumplestiltskin remix and you could have knocked me over with a feather. Dreams really do come true!*

This book is something special, and I'm not just saying that because I'm biased (though I am!). Sometimes, you pick up a story, and you can just feel the author's giddy delight coming through every word. This is one of those. I gasped. I giggled. I kicked my feet in pure joy. I cannot wait for you to read this one...

Katee Robert

CONTENT GUIDANCE

TROPES AND TAGS: Forced marriage, Mafia, virgin heroine, blackmail, male escort, sex club owner, oops I thought you were the guy I was supposed to marry, I'll help you…for a price, marry him but I'll be dripping down your thighs when you say your vows, he's not a good man but he's the kind of bad you want on your side, make better choices or I'll make them for you.

CONTENT WARNINGS: Explicit sex, death of parent and sibling (off page, in the past), depictions of domestic violence, murder, death of a pet (off page), graphic violence, cheating (he deserves it), forced marriage.

PLAYLIST

Throughout *Irresistible Devil*, you'll find footnotes referring to songs that inspired a scene, might be playing in the background of a scene, or may otherwise enhance your reading experience. We encourage you to queue up these songs so they're ready to play whenever you see them referenced. For a handy Spotify playlist  tailored to each book, go to read.sourcebooks.com/blackroseauction or scan the QR code and search for *Irresistible Devil*.

REQUIEM—Allison Russell

EVERYTHING I WANTED—Billie Eilish

TO BE ALONE—Hozier

SIDEWAYS—Santana feat. Citizen Cope

MOMENT'S SILENCE (COMMON TONGUE)—Hozier

DINNER & DIATRIBES—Hozier

GOLD ON THE CEILING—The Black Keys

TALK—Hozier

OH MY GOD—Adele

RENEGADES—X Ambassadors

DREAM GIRL EVIL—Florence + the Machine

INDIGO CHILDREN—Puscifer

BURY A FRIEND—Billie Eilish

CONDITIONS OF MY PAROLE—Puscifer

POLAR BEAR—Puscifer

AS IT WAS—Hozier

ARSONIST'S LULLABYE—Hozier

SOUR TIMES—Portishead

STRANGERS—Portishead

THE HUMBLING RIVER—Puscifer

HORIZONS—Puscifer

LONELY BOY—The Black Keys

REV 22:20—Puscifer

GIRL WITH ONE EYE—Florence + the Machine

MOVEMENT (MAYA JANE COLES REMIX)—Hozier

GLORY BOX—Portishead

CHERRY WINE (LIVE)—Hozier

BAD GUY—Billie Eilish

THREE ROUNDS AND A SOUND—Blind Pilot

NFWMB—Hozier

YOU SHOULD SEE ME IN A CROWN—Billie Eilish

ANGEL OF SMALL DEATH AND THE CODEINE SCENE—Hozier

SUNLIGHT—Hozier

COME TOGETHER (LIVE)—AnnenMayKantereit

CLOSER—Nine Inch Nails

ANIMAL I HAVE BECOME—Three Days Grace

TOO SWEET—Hozier

1

Y ou're getting married, sugar."*

The term of endearment rolled off my father's tongue, but there was a bite to it. He'd barely been able to look at me for days.

He sat there in his perfectly tailored tuxedo, his hands folded calmly on the desk in front of him, even though the tension in his jaw gave away how angry he was.

My heart raced in panic, but I only allowed my cheeks to lift into a polite, hopeful smile, the reaction he expected of a Bryson woman. I'd known I was in trouble when he summoned me shortly before the gala he was hosting at one of his hotels, but I hadn't expected it to be this dire.

He slid a stack of printed papers across the desk with enough angry force that they rained down across my lap. Tabloid after tabloid with mortifying pictures of me. I was in a dance club,

* REQUIEM—Allison Russell

showing more skin than I'd ever shown in public before, my raven hair fanned out in wild, sweaty curls with parts of it sticking to my neck and shoulders.

Bryson Heiress Goes Wild. Bryson Sister Gets Dirty on the Dance Floor. Juliet Bryson: Virgin No More?

A strategically placed cameraman below the elevated dance floor had captured me grinding on some guys, inadvertently flashing my panties at that angle. In one image, a guy's hand was under my skirt. Though I swatted it away seconds later, the pictures kinda made it look like I was letting someone touch me intimately in the club. I'd admittedly been trashed, too trashed to think about things like my image, but I slept in my own bed alone that night, which was more than anyone I'd been out with could say.

I was just out dancing with friends!

I didn't dare try to defend myself. The facts didn't matter, not to my family. Public perception was everything.

"You think I need this right now? I buried your brother a few months ago, and *this* is what you think I need right now?" He waved an errant page at me, barely containing his fury.

I bit my tongue and shook my head.

I buried my brother a few months ago too, Daddy. The grief was like a fist around my windpipe, but I held my breath until it felt like I could release it without sobbing. All I'd wanted when I went out dancing was to escape the feeling. I thought maybe if I drank enough and did the things normal people did to have fun, then I'd manage to forget for just a few minutes that my brother was dead.

It hadn't worked.

My father's angry expression drained away until he just looked grim. "There's blood in the water after your brother's murder, and the sharks are circling, wondering just how weak we are. On top of that, the business is bleeding money, and I can't figure out why—something I'm barely managing to keep out of the news—and now you go and do this."

"Daddy, let me help! I can look into the business." I'd been begging to be given more responsibility for years, but my father was fundamentally old-school. Women had an important role to serve at their husband's side, but it wasn't in the office.

"The accountants are already on that," he said dismissively, flicking his hand like my degrees in finance and accounting and the fact I'd been working as a forensic accountant for years were meaningless. "You can help by securing the partner I need to solve all three problems. You settle down and start rebuilding your reputation, we gain a strong ally to weather this storm, and he infuses my businesses with cash. With your brother gone, I need an heir."

Geoff had been my only brother, the only person my father had ever considered as his replacement.

"What about Brenner?" My older sister's husband wielded considerable influence in political circles.

"Brenner serves his purpose, but he's not ruthless enough to be a territory leader. I need you to marry someone who isn't afraid to get their hands dirty, but who's smart enough to keep their image clean."

What about what I need? "Mama said that I could choose

who I married." I was on dangerous ground questioning him, but when they'd decided to parade me in the press as a virgin who'd chosen to wait for marriage, I'd gone along with it eagerly because it came with the promise of a choice. I was willing to abstain from sex and keep my image squeaky clean if it meant I wouldn't be forced to marry someone of their choosing. Or at least I'd managed to keep it squeaky clean until that night in the club.

He fixed me with a cold stare. "Your mother is in the ground with your brother. You made your choice by acting like a whore."

He let out a deep breath and straightened all the objects on his precisely organized desk. We were in one of his hotels, but this floor was set up as a residence for our family, so this office was an exact replica of his office in our home. When he looked back up at me, it was with a gentle smile on his face. To anyone else, he would've looked calm, but I'd seen that look before.

"I need this alliance, Juliet. *We* need this alliance. If you fight me on it, I'll offer him your sister."

I gasped. "Sophia's already married!"

"Jacque isn't."

This time I didn't gasp because I'd stopped breathing. "Daddy, she's eighteen."

He shrugged, and I knew he meant it. Girls had always been secondary to him—more of a liability than an asset but potentially useful as a bartering tool. He'd married Sophia off to a senator, a match that had secured my uncle his second term as president of the United States. To the public, Uncle Charles was the head of our family, the powerful one. But Daddy was the true puppet master pulling all our strings.

Jacque was the baby of the family, ten years younger than me. I had Daddy's dark hair, but Jacque looked so much like Mama that it sometimes made my chest ache. She was willowy and blond, with a million-dollar smile, but we both had Mama's cornflower-blue eyes. All I wanted was for her to have a normal youth. I couldn't possibly give it to her, but I could protect her from this.

I sighed. "Okay. Who is he?"

Daddy laughed, already more relaxed now that I was cooperating. "I'm not telling you yet, sugar. I don't need you arriving to meet him having done full opposition research on the poor bastard."

He'd tried once before, much less forcefully, to send me on a date with a business partner's son, and it hadn't gone well. It wasn't my fault the smug jerk hadn't come to dinner prepared to defend his questionable political stances.

Daddy spread his hands, still wearing that effortless smile, the vicious one people mistook for charming. "You're not to debate him. You're to charm him. Make sure he sees the *full value* of having you as a wife."

The way he said it turned my stomach. I folded my hands neatly in my lap, trying to hide how badly they were shaking. "Are you telling me to sleep with him?"

He narrowed his eyes just a fraction. "I don't want him thinking my sweet pea is a slut to be used and discarded. *Charm* him. If offering him a taste is what it takes to show him the long-term value in a potential partnership?" He shrugged.

I was really having this conversation. With my father.

I didn't have the first clue how to seduce someone. I'd spent my entire life trying *not* to seduce people...because I'd always known putting a single toe out of line would lead here. No moment of fun was worth the loss of my autonomy, and the second anyone in my family caused a scandal, they rarely got a say in how it was resolved.

I was an *accountant*. A magnificent forensic accountant, but an uptight, number-crunching nerd nonetheless. Deep down, I wasn't like the polished women who ran in our circles, the ones who could derive power from nothing but conversational charm and sex appeal. He was sending a virgin to do a siren's work.

"What if he doesn't like me?"

My father cocked his head like I was being ridiculous. "You're a Bryson. Make him like you."

He gestured to the door with an upturned palm—a firm dismissal since this matter was settled and we needed to get dressed before the guests arrived.

I stood and let him escort me out, grasping for some way to tell him I couldn't do it.

"What if I don't like him?" I said in a small voice, the weak one he hated.

His expression turned hard. "Find a way to like him, sugar. I know you won't let me down again."

2

know you won't let me down again.

Again had punched me in the gut just like he'd known it would. That word had driven me to go for a walk before the gala, which in hindsight was a nonsensical idea. It had taken a team of people two hours to make me look like my supermodel sister. The diaphanous peach layers of the gown they'd chosen perfectly complemented the pearls they'd used to pin my hair up in soft curls and the subtle pink tones they'd picked for my makeup. The vintage couture gown probably had more business being in a museum than it did being dragged across a hotel lawn.

And that was before it started to pour.

I stood in the boathouse, watching rain come down outside in torrential sheets, wondering how things could possibly get worse. Being a Bryson had taught me that they could always get worse. People said my family was cursed—too many tragic

* EVERYTHING I WANTED—Billie Eilish

deaths and bizarre accidents. Some days I wasn't sure they were wrong.

With no phone, I had no way of getting back without showing up to the party a disheveled, soaking-wet mess. How was I supposed to explain being foolish enough to get caught in the rain...or why I'd been in the boathouse in the first place?

No matter what excuse I came up with, Daddy would conclude it was because I'd thought about running away. He'd be even more disgusted to know I'd really just sought solitude and been too freaked out to use common sense. In his eyes, at least running away would show some initiative. He had no tolerance for this kind of pointless emotional weakness.

I didn't have any illusions about what would happen if I ran. As though Nathaniel Bryson wouldn't hunt me down. There was nowhere I could hide from his power and influence.

If his enemies didn't find me first. They'd executed his son. They'd be far more creative with his daughter.

I shuddered, fighting back tears. The boathouse wasn't technically off-limits, but since it was far from the main property, all the way across the hotel grounds, it was outside the perimeter my father's security team expected me to adhere to, especially after what had happened to Geoff.

I was fucked.

The gala would already be starting. If I got soaked, there'd be no way to fix my appearance before I was supposed to meet my prospective husband.

I glanced around the interior of the boathouse, looking for an umbrella, a tarp, anything that might make this less bad. Because

I was definitely able to carry my shoes and the enormous skirt of my gown while I held a tarp over my head and ran across a wet lawn.

Solid plan, Juliet.

Lightning split the sky, and even though summer storms were a near-daily occurrence, it still felt like a bad omen. I'd never believed in fairy tales, but I'd also never expected to become a cautionary tale.

My gown swished as I walked to another window, as though there'd be some magical solution in the other direction. They'd gone old-school and laced me into a corset underneath the gown to make the bodice sit better, and the combination of it squeezing me and the heavy weight of the dress was making me feel like I couldn't breathe.

I wasn't going to cry and mess up my makeup, but I couldn't seem to slow my breathing. I was already lightheaded. I needed to take deeper breaths, but I couldn't expand my ribs enough, which was exacerbating my anxiety.

In a moment of desperation, I reached back and managed to contort myself to push the zipper down, then pull it the rest of the way to reach the corset underneath. I tugged on the only part of the corset strings I could reach, but it didn't seem to want to come loose. I was used to shape wear that didn't tie, and my fumbling fingers seemed to be tightening the knot instead of releasing it.

I can't fucking breathe!

I frantically tangled my fingers between the strings until I felt what I thought could be a knot, but all that seemed to do was tighten the corset further. I almost fell off my heels but leaned

against the wall and kept tugging, well past being able to use reason.

"*God damn it*," I said aloud, giving voice to all the frustration and fear knotted inside me. This wasn't really about the corset, but fuck if it wasn't the perfect metaphor for being trapped in a world where I didn't belong.*

"Need some help with that?" A deep voice rumbled in the darkness behind me, and I jumped with surprise.

I was mortified someone had been sitting there, witnessing my breakdown. My family couldn't afford to show any more weakness. I dropped my hands to my sides and whipped around. "Absolutely not."

My panic didn't conveniently vanish just because I had an audience, but I knew a thing or two about hiding my feelings in front of other people, no matter how extreme they were. I breathed through my nose as I peered into the darkness.

In the shadows sat a man whose long hair was such a white blond, it caught even the limited light from the muted boathouse sconces. He was shirtless and relaxed, his legs sprawled wide like he was entitled to as much room as he wanted. He didn't need to stand for me to know he was tall. Wiry, chiseled muscles covered his torso and corded his arms, but he looked more like some kind of rebel prince than a warrior. His nipples were pierced, and tattoos wound across his skin in disorderly patches.

He certainly wasn't the type of man who'd been invited to this gala. It was all upper-crust and political types.

* TO BE ALONE—Hozier

Was he from a rival territory and somehow managed to get past security?

He reached into his pocket and flipped out a knife.

Years of training overrode my fear, and before I'd even consciously decided to reach under my skirts, I dropped my clutch and pulled a handgun from my thigh holster.

I aimed at his chest. "Drop it."

I might've been the refined granddaughter of a former president and the niece of the current one, but I was also the daughter of a ruthless territory leader. My father had made sure I could defend myself.

"Easy, princess," the guy said with laughter in his dark eyes, holding his palms up and gesturing to my cinched waist. "Just trying to help."

The adrenaline made my heart race more than it had before, and I still couldn't breathe. I was pretty sure I was going to pass out.

The reckless motherfucker walked straight toward the barrel of my gun, not even hesitating as he stepped into the light and got close enough that I could see scars marking his body along with his tattoos. If he'd wanted to attack me, he would've used the element of surprise that he'd freely given up, so surely that wasn't his intention.

"Just trust me," he said, like he was asking me to try a new food and I was being ridiculous about it. Not like he was attempting to cut off my clothing.

He turned me around with one hand on my shoulder, and his huge palm felt shockingly warm against my bare skin. With

one quick slice, he relieved the worst of the tension. He pocketed the blade and tugged on the strings, causing the garment to come loose. When he started to pull it off for me, I nudged him away. "Enough help, thank you very much."

He shrugged and returned to the bench he'd been sitting on, making no effort to pretend he was doing anything but watching me. It was tricky to get the whole corset off without removing the dress, but after some completely undignified wiggling, I was free.

He was still staring, his expression unreadable from where he was in the shadows.

I took slow, deliberate breaths, marveling that taking the corset off made a world of difference. "The knife was a little overdramatic, don't you think? You couldn't have just untied the knot?"

He shrugged. "If my sub's panicking in bondage, I don't fuck around. I cut the rope."

"It's hardly the same situation," I said, as though I knew anything about bondage.

"Are you denying you were panicking or denying you're a sub?" he asked, his voice edged with teasing humor.

I wanted to snap at him, but all comebacks eluded me. I just stared back at him, fighting not to look at his body again. I was pretty sure the pile of clothes next to him was a server's uniform for the gala, but there was an arrogance to his features that made him seem more like a territory leader than staff. His high, pronounced cheekbones gave him an almost elfin quality, but the intensity of his dark eyes was more devilish than ethereal. He wasn't quite smiling, but his full lips lifted just

enough to tell me he was amused, which made my heart flutter nervously.

Great, now I'm ogling one of Daddy's employees. Could this get any more embarrassing?

I turned my back to him to make myself stop staring, set my gun on the ledge in front of me, and picked up the clutch I'd dropped when he'd taken out a knife. My stupid clutch was too small to hold a phone…but there was one cigarette and a lighter in there, hidden in a special pocket in case of emergencies. Tonight certainly qualified. What did I care if this guy saw me smoking?

The one time I'd been photographed smoking outside an event when I was in college, it had made tabloid headlines: *Bryson Heiress Lights Up.*

The Bryson heiress has bigger problems right now.

With shaking hands, I slid the cigarette between my lips and struck the lighter again and again, but it only sparked. The more I tried, the more I looked incompetent, but I also became more determined to make the damned thing work. I could feel the smug bastard smirking behind me without even looking.

I sighed and dropped the traitorous lighter back into my clutch. If the guy was silently enjoying my struggle with the means to put an end to it, I wasn't about to give him the satisfaction of asking for help.

"Am I supposed to feel sad for the poor little rich girl?" he said, the amusement in his tone mocking me now.

"Fuck off." It felt good to snap at someone, to lash out with a fraction of the anger I was feeling.

Dark laughter rolled out of him. "The princess has a mouth on her."

"Keep it up and I'll have to mention to my father that one of the staff was lurking in the boathouse, disrespecting his daughter instead of doing his job."

Why the hell did I say that?

"That how you solve all your problems? Running to Daddy?"

It wasn't. I didn't think I'd ever gone running to my father over anything, not since the third grade when I'd told him that Charlie Robertson was mean to me, and the next day, my brother beat the hell out of the kid on the playground. Charlie's dad had then been fired from his job, and Charlie had gone to public school after that.

If he heard the way this guy was talking to me, my father would have one of his enforcers cut out the stranger's tongue.

The threat had just slipped out. This stranger had seen me exposed, and I was out of my element, flailing as I fought for steady ground.

"I'm sorry." I sighed. "But I don't need this right now."

I heard him stand, and by the time I picked up my gun and turned to see what he was doing, he was crowding my space. I gave ground too easily, so he backed me into the wall, seeming unconcerned that a gun was pressed against his stomach.

He reached up slowly, holding eye contact with me as he struck a match on a piece of metal above us to light it.

He was tall and dangerously good-looking.

And he knew it.

Lord, did he know it.

The light of the match made the lip ring in the center of his bottom lip glint, drawing my eyes to a mouth made for sin. His bottom lip was fuller than his top, and it looked pillowy soft as his mouth lifted into a nearly irresistible smile.

I had nothing to smile about. My life had been falling apart before I'd somehow ended up trapped in a boathouse with fucking Lestat.

When he held the flame to the tip of the cigarette still dangling from my mouth, I automatically puffed gently to light it. I knew smoking was bad for me and unladylike and generally frowned upon by society at large, but something about it soothed me like nothing else could. It was a choice between smoking to steel my nerves or sobbing until I felt empty.

I held the cigarette and exhaled slowly, turning my head to the side so I didn't blow smoke in his face, even if he deserved it.

He was still in my space, watching me too closely.

"*What?*"

His lips quirked. "They teach you to pull a gun like that in princess school, but they don't teach you manners?"

I gritted my teeth. "Thank you."

He wrapped his fingers around my wrist and tugged it toward himself, taking a deep drag of my cigarette while still holding me, his face only inches from mine.

Irrationally, all I could focus on was that his mouth was exactly where my mouth had just been, where my mouth would be again in a moment.

His thumb drew a tiny circle on the inside of my wrist, and my heart instantly started to pound like he'd touched me somewhere

far more intimate. He released me, but I could still feel the heat on my skin where his hand had held my wrist.

I angled my head up to meet his eyes, and we stared at each other for long, charged seconds. He was a complete stranger to me, and yet I was drawn to him on a level I couldn't understand. I wanted him, and I didn't even like him. I had far bigger things I should've been focused on, but there was no focusing on anything with this guy in my space.

It wasn't like I'd never been around shirtless men before—we spent summers on yachts and at beach houses—but something about *this man* shirtless felt inappropriately intimate. Maybe it was the scars marking his body that made me feel like I was seeing more than I should.

As though my fingers no longer belonged to me, I reached out and traced a round scar on his rib cage. The muscles on his stomach tensed, but he didn't pull away. "Someone shot you," I said, like a fuckwit.

He smiled, slow and arrogant. "It was worth it."

Wait, what does that even mean? "What could possibly be worth getting shot?"

He huffed a laugh and picked up my wrist again to steal another drag of my cigarette, effectively making me his cigarette holder. It shouldn't have been hot.

"What are you running from?" he asked as he exhaled.

"I wasn't running. I went for a walk and got caught in the rain. Who would try to run in this?" I gestured to the frothy layers of my peach gown.

He pinned me with a look. "Someone desperate."

Someone like him wouldn't have freaked out and just started walking across the grounds in a frantic effort to be alone for five minutes. Someone like him certainly wouldn't have any trouble seducing a stranger. He could probably seduce a light pole if he so much as leaned on it.

I let out a shuddering sigh at the mess I'd made for myself.

The man's smile fell, replaced with a deadly stare. "You need me to slay a dragon for you, princess?"

I wanted to tell him to stop calling me that, but then I'd lose our unspoken game. Instead, I said, "Would you?"

This was dangerous. *He* was dangerous.

He cocked his head, considering. "What kind of help do you need?"

There was a challenge in his tone, like he knew what I was going to ask for wasn't what I really wanted.

"Can you help me get back to the party without getting rained on?"

"Even if there's a price?" he said.

Somehow, I knew he didn't mean money. It felt like I was making a deal with the devil, but I nodded anyway. I looked the dangerous man in the eye and said, "Please help me."

I meant to sound assertive, but it came out breathless and laced with desire.

He turned me around again, so my back was to him, and then he slowly pulled the zipper back up on my dress, letting his fingers brush my bare skin as he did. It was shockingly intimate.

With a hand on my waist, he spun me to face him, standing close enough that I was almost against his chest. His eyes were

so dark, they were nearly black, and they swam with unchecked intensity. In my world, feelings were worn like outfits, specially selected for the occasion and honed to be appropriate and polite no matter what.

There was nothing polite about this man.

With his face so unguarded, I saw the moment he decided to kiss me. I closed my eyes, my heart racing, and arched up, ready to feel the first brush of his warm, soft mouth against mine.

It never came.

When seconds had passed, I opened my eyes and found he was no longer standing so close. His expression was scathing, like he couldn't believe I'd thought he was going to kiss me.

What else is a girl supposed to think when you lean that close with that stupid smoldering look?

Had he done it on purpose to make a point?

I'm going to die of embarrassment!

I wrapped my arms around myself, shivering, but it wasn't just because I was cold.

"Come on," he said, pulling open a door at the back of the boathouse. One of the staff golf carts was parked there, and he pulled a key from his pocket.

I slid behind the wheel, getting a little wet in the few steps I had to take into the rain, but it wasn't bad. He followed me out, standing in the downpour, letting it soak him like he didn't even notice. He leaned over me to drape a well-worn black leather jacket around my shoulders, enveloping me in his scent.

Just as I was about to protest, he brushed his mouth against

my ear. "Go back where you belong, princess, before you get yourself into trouble that Daddy can't solve."

I turned my head, leaving our faces so close, we were almost kissing. I saw the flash of amusement in his eyes when I said, "Go fuck yourself."

The bastard was still laughing as I drove out of earshot.

3

The night hadn't even truly begun, and I was rattled as I finally reached the ballroom.*

I was never rattled. But at least I'd managed to sneak back inside with only a slightly damp skirt. A back stairway got me safely up to my room, where I'd stashed the guy's jacket and taken a quick second to touch up my hair and makeup.

I greeted some of our guests, waiting to spot the mysterious man I was supposed to marry, but I knew everyone so far.

"Glad to see you getting back out there," said an elderly billionaire as he kissed me on the cheek. "Don't let the gossip get you down."

Knowing him, he'd turn around and instigate more gossip about me the moment he was out of earshot. Hell, I was pretty sure he owned one of the tabloids that had run the worst pictures

* SIDEWAYS—Santana feat. Citizen Cope

of me. I smiled vacantly as he patted my shoulder before heading toward the bar.

The next man who spoke to me grasped my hands in greeting. "Can we expect a dance from you later, Juliet?" He winked, leaving no mistake about what kind of dance he was hoping for.

I'd been planning to avoid my father, but maybe it was worth being in his presence to put an end to this garbage. They'd never say such things in front of him.

What does it say about me that they'll do it to my face?

My family was bona fide American royalty. My grandfather and uncle had both served as president. I'd grown up playing with my two sisters on the White House lawn in shiny patent leather shoes and matching dresses.

The Bryson Sisters, they called us—the surrogate First Daughters. My aunt and uncle had never had children of their own, but my family wanted to make sure Uncle Charles still looked like a doting family man to voters. Our older brother had been the model Bryson man long before he was grown, destined for great things. He'd been heir to the Bryson dynasty, and now I was supposed to marry a man who'd step into that role...which meant our children would be under the same pressure I'd been under my whole life.

I wasn't even sure I wanted children, but my opinion wasn't going to matter. It was like my life had never fully belonged to me, like the public was entitled to parts of me that normal people didn't have to share, and the rest belonged to my father.

The public's fascination with the minutiae of my life had first come to my notice when I was only five and a picture of me with

my first missing tooth had ended up in a newspaper. I asked my father why I was in the paper, and he said, "Because you're their special princess, sugar."

While we were children, our images were tightly controlled by the family, and they fed the press only what they wanted the public to know. The day each of us had turned eighteen, all bets had been off.

Humans loved to build someone up, to put them on a pedestal. The only thing they loved more was to tear those same people down.

I was lucky to be the middle daughter, so my sister Sophia had run that gauntlet before me. Her senior year of high school, weeks after her eighteenth birthday, she sent a picture of herself wearing nothing but some lingerie to a boy. The next day it was all over the tabloids.

Bryson Heiress Is All Grown Up.

There was no changing her image after that. She was the sexy one forevermore, the risqué one, so my parents leaned in to it and put her on the modeling path. If she owned her image that way, they could reclaim the message. Soon, pictures of her in lingerie were on billboards in Times Square, and no one cared about that first photo. Models were allowed to be in their underwear and still maintain their dignity.

Did she want to be a model?

No one ever stopped to ask.

She didn't go to college. She modeled until they decided it was time for her to settle down and be a political wife. Then she retired from her career to start popping out babies.

My parents had decided that I'd be the virginal sister to make up for Sophia's misstep, and after I turned eighteen, they sent me to do a round of interviews talking about how I was waiting until marriage to have sex. The public lapped it up, but it raised the stakes considerably because they were just waiting for me to fail. I couldn't sit next to a boy without speculation, so I avoided any kind of dating just to prevent the press circus that would follow.

I'd learned two lessons from Sophia's big mistake when I was fourteen. The first was that if I wanted any chance at having control of my own life, I couldn't put a toe out of line or decisions would be made swiftly on my behalf. The second was that I couldn't trust a soul.

I turned to find my father watching me from across the gala. He appraised everything from my hair down to the bottom of my dress, and I held my breath, certain in my panic that he'd be able to tell I was no longer wearing the corset underneath…and that he'd somehow know the circumstances that had led to its removal. In the few minutes I'd been in my room after the boathouse, I'd checked and double-checked that every pearl in my hair remained perfectly in place, but I still had to fight the urge to lift my hand to smooth my flawless curls as he studied me.

He finally gave me a tight smile and inclined his head in approval. I exhaled slowly, too nervous to feel any real relief.

I'd never been in this situation before, had never let him down over something serious. It was…terrifying. He wouldn't physically hurt me, but there were far worse things than broken bones.

He hadn't explicitly said it, but if this guy decided he didn't

want to marry me, my father would punish me with something far worse.

I almost blew it over my stupid feelings! What if the random guy hadn't been there to save my ass?

As the minutes ticked by, I found myself watching the periphery of the party, wondering if I'd see Mr. Dark and Dangerous. Every time a server passed with a tray of drinks, I checked to see if it was him. As though I'd have to look hard to find someone who reminded me of Jareth the Goblin King in this crowd.

Was I hoping I'd see him or hoping I wouldn't?

Why was I even thinking of him when there were far more important things to worry about?

"Trying to find him?" my father asked, appearing at my side.

I blinked, realizing he meant his prospective new ally, the man I was supposed to be focused on tonight. I pasted a smile on my face, making sure I kept my tone light. "How can I find him when you won't tell me who I'm looking for?"

He chuckled like this was a fun game and not my life he was toying with. "I think you'll know him when you see him. He'll be here soon."

"Can you tell me anything about him so I can be prepared to *charm* him?" My stomach clenched as I bit the words out around chattering teeth.

"He's got more money than anyone else here, and I'm told he's good-looking." He nodded to someone from security. "Why don't you go on to the Kennedy Room, and I'll bring him to meet you, give you a little privacy that way."

Privacy. I almost laughed.

I kissed him on the cheek automatically. "Yes, Daddy."

He stopped me as I started to walk away. "Sometimes he can be direct, speaks his mind. Show me you can be a Bryson woman and bite your tongue. I know you won't disappoint me, sugar."

I exhaled tightly and nodded, my entire body shaking.

When I got to the private banquet room he'd directed me to wait in, I didn't know what to do. First impressions were everything.

Should I stand? Sit at a table?

When the rising swell of fear felt like it would drown me and I wanted to run, I forced myself to go to the bar against the wall and make a drink instead. Maybe he wouldn't be so bad.

The door on the far side of the room opened and closed. I craned to see if it was a member of the staff checking on me and nearly dropped the bottle of gin I'd just picked up when I saw Mr. Dangerous.

He stood there in an immaculate tuxedo, his blond hair pulled back into a bun. The tux couldn't hide the tattoos on his hands or the glint of his lip ring, though it made him look more refined, almost civilized. But something lethal lurked beneath that veneer.

I was stunned into silence, standing there staring at him mutely.

His grin nearly reduced me to a puddle on the floor. "You weren't expecting me?"

4

set the bottle down and gathered my wits, turning to greet him properly. *This* was the man my father wanted me to marry?*

Oh god, I'd been vicious with him in the boathouse.

I aimed a loaded pistol at him! I told him to go fuck himself!

But he'd kind of deserved it.

The son of a bitch must've known the entire time that we'd meet later. Why had he let me humiliate myself like that?

It didn't matter. I could salvage this. I had to salvage this, or he might tell Daddy the whole story.

I extended my hand, giving him my sweet smile. "I'm Juliet. I'm sorry I wasn't myself earlier."

He grasped my hand, but instead of shaking it, he tugged it up to his mouth and planted a gentle kiss between my knuckles. His lips caressed my skin, every bit as soft as I'd imagined, but it was the light brush of his lip ring that made me shiver.

* MOMENT'S SILENCE (COMMON TONGUE)—Hozier

This was bad. This was really bad. I had absolutely no chance of keeping my wits about me with this guy.

I wanted to run from the room instead of facing him, but I fell back on a lifetime of training. *Be polite. Do as you're told. Don't make a fuss.*

"So we meet again. Drink?" I tried to sound relaxed.

"Whatever you're having."

I was still freaking out, but my hands were steady. I went through the ritual of making the drinks: measuring the gin and ice in a shaker, executing a perfect pour into a chilled glass, perching two olives daintily on the rim. It gave me a moment to compose myself, to feel like I was back in control.

He watched my every move. "A martini? I would've pegged you for a champagne girl."

It was decidedly not a compliment. His eyes scanned from my hair to my makeup to my gown, seeing me in the bright lighting for the first time.

"Champagne gives me a headache." I smiled prettily through gritted teeth as I passed him one of the glasses.

He narrowed his eyes. "Drop the act."

"What act?" I took a drink to stop from swearing at him again.

"Trying to pretend you're a docile kitten when you were ready to shoot me an hour ago."

I lifted the toothpick from the rim of my glass and slid an olive off with my teeth, watching him watch me.

A challenge glimmered in his eyes.

I raised my chin.

"I thought this meeting was with your father," he said with a smirk that would've made Casanova blush. "You're the one he sends to do his dirty work?"

Motherfucker. He didn't even need to emphasize the word *dirty* for the innuendo to roll off his tongue. He knew exactly why I was there.

"If you'd prefer to marry him, I'd be happy to retrieve him for you."

Fuck, fuck, fuck.

Seduce him, Juliet. Don't be a bitch to him.

Even his laughter sounded predatory, low and rumbling, somewhere between a warning and an invitation. "Based on your little performance in the boathouse, marriage isn't what you want." I opened my mouth to deny it, desperate for that not to get back to my father, but he cut me off. "Don't bullshit me, Juliet. Why are you doing this?"

I blinked. "Because my father told me to."

He stalked closer, placing a hand on each side of the bar next to my shoulders, effectively trapping me there. "Do you always do as you're told?"

My heart thundered at his closeness. This wasn't polite or proper, but instead of wanting to push him away, I wanted to pull him closer, to feel the hard planes I knew were hidden beneath his perfectly tailored tux.

I managed to keep my voice steady and aloof. "Not always. As you witnessed earlier." I pressed my lips together, frustrated that he'd seen me so vulnerable. "But most of the time."

He leaned closer, almost letting our bodies touch. "What

about when you belong to another man? Will you still be obedient to your father then?"

I had to pause. Some naive part of my brain had assumed my father's interests would always align with my future husband's, so it wasn't something I'd ever considered before. I twisted my fingers into the layers of my skirts, quickly trying to come up with the right answer. I wasn't prepared for any of this.

I looked up at him from under my lashes. "I'll still be loyal to my father. Not obedient."

He smiled, and I felt it low in my stomach. I was desperate for what he promised with that smile...and it scared me. This was a man I could lose control with.

I swore he could see the fears swimming in my eyes, and it brought out the predator in him.

"If you belonged to me, would you be obedient?" He ran a thumb along my bottom lip, like he already owned me, and it sent delighted chills skittering down my spine.

I was shaking, but I felt alive and molten. I wanted him like I'd never wanted anyone in my life, and it had nothing to do with my father's expectations.

"Yes," I breathed.

He pulled me away from the bar and turned me around, placing my hands where his had been. He wrapped my hair around his hand and lifted it to brush possessive, searing kisses along the nape of my neck. In the mirror behind the bar, I could see the frown that creased his brow, which made him look like he was intently focused on devouring me. I was breathless from nothing more than kisses on the back of my neck.

He used his other hand to pull my skirts up. Then his rough palm suddenly skated over my thigh, and he pressed me back harder against his arousal. It was thrilling to feel how he wanted me too.

Touch me. Oh god, yes...more.

I didn't say it, but he could feel my trembling thighs and panting breaths, the way I parted my legs wider, begging for it. I'd never let anyone touch me like this before, and I was desperate to know what came next. Sophia had taught me how to watch porn in secret, and I'd stolen some of my mother's romance novels, so I knew the mechanics but had never expected to feel like I was combusting the very first time this happened.

I felt...reckless and needy, helpless and still somehow powerful because this man wanted me.

I gasped when his fingers slid over the satin of my panties. I didn't want the smug bastard to feel how soaked they were, but I needed him to touch me more than I wanted to hide the effect he had on me. He teased his fingers under the side of the fabric, sliding up and down without touching me where I needed him most. I whimpered and rolled my hips, unsure of what I was even coaxing him to do.

"You really want this..." It wasn't a question, not quite, but there was surprise in his gruff tone, like I'd done something unexpected.

"*Please...*"*

He stopped moving. "Would you still want this if your father hadn't sent you to *charm* me?"

How did he know the word my father had used?

* DINNER & DIATRIBES—Hozier

I panted, trying to think clearly. I reached for some kind of answer that made me sound less pathetic, but all I could come up with was the truth. "I wanted this in the boathouse before I knew who you were."

Like that was all the answer he needed, he tugged my panties to the floor in one swift movement, letting me step out of them before his fingers returned and obliterated my understanding of pleasure. He pressed and rolled in clever controlled movements, swiftly bringing me close to release. I moaned and writhed, simultaneously reveling in the new sensation and yearning for something more.

He growled against my ear, "Would you let me sink into this tight pussy right here?"

"*Yes.*" I was willing to let my first time be bent over a barstool if it meant I got to feel this with him.

He groaned. "You should demand your own pleasure first, princess."

He lowered himself to the ground under the bar, kneeling before me in a ten-thousand-dollar tuxedo like it didn't matter.

His dark eyes never left mine when his hands roamed under my skirts again, ever so slowly tracing a path to where I ached. He watched me with a hungry expression as he reached the apex of my thighs, like he was savoring my reactions as much as I was melting for his touch.

At first it was too light, but then I realized he was slowly building to something, deliberately drawing this out instead of getting me off as quickly as he could. He kept taking me higher, then letting the pleasure subside, then coaxing more from me again.

I fisted my hands, fighting the wanton part of me that wanted to weave my fingers into the long strands of his white-blond hair. I needed to stay in control. There was too much at stake.

He looked at me curiously. "Why do you fight it, darling?"

I thrashed my head, trying to remember how to form a sentence that went beyond begging him for more. "We shouldn't be doing this where anyone could walk in..."

His grin was dangerous. "If you still remember where you are, I need to try a little harder." He ducked under my skirts, and the next thing I felt was the hot, wet slide of his tongue against my core. I gripped the bar harder and spread my thighs wider. It was like he knew my body better than I did, knew just what to do to make me mindless.

I didn't know anything could feel this good!

He rolled his tongue over my clit with delicious pressure, holding my hips in place as I shook and moaned. I was coming apart with sensation, but he just kept going, never so much as pausing while I was slowly stripped of reason, existing only for the pleasure he drew from my body. I couldn't breathe, couldn't speak. I was so close, so desperately close.

He thrust two thick fingers inside me, and my knees started to buckle. The stretching pressure was intimate and intense, leaving me to wonder for a split second what losing my virginity with him would feel like, but then I lost the ability to think altogether. I rode out the most intense orgasm of my life, bucking and whimpering as he let me finish, still gripping my hip with one hand to keep me steady.

He stood slowly, meeting my gaze with an expression that

was equal parts smug and lustful. Then he slid his fingers into his mouth and licked them clean.

He had every right to be smug. The man was a god of sex. Not that I'd ever had sex, but if there was something better than that, I wasn't sure I'd survive it.

"What about you?" I asked in a husky voice I barely recognized.

He pushed me down to my knees. I'd never given a blow job before, but that didn't stop me from scrambling to unfasten his pants.

He knocked my hands away. "Not yet, greedy girl. Turn around and show me how wet you are first."

He leaned back against one of the stools, waiting for me to comply.

When he'd been in control, it had been easy to surrender and let it all happen, but this was harder. I bit my lip, hesitating.

"Typical spoiled brat," he growled. "You promise to be obedient to get what you want, and then you immediately start to disobey. *Show me.*"

I gasped at the barked command even as I wanted to claw at him for calling me a spoiled brat. I gathered the voluminous layers of my skirt, trying to kneel and hold it all up, but he pushed me forward onto all fours.

"Let me help you," he said, hiking the skirt up over my back to reveal my bare ass and pussy to him.

He teased a finger inside me. "I bet no one has ever made this pretty pussy come like that." From the way he said it, he already knew the answer, and I hated him for being such a cocky bastard about it.

"No one has ever made me come, so it's not exactly steep competition. Do you always fish for compliments?"

He ground his knuckles over my clit, and I moaned without meaning to, giving him yet another wordless compliment he obviously didn't need. "Seems like your past sex partners weren't trying very hard." He rolled his thumb over my clit in torturous little circles as he thrust his fingers into me deeply this time. "I could make you come again in seconds."

I bit the inside of my cheek, struggling not to moan again. "I don't have any past sex partners, jackass. Have you been living under a rock?"

Fuck, I was supposed to be nice to him, but I could barely remember why when he did that with his fingers. It felt so agonizingly good.

He went still, and I wanted to cry at the loss of sensation. "You've never...?"

I sighed at the disbelief in his tone. "As though it isn't a publicly known fact?"

He smirked. "A *fact* created by the Bryson PR machine."

"Well, it's true," I snapped. "One more thing for you to be smug about, I suppose. Isn't a virgin bride what men like you value? Should I make you wait until the wedding?"

I was half venting and half taunting, still wanting him to just lose control and fuck me right there on the floor.

When he didn't move, I turned around, but when I reached for him, his watch buzzed. He glanced at it. Then there was a brief second where he looked like he was considering something.

"I have to go," he said definitively.

My stomach dropped. Now he didn't want me?

I opened my mouth to question him, but he pressed his damp fingers against my lips. He lifted my chin, his eyes boring into mine. "Demand more for yourself, Juliet."

What the fuck is going on?

"What...w-was this?" I stammered. Had he been testing me, and I failed? Was I too easy? Not experienced enough?

He shrugged. "I told you there'd be a price for my help."

It felt like the floor had opened under me and I was Alice tumbling into the void.

He strode out through the room's back entrance without another word.

Angry, confused tears burned my eyes, but I swallowed them back, not willing to fall apart.

I'd barely stood and straightened my gown when the other door opened, and my father walked in with a handsome dark-haired man who looked vaguely familiar.

"Kevin, this is my Juliet. *Your* Juliet if we can come to terms. Juliet, this is Kevin King."

I could only stare at them for a horrifying moment, completely lost as to what to say.

Sorry, I thought the other guy was you and I let him go down on me and I've just realized I don't even know his name, and ohmyfuckinggod, where are my panties?

5

shook Kevin's hand and tried to keep the alarm from my expression as I searched the floor for my missing undergarments. How was I going to explain what they were doing on the floor?*

I was briefly too distracted to focus on Kevin, but I'd caught a glimpse of a white guy with a strong chin, blue eyes, and dark hair that was just the slightest bit wavy. He was probably in his late thirties and probably just shy of six feet. That morning, I might've described Kevin as extremely attractive, but Mr. Dangerous had redefined my understanding of attraction.

If Kevin was like the soothing glow of a pretty candle, the other guy was like staring into the sun—the involuntary desire he stirred made him physically uncomfortable to behold.

"Juliet?"

I glanced back and realized they'd moved to a table and were waiting for me to sit.

* GOLD ON THE CEILING—The Black Keys

"Would either of you like a drink?" I asked, retrieving my martini to give myself one more chance to glance around the room.

Is this even my martini, or is it his?

There was a pause, and then my father said pointedly, "We both have drinks, Juliet."

I blinked, focusing on the glasses in front of them. I pasted a smile on my face and slid into the waiting seat across the round table from Kevin, which left me facing the bar where we'd just... where *he'd* just...

My cheeks heated.

After a pause, Kevin sighed heavily. "I thought I was meeting the other one." He looked around like another woman was going to be brought out. "The model? She's the one people recognize."

My father bristled. "The Bryson name is all you need for recognition. Sophia's married already. Juliet's just as lovely as her sisters."

Kevin looked me up and down, then turned back to my father. "So there's another one? A different one than this one and the model?"

That snapped my focus back to their conversation. "She's still a child. I'm afraid if the goal is to marry a Bryson, I'm your only option."

There was a painfully awkward long pause where it seemed like Kevin was contemplating whether I was worth the effort. Then he cleared his throat. "Your father tells me you like art. I'm something of a collector myself," he said, offering a thread of connection.

I seized it with both hands. "I'm mostly a fan of the old Renaissance masters, but I'm learning to appreciate modern art. What do you collect?"

Had there been a quiz later about his art collection, I would've missed every question. His mouth was moving, and words were coming out. I was giving responses that made it seem like I was engaged. But through the entire conversation, my mind was spinning.

Who the fuck just got me off?

I should've felt violated, but I'd wanted it, and I'd have been lying if I said I didn't want more. I felt...*awakened*. I hadn't even known what my body was capable of.

"You know, I think I will take that drink now."

Kevin had spoken, and I nodded knowingly at whatever he'd said.

The words only sank in when I caught my father's annoyed expression.

This was a disaster! I couldn't even act like a competent adult, much less convince this guy he should marry me.

I jumped up from my chair. "A drink. Absolutely. May I fix you a cocktail?"

"I'll take an old-fashioned," Kevin said.

I smiled uncertainly, realizing how ridiculous it was for me to offer to make cocktails. I could make a martini and pour a basic mixed drink, but I didn't even know what kind of liquor went in an old-fashioned. "Unfortunately, that exceeds my bartender knowledge. What if we get you one from the ballroom and then I show you the small gallery on the second floor?"

What if I get you the fuck out of this room before Daddy questions the second martini glass I just noticed on the bar and someone very possibly finds my underwear?

Instead of answering me, Kevin sat back, looking at my father and spreading his hands. "Let's be frank…she's lovely, and a few weeks ago, I wouldn't have hesitated."

There was a *but* coming, so my father interrupted him. "She's your ticket to the White House, son. A union of powerful families—the sky's the limit."

Kevin sighed. "I need a wife who's going to be an asset and not a liability. Someone demure. She's your daughter and a Bryson, and I understand the power that brings…but she has a history of scandalous behavior. How can I trust she won't be an embarrassment?"

Scandalous behavior? He made it sound like I'd been caught hosting a drug-fueled orgy in rehab. The only time I'd ever been caught with a toe out of line was at the club that night, and all I'd been doing was dancing a little provocatively with some guys. It wasn't like I'd had sex with them in the club for all to see.

Daddy's mouth lifted into his charming smile. "She's a spirited girl, but you'll find you like that in a wife. Her mother was the same way. It was a momentary lapse that taught her she never wants to behave like that again. She's ready to settle down. Aren't you, sugar?"

Oh, is the spirited girl *allowed to speak now?*

I'd been treated like this my whole life. Why was I suddenly mad about it?

Demand more for yourself, Juliet.

I swallowed back a scream because that bastard had somehow become a voice in my head. "Yes, Daddy." I felt like a child being paraded out to meet the adults and give the requisite answers to inane questions.

My father nodded. "And no matter what assumptions you might've made from those pictures, my security can confirm nothing happened. She remains a virgin, something you'd be hard-pressed to find in another bride."

Kevin stared at me like he was taking another look at a vintage car he might want to buy. "Why don't you grab me that drink, and I'll meet you in the ballroom?" He turned back to my father. "There's actually another piece of business I'd like to discuss with you..."

There was a pause I was all too familiar with. I'd been dismissed, and they were waiting for me to leave.

Another piece of business. That was all I was to him.

I strode from the room and headed back toward the party, hoping to resolve some business of my own. If I didn't find Mr. Dangerous and make sure he planned to keep his mouth shut about what had happened between us, my life would be ruined.

6

was hyperaware of my missing underwear as I crossed back into the main ballroom and headed for the bar. I'd never gone commando before, and I felt scandalous. I tried not to look around for the mystery guy but couldn't help nervously scanning the crowd, as though he would appear and announce what I'd let him do to me.*

It seemed like everyone was watching me, like they already knew.

That shame twisted something inside me, like a perverse part of my mind was turned on by the idea. Like I *wanted* them to know.

He broke my brain with that orgasm. What am I even thinking?

I ordered our drinks and made my way upstairs to one of the cocktail tables at a balcony railing where I could see everything

* TALK—Hozier

happening in the ballroom. It took only minutes for my father to appear, his eyes alight with irritation. "That was a disaster."

I opened my mouth to apologize, but he said, "First, he was expecting your sister. He's got more money than god, and he can't do so much as a Google search? Then he throws me a curveball I don't have an answer for."

"What kind of curveball?" I kept my tone soft and neutral, hoping he would actually tell me what was going on.

"Senator Macallan won't stop pushing for King to be investigated. King was under the mistaken impression that I could make it go away. He's testing the power of our name, asking me to demonstrate what it'll do for him."

"You're Nathaniel Bryson. Surely you have some sway with Macallan."

He rubbed his temples. "Not enough to make a federal investigation into King go away. He's pulled all the right levers already, but the good senator is like a dog with a bone and won't stop insisting. He can't be bought or reasoned with."

"So King doesn't want to marry me now?" If it was because Daddy couldn't manipulate a senator and not because I'd failed, surely he couldn't punish me for it.

"It would help if you could give him a reason to want to."

"But if you can't make the investigation go away, do you even want me married to him? Won't that bring scandal?"

He barked a harsh laugh. "He'll stop at nothing until it goes away—of that, I'm sure. You've got nothing to worry about there, but the senator might if he doesn't back off soon."

It sounded like a whole lot to be worried about.

My stomach sank as I spotted the son of a bitch who'd tricked me at the railing across from us, midconversation with a judge my father had handpicked to be appointed. Judge Rodgers looked entranced, as caught in the mystery guy's spell as I'd been.

I didn't even think the judge was into men, but he sure looked ready to take the fuckhead upstairs.

"Who is that?" I blurted before I could think better of it.

My father looked over at the man who'd just been up my skirts, and they locked eyes across the room. The devil himself raised his glass, toasting us with a roguish grin, like this was all some kind of game to him.

I wrapped my clammy hands into the folds of my skirt to keep myself from flipping him off.

"Stay away from him, sugar," my father said, going rigid beside me. "You don't need to know his name. He gets ahead in the world by knowing other people's secrets, by having leverage."

I was going to be sick. Was that what it had been about? Leverage over me, something to blackmail me with? "Why's he even here if he's that dangerous?"

My father's voice was bitter. "Because he didn't give me a choice in the matter."

That rocked me back on my heels. This guy not only had the guts to antagonize my father but had the power to keep him from doing anything about it.

As though in slow motion, the bastard raised his hand and dabbed the corner of his mouth with the unmistakable lavender fabric of my panties, then put them in his tux pocket like a trophy.

I squared my shoulders and straightened my back, presenting the posture that had been taught to every generation of women in my family. The posture of a woman with whom you did not fuck.

The asshole's head tilted like I'd done something interesting, so I pulled my eyes away from him and glanced at a random person in the crowd as though he hadn't been any more important to me than the next person.

I swore I heard the rumble of his laugh over the sound of the crowd.

My father looked me in the eye, his expression almost frantic in its seriousness. "He's a dangerous son of a bitch, and I don't want you anywhere near him."

"Yes, Daddy."

Too fucking late...

———

"An old-fashioned," I said, as I passed Kevin's drink to him.

He'd come to join me at the cocktail table on the upper level, after my father strategically left me alone to attend to other business. Which had also left me still avoiding eye contact with Mr. Dangerous, who was leaning all too casually against the railing on the far side of the upper level. I'd been terrified he was going to come over when my father left and cause a scene in front of Kevin.

"You must think I'm an asshole..." Kevin had a faint smile, like he was waiting for me to confirm it.

Instead, I said, "You're direct. It's refreshing. I know exactly where I stand with you." I gave him a playful look. "It's

unfortunate I happen to be standing on the wrong side of my sister...but I can't blame you for thinking she's the more strategic choice."

His smile this time was genuine. It was warm and charming but didn't trigger the wild feelings another smile had earlier in the night. "I might be warming to the idea of a match with you."

A phone on the table buzzed wildly.

"Are you going to get that?" he said.

"It's actually not—" I turned it over and stopped talking.

Unknown: He is an asshole. Ditch him so I can taste that pretty pussy again.

My cheeks burned with shame. I wanted to chuck the phone all the way across to the other railing and smack Mr. Dangerous in the head with it.

How could he even hear our conversation? And how the hell had he gotten a phone onto the table without me noticing?

I refused to look at him but could still feel his eyes boring into me, waiting to see what I'd do. I couldn't put the phone down and pretend it wasn't mine now, so I picked it up and said, "Interested in that tour of the gallery?"

I discretely dumped the phone in the nearest trash can and made sure he saw me taking Kevin's arm as we left the ballroom.

———

"Who's your favorite artist of all time?" Kevin perched next to me on a bench in the hotel's art gallery. It was a pretty sparse

collection of paintings, but it had given me an area of competence to focus on that had the bonus of letting me escape the ballroom.

"Any medium? Not just painters?"

"Any artist." He stared at my face as I looked at the ceiling and considered my answer.

"Bernini. He was a Renaissance sculptor, and a piece of his, *The Rape of Proserpina*, brought me to tears the first time I saw it. The way he could turn marble into a thing with such life and movement and...*feeling.*"

He looked skeptical but amused as he tucked a piece of hair behind my ear. "I prefer living beauty over marble made to look alive."

I leaned into his touch just a little, hoping it was okay to encourage him.

"Living beauty fades, though," I pointed out.

"Maybe." He shrugged. "But maybe that's what makes it so precious."

"And what about you?" I asked softly. "Do you have a favorite artist?"

He tilted his head back and forth, then shrugged again. "Art isn't really my thing. I love hunting the way you love art. Being outdoors, outmatched by some beast I ultimately conquer. Big game is my passion."

I let him see my eyes flare with surprise. "It doesn't scare you?"

He grinned. "Oh, it does. That's the part I'm hooked on."

I lowered my eyes, and when I looked back up, he'd shifted even closer. Just as Kevin started to kiss my neck, Mr. Dangerous

sauntered into the gallery and pretended to be studying the paint-ings for a split second before pinning me with a smoldering look. Kevin's kiss didn't make me feel anything except the urge to pull away, but when Mr. Dangerous's mouth hitched up into a know-ing smile, my stomach swooped with desire.

I pulled away from Kevin awkwardly. "It's getting kind of late. Do you think you could walk me back to my room?"

Why did I say that?

I knew exactly why I'd said it; it had nothing to do with my father's goals and everything to do with wanting to make the arrogant bastard jealous.

What if Kevin thinks that means we're going to have sex? Do I want to have sex with him?

Oh, I wanted to have sex with someone, but it wasn't Kevin, and it wasn't happening.

"I'd like that," Kevin said with a twinkle of interest in his eyes.

I dared a glance back over my shoulder as we left the room. Mr. Dangerous looked at where I was holding Kevin's arm, and his eyes narrowed into an irritated glare.

Good.

Die mad, asshole.

7

"Can I be honest with you, Juliet?" Kevin asked as the elevator doors slid open.*

I gave him a sideways glance. "In our world? That'd be refreshing."

He let out a slow breath. "I didn't mean to insult you by asking about your sisters. You're beautiful and charming, and any man would be lucky to have you." The elevator stopped at my floor, and he escorted me down the hall.

"But?" I asked with a wary smile, knowing from the way he inflected the sentence that there was more to it.

"It's just that I know what I'm looking for in a wife, and I have my doubts that a meek little thing like you is suited to my needs."

It was a test, a challenge even. It was right there in his tone—he wanted me to prove him wrong.

* OH MY GOD—Adele

Kiss him! Grab him and kiss him!

Will he think I'm a slut if I do that?

Daddy needs this!

I *need this, or there'll be hell to pay.*

I tried for a seductive look. "Maybe I'm not as meek as you think I am."

When I pulled him closer by the lapels of his jacket, he leaned down, letting me press my lips to his. I'd had a few stolen kisses with men over the years, but I'd never been the aggressor, and I was unsure of myself.

His mouth was warm and soft, but there were no sparks, no intensity as I tentatively moved my lips over his. It was painfully awkward, especially because he just sort of allowed it without really participating. After a few seconds, he pulled back, then nodded like I'd confirmed his suspicions.

He kissed me on the cheek. "Good night, Juliet."

I slid the key into my door and pushed it open, then shut it without looking at him again. He didn't need to see how red my cheeks were.

"No, no, no!" I said aloud, flopping down onto the bed.

I just blew it. I had one job, and I blew it!

I was an undesirable, awkward shrew who couldn't even get a kiss right. Kevin King didn't want me. I'd thought the guy from the boathouse wanted me, but it had been some kind of game for him. He was probably out there laughing right now, mocking the way I'd been putty in his hands.

I was so embarrassed, I wanted to pull the covers over my head and never reemerge.

I buried my face in the blankets and groaned, letting the comforter muffle the sound. When I breathed back in, I was enveloped in the scent of leather and the light, clean smell of the man from the boathouse.

His jacket.

I pulled the covers back to find it and sank my fingers into the buttery-soft texture of it. I groaned again because no matter how pathetic it made me, the scent took me right back to the rush of being alone with him and the forbidden thrill of letting him touch me.

No one had ever made me feel like that.

Evidently, no one was going to anytime soon.

The shame fell away just enough for me to remember what he'd coaxed from my body. I hated him for being a devious bastard. But my stupid lady parts didn't give a fuck about any of that.

I'd never had a particularly strong appetite for sex because it had never seemed worth the risk of blemishing my image, but it was suddenly all I could think of. I *ached* to feel alive like that again. I wanted to live in a reality where I wasn't chum in a pool of sharks, where desire wasn't either a weapon or a weakness.

I stripped out of my gown and climbed back under the covers. Then I slid my hand down and explored, finding the place where the ache seemed to originate. When I moved my fingers, a rush of sensation uncoiled in my belly, somehow making the ache better and worse at the same time. I whimpered, moving them again.

It always took me a long time, but it wasn't that I'd never

made myself come before. I'd just never come like *that*. It was like he'd unlocked something inside me, or maybe he'd unlocked the knowledge that what I'd been doing wasn't all my body was capable of.

I parted myself with my other hand like he'd done, but I was too timid to push inside, as though I weren't allowed to touch myself like that. I was a fool for being uncertain of my own body when a stranger hadn't been.

Meek. I was meek with my own body.

The thought ignited a wave of defiance in me. I was only meek because that's what they'd trained me to be. If I was going to be shamed regardless, I might as well have ownership of my own body.

I thrust a finger inside myself, then added another, curling them and seeking the sensation he'd coaxed from me.

Oh...

I repeated the motion, breathless to have discovered something new.

A tap on the balcony window shattered the silence, making me jolt upright and yank my hands away.

I gasped. "What the...*fuck?*"

It was Mr. Dangerous peering through the curtains and tapping again like he had every right to be there and I was being rude by not letting him in faster.

He's a dangerous son of a bitch, and I don't want you anywhere near him.

If I summoned security, I risked his telling everyone what we'd done earlier—and producing my panties as evidence.

I wrapped a sheet around my nakedness, then pulled the sliding door open a crack to whisper, "One scream, and security will make your life hell."

He caught his lip ring between his teeth and rocked back on his heels, the picture of nonchalance. "I just came to get my jacket back, but if you want me to make you scream, princess, I'm up to the task."

I clenched my thighs together at the pictures that put in my head and opened the door the rest of the way, more worried someone would hear him than I was afraid of him.

Oh god. His jacket. I'd been so distracted by his innuendo that it took a second for the rest of what he'd said to sink in. His jacket was in my bed, tucked under the blanket like I was a pervert creeper who'd been sniffing it while I touched myself.

Because that's exactly what you were doing.

"I don't have it," I insisted as he stepped inside and slid the door closed behind him. "I left it on a chair downstairs, so you'll need to check with someone from the staff."

He rubbed his chin like he was trying to hide a smile. "How are you a Bryson who can't lie for shit? Lying is basically in your DNA."

I sucked in a breath. "How dare you!"

"Apologies." He took my hand and pressed a slow kiss to my fingers, a gentle slide of lips, tongue, and teeth. It was all I could do to bite back a pathetic sound.

His mouth. I know exactly what he can do with that mouth.

He paused with my fingers against his lips and tilted his head. "Were you already asleep when I disturbed you?"

He knew. From his tone and the look in his eyes, he knew exactly what I'd been doing.

"Yes," I said too quickly.

He narrowed his eyes. "Was it me you were thinking of?"

I jerked my hand away, my cheeks flaming. "My father said you're dangerous. That you manipulate people by learning their secrets."

He flashed that grin again. "Do you believe everything your father tells you?"

"Is it true?"

He sat on the end of the bed, waiting for me to object to him acting like he belonged there. I wasn't going to give him the satisfaction. I pressed my back against the wall, staying rigid and maintaining distance between us. I didn't trust myself after the way I'd behaved earlier.

He shrugged. "People willingly tell me secrets. If they're then scared of what I might do with the information, that's not my fault."

I held out my hand. "Give my panties back."

He narrowed his eyes in challenge. "Admit you were thinking about me when you were touching yourself, and they're all yours."

I managed to hold his stare. "I wasn't touching myself."

"You think I don't recognize the scent of that perfect pussy? That I can't remember what it tasted like?"

If my cheeks got any more flushed, they were going to catch fire. "Cherish the memory, dickhead, because you'll *never* taste it again."

The man was sex incarnate. Everything about him, from the way he moved to the way he spoke to the way he smiled, conjured erotic thoughts. It gave him a completely unfair advantage in a conversation.

I crossed my arms. "So how does this work? What do you want from me to buy your silence?"

He studied me. "It's fascinating that you think hooking up with me is so beneath you that I could blackmail you with it."

He almost looked...hurt? When he said it like that, I sounded like the asshole. He had me all tied up in knots, questioning everything.

I hugged the blanket closer around myself. "Everyone knows I'm the virgin Bryson heiress. It's not about you. There will be consequences if I hook up with anyone except whoever my father chooses."

He winked. "Except you did...and there weren't...because we didn't get caught."

He looked around slowly, drawing attention to the fact we were shut in a room together and no one would know if we did something now. His eyes traced the outline of the blanket I clutched, reminding me I was naked beneath it.

"*This* is why you're dangerous, isn't it?" I asked, contemplating. "You know exactly what buttons to push to keep people off-kilter."

His eyes flashed with intensity. "One word from Daddy, and you're so sure I'm your enemy."

"So, what's your plan here? We fall into bed together, where I reveal my deepest, darkest family secrets?"

His voice was a low rumble. "Fall into bed with me, and I'll make sure you don't remember your own name, much less your family's filthiest secrets. I don't need you to tell me those. I was there."

"What the fuck does that mean?"

"Ask your father."

I felt like a toy being passed between a pack of rabid dogs: helpless and likely to be ripped to shreds if I didn't grow some teeth and claws of my own. I was sick and fucking tired of being the *meek little thing* they could manipulate—all of them, my father included.

Like he could tell I'd been pushed too far, he shook his head and turned to slide the balcony door open. Then, as if he'd changed his mind, he came back into the room, but it was only to set a card on the nightstand. The card only had a number on it.

"You ever find yourself in need of another favor, give me a call."

He was outside, already gripping the third-floor railing to climb over, when a reckless idea struck me.

"What if I need a favor now?"

He turned back, his expression carefully neutral. "Oh?"

"Senator Macallan. What kind of leverage do you have on him?"

A grin spread across his face. "Now *that* is a *big* favor. Some gossip is cheap, but no one has dirt on the good Senator Macallan."

I rolled my eyes, knowing what he was going to say. "Except you."

He put his hands on the top of the doorframe, leaning just barely inside. "Are you asking this in the hope my price will be

the same as last time? Because if you want me to make you come again, all you have to do is...beg."

I sighed in exasperation, partly because he turned everything back to sex and partly because some treacherous part of me thought begging didn't sound like too steep a price for what he could deliver. "Which part of *you'll never taste it again* was unclear?"

"Darling, my tongue is hardly the only way I can make you come."

"God damn it, why are we even talking about this? Do you have information I can use?"

"Naturally."

"Name your price."

"You'll come to my office tomorrow, and for six hours, you'll do anything I ask."

The very idea of it sent my heart racing in a combination of horror and excitement. "Fuck you. Absolutely not."

"Fine. Enjoy your evening. Give my regards to your father." He sketched a bow.

God damn it! "Three hours."

His grin made me shiver with the kind of fear you could learn to crave. "I think you'll find you want more time. But it's a deal."

He pulled out his phone and tapped through a series of screens. Then my phone buzzed on the nightstand.

"You have my number?" I said incredulously as I picked it up, but I promptly forgot it even mattered when I clicked into some kind of portal and skimmed through an email. "This can't be real."

He shrugged. "I don't believe in faking it."

It was what I was coming to recognize as his usual innuendo, but there was nothing playful about it. He knew what he'd just handed me, and he studied my every move to see what I'd do with it.

Holy fuck!

"Holy fuck," I said aloud this time, my mind reeling at the email on my screen and what it would mean for the senator if it got out.

"I think I was expecting a kinky sex tape or something…"

Mr. Dangerous sighed and leaned closer. "Sexuality is sacred. I'd never use it as leverage." He smirked. "But don't tell anyone that."

This was the kind of financial crime that would cause more than a scandal. If I showed this to the senator, he'd have to stop pushing to investigate King or risk losing his seat and possibly getting jail time. It was a dangerous plan that had all kinds of risks, but it wasn't like I was actually going to release it. I just needed the senator to think I might.

I tried to picture standing in front of him and showing him the email…threatening to ruin his life with it if he didn't do something unethical…

Who am I that I'm even thinking about doing this?

Was I scared enough of letting my father down again to do something this reckless? I thought of Jacque and realized I'd do anything to protect her.

But there was another, more selfish layer to it. If I pulled this off, it would make me a shark, a real player in their dangerous political games.

What will you even say to him?

I played the words through in my mind, trembling nervously.

The devil I'd just made a deal with leaned against the wall, completely at ease. He probably did this kind of thing over his morning coffee without a care in the world.

"Can you...be the one to deliver the message?"

He pushed off the wall, looking disgusted. "You want me to blackmail a sitting U.S. senator while you hide behind this innocent charade? Typical fucking Bryson. It's time you got your own hands dirty."

The anger in his tone made me flinch, a reminder that I was alone with a dangerous man I knew nothing about.

I wasn't a shark. Not yet.

Like he knew he'd scared me, he let out a deep breath and allowed his mask of cool indifference to slip back into place. "Besides...they wouldn't let me get close enough to deliver the message. But he'll be expecting you."

Fear gripped my chest. "You already told him I'm coming?"

"No." He smirked. "He sent for an escort."

8

asked for a blond."*

Of all the things I'd expected Senator Macallan to say when his security frisked me and led me through to the bedroom of his suite, that didn't even make the list.

I'd been convinced he'd recognize me, given that he'd known me socially since I was a kid.

As my enigmatic partner in crime had dug through my makeup bag to make me a convincing escort, he'd said, "A man who's waiting for his call girl only sees what he wants to see." He brandished a makeup brush. "C'mere."

He said it so softly, it was how I imagined a lover might sound summoning me to bed, but not even in a sexual way. He had this way of making it seem like he belonged and that whatever he was doing—no matter how unreasonable—was absolutely acceptable.

* RENEGADES—X Ambassadors

He applied eye makeup and contour with all the ease of a seasoned makeup artist. When he touched my face, staring this closely at me, his body once again touching mine...it couldn't have been more intimate.

Well...it could've. As deft as his fingers were at applying an absolutely flawless cat eye, he was even more skilled at...other things. Things I absolutely wasn't going to think about while he was that close.

So I took my chance to stare back, finding myself watching his mouth, noticing the way he toyed with his lip ring as he focused.

"If you look at the good senator like that, you might not need to threaten him with the email," he said as he swiped eyeliner across my other lid, flashing his white teeth. "He'll forget he's got any morals and do whatever you ask."

"You're so full of shit," I muttered.

He gathered my hair into a ponytail in his giant hands and tugged on it roughly, making me gasp—but not purely with pain. "Watch your mouth, princess. Do you have a hair band?"

"No."

He transferred all my hair into one of his hands and pulled the band out of his bun with the other. His beautiful white-blond hair cascaded onto his shoulders when he released it, and I was hit with the clean sea breeze scent of what could only be his shampoo. It was the same scent that lingered on his jacket.

"Delicious," he purred, and for a second, I thought he was reading my mind, but then I realized he was looking at me in the mirror.

Or the person who used to be me. With a little makeup and a sleek high ponytail, I was barely recognizable. It was like he'd done a magic trick.

"I'm not usually a fan of makeup, but that's remarkable," I said, still in awe.

He stood behind me and appraised his work in the mirror. "You're not a fan because they make you up to look like a delicate little lamb being led to the slaughter. I think you'll find it's more fun to be the huntress," he said with a wink.

For the first time in my entire life, I looked like a temptress... and he was right, I didn't hate it.

I was still only wearing a blanket wrapped around myself, and he eyed it thoughtfully. "I'm guessing you don't have any hooker attire in that closet?"

"Sex worker," I corrected, and laughter danced in his eyes. "And no, I don't have anything risqué in there."

He rifled through my closet, then stopped suddenly. "Is this *the* Bryson Blue Dress?" It wasn't the flashiest dress by a long shot. In fact, it was the definition of subtle class, with a high neck and an A-line shape that nipped in at the waist. The rich shade of cornflower blue was its most striking feature. The Bryson Blue Dress wasn't notable for how it looked but rather who'd worn it and what had happened to them afterward.

I shrugged. "I had it out for a photoshoot. It needs to go back in its bag."

It was a lie. The shoot had been months ago. I hadn't been able to bring myself to put it away again afterward because just seeing it, touching it comforted me. My grandmother had worn it

to my grandfather's inauguration, and my mother had worn it to my uncle's. I had such vivid memories of her wearing it that day, how beautiful she'd looked and how happy we'd all been.

I missed her. I missed my brother—and my sisters, even though they were still alive. The day my mother had worn this dress was one of the last times I remembered us feeling like a real family.

"Am I cursed now that I've touched it?" He said it with a hint of intrigue rather than fear. Both my grandmother and mother had died in tragic accidents not long after wearing the iconic dress, so people said it carried my family's curse. There were entire corners of the internet dedicated to obsessing over the power of this dress.

"Yep. You're a dead man. You should get your affairs in order."

His mouth lifted into a surprised smile, like he hadn't expected me to make a joke. *I* hadn't expected to make a joke, but he coaxed out confidence I'd never had before.

"You just might be the death of me, darling." He caught his lip ring between his teeth, studying me with those intense eyes.

I shrugged and looked away, scared I might let my guard down too much with him.

"I lost my mom in an accident too," he said. "I was so young, I don't really remember her, but that might be worse than missing her—knowing she's been forgotten."

My stomach hollowed at the unexpectedly vulnerable statement. It hit close to my own fears about forgetting things about my mother and brother.

"Who raised you then?" I asked, trying to shake the heartache that always accompanied those thoughts.

He shrugged. "My dad was never in the picture. My grand-parents did as much as they could."

The soft way he said it made me wonder if he'd been the caretaker in that relationship.

"You don't seem like someone with grandparents," I blurted, not really meaning to say it aloud.

He pouted sympathetically. "They didn't teach you biology in princess school either?"

I shoved his shoulder with my hand, then immediately regret-ted it because it put us so close together, and my whole body practically buzzed with awareness anytime I touched him.

"I know how biology works, but you seem more like you were spawned from darkness or are the progeny of a vampire or something."

He blinked and let out the first genuine-sounding laugh I'd heard from him. It was so infectious, I smiled back, then realized what I was doing and wiped it from my face. He looked just as surprised and stroked a thumb along my jaw. "I could get used to making you smile like that."

What am I doing?

"Don't," I said, walking back toward the bedroom to put some distance between us. There was too much at stake to be flirting with my father's enemy.

He turned back to my cherished blue dress. "Well, that clearly won't work," he said, reverently sliding it to one side. When he didn't find anything deeper in the closet, he returned to the bedroom.

He stripped off his tux jacket and then his shirt, then pulled

off his tank top undershirt so fast, I didn't have time to protest. And I apparently lost the ability to speak when faced with his bare chest. Because all I did when he tugged my blanket off and pulled his undershirt over my head was stand there and let him. His ribbed shirt hugged my body, barely covered my ass, and plainly displayed my nipples through the white fabric.

I put my hands over them indignantly. "You cannot tell me an escort would walk through a hotel like this."

He laughed. "What, barefoot? You're right. Put those strappy fucking heels back on."

How had he even noticed my shoes?

I did as I was told even as I said, "You know that's not what I meant."

His expression turned serious. "Of course you can't go like that. You'll wear my leather jacket over it."

The devious bastard had cornered me. I could walk out there like this, or I could admit I had his jacket.

I stormed over to the bed and retrieved it from the blankets it was buried under. "Happy?" I snapped.

He bit his bottom lip, fighting a smile but not saying a word.

The embarrassment served as a useful distraction from what I was about to do. Any excuse to run away from him after just pulling his jacket from my bed. I picked up my phone, then squared my shoulders as I headed for the door. I was scared and uncertain, but the adrenaline flooding my system felt different from the nervous fear that usually drowned me in the face of my father's expectations. I was doing this to keep Jacque safe and to avoid disappointing Daddy...but on some level, I was doing it

for me. It felt good to be taking charge. Good...and absolutely terrifying.

"Now pardon me while I go commit my first felony."

———

Senator Macallan stood there leering at me after observing that my dark hair was the wrong color. It felt like he was a Karen in a restaurant, complaining about something trivial to get a discount even though it didn't actually bother him.*

"Okay, I can leave and see if someone else is available. Not sure how long it'll take, but..."

I was bluffing, and we both knew it, but some scared part of me wanted him to send me away so I could turn tail and run but still tell myself I'd tried.

"Stay," he said. "You look just like Juliet Bryson... I like that."

"Oh yeah?" My voice wavered uncertainly. Did he know? I was freaking out.

"Yeah. I'm gonna enjoy pretending I'm balls deep in that frigid bitch."

My god. This was one of the softest-spoken, most polite people I'd ever met, but apparently not when he got to be himself. I'd only ever been nice to this douchebag.

"Well, don't get too excited yet. We've got something to talk about first."

He circled me creepily, only half listening to anything I was saying. "I already know the rules," he said dismissively.

* DREAM GIRL EVIL—Florence + the Machine

Am I really going to do this? Shit, shit, shit!

"I've got a new rule for you. You stop pushing to have Kevin King investigated."

Now *that* got his attention.

"Who the fuck do you think you are?" He suddenly looked angry.

"Someone who knows what you've been up to..." I passed him my phone with the email open, and it took only seconds for his eyes to get huge.

For an instant, he looked like a wounded animal about to strike, and I was scared he'd hurt me, but then he deflated in shame. "What do you want?" he said with disgust, but he was the one who'd been stealing from impoverished kids and saying... unkind things about them.

"Already told you. Kevin King is off-limits. You don't push for him to be investigated, and if you hear anyone else stirring up trouble, you put a stop to it."

The sigh he let out was as heavy as his mistakes. "Fine. Get out."

Holy shit, I did it!

I wondered whether I needed more concrete reassurance than that, but it was written in his posture. He was defeated and would've done anything to stop that shame from becoming public knowledge.

"You *are* Juliet Bryson," he said softly, not really speaking to me.

"The frigid bitch herself." I flashed him a look of disgust and turned for the door.

Once I left his room, I made it three steps past the corner

before someone snatched me around the waist and yanked me into a hotel room. I tried to scream as the door slammed, but his hand clamped over my mouth.

"You are a lucky, lucky girl…"

I knew that low, melodious voice, even if I still didn't know his name. I knew the feel of his body against my back as well. I was far too comfortable with his arms banded around me.

Like he could feel that I'd recognized him, he released his hold on me.

I whipped around. "You were lurking here the whole time? Why?"

"You went charging in there with no plan and no backup. What if he'd gotten violent to stop you from outing him?"

"You told me not to take my gun."

"That didn't mean you should go in there with your real phone, no plan to check in, no fucking plan at all." If I didn't know better, I would've said he was worried about me.

"Why didn't you bring any of this up *before* I went in if you were so worried about it?"

"Because I wanted to see whether you'd have the sense to give a single thought to your own safety."

"Well, it worked out fine." Adrenaline pounded through my system. I was buzzing with power like I'd never felt before. I'd handled my own shit. More than that, I'd handled something neither King nor my father had been able to manage.

I'm a goddamned shark. Maybe still a little one in a sea of great whites…but no longer chum.

He studied me. "You…enjoyed that, didn't you?"

"Hell no, I was terrified." My heart rate still hadn't come back down anywhere close to normal.

"Ah, but you liked the rush, the thrill of bringing a powerful man to his knees."

On some level, he was right. I felt daring, like I could do anything.

He lifted my chin, staring like he could draw the feeling from me and savor it. He looked *hungry* for it.

"Do you miss this, Mr. Jaded? I bet you haven't been scared like that in a while." My chest rose and fell rapidly to match my thumping heart rate, but I leaned closer, refusing to back down from his closeness.

He tilted his head in that predatory way I was becoming familiar with. "You'd be surprised..."

The moment was there. I wanted to kiss this wildly inappropriate man. When I'd wanted him before, I'd had the excuse of ignorance, but now I knew precisely who he was: an enemy to my family and a danger to the careful plans my father had for me—plans I'd just risked everything to keep alive.

I stepped back, putting some distance between us.

A sudden memory of the brutal awkwardness of kissing Kevin struck me. For this plan to work, I had to do better than that.

Maybe kissing Mr. Dangerous isn't such a bad idea... I need the practice.

He leaned back against the wall, tucking his hands into his pockets like he was trying to avoid touching me. "I've seen that look before, princess. You go hunting for trouble, you're going to find it."

Like he already knew what I was going to do, his arms were there to pull me closer when I took the two steps to reach him.

He tugged my hips against his, folding me into his arms like I was something precious.

Did he really want me, or was this all a game?

Did it matter?

His lip ring was the first thing I felt as he lowered his mouth to mine, which only made me notice how soft his lips were. When he slanted them over mine, I became shockingly aware of my entire body. He was gentle but dominant, viscerally sexual but still sensual in a way that almost felt romantic. He kissed me like he'd been waiting for it his whole life, which was ridiculous because he'd probably kissed hundreds of people.

There was nothing awkward about kissing this man. He didn't leave room for awkwardness or thoughts or anything but *the feel* of him. Why couldn't he really have been the man I was supposed to marry?

Because he's dangerous!

His hand started to work its way ever so slowly under the hem of the shirt I was wearing, and I had to stop this. Now that I knew exactly what he could do with that clever, clever hand, I'd be a traitor to my family if I kept going beyond what I needed from him.

I pulled away, panting with the effort it took.

He dropped his hand and feathered tiny kisses on my cheeks and up to the shell of my ear. "We can go slow," he said, his voice dripping with temptation.

"I can't do this with you," I said, not meaning to explain myself.

"Why not?" He still had that hungry expression, but there was a dark, unreadable layer to it now.

"Because I don't trust you," I said.

He shook his head, smiling, but there was no joy to it. "Yes, you do. You don't trust yourself with me. There's a difference."

"Thanks for mansplaining my feelings to me. You're a lying, manipulative motherfucker." I tossed it out as a fact, but there wasn't the anger behind it that there should've been.

"You already knew that when you kissed me." His teeth grazed my neck lightly, but when I gasped and arched into him for more, he bit me harder. "And watch your mouth, darling."

I pushed away from him, stepping back while I still had the self-control to stop him. "I kissed you to learn how it's done properly. Mr. King found my skills lacking, and I might not get another chance if I mess it up again."

He narrowed his eyes. "Who's the manipulative one now?"

I shrugged, feeling like a goddamned warrior, and opened the door.

"Where are you going?"

"To make a few more rash decisions."

———

I hammered my fist on Kevin King's hotel room door like I had every right to be there. A quick call to security had gotten me the room number. My father had called me immediately to see what I was up to, but he could wait. He wouldn't dare interrupt if he thought I was down here securing what he wanted.

Seconds later, King flung the door open with a gun aiming

straight at my face. Up to that point, I hadn't seen what made my father think King was ruthless enough to be his successor, but I could recognize it now: the vicious expression, the penchant for violence he disguised far too well the rest of the time. He wasn't just prepared to use his weapon—he was eager to do it.

I'd been around violent men my whole life, but this one worried me.

"Juliet," he said curtly, lowering the gun but still not looking friendly. "Was I not clear enough?"

Yowza. As far as he was concerned, I'd been dismissed. Now I was an annoyance.

I took a steadying breath. "You were clear, but you were wrong. May I come in?"

He sighed heavily but stood aside to let me enter and close the door.

"Macallan is going to stop pushing for you to be investigated. I have his word."

He looked like he was working out a puzzle. "Your father said he couldn't help. He talked to Macallan?"

The pounding, thrumming thrill of triumph kicked back into my system. "No. I did."

He failed to hide his surprise. "How did you pull that off?"

"Does it matter?"

He looked me up and down, not missing my flushed cheeks and scandalous attire, the bite mark on my neck. Whatever he thought was better than the truth that I'd conspired with the enemy.

The look he gave me was covetous, like I was suddenly an

auction item he had to own. "Not so meek after all. Are you still a virgin?"

I raised my chin indignantly. "Of course. Until my husband claims me."

Oh, he liked that answer...

His eyes skated over my body possessively like he was determined to be that man. Was this how he looked when he was hunting?

Before I could lose my nerve, I crossed the room in three quick steps and tugged his head down to mine. I kissed him like Mr. Dangerous had kissed me, claiming Kevin's bottom lip between mine before letting my tongue trace the seam of his lips. I was too focused on his reactions to enjoy it.

This time he responded, cupping my ass and grinding me against his erection. He took control, plundering my mouth with his tongue as he backed me toward the bedroom. Things were escalating quickly, but I stopped him. I wasn't positive I wouldn't be disappointing in bed with my lack of experience, so it was better to quit while I was ahead.

I pulled away, then kissed him on the cheek. "Good night, Mr. King."

He laughed disbelievingly. "That's it? You're leaving?"

I threw him a saucy look over my shoulder. "I have my doubts that a meek little thing like you will suit my needs."

There was a flash of anger in his expression, and I thought I'd gone too far, but it was quickly replaced by a wolfish smile. "We'll see about that, Juliet."

———

I'd barely made it to the elevator when I got a text.

Unknown: This is Kevin. Have dinner with me tomorrow.

I thought about asking if it was a question or a command, but I'd challenged him enough tonight. Compliance was safer.

Me: Where and when?
Kevin: My plane will pick you up on the airstrip at 8.
Me: Looking forward to it.

Was I looking forward to it? I was excited to tell my father the news. I was still nervous that I'd blow it with Kevin but determined not to lose my upper hand.

As I got back inside my room, my phone went off again, this time with a message from a different unknown number, but it was immediately clear it was Mr. Dangerous.

Unknown: Well played. I'll see you tomorrow.

He attached a map location that was half an hour away, obviously where he expected me to meet him to fulfill my end of the bargain. Forget worrying about what he was going to make me do in the three hours I belonged to him—how was I going to sneak out and explain being gone for that long when I was being watched this closely? After Geoff's murder, Daddy had begun insisting a driver take me everywhere.

Me: I don't know if I can get there without getting caught.

Unknown: A deal's a deal. You'll figure it out.

Seconds later, a video came through.

I hit Play with dread coiling in my stomach. Was it a video of what I'd done with him in the Kennedy Room?

As soon as the thumbnail loaded, I knew it was far worse.

A clip of me blackmailing Senator Macallan.

I'd walked straight into his trap.

Unknown: Three hours. Anything I want.

9

The address my blackmailer had given me turned out to be some kind of private helipad with a swanky lounge to wait in, but there was no one else there except a pilot who escorted me silently out to the helicopter.*

I'd tried searching the address online, but it was the strangest internet black hole I'd ever encountered. I couldn't track down any records, anything associated with it, even a satellite image. I hated being this unprepared.

When we landed, he pointed me from the helipad to an enormous house. I didn't know what I'd been expecting for this guy's "office"—it irked me that I still had no idea what his name was—but a palatial estate an hour from the city wasn't it.

I followed the obvious path to the front door, feeling nervous and overwhelmed. But neither of those words was entirely accurate... I was scared shitless, scared in a way I'd never been scared before.

* INDIGO CHILDREN—Puscifer

I was terrified of what he might do to me but even more afraid that I might not hate every moment of it.

He had enough evidence to send me to prison, so he basically owned me...and there was no escape from it because I'd never be sure he'd destroyed the footage even if he said he had. I'd made a serious, unforgivable mistake.

You're a Bryson. Get it together.

If he was going to play dirty, I could do the same. An enemy was letting me into what appeared to be his home, and I had every intention of exploiting every last weakness to get information that I could use later. Mutually assured destruction was the only way to free myself from the power he had over me with that footage.

I had to find a way to ruin him.

The area around the entrance to the house featured enormous wooden double doors with tasteful marble sculptures placed around the space. I rescinded the word *tasteful* once I got a closer look. Every sex act I could conceive of was being performed by said sculptures in far more graphic detail than the Italian masters would've gotten away with. It was just subtle enough to be spectacular and must've cost an absolute fortune.

I guess being a manipulative bastard pays well...

I'd gotten myself to the front door by not thinking too much about what would happen on the other side of it. I'd had smaller problems to focus on, like what to wear and how to get here. A demure black wool coat had covered a dress that might've raised some questions, since it was sexier than my usual style. Now that I was standing on the precipice, my heart was pounding.

I blew out a shaky breath and knocked on the door, fully expecting a staff member to answer, and was stunned when the bastard himself opened it wearing nothing but a pair of low-slung sweatpants, looking like he'd just gotten out of bed.

"Your three hours started when I got on the helicopter," I said, glancing at my watch.

He ushered me inside and held out a hand for my coat. "If that's how you want to play it…"

I shrugged off my coat and placed it into his waiting palm, managing not to actually touch him. He took in the teal dress I'd chosen after much debate about what one should wear to face their blackmailer. Being a femme fatale best suited my mood, so it was a tastefully curve-hugging, fifties-style dress, but it didn't show an inch of skin between my throat and my knees.

"You dressed up for me, darling. I like that."

His praise shouldn't have made me want to preen. It was too easy to relax around him, too comfortable to let my guard down, but I could see through his manipulation now. This was the same man who'd set me up last night and wouldn't hesitate to use the evidence against me.

"Don't flatter yourself. I have a date later."

He cocked an eyebrow. "With Kevin King?"

"You have to ask? Don't you supposedly know everything?"

His eyes flashed. "Everything I care to know."

Ouch.

"Oh yeah?" I challenged. "Do you know what Kevin King is into? That would be *extremely useful* information to have…"

"Give me a few hours, and I'll find out for you, princess..."

"Wait, don't actually go snooping—"

He turned and headed straight for a magnificent staircase in the center of the foyer, then started to climb. I followed him without question, in awe of the flashes of marble and dark wood I saw as we walked. It was an interesting cross between Versailles-level finery with ancient Greek extravagance and maybe a dash of High Renaissance charm thrown in. The man had expensive taste.

"I think I was expecting a dungeon or something," I said begrudgingly as he pulled open a heavy door.

"Maybe you just need to expand your understanding of what a dungeon looks like," he said with a wink. He gestured for me to follow him into the room.

It was...an office. Again, a lavish, enormous, richly appointed office...but an office just the same. No implements of torture on the walls, no sex swing, nothing at all like I'd lain awake imagining the night before. Just a huge desk in the center, a few smaller workspaces around the edges of the room, and a seating area close to the far wall.

"What is it you do for work?"

He perched on the edge of the desk and crossed his arms over his bare chest. "You don't know?"

"Unless you bought all this with blackmail and hush money, I have no idea what you do professionally."

He grinned. "Let me know when you figure it out."

Cryptic, manipulative bastard.

His titles just kept growing, and I still didn't have a name

for him. But I wasn't about to ask, not after that bullshit answer.

"Can I get you anything? Water, booze, fresh cherries from my orchard? They're perfectly sweet and ready to be picked."

I rolled my eyes. "You think I haven't heard every variation of a cherry joke there is to hear as a twenty-eight-year-old virgin?"

He frowned. "Not a joke, Juliet. Actual cherries. One of these days, you should examine why you interpret everything as innuendo... Some repressed feelings perhaps?"

Infuriating, cryptic, manipulative bastard!

"Everything *is* innuendo with you, even if, in that one instance, you were being literal."

"If you say so..." He circled the desk to stand behind a massive leather chair and placed his hands on the back of it. "Please, have a seat."

Everything in the room felt suspiciously straightforward compared to the wicked things I'd imagined. "Why?" I asked, eyeing the chair like it might have secret restraints that would pop out and trap me the second I sat down.

He sighed and circled back around the desk to flip a laptop open. "There's a discrepancy in my books. I want you to find it."

He wanted me to do *accounting*? I was so stunned, you could've blown me over with a feather. Of all the depraved things I'd imagined him forcing me to do...

"You expect me to do it here? This kind of review could take weeks."

"You have..." He grabbed my wrist and gently turned it over to look at my watch. "Two hours and fifteen minutes."

I think you'll find you want more time.

He'd played me once again.

"It doesn't work like that."

"You're the one who cut the time in half. Do it or—"

"Or you'll release the tape?" I snapped, unable to keep the frustration from my tone.

His dark eyes flared with mockery. "So *dramatic*... Do it, or you'll have to come back another day to finish."

I huffed out an angry sigh and flopped down on the chair. Bickering was only going to waste time, and I didn't want to be here a minute longer than we'd agreed.

Besides...he was giving me access to his books!

I pushed closer to the computer and started to click through the documents. As soon as he left the room, I'd take pictures of as much of it as I could to review later.

Like he was reading my mind, he held out a hand. "Phone."

I rolled my eyes and gave it to him. It had given me the illusion of safety, but I'd have to be in mortal peril before I called someone for help and was forced to explain what I'd been doing there. My blackmailer was dangerous, but I was useless to him dead.

It took me a little while to get my bearings with all the documents, since much of the information was hidden. It was a giant mess of a data dump and included a vast number of transactions.

Was he an art dealer? An arms dealer? Some kind of fixer?

Everything was labeled with a numeric code, so there were no personal names or business names, nothing I could use

against him. Of course, he'd be too clever for that. I'd have to be smarter.

He'd moved to the seating area, but I could feel him watching me from across the room. I looked up to find him sprawled almost exactly like he'd been in the boathouse, assessing me with those predatory eyes.

"Are you planning to watch me the whole time?"

He stretched, drawing my eyes to the wiry definition of his abs. "Of course not. I'm far too busy and important for that."

"Then why are you still watching me?"

"Because I can. Is it distracting?"

Fuck yes, it's distracting! He had all the power in this situation, and I hated it.

I kept scrolling through records, exporting things to a clean spreadsheet for comparison, until he stood abruptly.

"If you'll excuse me, I need to get dressed before my meetings start." He said it with a teasing, superior air that made me wonder just what kind of meetings he'd be taking.

I couldn't tear my eyes from him as he strode across the room, parading his physique in those stupid sweatpants: His lean waist that dipped into a V of muscle at his hips. The outline of his package. The rounded shape of his ass. It was obscene how revealing a simple pair of sweatpants could be. Just as he was about to leave, he looked up and gave me a tiny wink that told me he knew I'd been watching...and that I appreciated the view.

Damn him.

When he shut the door, I sat there being eaten alive by the temptation to snoop. There was no way he didn't have cameras

in here. He'd probably left on purpose just so he could humiliate me by showing me the snooping footage later.

Fuck that. Not this time, asshole. I'm going to beat you at your own game.

10

lost myself in the trail of money, using every trick of forensic accounting I could come up with until I finally started to discover what I was looking for. He'd simply instructed me to find the discrepancy, but one issue led straight to another until I found a trail of breadcrumbs to follow.*

I heard the office door open and close, but I managed to keep my eyes glued to the screen until he came into my peripheral vision. I'd taken *getting dressed for meetings* to mean he'd be putting on a suit. Instead, he stood there in a pair of leather pants and biker boots. He'd pulled his hair back into a high bun and wore just a trace of eyeliner that made the black of his eyes seem ancient and omniscient. A pair of dangly silver earrings hung from his ears, and an intricate black necklace hung all the way down to his navel. It shifted on his chest and stomach every time he moved, drawing my eye there.

* BURY A FRIEND—Billie Eilish

"Are you allergic to wearing a shirt?"

These pants were cut even lower than his sweatpants, and the line of muscle that led down into them was impossible not to follow. I tore my eyes away and looked up to find him smirking.

"People try to use shame as a weapon; I turn it back on them. Someone goes to the effort of wearing a suit, and I don't even bother with a shirt—who do you think has the power in that situation?"

"So, you do it to deliberately make people uncomfortable? That tracks."

He opened his mouth to respond, but the door thumped open, and a man the size of a giant charged in. He looked six and a half feet tall and *thick*, with a short beard and shaggy dark hair that was shaved on the sides.

And he was pissed.

On instinct, I jumped up from the chair and moved to the corner, putting more furniture between us. He glanced in my direction and paused like he didn't want to scare me, but then he continued his advance on my blackmailer.

"Did you fuck her?" the giant growled in the deepest voice I'd ever heard.

The devious bastard calmly stood his ground. "Did I fuck whom, Azrael?"

He's seriously called Azrael?

"Don't play bullshit games with me. Styx. Did you fuck her?" The menace in Azrael's tone should've had the other guy cowering if he had any sense.

"No," my blackmailer said simply.

Azrael reeled back, but his expression was disbelieving. "Come on, Reaper. I saw the bruises."

Reaper! His name is Reaper? *A code name in their organization, maybe? Also...what the fuck? Reaper beat a woman?*

Reaper reclaimed his place on the couch, looking unconcerned. "She's a little pain slut. The impact play was entirely consensual."

He bruised someone because she wanted it?

Azrael pointed a finger. "Don't fucking touch her again." He turned to leave.

Reaper's smirk had a vicious edge. "You're lucky it was me she came to."

Azrael whipped back around, his hands clenched into fists. "What's that supposed to mean?"

Reaper was still perfectly calm, even though, from where I was standing, it looked like he was a hairbreadth away from being crushed beneath Azrael's massive fists. "If you don't give her what she wants, she's going to look for it elsewhere."

Azrael raked a hand through his hair, and all the angry energy seemed to drain from him. His voice was gravelly. "She's...been through some shit. She doesn't talk about it, but I know enough."

"And you think treating her like she's going to break is the answer? She wants to feel normal. Wanted. She wants it with you. You're a bastard if you won't give her that."

My jaw almost dropped at the desperate look on Reaper's face and the intensity in his voice. He cared about these people, and he was letting me see it. There had to be an angle.

Azrael just nodded once, then looked at me. "Is that Juliet Bryson?"

Fuck!

I hugged shaking arms around myself like I could somehow hide my identity now.

Reaper reclined back with his arms folded above his head. "Yes."

Azrael frowned at the laptop on the desk. "And is that…?"

"Yes."

Azrael shook his head slowly. "You're a real fuckin' piece of work."

It was said with a mix of fondness and disgust. Evidently, he didn't love Reaper giving me access to his books.

"So I'm told. Is that all?" Reaper sounded bored.

"No. Grim's waiting."

What the hell have I stumbled into where these are seriously their names?

Reaper made a graceful gesture with his fingers. "Tell the traitor to come in."

Azrael left and was replaced by a guy who was built more like Reaper but a little bulkier. He at least had deigned to put on a black T-shirt that matched his shoulder-length dark hair and his black pants. His eyes were the palest blue I'd ever seen, which gave him an otherworldly quality. If Reaper was sex incarnate, this guy was more like death incarnate. I wouldn't want to be left in a room alone with him. He creeped me the hell out.

Reaper tilted his head. "You couldn't have warned me Az was out for blood?"

Grim's expression remained stony. "Told you what would happen if you meddled." His eerie eyes flicked to me, then back to Reaper. "The candidates are here."

11

andidates for what? I was becoming more and more convinced this was some kind of bizarre cult. Reaper certainly
had all the magnetism of a cult leader.*

He clapped once like he was pleased. "Ah, perfect. Start
sending them in."

Grim left the room, and my breathing returned to normal.
I made my way back to the desk and sat in front of the computer. After a few deep breaths, I refocused on the screen. I'd
complained about Reaper sitting there while I was working, but
now I hoped he stayed just so I got an answer as to who the hell
the candidates were.

When nothing happened and the silence dragged out, I asked,
"Are you in some kind of death cult?" His eyes widened in mocking
question like he had no idea what I was talking about. "Reaper,
Grim, Styx, Azrael. You've got a bit of a death theme going there."

* CONDITIONS OF MY PAROLE—Puscifer

"Ah, that…" He nodded knowingly. "My organization is called Petite Mort."

My cheeks flushed. Petite mort, the French concept of an orgasm being like a *little death*.

So an…orgasm cult then?

There was absolutely no way I was asking that aloud.

He smirked like he knew where my thoughts had gone. "You're *so close*, darling. Let me know when you figure it out…"

A tentative knock at the door saved me from embarrassing myself further.

"Enter," Reaper called without getting up from the couch.

A stunning woman with chin-length purple hair stepped in, looked between us, then took a few more steps toward the seating area. She oozed confidence and had every right to. She was voluptuous and pretty at the same time.

"I'm Peg."

I tucked my chin, suddenly cognizant of the fact I was easily recognizable and somewhere I wasn't supposed to be. It wouldn't have mattered. She had eyes only for Reaper.

He fixed her with his mesmerizing stare. "Impress me, Peg."

The charged vibe between them made me want to leave the room, but I sat glued to my chair, no longer even pretending to work. I was a different kind of nervous now where I felt out of my depth, like I was supposed to look away, but I couldn't.

Peg started to peel off her strapless dress in a slow, sensual show, but Reaper held up a hand. "Hang on for a second, love." He turned toward me. "Would you prefer to work in another

room while I'm conducting interviews? Wouldn't want to distract you."

And miss the chance to figure out what the fuck was going on here? "I'm fine." I said it too quickly and wanted to cringe.

Reaper shrugged. "Let me know if you change your mind."

He gestured for Peg to continue, and she slid her dress the rest of the way off, revealing that all she had on under it was a minuscule thong. As she stripped that off, she turned around so that when she bent over, Reaper was offered an unobstructed view of her most intimate parts.

She stood there in nothing but a pair of heels without the slightest hint of insecurity. To be fair, she didn't really have anything to be insecure about. She had sun-kissed copper skin and generous soft curves that probably made people's mouths water. Her full breasts were tipped with perfect little brown nipples, and the piercings looked like invitations to touch.

She's completely naked! Has no idea who I am or why I'm here. This has to be a cult. What the fuck have I stumbled into, and are they going to let me leave?

Reaper's expression didn't change. He just sat there expectantly until it was clear getting naked was her party trick to impress him.

After a long pause, he sat forward, bracing his elbows on his knees. "That's it?"

She straightened and nodded uncertainly, crossing her arms over her breasts.

Mother of god. I'd be mortified if I stripped naked and a man's response was, That's it?

His laugh was dark and menacing. "Get on all fours." When she didn't immediately move, he snapped his fingers, and she dropped to the ground in front of his chair.

I was sure he was going to spank her or fuck her or something. From the look on her face, he could've done whatever he wanted, and she would've enthusiastically complied. I was *transfixed*, drunk on the anticipation.

But all he did was prop his boots up on her back. "You do make a very pretty footrest," he purred.

He'd just called her a piece of furniture, and still she glowed at the compliment, absolute awe on her face.

"Next," he called loudly.

He just left her there as a footrest. She couldn't have looked more deeply content.

Oh shit. The next person is going to come in and not only potentially recognize me, but they're going to tell people I was part of...whatever that is.

I shifted lower in my chair and angled my face away from the door, like that was going to do anything to help.

Reaper waved a hand in my direction. "You can relax, darling. No one here will breathe a word about you. They've all been vetted and signed NDAs, but more importantly, they know I'd destroy them if they did."

Even though I didn't trust him, I had no doubt he could follow through on that threat.

I stared blankly at the computer in front of me for a second. I'd completely forgotten my task. The bastard was probably doing this on purpose so I'd run out of time and have to come back.

Not happening.

I threw myself into the numbers, not looking up when the next candidate came in. Not even when Reaper said, "Impress me, Acacia."

Those words were going to haunt me long after I left. What would I do if I stood in her shoes? As a command, it was devastatingly effective at making the recipient feel small. The very nature of it made me second-guess whether anything about me could be enough to impress this man. I certainly lacked the kind of skills he seemed to be looking for...

I kept my eyes on the screen when she moved around...and when she started to make obscene noises. It was only when she lay down on the desk I was working on and brought herself to a screaming, back-arching orgasm that I lost it and looked up to find a very beautiful, very naked white woman. Evidently, no one kept their clothes on long around this man.

She'd barely stopped writhing when he said, "Absolutely not. Next!"

I looked at him and must've had confusion stamped comically on my face because he stage-whispered, "Nothing impressive about a fake orgasm. I can always tell."

I blinked in surprise and looked back at the numbers, determined not to get sucked into the next candidate's antics.

I made it through two more candidates without tearing my eyes from the computer screen for more than a few stolen glances. One tied the footstool woman up, and the other sounded like they might've been a guy. I didn't know exactly what they were doing, but the bound footstool woman sounded like she came. It

seemed like they all knew one another somehow. Not that I was listening as intently as I was *not looking* or anything.

The next woman who entered the room spoke before Reaper did. "I think we both already know I can impress you, baby."

He huffed a laugh. "You certainly aren't impressing me right now. You think the process doesn't apply to you because we fucked? The sex wasn't that good, love."

Her heels clicked on the floor as she sashayed her way over to him.

The metal snap of a purse sounded, followed by "May I?"

My fingers froze on the keyboard when a zipper being pulled down broke the silence. There was some shuffling, and then, out of my peripheral vision, I could see she was doing something with a thin white cord.

She gave a satisfied chuckle. "You can say you're not impressed, baby...but your cock says otherwise."

I will not look at his penis. I will not look at his penis.

He was watching me. I could feel him watching *me* while someone else was touching him intimately.

I met his eyes first, and they dared me to look down, challenged me to stop being so afraid.

He didn't speak, but I swore I could hear what he was saying with that look: *It's just a body, darling.*

I let my eyes slide down his torso until I saw what she was doing with the cord. His erect cock was out. Even using that word in my mind felt wicked, but to use anything less sexual to describe what I was seeing would be inaccurate. She'd rapidly crisscrossed the cord around his cock into something that looked

more like erotic art than bondage. Even if he wasn't impressed, I was.

And not just with her handiwork. I'd seen cocks in porn before, but seeing his in real life had me shifting in my chair. It was thick and rock-hard beneath the cord. I was flustered and hot and inexplicably frustrated. I wanted to banish the siren who was tying him up—and the woman who still rested at his feet—so I could toss all reason to the wind and climb on top of him.

They were on their knees to serve him...but he was looking at me.

He snapped his fingers. "Thank you, Kenzie. We'll let you know."

She huffed and released his cock more quickly than she'd tied it. Then she stormed from the room.

"You too, Peg," he said far more gently, and the other woman scrambled out of the office obediently.

The trance broken, I looked back at my screen and pretended that moment hadn't just happened.

The next woman who came into the room had such an intense presence, it was like I was compelled to look at her. She was a tall, curvy Asian woman with chin-length black hair and an imperious air about her. Even the click of her heels on the floor was assertive, and the way she looked down her nose at Reaper made me want to laugh delightedly. What would it be like to not be intimidated by him?

"Impress me," Reaper drawled.

"Are you fucking kidding me, you sniveling little shit?" My jaw fell open, but she crossed her arms and continued. "You like

to sit on your throne feeling all high and mighty, but don't think for a second I couldn't rip you down from it and toss you back into the gutter where you belong."

Reaper groaned like she'd done something intensely erotic, a sound that would've made my knees wobbly if I'd been standing, then let his head collapse back onto the couch. "God, you're good. No other Domme can hold a candle to you, love."

"Don't forget it."

He grinned lazily. "Consider me impressed."

She arched a delicate eyebrow. "We both know I'm not here for your stupid little open call."

"Oh?" He sat up, focusing on her more intently. It was clear he knew exactly what she was going to say, but he was making her say it anyway. No matter what she'd just said about tearing him off his throne, he seemed to be the one in power in this relationship.

"You ever lay a hand on one of my subs again without my permission, and we'll no longer be doing business together."

He steepled his fingers, still the picture of calm. I wanted to know what it took to rattle him, to shake this infinitely relaxed demeanor. "As I mentioned to your brother, it was entirely consensual. Did the lady suggest otherwise?"

Az was her brother? They looked absolutely nothing alike.

She let out a breath. "I don't give a fuck if it was consensual. If I thought you'd cross that line, we wouldn't even be having this discussion. She's under my care—you give me the respect of checking first."

She was terrifying. I wanted to be her when I grew up.

"Noted," Reaper said lightly.

She seemed satisfied with that answer and turned to leave.

"One more thing, O..."

She whipped back around, flashing a look that promised a painful death she'd enjoy drawing out. "What?"

"You're acquainted with Kevin King. Anything you can tell me about him?"

I stiffened at the sudden reminder of what awaited me when I left this bizarre situation.

She tilted her head and took a step back into the room. "Fuck that guy. No idea what he's into, but he...crossed me once." She sounded disgusted by the memory.

He rolled his eyes, turning to address me. "Ophelia doesn't hold grudges—she nurtures them in a goddamned nursery until they grow into little demons just like her. Evidently, she doesn't have anything useful to share with us."

He flicked his fingers, daring to dismiss her.

She squared her shoulders. "You're not sending her to that guy. She's green as the bowl I'm about to smoke to relieve the stress you've caused."

She didn't seem to recognize me. I worked up the nerve to speak up, needing to know if there was something more specific she could tell me about him. I wanted whatever info I could get. "I don't work for him. I have a date with Kevin King later." I tried to sound confident, but the waver in my voice gave me away.

Her expression softened into something resembling pity. "I'd cancel it, sweets. He's a real piece of work. It's not worth the

money when you haven't learned how to handle yourself yet. I can refer some easy regulars your way to get you started."

She thought I was...a sex worker? Was that what she was? Did that mean Reaper was some kind of...pimp? I wasn't about to explain the intricacies of the situation, so it was time to back off. I met her eyes. "Thank you. I'll think about it."

She turned to leave, but at the door, she turned back to me. "If you like being an independent escort, I respect it. But think about working for Reaper. The dispute you just saw was personal. He's..." She looked him up and down, searching for the right words. "Well, he's not a *good* man. But he's the kind of bad you want on your side."

12

We hadn't engaged again after Ophelia left, and I was quickly approaching the end of my three hours. I'd learned his name, or at least his code name, and I was pretty sure I knew what he did for a living, but I hadn't discovered anything I could use against him on this computer. I still had a last-ditch trick up my sleeve, though, if I could distract him long enough to plant it.*

"How would you do it?" Reaper meandered around his office, filing paperwork after his interviews were over.

"What?" I looked up from the computer screen.

He perched on the edge of the desk in front of me. "How would you impress me? I know you've been sitting there thinking about it, wondering what you'd do if you were in their shoes."

He wasn't wrong. Each time one of them had come in, I'd

* POLAR BEAR—Puscifer

wondered what I'd do if faced with the same command. I tried to hold back a smug smile. I might not have bedroom skills, but I was a goddamned wizard with numbers. "You've got three million dollars missing. And I know where it went."

It took him a second to register what I'd said. Then his smile dropped. "Show me."

"They've covered their tracks pretty well, moving it around the accounts first. The way you've got all this accounting segmented out makes it a nightmare to track. It ended up being exactly three mil after the final transfer was completed a few months ago."

I walked him through where the money was moving and the account it was all ending up in.

He opened something on his phone. "What's the account number?"

I read it off.

He was silent for a minute, studying his phone screen. "Interesting..." He scribbled the number down on a sticky note with the initials *TW*.

"Do you know whose account it is?"

He didn't bother to look up. "Of course."

"If I asked, would you tell me?"

He smirked. "For a price."

I laughed. "I wouldn't make another deal with you if my life depended on it."

"I'll remember that," he said, closing files on the laptop and putting it into a case.

"So you're a pimp? That's what you do for a living?" I asked.

He shrugged, perfectly at ease. "I guess you could say that. I facilitate connections."

I crossed my arms, trying to sort through everything I'd just seen and heard. "You *facilitate connections*? Using euphemisms to distance yourself from your affiliation with sex work is a bit cowardly, don't you think?"

He threw his head back and laughed. If someone found a way to bottle his laughter, they could use it as a weapon to bring people to their knees. "Darling, I'm being polite for your sake, but if you'd like me to spell it out...I own a sex club and employ only the finest sex workers to provide the types of erotic services powerful people don't dare to ask for elsewhere."

Nervous excitement thrummed through me at the mention of an illicit sex club. "And that's what they were candidates for?"

He shook his head. "None of them were experienced enough to work for me in that capacity yet. They were auditioning to be the entertainment at my monthly party. First Thursday of every month. I'd invite you, but you'll be otherwise...*engaged*."

I narrowed my eyes. "So you use sex workers to get information?"

"Hardly. Powerful people are only too happy to trade information to gain a favor." He tilted his head back and forth like he was thinking. "That, and as an escort myself, I've fucked half of them...or their wives. Or their wives and their *daughters*." His eyes flashed on the last word.

He was a sex worker too? *He must have a waiting list a mile long.*

He was watching me expectantly like he'd just wound up a toy and released it.

"You're trying to shock me."

He grinned wickedly. "Is it working?"

I wasn't going to give him the satisfaction of blushing and cowering. "What's it like?" It was a completely inappropriate question, but when was I ever going to have another chance to ask it?

"Surely you'll be able to tell me soon enough... Isn't that what you're about to do with Kevin King?"

I gasped. "Are you calling me a whore?"

"My darling, I have nothing but respect for my profession. I hope your marriage brings you the same joy that fucking people for astronomical sums of money brings me. And if it doesn't?" He winked at me. "Well, you have my card."

There was a facetious bitterness to the way he said it that told me he didn't actually want me to hire him.

"How did you first...? Sorry, it's none of my business." I looked away.

He tucked his thumbs into the top of his pants, teasing me with a glimpse of body hair. "What, turn my first trick? Fuck my first john? Stop being so scared you'll use the wrong words." He shrugged. "It's just work."

"So...?"

He looked up like he was searching for the memory. "This older guy wouldn't take no for an answer, so I joked that he'd have to pay me. Then he offered me enough to live on for months in exchange for one night."

I studied his expression. "How did you feel afterward?"

"You mean did I hate myself because I was now a dirty hooker? Hell no. I felt like a fucking god. In those early days, it was my clients who seemed pathetic to me. I didn't respect them. Hell, I didn't even like most of them. And that was how I discovered my true calling."

"Which is?"

"Kink. Being a Dom. The meaner I was to them, the easier it was to stay hard. And the more they were willing to pay me for the privilege. I know better now—know all about consent and aftercare and the textbook way to do things. But back then I was pissed and raw, and I didn't give a fuck about anyone's feelings. And they loved me for it. Because that's the thing...the textbook version of kink is safe and healthy, but it never quite feels real... I gave them real."

He paused like he was surprised he'd said so much. This was a glimpse into a world I'd probably never get to see again.

"How did you go from that to owning a sex club?"

"I thrived when I started working in a dungeon. But it was too restrained for me, too polite, too controlled. To stay on the right side of the law, there was no sex allowed—no penetration, no exchange of bodily fluids. What's the fucking point if you're going to hold back the good stuff?"

I could only nod in agreement like I had any idea what he meant.

"So I went independent, working for myself for a while until other pros came to me looking for a safe space to push the boundaries. My business partners, Az and Grim, and I found ways to make it safe."

Like blackmailing and manipulating powerful people.

I was so out of my element, I didn't know what to say. The silence dragged out, and with it, my uncertainty grew. My task was done, my time was almost up, and that meant I was about to go and face my real challenge. I couldn't make another mistake with Kevin.

"King thinks I seduced the senator," I blurted.

He stopped what he was doing to look at me quizzically. "And?"

I sighed, surrendering to my mortification. Better now than later. I twisted my fingers together nervously, unable to meet his eyes. "Now he has...expectations. For me to be some kind of ruthless seductress."

I expected him to mock me, but he was still studying me. "And you don't think you are?"

I gave him a sideways look.

He sighed dramatically and hopped down from the desk. "*Fine*, I'll give you sex lessons."

"What? No! That isn't what I was getting at."

He gave me a suggestive smile that made my stomach flip.

"That!" I said, pointing at his stupidly attractive face. "Teach me how to do that."

"How to smile?"

"You walk into a room, and I think about sex. You lean on a doorframe, and I think about sex. You smile like that, and I feel it all the way to my goddamned toes. You have this...magnetism. Teach me that. Or at least the beginner's version of that."

He came toward me, and my breath hitched when I backed

into the desk and realized I had nowhere else to go. He planted a hand on either side of me, leaning into my space to graze his teeth along my earlobe. "Princess, you walk into a room? I think about sex." With his hands on my hips, he lifted me onto the desk, and I instinctively tried to part my knees to let him stand between them, but my dress prevented it. He grabbed the fabric and hiked it up around my hips, and I let him because it meant he could get closer.

His smile was gone, replaced with an intense look of longing. "You bite that full bottom lip, and I think about sliding my cock into your mouth."

I gasped when he jerked my hips forward, rolling my body instinctively against him and the hardness I could feel through his leather pants.

"You gasp like that, and it makes me rock-hard." He planted a tiny kiss on my temple. "Darling, there's nothing to teach you."

I looked up into his eyes, seeing a question there and a tether he'd snap if I only answered it. I panted, feeling wild and desperate for him to simply take what I didn't dare offer.

"For thirty more minutes, I have to do anything you ask," I said softly.

He looked disappointed. "You'd like that, wouldn't you? To do what you want but still tell yourself you didn't have a choice. You want me? Come back when it's not part of a bargain and own it."

Duty and safety and common sense be damned, I needed this with him. I'd spend the rest of my life wondering if I didn't explore it. "I don't know what time I'll be back from my date later, but—"

He looked surprised, but then he swiped a hand across his mouth. "You won't. Be back later that is. He's taking you to Rome and planning to stay for a week. He'll propose before you come home—already has the ring."

I sucked in a breath, feeling like the room had suddenly gone topsy-turvy. So fast—everything was moving so fast! "How do you know these things?"

"You asked me to get you info. What's important is if you go on this date, that's it. The rest of your life is decided."

I laughed bitterly. "It was decided before I was born. I don't have a choice."

"Why? Because of your sister?"

Of course, he knew what my father had threatened. "And a thousand other reasons. If you know my family history so well, how can you even ask that? Do you know what happens to people who defy my father?"

"I defied him." He dropped it like a lead weight between us, indisputable proof that someone could cross Nathaniel Bryson and escape the consequences. "Stay with me."

"It's not that simple." I was his daughter. There was no escaping.

"One day, you're going to learn that it is. Until then, you're wasting my time." He backed away so quickly that my ass slipped off the desk, and I had to scramble to keep myself standing, tugging my dress back down in a losing battle to regain some dignity.

He held out the laptop I'd been working on. "You can return this for me."

I frowned in confusion. "Return it?"

"To Kevin King."

I gasped. "You just had me snoop through his files?"

He poured himself a drink from a liquor cart that he'd pulled out from behind a cabinet door. "I suspected he was bribing someone, and I needed to know who. You got there faster than I would've."

"What will you do with the information?" Had I just accidentally conspired with my future husband's enemy? My future *husband...* I was going to be someone's wife, and no one was going to give me any say in the matter. Would my mother have been able to intervene if she were still alive, or had those always been empty promises, that she'd make sure I got to choose who I married? I was irrationally angry with her, angry she'd left me alone and angry that she might've told me what I wanted to hear, all the while knowing it was a lie.

Reaper smiled wickedly. "I'll make them a better offer."

"Why?"

"Because if King is up to what I think he's up to, I'm going to need help to bring him down. If he's marrying you, he's obviously got political aims, which will only make it easier for him. I'd prefer he didn't succeed."

"Then why did you let me blackmail Macallan to drop the investigation? Why not stop him that way?"

"Because having Kevin King's wife wrapped around my finger is the stuff of wet dreams."

I'd been so mortifyingly naive. I felt something special with Reaper, some inexplicable pull that made me want to be in his arms. From what I'd seen with those interviews, though...so

did everyone else. I wasn't special, and this was all part of some bigger game to him.

"I thought you just told me you wanted me to stay."

His face was beautiful even when his expression was ice-cold. "And you made your choice. Now run along, darling. Mr. King won't like it if you're late."

"What about the remaining twenty-five minutes?"

He didn't bother turning back on his way out of the office. "I got what I needed. Your debt is paid."

On my way out, I braced a hand on one of his shelves, pretending to balance as I adjusted the strap on one of my shoes, but really, it let me place a tiny camera next to his books.

He was fifteen moves ahead of me, but I was swiftly learning his game.

Let's see how you like it when the tables are turned...

13

As soon as I got back into my room, I put my headphones in and pulled up the video feed from the tiny camera I'd left in Reaper's office. It started with me planting the camera, so I scrolled until Reaper returned to his office moments after I left.*

He put his hands on his head and stood still, looking out the window for so long that I checked to make sure the video hadn't frozen.

He suddenly cursed and started pacing, raking his hands through his hair. I'd wondered what it would take to break his cool, and apparently whatever I'd discovered for him in Kevin's books was the answer. Who could Kevin be bribing that would make Reaper this agitated?

He picked up his phone, started to type, then threw it across the room with another curse.

Grim came charging in. "The fuck was that?"

* AS IT WAS—Hozier

Reaper threw his hands in the air. "The fuck do you care?"

"We're business partners, asshole. We had a fucking plan. First, you decided you were gonna be balls deep in Bryson's daughter when he walked in with King. Then you suddenly changed your mind. And now you bring her here without so much as a heads-up?"

I stopped breathing, and I wasn't sure I could take in air without puking. If he'd stuck to his plan, my father and Kevin would've walked in to find us having sex. I'd known it had been a close call, but he'd *intended* for it to happen, had planned it with his business partner. Had Grim been watching the whole thing? It was all too vile to even wrap my head around.

Reaper sat on the couch, back to being completely at ease. "I made the call to leave the daughter in play. It would've been instant gratification, but she'd be useless after that. If we really want to destroy Bryson, it's gonna take the long game."

My father had said Reaper was dangerous, but did he know Reaper and his club were actively plotting against him? The issues with his business, the unrest in his territory...my brother's murder? Had all of it been orchestrated by Reaper? If that was the case, not only had he taken my brother from me, but he was the reason I was being forced to marry King.

Grim poured himself a drink. "Did she find anything?"

"Fuck yeah, she did. Grab my phone, and I'll show you."

"Get your own phone, you lazy shit."

Reaper rose and disappeared off camera to pick it up.

When he spoke again, his tone had changed. "Send Katya up. And Damian."

Grim looked up in surprise. "Reaper, we haven't—"

"*Now.*"

Grim left, and Reaper crossed the room again slowly. He unbuckled his belt and dropped his leather pants so fast, my jaw actually dropped. I was so flustered, I almost slammed my laptop shut, but as he took his cock in his hands and started to stroke it, I couldn't tear my eyes away.

Good god, he's beautiful.

From behind the safety of the screen, I could stare as much as I wanted. He was so lean that when he was naked, it was easy to see the carved muscles on every part of his body. The dip that always caught my eye when he wore low-slung pants drew my eye straight to his cock when he wasn't wearing them. His intriguingly thick cock that I couldn't quite imagine having inside me...and yet I couldn't stop trying to imagine it as I stared at the screen. Every part of his appearance made me want to know more. His scars and his tattoos all had stories I was desperate to hear. I wanted to know what his hair looked like when he first woke up and what his lip ring felt like on every part of me. I wanted to know if the effortlessly sexy way he moved and sat and breathed was a practiced art or just how he was made.

No one should be allowed to have that much sex appeal.

The two people he'd sent for entered the room, and he commanded them to strip and crawl to him.

I should stop watching right now. These people didn't consent to me watching them.

But as they became a tangled, writhing mass of pleasure, my self-control—and my morals—fled in a haze of lust. I'd been on

the receiving end of Reaper's ministrations, but to watch the way he so carefully and masterfully doled out pleasure while remaining in control was mind-numbingly sexy. I was breathing hard, clenching my fists against the urge to touch myself while watching the scene play out before me.

My phone vibrated, yanking me from the filthy, traitorous, unbelievably inappropriate fantasies I was lost in.

Reaper: You're still watching, aren't you, Juliet?

I fast-forwarded from the recorded feed back to the live feed, only to find that the two people were no longer in the room with him, and he'd put his pants back on. He'd moved the camera to the desk in front of him, so I had a close-up as he lounged in his desk chair, staring at the screen with a teasing smirk on his face.

In a fit of rage, I called him and watched on camera as he picked it up with a grin. I snapped, "You set me up! You were going to let my father and King walk in and find us—like that!"

There wasn't a hint of remorse in his honeyed tone. "I'm getting hard again just thinking about it."

I gasped. "What kind of sick son of a bitch does that to someone?"

He huffed a laugh. "From the mouth of a Bryson no less..."

"Leave my family out of this. You didn't even know me! What had I ever done to you to deserve that?"

He sighed into the phone. "If you're waiting for an apology from me, darling, you're going to be disappointed. I'm not sorry. Hell, if you must know, I've been eaten alive by regret that

I stopped. I should've ruined you and taken you home and fucked you until we both forgot you were a Bryson. We could still be in bed right now."

My cheeks flushed because, despite his betrayal, my body responded to the silken invitation in his tone. It was like he really was some kind of mystical being and could control my mind with his voice. It was enraging that I was wildly attracted to such a prick.

I made an incoherent scoffing sound, too outraged to get words out at first. "You don't seem to be having any trouble finding willing bed partners."

Why would he even want someone with no experience? He's still playing games and manipulating me.

I could hear the smug smile in his tone just as plainly as I could see it on his face. "Thank you for noticing. Now stop worrying about things that didn't even happen and come back to me...before you do something foolish like follow Daddy's orders to marry Kevin King."

"King hasn't lied to me or tricked me or tried to ruin me."

He was silent for the span of four of my rapidly pounding heartbeats. "They will *extinguish* you, Juliet. Because they don't really see you."

I gritted my teeth. He hated my father enough to have been plotting to make me collateral damage in his vendetta. He was toying with my feelings, convincing me my father and King were the enemy. How much pleasure would it bring Reaper to turn Nathaniel Bryson's daughter against him? I might've resented my father, but I'd remain loyal to him no matter what this man said.

My whole body was trembling with indignant rage. "You're a monster."

I could practically hear the shrug in his cool tone. "Better a monster than a silly little lamb led to the slaughter."

14

Two days later, I stood in Rome's Galleria Borghese in front of the sculpture I'd told Kevin King about, my every move echoing through the empty gallery. I didn't bother questioning how he'd gotten us private access, without so much as a security guard present, because I knew the answer was money.[*]

Bernini's works of marble were stunning in the soft evening light that let the shadows heighten the drama of each piece. They highlighted the harsh determination on Hades's face when he claimed Persephone as his prize and cast an even more desperate feel to the tears that ran from her cheeks. It was beautiful and frightening and maddening all at once.

Much like Reaper...

No. I absolutely refused to waste another thought on that devious bastard. He'd manipulated my feelings; he'd been plotting to humiliate me the entire time. My father may not have given

* ARSONIST'S LULLABYE—Hozier

me much of a say in matters, and Kevin was using me for his own political aims, but they'd both always been forthright about it. If an alliance with King would strengthen Daddy's position and potentially protect all of us from Reaper, then I'd do whatever it took to make it happen. He'd said my debt was discharged, but if he continued trying to blackmail me, I'd have to figure it out.

Kevin's arms slid around my waist from behind, and I let him pull me gently against his body. I was so unused to affection that it felt strange to let someone hold me whenever they wanted, but it wasn't unpleasant. I was nervous but tried not to let him feel how stiff I was.

"All this art, and it's you I can't take my eyes off," he murmured against my neck.

I squirmed uncomfortably at the praise, and he smiled like my shyness pleased him. He was acting besotted, but he was interested in me for political reasons, not personal ones. Or that was what I'd thought, but now I couldn't tell. My judgment had been so off with Reaper that I was still reeling.

Kevin pulled his arms back and turned me by the shoulders to face him. "I was planning to wait until the end of the week for this, but my mind is already made up, and this feels like the moment." He lowered himself onto one knee and presented me with a diamond ring so massive, I could only stare at it in shock. "Marry me."

If you go on this date, that's it. The rest of your life is decided.

I imagined Reaper's sneer if he could see Kevin so predictably down on one knee. Then I wiped him from my mind again and defiantly said, "Yes."

Kevin slid the massive rock onto my finger and stood to kiss me, sealing a perfectly romantic moment that still felt somehow forced.

"I overlooked you when I thought you were too timid, but then you showed me a spark of that Bryson ruthlessness, and it triggered my hunter's instincts." He backed me into the base of the sculpture, and I waited for someone to come and tell us we couldn't make out against the priceless work of art, but the silence mocked me for thinking the rules applied to Kevin King. "You're exactly the partner I need, Juliet."

It was a word I'd dreamed of far more than *wife—partner*. A word I hadn't quite dared to hope for.

I wanted a man who saw me as his equal, who valued my opinions and not just my ability to decorate his arm. Kevin hadn't wanted me when he thought I was just a pretty object. He'd only taken an interest once I showed some initiative. He was assertive, and I was learning that he'd make most of the decisions when we were out together, but he'd brought me to this gallery purely because I'd mentioned it. Even if the chemistry wasn't there between us, that could come with time.

He twisted the engagement ring back and forth on my finger. "You're already wearing my ring. You belong to me. Are you really going to make me wait until the wedding to be with you?"

I looked down to hide my startled expression. Daddy would expect me to deny Kevin to be sure he couldn't go back on his word. It would be far smarter to make him wait, but maybe this was the best way to move forward and wipe what had happened with Reaper from my mind. I wouldn't still be thinking about him if I were fantasizing about Kevin.

I pulled his head down for another kiss, and against his mouth, I said, "Make me yours, Mr. King."

I felt his smile. Then I let out a tiny squeal when he lifted me so I was perched on the edge of the statue base. He pressed his lips to mine as he tugged my panties off and unzipped his pants.

The minutes that followed were...fine.

My shoulder was grinding against the Cerberus part of the sculpture awkwardly, and I couldn't seem to stop thinking about the fact I was touching something Bernini had touched while I was losing my virginity.

Kevin's fingers dug into the flesh of my thigh, and I flicked my eyes up to where Hades's hand did the same to Persephone, wondering for the thousandth time how Bernini could've made something carved of stone so lifelike.

There was a foreign stretching pressure but no real pain. It was exhilarating to feel Kevin slide into me and know I'd finally shed the brand of being a virgin. I felt a measure of satisfaction when he climaxed quickly because I'd managed to please him my first time.

Afterward, he helped me down, and I was unsteady on my feet, numb with overwhelm at what had just happened. Everything had a surreal quality as he led me to a bathroom. He didn't seem to notice I was completely out of it, which was good. I didn't want him to think I was anything but happy. Before he released my hand, he softly kissed my knuckles just above my engagement ring. "Don't be long, Mrs. King."

I went into the bathroom, and after I'd finished cleaning up, I stared at myself in the mirror. Besides being a little disheveled, I

still looked exactly the same. My pink lipstick was smudged, so I went through the motions of wiping it and taming the curls Kevin had swept out of place with his hands in my hair.

As the adrenaline settled, a hollow feeling slowly sank into the pit of my stomach.

That's it?

After all the years of anticipation, it was…fine.

Demand your own pleasure first, princess.

I'd been engaged for less than an hour, and I was thinking of another man, remembering what he'd done with his mouth.

What he'd done with his mouth when he'd been about to ruin my life by deliberately letting Kevin and my father catch us.

Pleasure and shame had always been tangled for me because I'd been told sex was only for marriage, and now they were inextricably linked. Maybe it was better if my marriage was purely about Kevin's pleasure. My own had only brought me trouble so far. As long as my fiancé was happy, it didn't really matter.

I found him waiting for me outside the bathroom door, and we made our way slowly out of the gallery.

I wanted…something. A hug? Some kind of reassurance. Maybe just to be held while I made sense of it all.

But I couldn't bring myself to ask him for it as he ushered me toward our waiting driver. Surely the other women he'd slept with didn't need to be cuddled like an emotional wreck after sex.

His head of security, a muscular white guy named Eric who wore his clothes just a little too tight, opened the door to the SUV for us. He looked me over and smirked, like he knew exactly what we'd just done.

I tried to think about something concrete. "You mentioned staying all week," I said carefully, stopping to clear my throat because I sounded so shaky. "Do you think we could cut that short by a few days? I need to be back for a work thing by Tuesday."

He beamed at me like I'd made a hilarious joke. "You don't need to stress about working anymore, babe."

My heart pounded faster. "It's really not a stress. I love my job."

His smile fell. "I'm not interested in competing for my wife's time."

The hollow feeling in my stomach dropped into free fall. "You want me to quit my job?"

He tilted his head, looking annoyed now. "Is that a problem?"

I was in dangerous waters, and I needed to get out fast. I was a fool for not anticipating this, given that none of the women in my family had ever maintained their careers after marriage. I pasted a smile onto my face and shrugged. "Of course not. Whatever you think is best."

Eric continued facing out the window in the front passenger seat like he'd done for the whole drive, but he met my eyes in the rearview mirror and smirked again. He was weirdly unnerving.

The driver took us back to the monstrosity of a villa where we were staying on the outskirts of Rome, and I sat in silence as Kevin took care of some work calls along the way. He was a busy man, so I couldn't be mad at him for using the time productively. It just felt like I was an afterthought now that our business was concluded.

When we got to the house, I sat out on one of the patios while

Kevin went inside to finish his calls. It was fully dark by then, but I didn't bother turning a light on. The darkness felt soothing, like I was part of it and no one could see me if I just sat still.

I sipped a glass of wine, trying to stop my mind from spiraling. I was marrying Kevin King. There was no backing out now, and my only option was to make the best of it.

I had sex with Kevin King.

I'm not a virgin anymore. What if he changes his mind before the wedding?

The wine wasn't working. Going in search of a stronger drink would mean leaving the comforting safety of the darkness, where I didn't have to worry about whether I was wearing the correct facial expression.

Kevin had left his cigar box on the table, but cigars made me feel sick. Out on the driveway, I could just make out the glow of a cigarette and the outline of our driver standing against the car, smoking.

When in Rome...

I walked over to him, desperately craving that steadying hit of nicotine. I wanted it so badly, I was ready to beg.

In broken Italian, I managed to explain what I needed, and the kind gentleman delightedly handed me a cigarette from his pack and held up the lighter for me to light it. I was so grateful, I could've wept at his feet, but I gave him a nod of thanks and wandered back over to the patio.

It was the first time I'd smoked since the boathouse. Had it only been a few days since then? Maybe I felt so vulnerable because I was strung out from the emotional roller coaster I'd been on for days.

I set my cigarette on the ashtray to take a quick picture of my engagement ring and send it to my father. He immediately texted me back.

Daddy: Proud of you.

I wasn't ready to unpack finally hearing those words from him now.

I took another drag of the cigarette and sent the picture to the group chat with my sisters.

Jacque: OMG you're getting MARRRIED!!!
Sophia: Show-off.
Sophia: Seriously, tho. Congrats. Quite the catch.

I was still typing a response back when someone smacked my hand so violently that the cigarette and my phone went flying onto the gravel. I lurched from the chair, reaching for a gun I wasn't carrying because Kevin had said it wasn't necessary with his security.

But it was only Kevin himself standing there with a sneer on his face.

He aggressively pointed a finger at me. "Don't you ever let me catch you smoking again."

I shrank in on myself, ashamed I'd upset him so quickly. Smoking was a stupid thing to do, and I knew better.

"I'm so sorry. I won't ever do it again." I hoped he could hear the sincerity in my voice.

He picked up his cigars and stormed off without another word. Movement at the patio door caught my eye, and I turned to find Eric staring at me again. From the way he smiled, I had the feeling he'd been the one to tell Kevin I was smoking. He disappeared into the house.

I sat back down and shivered for what could've been hours but was probably only minutes. I was so alone and so raw. I couldn't talk to my sisters. They'd only worry, and there was nothing they could do to help.

If Kevin didn't want someone timid, why did he make me feel scared to be anything but timid with him?

I thought back to my angry phone call with Reaper, how no matter what he'd said, it had only made me madder. In a twisted way, he made me feel safe to be angry or defiant. I wanted to be that version of myself and not this new version who was even more terrified than usual to put a toe out of line.

In a moment of frustrated angst, I unlocked my phone and sent a text to Reaper.

Me: Not a virgin anymore.

As soon as I'd sent it, I wanted to smack myself. Why would I willingly give him that information?

But what did it even matter when he already had enough to ruin me multiple times over?

Reaper: Are you okay?

I swiped a hand over my face as the darkness spun a little. I couldn't handle kindness from him, not when I knew he always had an ulterior motive and not when there was nothing he could do to help even if we struck a bargain. I didn't need him to be gentle. I needed him to fight with me, to remind me that I was stronger than this.

> **Me**: Why would you ask that?
> **Reaper**: Because you're texting me about it?

Shit.

> **Me**: Maybe I wanted to gloat.

He sent back a short video of him winking, then panning to where a blindfolded man's lips were wrapped around Reaper's cock.

It was jarring and shocking and irrationally erotic...as all things about him were. I'd once looked up the term *pansexual* online after I heard someone say it at a party, and it only truly made sense once I'd met Reaper. He defied labels and boxes, and I was pretty sure he also confused the labels and boxes most people thought they belonged in.

> **Me**: wtf??
> **Reaper**: Sorry, I thought we were gloating about being with other people. Did I do it wrong?

I turned on my phone's flashlight and took a short video winking, then panning to my engagement ring.

Ellipses appeared, then disappeared.

They appeared again, then disappeared.

I held my breath when he started to type a third time.

Reaper: Delete this conversation and my number. Wouldn't want your fiancé to find out about our arrangement.

Me: What arrangement?

Having Kevin King's wife wrapped around my finger is the stuff of wet dreams.

He'd said my debt was discharged, but he must've been planning to use the leverage he had over me to his advantage.

Reaper: I'll be in touch.

A YEAR LATER…

was in the trunk of a car.[*]

It had been a recurring nightmare for me ever since they'd found my brother's body in one, but I tried not to think about that as I got tossed around in complete darkness. I'd climbed in here on purpose after all.

The car jostled over a particularly bad bump, and I nailed myself in the face with my engagement ring. With a diamond that size, it was a wonder I didn't hit it on things more. I switched it to my right hand and turned the stone toward my palm, tucking it in where people wouldn't notice it if I kept my palm down.

I should've left the damned thing at home, but I'd been in too much of a hurry, afraid to miss my chance.

Home.

Was that really how I thought of Kevin's house now? I'd been living there for almost nine months, and it was more of a gilded

cage than a home—a lavish monstrosity where it didn't matter how many rooms there were; I was never truly alone.

I swore the walls watched me when Kevin didn't. And if the walls weren't watching, Eric certainly was.

But Kevin was out of town this weekend, off to his private island for his bachelor party, and he'd taken Eric along. He'd made it clear he expected me to stay home, had left some of his goons to make sure. But I'd managed to pretend I'd gone to my room for the night, and then I'd snuck to the garage and hidden in the trunk before one of his drivers left for the weekend. I'd spent months studying his surveillance systems just to pull it off, and I was still crossing my fingers I hadn't missed something.

I didn't know where I'd end up, so I'd spent weeks studying bus routes and had memorized multiple taxi numbers so I'd be able to get back in a way that wasn't traceable. It was rash and dangerous, a half-cocked plan that could go wrong a thousand different ways, but I needed to know I could do it. When my chance had come, I'd grabbed some cash and made a run for it.

Josh was my unwitting getaway driver. He'd driven me every-where for months, and the only things I knew about him were that he liked dogs and was a Virgo. The former I assumed because he always offered to walk Lola, the dachshund puppy Kevin had given me when I mentioned that I missed seeing my friends. And I only knew he was a Virgo because I'd complimented the sapphire in his pinky ring. He'd told me his mother had given it to him because it was his birthstone.

Josh was sweet. Protective. The kind of guy I might've dated in another life. He was the only one who still met my eyes after

the especially bad days with Kevin. To everyone else it was like I was invisible. It was easier for them to pretend they didn't see.

Kevin didn't like it when I got too friendly with the staff anyway, and I was pretty sure they'd been told not to talk to me more than they needed to in order to perform their jobs. I didn't want to get anyone fired, so I hadn't pushed.

But I was so fucking lonely. All I wanted was one unsupervised visit with my little sister before the wedding, one night of freedom. Kevin had seen to it that I hadn't been alone with her in months, always accompanying me or sending someone from Eric's security team to watch over me.

Watch me was more the truth of it.

I had no idea where we were driving, but that was a problem for later. I'd have to be back before anyone noticed I was gone, or all hell would break loose. I'd deliberately left my phone at home since Kevin always tracked me with it, so I wouldn't even know if they discovered I was missing, not until they caught up with me.

One night. One night to feel like a person again. One night of hugs and movies and uninhibited girl talk. If no one knew, I wouldn't get anyone into trouble.

A year had been enough time to realize King was more dangerous than my father. He was volatile like a volcano that could be triggered by the slightest provocation—or no provocation at all.

I was used to being tightly controlled and watched, but I wasn't used to the casual cruelty that had become a part of my daily life with him. He constantly found new ways to strip away my self-esteem and erode my confidence.

I was always compliant and attentive to him in the bedroom, and I was thankful that was where he was the least cruel. It wasn't usually terrible, but it was an unwelcome burden I had to attend to. He'd never once given any thought to my pleasure. I didn't dare ask because I wasn't even sure I wanted him to touch me in that way.

Surely the novelty would wear off, and he'd begin to take mistresses, if he hadn't already.

We'd been driving for what felt like half an hour when the car made a turn and stopped abruptly. The driver's door opened, then slammed closed. I didn't dare move.

Please don't open the trunk. Please don't open the trunk...

I made myself wait twice as long as I thought I should before I pulled the emergency-release handle to pop the trunk. I peered carefully out of the crack, trying to make sure no one was about to see me emerge.

I climbed out awkwardly, relieved to find there wasn't anyone nearby. It took me a second to get my bearings, but when I did, nervous butterflies fluttered in my stomach.

Josh had come to a biker bar on the outskirts of town, a bar with nothing else around it. I'd never been somewhere this seedy before and had only ever seen bikers on TV. A biker gang was a key component of the shadier side of my father's business, but I only knew that from snatches of overheard conversations. He considered them the low-life, expendable infantry who'd take the fall if there was a failure at that level of their operation. He was deeply insulated from the illegal branches of his dealings, so I'd never been allowed anywhere near people like this.

There didn't appear to be a bus stop nearby, which complicated matters, but I was sure someone at the bar would let me use a phone to call a cab. I just needed to make sure Josh didn't spot me and keep my head down enough not to be recognized.

I looked nothing like the Juliet Bryson anyone had ever seen in public. That Juliet Bryson was the epitome of subtlety and class, always wearing soft pastels and demure clothing tailored not to hug too tightly. Today I'd opted for casual denim cutoff shorts and Reaper's tank top; then, at the last moment, I'd dug Reaper's leather jacket from its hiding place in my closet and pulled it on. I hadn't gotten caught that night; maybe it could bring me luck again.

Reaper hadn't been in touch. It had been a year, and I hadn't heard so much as a whisper from him. But our last conversation had left him as a specter in my life. I waited for a call, an email, a letter...anything. I began to think he was waiting until King and I were married to hatch some kind of nefarious plan. If only that were the only reason I was dreading my wedding day.

As I encountered the first bikers milling about outside, a flare of fear reminded me just how risky this was. I was a public figure they could easily recognize even if I'd attempted to copy Reaper's makeup handiwork, with slightly less dramatic results.

I'd been too scared to practice doing my makeup like this during the hours other people were awake, so I'd waited until the middle of the night and shut myself in my closet to practice once. Kevin didn't like to share a room, so I at least had my own bedroom he visited only when it was convenient for him, but I didn't trust that he didn't have cameras in the bathroom. It

seemed unlikely he'd bother with my closet. The next morning I woke up feeling victorious, like that minuscule act of defiance meant something. It had given me the confidence to study his security system more closely, testing it in small ways to see what he noticed.

When I walked toward the bar, my heart thundered even faster. Kevin was in a completely different time zone, partying with his friends. With any luck, he'd done a bunch of drugs or was too hammered to even think about me. If he assumed I wouldn't leave the house, there was no reason to waste his bachelor party watching me.

Maybe some twisted part of me wanted to get caught. Would he call off the wedding if I disobeyed him? I knew in my bones that there'd be no sending me back to my father in shame. I'd simply become the next victim of the Bryson Curse.

But my instincts told me King wouldn't call it off. He'd be angry, but once he knew I'd just gone to see my sister, he'd calm down enough to see reason. He'd face a scandal too if we called it off two weeks before, and he'd been enjoying making the political rounds with a Bryson on his arm. In this instance, the public interest worked in my favor because they were ravenous for our love story. Parts of our wedding were going to be televised, and no matter how much money he had, Kevin couldn't buy the positive press that came from being with me.

As long as I didn't cause a scandal, he'd still marry me.

I didn't need to worry. Not yet anyway. These men didn't care who I was any more than they cared about the identity of the beers they were holding. I was an object to them.

"Goddamn, look at the legs on that bitch." The muscular man who'd spoken elbowed the one next to him, who bit his fist in response. The second man had a tattoo across his throat that said *Die Free*.

"You here with someone, sweetheart?" He eyed Reaper's jacket.

Who owns you? That's what he was really asking.

"No," I said simply, too worried my voice might tremble with fear if I said more.

Their eyes lit with interest, and the youngest one took a step toward me. I backed up and ran into a wall of a human. When I turned, I found a hulking bearded man who was attractive in a gritty, imposing way. He had salt-and-pepper hair, sharp blue eyes, and broad shoulders. He looked fully capable of tossing me over his shoulder and taking me back to his cave, and he seemed to be considering doing just that as he flicked his eyes from my legs, to the sliver he could see of my breasts, then finally to my face.

"Only one reason a girl like you comes to a place like this." His voice was like a rumble of thunder, and he stood there with the self-assurance of a man who was used to being in charge. The patch on his cut denoted his role as president of the Serpents of Death MC.

Shit. That was the gang that worked for my father. There was no reason for a man like this to care enough about Nathaniel Bryson's middle daughter to recognize me, but it raised the stakes if he did.

The other guys watched us with smiles on their faces, eager

to see me submit meekly to their leader. Like I'd been meekly submitting to Kevin for months.

Fuck that. Not tonight.

"You seem to know an awful lot about me when I don't even know your name. I'm...Julie."

"Thor," he said, and I fought a smile.

Of course your name is Thor.

"I was just about to grab a drink, Thor. Care to join me?" He absolutely didn't need to know I was stranded there and needed to use the phone. Something in my lizard brain screamed at me not to show him weakness.

It was clear I was being viewed as fresh, very available meat. Might as well head in there with the apex predator.

I was so scared, my lower back felt like it was going to spasm from the tension...but I'd *chosen* this. It was the first thing I'd chosen in a very long time.

He put a hand at my back and steered me inside the noisy, filthy bar. It was a huge, sprawling building with rooms off to the side and a large back area that had at least a dozen pool tables. It was dark and loud and uncomfortably crowded...which meant no one had any reason to notice me specifically in there.

Two guys moved out of the way when we got to the bar to make space for us to sit. The bartender dropped what she was doing to come over, but to her, I didn't exist. She looked to Thor and only Thor, who said, "Whiskey."

Two shots appeared in front of us. For a split second, I debated explaining that I didn't drink whiskey but decided it was

* STRANGERS—Portishead

better not to push my luck. I wanted to look like a normal girl...
He was certainly treating me like one. In this situation, a normal
girl would take the drink she was offered.

We clinked our glasses together, and I knocked the shot back,
cringing at the sickly-sweet taste. I choked a little on the cough
I tried to hold back and caught the way a hint of a smirk played
across Thor's face. He immediately signaled for another, and two
more shots were set down in front of us.

I knocked that one back too, beginning to wonder if this was
Thor's idea of foreplay. When he signaled for another, I put my
hand on top of his. "I'm kind of a lightweight. If I don't slow
down, I'll be puking soon."

He grasped the hand I'd touched him with and slid the rock
of my engagement ring around to the top of my hand. "You
married, Julie?" He said it lightly—or as lightly as a man who
sounded like thunder could ever say anything.

Something told me lying to this man was a bad idea. Cunning
intelligence flashed in his glacial-blue eyes, just waiting for me to
slip up.

"Does it matter?"

He shrugged. "Not to me. Not like we haven't seen your type
here before."

The warmth of the back-to-back shots was settling into my
belly and perhaps loosening my tongue. "Oh yeah? What type
is that?" I sounded flirty and unconcerned...which was exactly
how I was beginning to feel.

"Bored housewives with more money than sense, looking for
a good time."

I laughed and took the third shot, feeling more than a little reckless. Liquid courage couldn't hurt at this point.

"I'm not married. Not for another two weeks." I glanced at my watch and realized I was going to have to show my hand a little with Thor. "My phone is dead, and I need to get somewhere. Any chance you could help me call a ride?"

He held out a hand to help me down from the stool. "Got nowhere to be. I'll give you a ride."

Walked right into that one, dipshit.

I automatically took his hand and followed him through the bar as I mentally scrambled for an out. "My fiancé won't like it if I ride with you."

Thor paused and turned back to cock an eyebrow at me. "Is he here?"

I drew a breath to respond but spotted Josh and three of Kevin's enforcers making their way toward us, and I practically shoved Thor in my urgency to get out of there before they saw me. A motorcycle ride with Thor was better than getting caught.

"Thank you for the offer. I'd appreciate a ride," I blurted.

I was in such a frantic rush to get away from Kevin's men that it wasn't until we were already on the road that I realized Thor hadn't asked where I was going before he started driving.

Doesn't matter. We're going toward town, which means closer to Jacque's apartment, and I got away from the immediate threat.

Minutes later, we were flying down an empty road. I clutched Thor's muscular torso as his motorcycle roared under us, and the wind whipped my face. Getting on a bike with some random

dude, who may or may not have been inebriated, was one of my more questionable life decisions, but in that exhilarating moment, I didn't care. I'd escaped.

Thor kept driving until he turned into what looked like a compound with huge gates and barbed wire fences around it.

"Where are we?" I asked when he'd parked and taken my helmet back.

"Clubhouse," he said. Then he grabbed my head and kissed me forcefully.

After nine months of living with Kevin, I was all too used to having to endure the attentions of a man I wasn't interested in. Kevin kissed like I was a possession he expected to please him. Thor kissed like he was trying to take something from me. He held the back of my head so I couldn't pull away, then pillaged my mouth with his tongue, depriving me of the ability to breathe.

When his other hand slid down the front of my top to cup my breast, I managed to thrash out of his hold.

"Come on," he said with a hand at my lower back to guide me toward the building.

I twisted away. "I need to get home. People will be looking for me." I put some force into my tone, daring to challenge him.

People *would be* looking for me if I didn't make it home, but they'd never find me there.

"Didn't ask," he said, grabbing my arm this time and all but dragging me forward.

It was only when the gate to the compound slid closed that it truly sank in how fucked I was.

16

My night had started in a trunk, progressed to a motorcycle ride, then rapidly ended up with me hiding in a bathroom at a motorcycle club with a phone I'd stolen from a man named Thor.*

You wanted an adventure...

Hell, maybe sex with Thor would be fun, a change from what I'd experienced with Kevin. But kissing Thor hadn't been fun. If he fucked like he kissed, I might as well be a blow-up doll.

I was in so far over my head, I couldn't see the surface, and it would only get worse if someone recognized me. Was being forced to fuck Thor better than having my fiancé find out where I was?

It was devastating to realize it probably was.

I stared at Thor's phone, trying to think of who I could call. I didn't dare put my sisters at risk by calling them, and I wasn't

* THE HUMBLING RIVER—Puscifer

even sure what they could do to help. One call to my father would probably have Thor returning me safely to one of Daddy's properties, but I didn't have any way of knowing how things stood between them. For all I knew, Thor would deliver a ransom note and hold me prisoner, and all hell would break loose. Or worse, it was possible that the Serpents of Death had grown tired of being my father's *expendable infantry*, and they'd hurt me to punish him. I could call Josh, but he'd either have to tell Kevin what was happening, or I'd be putting him at serious risk by forcing him to lie to his employer. I couldn't put my safety above his, not when he'd always been kind to me.

There was another desperate option. Someone whose safety I was significantly less concerned about; someone who hadn't always been kind to me.

I dug through the jacket pockets until I found the card Reaper had left for me the night I'd met him. I started to dial before I could think about all the reasons it was a bad idea.

I was surprised when Reaper came up as a saved contact on Thor's phone as soon as I dialed the number but didn't have time to think about it because he picked up on the second ring. "The fuck are you doing calling us tonight? Do we have a problem?" Reaper's unmistakable sultry tone was seductive even when he sounded angry.

Fuck. Fuck!

Shit…what was his relationship to Thor? Would they both turn on me and call my fiancé to gloat? No, Reaper didn't operate like that. There'd be a price for his help, but he wouldn't rat me out. I was only useful to him if I married Kevin.

"*Thor*," he barked when I didn't respond.

"It's Juliet Bryson," I whispered, hoping he'd be able to hear me over the loud music in the background wherever he was. "I need a favor."

For an agonizingly long moment, there was only that heavy bass thumping at half the speed of my heart, as though it were mocking me with its languorous rhythm.

"Care to tell me why you're calling me from Thor's phone, princess?" His tone was tight and even angrier.

"I...went out. Ended up at the biker bar off Forty-Seventh. Long story short, I took a motorcycle ride with Thor, and he brought me back to his clubhouse. I need to get out of here, but he's...insistent that I stay."

"I take it your fiancé doesn't know you *went out*?"

I exhaled slowly, audibly shaking. "No. I just...I don't have anyone else I can call."

He cursed, but it sounded far away, like he'd put the phone down to do it. "Does Thor know who you are?"

"I don't think so."

He let out a breath. "Listen to me very carefully, Juliet, because if you don't play this right, you'll get us both killed. The risks of coming to get you tonight are astronomical. The price for this favor will be too. But we have to get out of there in one piece first." There was no longer music behind him, and an engine hummed to life in the background. He was on his way.

It was a bitter pill to need to be rescued by a man who'd set out to ruin me and ended up blackmailing me, but I almost cried

with relief. I'd been holding it together, trying not to admit how scared I was.

"The only way this works is if he believes you're mine. So you better be comfortable acting like you're mine...and like you're fucking happy about being mine. If you've got any reservations about that, tell me now. I'll come up with another solution, but it'll take time."

"Whatever it takes. But he knows I'm engaged. If someone recognizes me, they're going to know it's not to you."

"Darling, no one in my world would think marriage could stop you from being mine." His engine revved like he was flooring it.

"How long will you be?"

"Ten minutes, maybe twelve. Stall."

"Thank you," I said softly.

He laughed. "Let's see if you're still thanking me after this little charade..."

17

made it eight minutes hiding in the bathroom.*

It would've been fine if Thor hadn't noticed his phone was missing. The bathroom door didn't lock, so he wrenched it open and found me holding his phone. I should've hidden it in the cabinet or something, but it felt like my lifeline, and I didn't want to let it go.

He yanked me up by the arm, and I yelped. "The fuck are you doing in here with my phone?"

"I told you mine was dead, and I need to get home." My voice was high and pleading; all pretenses of being brave had abandoned me.

He dragged me into the front room and tossed me onto a couch. "You a fuckin' cop?"

"No! I just really need to get home."

He smiled cruelly. "So you called your fiancé to come pick you up? How do you think that's gonna go?"

* HORIZONS—Puscifer

"No, not my fiancé! I belong to someone else."

Skepticism marked every line of his face, threatening violence if I didn't come up with a better answer fast. He snatched me by the jaw. "Doesn't matter, darlin'. He ain't here, is he?"

There was a commotion outside, but Thor didn't seem to notice. Not until Reaper strode through the front doors with six bikers trailing him.

"Theodore," Reaper barked as he sauntered in, shirtless as usual but wearing an outfit that would've made Jareth the Goblin King proud. He'd left his long hair unbound, and it cascaded over his shoulders like an eighties romance heroine's locks. His knee-length black kilt hung so low on his hips, it was obscene. He wore biker boots and leather gloves that he slowly pulled off one finger at a time and tucked into the back of his waistband. His painted black fingernails, heavy eyeliner, flowing hair, and jewelry—from his lip ring to his thumb ring to the silver torque that adorned his bare chest above his nipple rings—gave him a feminine edge that clashed with Thor's overblown masculinity. "I see you've found my errant brat."

Thor rounded on him. "It's Thor, motherfucker."

Reaper's eyes flashed with amusement. "Ah. I see you've learned my real name too. I did rather enjoy fucking your mother. Celia, right?"

Thor roared and took a swing at Reaper, who leaned left so fast, it looked like Thor's fist was moving in slow motion as it swung harmlessly past Reaper's head. Then he knocked Thor on his ass with an efficient sweeping kick that hooked behind Thor's knee.

It shouldn't have been surprising—he'd always had the lethal vibe of someone who could handle himself in a fight, but I'd assumed it was from behind the barrel of a gun.

The six bikers pulled their weapons and aimed them at Reaper, who casually reached down to help Thor up. I didn't miss that he'd immediately drawn all the attention and violence from me to himself.

Reaper's gaze raked up my bare legs, cocking an eyebrow at the jacket before turning back to Thor. "You kept something of mine out of trouble tonight, and you have my thanks. I've come to retrieve her. Let's not blow our deal over a slut acting out."

Thor gestured for his buddies to lower their weapons and fuck off, leaving the three of us alone. He assessed us with those icy eyes that saw far too much. Why couldn't he have been a dumb biker?

"Known you a long time, Reaper." He stroked a hand along his beard thoughtfully. "Never known you to be possessive about a partner."

"This one is different," Reaper said with quiet menace.

Thor nodded. "I'll tell you what I think is happening here. I think you sent her to get dirt on me so that if this deal goes south, I take the fall for it. And I don't appreciate being set up."

Oh shit, this looks bad. That was precisely the kind of thing Reaper would do, given his ability to get leverage on literally everyone.

Reaper smiled and shook his head like it was just too funny. "You ever known me to be this sloppy, Thor? If I wanted to set you up—and I don't—you'd never know it happened."

Can confirm.

Thor walked to the fridge. "Have a beer with me then. If we're gonna trust each other, I should get to know your girl better. If she's important enough to rush over here for, she must mean a lot to you..."

He didn't believe our story, not for a second. If we couldn't make him believe we were together, we weren't going to make it out of here.

Reaper turned a look on me that was full of barely repressed rage. "I'm about done with her thinking she can act out and get what she wants. If she doesn't remind me why she's worth the trouble real quick, I might be leaving her here with you after all."

His threat was clear. He'd leave me there rather than go down with me if it came to it.

I folded my arms over my chest and raised my chin. "Maybe I got tired of waiting for you."

You want a brat? I'll show you a brat.

Delighted surprise lit Reaper's face, like he'd expected me to take the obvious path of fawning over him. "What's the matter, darling...your fiancé isn't satisfying you?"

Oh. We're not even pretending...

"I'm not going to talk about him with you."

Thor cleared his throat. "I've got a call to make. I'll give you two a minute."

As soon as Thor left the room, I opened my mouth to explain, but Reaper snatched me to him and obliterated every thought from my brain with a kiss. It was angry and rough, but I clung desperately to him, savoring the feel of his bare shoulders beneath my fingertips and his hands gripping my ass.

Against my ear he whispered, "He's trying to trap us. Don't say a fucking word." I felt his smile against my neck. "Unless it's *please...*or *more...*"

More.

Please.

Please make me feel alive again.

I was up against his bare chest, and all I could think about was how much I needed to touch him. All of him. I wanted to trace my fingers over the tattoos that covered his collarbone, then trail them down his abs.

What's stopping you?

It was the most liberating thing I'd ever experienced, to realize that while we were in this room, the rules didn't apply, and I didn't have to feel guilt or shame for it later. I could still hate him the minute we walked out, but right this second, our survival depended on me wanting him.

And, *god*, did I want him.

One of his big hands slid up and under my shirt, growling when he discovered there was nothing under it. "What the *fuck* were you playing at tonight?"

He rubbed my breast, then found my nipple, and I arched into his touch, gasping when he pinched it gently between his fingers. He watched me with a challenge in his dark eyes, like he was just waiting for me to stop him.

He didn't seem to understand that I needed him so badly, I could barely breathe. I gripped the wrist of the hand he had under my shirt, and he tilted his head like he thought I was going to pull it away. And I did...only to guide it down the front of my shorts.

"More," I breathed, and he obliged instantly. He unbuttoned my shorts with his other hand, giving him easy access to where I needed him.

When he ground a knuckle over my clit, the sound that came from my throat was as undignified as it was involuntary. He parted my folds, and I moved against him, pushing the tip of his finger inside me.

"Please," I begged, and he thrust a little deeper. "*More.*"

He closed his eyes and locked his jaw. "*Christ*, Juliet."

Did he know he'd just said my real name?

I forgot I even had a name when he twisted his hand to curl his fingers inside me at the same time as he pushed his other hand into my shorts to roll his thumb over my clit, moving faster when my breath stuttered. He dragged the pleasure from me relentlessly, finding the sensations that made me buck and gasp, then pushing me to the brink as he repeated them.

He claimed my mouth again, and I came apart at the seams, crying out as an orgasm rocked through me. He coaxed out every last wave of pleasure like he was wringing them from my body, then broke the kiss to meet my eyes. He looked as surprised as I felt, and then a line formed between his brows as he studied me.

To my mortification, tears started to burn my eyes; it was all just too much: The desperation and nerves of daring to defy Kevin. The terror of being caught by Thor. The confusing relief of being saved by my enemy. The bone-shattering release in Reaper's arms. Being touched when I actually wanted to be touched. Trust that didn't make sense. It was like the dam of my self-control had crumbled, and I teetered on the edge of falling apart.

"Don't you dare," he growled, kissing me again like he could chase away all my feelings that easily. Because he could.

His first kiss had been angry and rough, but this one was just fraught with intensity. He used his teeth and his tongue and his hands to pull me back into the moment where nothing else mattered but him.

"It's not polite to stare," he said, pulling back to glare at Thor.

I turned in Reaper's arms, but he held me against him possessively, idly stroking his fingers along my bare hip bone, not bothering to button my shorts back up.

Had Thor just seen me come?

It was obvious from where I was standing that he was hard, and I didn't understand why, but the knowledge he'd been watching only made me wetter. I wanted him to see.

I pushed back against Reaper's hardness behind me, and the look on Thor's face was ravenous. He licked his lips like a wolf about to take down his prey.

Reaper nipped the side of my neck. "Are you eye fucking Thor, brat?"

The charge of the room had shifted. Thor didn't look like he wanted to kill us. He looked like he wanted to join us.

I lifted a shoulder and let it fall. "What are you going to do about it if I am?"

Thor's mouth hitched into a brief smirk, like he wasn't used to seeing anyone talk back to Reaper. "You in a sharing mood, brother? Got a few ideas about how to put a mouthy brat in her place."

Reaper's hand on my hip tensed, though not enough that Thor would've noticed. "I'd normally suggest you ask the lady,

but the lady isn't allowed to make any more decisions this evening, given her questionable choices up to this point." I held my breath, waiting for his answer. I might've wanted Thor to watch, but I certainly didn't want to discover his idea of a punishment. "She doesn't put me in a sharing mood."

Thor covered his flash of irritation with a shrug. "Then get her the fuck out of here. She's caused enough trouble."

Reaper wove his fingers into mine and tugged me toward the door. He was the picture of nonchalance as he tipped a nonexistent hat at the bikers who were waiting outside.

As soon as we got in his vehicle, the charade would be over. I had to go back to remembering all the reasons I hated him, and part of me couldn't fathom shutting the door on everything we'd just unleashed again.

He sauntered toward his Range Rover, but just as we reached it, he pushed me against the side and claimed a quick but thorough kiss, a possessive kiss, with one hand on my ass and the other tangling into the hair on the back of my head.

"There will be a price for this," he murmured when he broke away.

I breathed a sigh and climbed into the passenger seat when he opened the door for me. "There always is with you."

18

"Did he touch you?" Reaper said it so softly, it was barely more than a whisper, but I still flinched. I'd grown so used to Kevin's volatility that I'd been bracing for Reaper to explode.*

"No," I said tightly. "You got there just in time. Thank you."

He nodded, rigid with tension. "Thank me by explaining how the fuck you ended up there tonight."

If I told him the truth, I'd have to own up to how right he'd been about Kevin, and he'd know how pathetic I was. He'd know I'd let myself get so desperate that I'd fled my fiancé's house in the trunk of a car and opted to be abducted by the leader of a biker gang rather than be caught. He'd know exactly how much trouble I'd be in if I didn't get home soon, and he could possibly use that against me. He'd pulled me out of the frying pan, but that didn't mean I was safe from the fire yet.

* LONELY BOY—The Black Keys

Not a fucking chance I was giving him any of that information.

"Kevin's at his bachelor party," I said, as though that explained it.

"I'm aware," Reaper said calmly.

I scoffed. "Why are you asking questions if you already know everything?"

He flashed a tight smile. "You won't distract me by being a brat. Answer the question."

"It was my bachelorette party."

He caught his lip ring between his teeth. "Uh-huh. Where were your sisters?"

I sighed heavily. "I said I'd meet them after. We're too recognizable together. It would actually be great if you could just take me to Jacque's place now."

It was his turn to scoff. "And lead the Serpents of Death who're following us straight there?"

I whipped around, and sure enough, I could see the lights of at least two motorcycles tailing us. "Shit! No, don't lead them there. Where are you going then?"

He looked at me like I was being obtuse. "Back to my party."

I shook my head roughly. "The last thing I need right now is to end up in a tabloid for attending a sex party."

He huffed a laugh. "You won't be anywhere close to the most famous person there. My parties are...discreet."

I hadn't been able to find a shred of information about them, despite plenty of covert digging. But that didn't seem like enough reassurance. "Who else will be there?"

He squeezed my knee gently, and the casual touch caught

me completely off guard. "It wouldn't be very discreet if I told you."

I looked out the window, resisting the urge to clutch his hand to keep it on my knee. I was so shaken, I craved the contact. How the hell was this night going to end now that it had gone this far off the rails?

He lifted his hand to open the glove box and pulled out a pack of cigarettes, the exact kind I'd smoked in the boathouse. Once he'd lit one, he offered it to me.

I instinctively reached for it, then remembered Kevin's edict and shook my head. "I don't smoke anymore." As though smoking were worse than any of his other rules I'd broken tonight.

Reaper opened the window, took a drag, and exhaled deeply. "Neither do I. Hold your hand out."

I had an instinctive flare of fear, thinking he meant to burn me with it, and I jerked away from him. He looked from me to the road and back again incredulously. He was too perceptive. If he examined my reaction too closely, he was going to learn things I wanted to keep private.

I held my hand out like he'd asked, and it shook violently.

"Take the damn cigarette, Juliet."

Two deep drags, and I stopped being at risk of sobbing and pouring my heart out to a man who'd comfort me one moment and use it against me the next.

One more, and I trusted my ability to reason out of this clusterfuck.

Reaper reached over and tugged my wrist up so he could take a drag. "Good girl."

Was he praising me for holding his cigarette or for getting it together? Didn't matter—the low purr soothed me as much as the cigarette.

He glanced at me sideways. "You were telling me a bullshit story about a bachelorette party... Do you want to finish it or spare us both and get to the part where you tell me the truth?"

I tensed, wondering what I could say. "It was a solo bachelorette party. A last night of freedom. That's the truth."

And it was.

He drummed his fingers on the steering wheel, and his tone suddenly turned lethal. "You expect me to believe it's just a coincidence you ended up at that bar and then on the back of that bike? On tonight of all nights. Tell me the truth right now, or you're going to be introducing Jacque to Thor in a few minutes."

God damn it, I had to tell him more of the truth, or he wasn't going to buy this.

I was shaking again, livid that he'd bring my sister into this. "It's not like I picked where I was going! I got there in the trunk of a car, for fuck's sake!"

He jerked his head to look at me. "Explain."

I cringed, knowing exactly how pathetic I was about to sound. "Kevin...doesn't like it when I go out, so I snuck out with one of his men." He could know that much without knowing how bad it was. Let him think I'd just been trying to cheat without getting caught. "I'm getting married in two weeks, and I didn't want to only have sex with one person for the rest of my life. I wanted an anonymous fling before becoming someone's wife."

"So you're a fucking defiant brat for him too. At least you're

consistent." His jaw tensed. "And Thor. *Thor* was going to be your anonymous fling?"

I shrugged nonchalantly like I'd been in any way a willing participant in that scenario. "A big bad biker seemed like an adventure until he started getting rough."

He slammed on the brakes hard enough that the seat belt hurt me. "If you're really that stupid, I'm taking you back to the big bad bikers."

"Fuck you."

He punched the steering wheel, uncharacteristically worked up before going ice-cold again. "Yeah. That would've been a much better solution. You want sex, Juliet? All you had to do was call me."

I had no way of calling you. Kevin monitors my phone too closely for that.

Like I hadn't thought of calling him on a near-nightly basis since I'd moved in with Kevin—sometimes because I ached with a need to know what sex with Reaper would be like and sometimes because I was achingly lonely.

"I don't want to have sex with you."

Then I'll know what I'm missing, and that might be worse than wondering.

He kept his eyes focused on the road, but his shoulders were tense. "We both know that's a lie. But that's fine. Makes no difference to me. Though you don't seem to understand what could've happened tonight."

Oh, I knew exactly what could've happened, and it was going to haunt my nightmares for a long time.

"Well, it's a good thing you were there to rescue me," I snapped. "The knight in shining armor who plans to claim an astronomical price for his aid. So fucking noble."

He opened his mouth to snap something back, but he closed it and tilted his head. "Wait. You're telling me one of King's men was at Thor's bar tonight? That's how you got there?"

I slowly said, "Four of King's men were there. My driver and three enforcers." Was that information I shouldn't divulge?

He cursed and picked up his phone. As it was ringing, he glanced at me. "You being there had nothing to do with your fiancé? You swear you were there only for a night of freedom?"

What the hell had I gotten tangled up in? "I swear."

The person on the phone must've picked up because Reaper said, "The deal is compromised. King had guys at your bar tonight."

He floored the gas, glancing in the rearview mirror. Thor was yelling on the other end, but it wasn't until I caught "Juliet fucking Bryson" that I realized I hadn't finished causing trouble for the night.

Reaper's tone stayed eerily calm. "She has nothing to do with King's dealings. She made some poor choices this evening, but the two aren't related."

He was quiet for a second. "You don't need to *discuss* it with her. I'm vouching for her. Go near her, and we're going to have a problem." The menace in his tone made me flinch.

He still wasn't looking at me, but that was probably for the best since he was breaking a hundred miles per hour. That, and he would've seen my stunned expression. He was *protecting* me.

He took two quick turns, and I began to recognize that we were approaching his property. "You're having some big feelings, Theodore. She's an asset to me, and that's as much as you need to know. This deal is too important to muddy it like this. We have to try again. I'll send one of my people to meet with you later, but Juliet Bryson is nonnegotiable."

An asset. Of course, he was protecting me. I was about to be a Bryson *and* a King, with access to information he couldn't get otherwise.

He hung up the phone, and we sat in silence as he pulled into an underground parking lot that must've been attached to his property. It was well lit and spacious, but it was clearly his private parking and not widely used by party attendees because there was only a small collection of expensive cars in a row.

A massive steel gate shut behind us, leaving the bikers where they couldn't reach us.

We both blew out a breath at the same time. "I'm trusting you, darling. If I find out you lied to me and you were there on your fiancé's business tonight, you're going to regret it."

Worry knotted in my stomach. I was hiding parts of the truth from him but not that. "I didn't mean to make such a mess for you. I'm sorry," I said softly, twisting my fingers together in my lap.

He lifted my chin with his thumb to force me to look at him. "You just saved our asses. If Kevin's men were there, he'd been tipped off to what we were up to, and the deal was going to go south either way. You probably just saved Thor's life even if the bastard can't see it right this second."

I frowned, trying to make sense of it all. "If I asked what was happening tonight, would you tell me?"

He cupped my face, and I leaned into his touch like a cat that was starved for affection—a pathetic cat who didn't care if he was using me as long as he kept touching me. "It's better if you don't know," he said.

For a charged second, we just looked into each other's eyes. I wanted him to pretend nothing outside the SUV mattered and kiss me.

His mouth lifted into a lopsided smile. "I know that look. That look is trouble, and we don't have time for trouble. I need to talk to my people."

He opened the door on his side and walked around to open mine. I took the hand he offered to help me down, but he released me as soon as we started walking toward a tunnel. "You need to stay here for at least a few hours until I can make sure things with Thor have settled and he isn't going to be a problem. Then I can have someone take you home."

Disappointment sank through me that I was now just another task he could assign to someone else. It was too similar to the way Kevin would hand me off to his people as soon as he was finished with me.

I'd been getting silly romantic ideas about Reaper, and that needed to stop. Maybe he wasn't as much of a bastard as I'd made him out to be, but he wasn't my savior either. As we got closer to the door at the end of the lit tunnel, I could make out the thumping bass I'd been able to hear over the phone with him. Through that door was a sex party.

"Can I just wait down here?" I asked in a higher voice than normal. "No one will find me."

He stopped and cocked his head. "You said you wanted a night of freedom. There is no greater freedom than what lies through that door. No inhibitions. No judgment. No consequences. No one will ever know." As he spoke, he got closer and closer, seducing me with both his words and his proximity. He was close enough to reach out and touch. "You want to fuck someone before you get married?" He made an extravagant hand gesture to lead me toward the door.

I didn't want to fuck *someone*. I wanted him. But I was terrified he was something worse than Pandora's box, afraid he'd ruin me. And I knew I shouldn't trust him.

I had to go back. Whatever happened tonight, I had to go back to Kevin and pretend none of it had happened.

Reaper misinterpreted my hesitation and tucked his thumbs into the top of his kilt. "Do you think the Juliet who threatened to shoot me in the boathouse will be joining us anytime soon? Or the one who devastated me with a kiss only to admit it was purely mercenary? What about the one who *impressed me* with her mind, then rejected me when I asked her to stay? Because that Juliet was hungry for life. So was the one who climbed into the trunk of a fucking car to sneak out tonight. You're really going to waste it sitting in a concrete garage when Eden awaits?"

I was in trouble no matter what happened now. "You promise there is zero chance that my being here will get leaked either to my family or the public?"

"Darling, you could murder someone in there, and no one

would ever hear about it." He flashed me a grin. "But don't. It's against the rules, and I'd hate to have to punish you."

The idea of being punished by him shouldn't have sent a nervous thrill swooping through my stomach. I raised my chin and pulled open the door.

19

As we ascended a flight of concrete stairs from the parking garage, the languorous bass grew louder and louder, and my heart beat faster and faster. We pushed through another door and crossed onto marble floors, but we were still in some kind of vestibule and not the main room where things were happening.*

I had to keep reminding myself to breathe, and I glanced over at Reaper. He looked perfectly relaxed, but of course he did. This was his home, his people, his domain. I was Persephone descending into his underworld, but he didn't have to drag me. Now that I was on the precipice, he would've had to drag me back out if he wanted to stop me from witnessing what was on the other side of the final door.

"Ready?" he asked with an eager twinkle in his eye.

I looked at his outfit, then glanced at mine. "Am I...

* REV 22:20—Puscifer

underdressed? Or wearing the wrong thing? Am I going to stick out?" I blurted the series of questions, and his mouth curved upward.

"You can wear whatever you'd like or nothing at all to my parties." With a hand on my waist, he leaned down to whisper, "I know which I'd prefer you in, but I'll admit seeing you in my jacket does things to me, darling."

I shivered at how low his voice dropped on the last word.

He offered his arm, so I took it, instantly feeling a million times braver. If I entered a room on his arm, no one would be looking at me. They'd be transfixed by him because it was impossible not to be. He must've had a different beautiful person on his arm every time they turned around. I'd be interchangeable with the others.

I focused on the feel of his muscled forearm under my palm, steady and absolutely sure of himself, as he pushed the door open and strode into a maelstrom of hedonism.

"You've been to my home, but this is your first experience with my club. Welcome to Petite Mort."

For a split second, it was sensory overload: the sultry music, the moody lighting, the body-painted dancers swinging from aerial silks, and the naked go-go dancers in cages. People were gathered in clusters around the periphery of what amounted to a ballroom, and a closer look revealed that in front of each cluster were people engaging in some kind of performance. Bondage. Flogging. Dancing. Fucking. Some things I didn't even understand at first glance...or second.

As I'd predicted, most of the people in the massive room

seemed to sense Reaper's entrance and turned to stare at their lord of the underworld as he led me deeper into his realm. But their eyes didn't stay on him like I'd thought they would. They shifted to me.

These people didn't just look at me…they *recognized* me. I was positive because I recognized many of them: The judge who'd been fawning over Reaper the first night I'd met him was kneeling at a man's feet, holding his drink like he was nothing more than a table. The secretary of state smirked at me from where he stood watching someone get tied up. I recognized models and actors among the crowd as well as billionaire philanthropists and some from the tech crowd. It was like some kind of kinky Forbes list.

They were whispering to one another as they stared, their eyes shifting from me to Reaper and back again. The reason finally dawned on me. It wasn't solely because Juliet Bryson had just entered their den of iniquity. It was because up until a minute ago, they'd all been sure I was a virgin. It was one of the only things most of them knew about me, outside the things they knew about my family.

Having sex with Kevin had been my normal for almost a year, but none of these people knew that. They'd all assumed I was still waiting for marriage…until I'd walked into this room on Reaper's arm. Now they were reassessing me entirely. Did they think it had all been a charade and I'd been a secret slut this whole time, or were they assuming my virginal vow had been no match for Reaper's sexual magnetism?

From the delighted looks on their faces, I was quite sure it was the latter. One look up at Reaper confirmed my suspicions.

He wasn't looking at anyone directly, but he had an air of satisfaction about him, like he was just so damned proud of himself.

He'd purposely strutted through the middle of the party with me on his arm! He wasn't trying to reassure me—he was gloating, letting them all believe we were lovers.

My cheeks flamed, and I knew better than to make a scene, but I pulled my arm away.

"Something the matter?" he asked softly, steering me across the right side of the room with the barest touch at my lower back.

"I wouldn't want people to get the wrong idea," I said, looking between us.

His shoulders stiffened, and for a brief instant, something like hurt flashed across his face. "Wouldn't want them thinking the pure Juliet Bryson had stooped so low, you mean?"

People moved out of his way respectfully, staring but not daring to approach, as he guided me down a hallway where it was quieter and there were fewer eyes watching.

I let my anger burn away the shame. "I *mean* deliberately parading through the middle of the party with me on your arm to gloat. You lied to me! You promised no one would tell, but these people know my father. They work with my fiancé. There is zero chance that little stunt won't make it back to one of them."

The repercussions started to sink in, and I spiraled into panic. Kevin would never marry me now, but he'd kill me rather than live with the humiliation. He might take it out on my whole family. And if he didn't kill me, my father would do worse. He'd punish Jacque because he knew nothing he did to me would be worse than that.

I was breathing too quickly, but I couldn't seem to stop. I'd just burned my whole life down in a moment of weakness in which I'd trusted this man.

He narrowed his eyes, and his tone was sharp and angry. "No one will tell."

I laughed bitterly. "You think NDAs magically stop people from opening their mouths when it's something that juicy?"

He smiled harshly and nodded. "I don't need an NDA. I'm in possession of information that could destroy every last member of my guest list, and they know it. There's something liberating about it, really. People at this party can be truly free because I won't take a violator to court. I'll make them wish they were dead."

I took deep breaths, seeing reason behind his words. What was happening at this party went far beyond mutually assured destruction, but I should've known there was more to it with him involved.

"Then if it wasn't to gloat, why would you parade me through the party on your arm like that? Don't tell me you didn't do it on purpose. There's always a reason with you."

He swiped a hand across his mouth, looking exasperated. "I was doing you a fucking favor. You said you wanted to fuck someone tonight. I just made you the most interesting person at the party—take your pick!"

I frowned. "You're saying they all want me now because they think I've had sex with you?"

He shrugged. "Something like that."

I was at a loss for words. I could call him arrogant or

presumptuous, but I *had* said I wanted to have sex with someone and that I didn't want it to be him. And there was no way him showing favor to someone wouldn't spark the interest of others. He could have bedded absolutely anyone he wanted. If someone was interesting enough to catch his eye, I'd want to know what they had to offer as well.

The emotion on his face was gone, replaced with his mask of cool indifference. "Now, if we're finished here, we do still have an ongoing issue with some *big bad bikers* to attend to before I can release you to have your last night of freedom."

We found our way to a room that had a formidable-looking bouncer outside, but they immediately moved aside with a nod when Reaper appeared. It almost looked like a boardroom inside, with a long wooden table surrounded by chairs, but there were couches scattered around the edges as well.

The music was much quieter in there, so it was abruptly silent when all six people at the table whipped around to look at us. I immediately recognized Grim lurking in the corner and Azrael's hulking form, but I didn't recognize the petite but tough-looking woman on the latter's lap. She had a faux-hawk and was lean yet muscular. She wore a tank top and a pair of loose sweatpants like she had nothing to prove.

Ophelia, stunning as ever, perched on the edge of the table in a shiny blue dress that looked like it was made from rubber that had basically been poured onto her. Another woman I didn't recognize sighed with what looked like relief at our appearance, leading me to believe they all knew exactly where we'd been. She studied me like she could read my every secret, but I held her

gaze, feeling like I was being tested. When she broke eye contact to look at the man with his arm around her, I almost choked.

Not the most famous person here was an understatement.

"You're Alex Chase," I spluttered, then immediately blushed. "I'm so sorry. I've never been on this side of the starstruck interaction before, and I think I'm going to die of embarrassment."

He gave me that devastating smile he was known for and extended a hand. "Just 'Alex' works. And you're Juliet Bryson. This is my wife, Elena."

I shook both their hands, suddenly placing Elena. She was a dominatrix, and they'd met when she was teaching him how to portray a dominant for a part in a movie. Apparently, sparks had flown. I'd read all about it online.

They looked at each other significantly in that way deeply connected couples could, conveying an entire conversation with a facial expression. Then Elena said, "I want no part of any of this. I just wanted to make sure he got back okay."

She nodded to me, then kissed Reaper on the cheek as she softly said, "Don't fuck it up this time."

She didn't look at me again, but I was positive she'd meant for me to hear. *Don't fuck what up?*

Alex and Elena worked their way around the room, hugging the others as Reaper said, "I believe you're acquainted with Az, Grim, and Ophelia. This charming little gremlin is Styx."

I frowned, wondering if that was a nickname she'd chosen for herself, but I extended my hand. "I'm Juliet."

"Even *I* know that." She laughed, shaking my hand without getting off Az's lap. "And I grew up in a cult that had almost no

contact with the outside world." She was one of those effortlessly charming, instantly likable people. She felt my engagement ring and flipped it over to see the enormous diamond. "I'm surprised King lets you out of the house alone with that thing on..."

He doesn't.

I sheepishly switched it back to my left hand. There was no point in pretending here where everyone already knew too much about me.

Reaper's expression darkened as he looked at it, and I wanted to cast it into the fires of Mount Doom.

The sounds of the party filtered in when Alex and Elena opened the door to leave, but as soon as it got quiet again, Az said, "What happened out there? You leave without a fucking explanation, then I get word the deal was called off, that Thor is out for blood, and then you waltz in here with Kevin King's fiancée on your arm!"

He was growing increasingly agitated, and Styx ran her fingers through the sides of his hair where it was shaved, like she was soothing him.

Reaper crossed to the window and leaned on it, staring out at darkness. "Juliet made some poor choices unrelated to her fiancé and ended up at the clubhouse with Thor. He refused to let her leave, and she called me for help. After we left, she shared that some of Kevin's men were at Thor's bar tonight, so I called the deal off. By then Thor worked out who she was and is convinced we set him up...which doesn't even make sense, but he'll figure that out when he calms down."

They all stared at him wide-eyed, but it was Az who spoke

first. "You just strode in there and challenged him on his own turf without even telling us where you were going? What if it had gone south?"

Reaper shrugged. "It didn't."

It was clear from the worry on their faces that this wasn't the type of business arrangement I was used to seeing with Kevin's associates. This was a family. Az wasn't mad about the deal. He was devastated Reaper had put himself at risk.

"I'm so sorry," I blurted. "I shouldn't have called him for help like that. It wasn't fair—"

Ophelia held up a hand. "Babycakes, you did the right thing. We're glad you're safe. It's this reckless motherfucker we've got a problem with."

Reaper rolled his eyes. "I told Thor I'd send one of my people over tonight to figure out how to put the deal back together. We don't have much time, or we'll lose our shot."

I looked between them, worried about what would happen if he sent Az and the two fought. Az looked like he could crush Thor in a fight, but surely Reaper wouldn't send him alone.

"Can you handle it, O?" Reaper asked, looking at Ophelia.

He was sending *Ophelia*?

She pursed her lips. "Not if I'm going to get in trouble again."

Reaper gave a long-suffering sigh and pinched the bridge of his nose. "I'd prefer you didn't reduce Thor to tears again, but if you must, I won't say a word this time. Just handle it please, O."

I...what?

She preened like she was pleased. "I'll head over there now."

She winked at me as she left, like she knew I was standing there dumbfounded. They were serious. This wasn't a joke.

"Ophelia can handle herself," Reaper said softly, like he was reassuring me he hadn't just sent her to her death.

"She's the only one who can *handle* Thor. I hope the poor motherfucker deserves what you just sent his way," Az muttered, shaking his head, reminding me that Ophelia was his sister.

"Can you pull security footage from the bar?" Reaper said, looking at Az.

"Yeah, you want it now?"

Reaper nodded, his expression distant like he was deeply focused on a problem. "What time did they get there?" he asked me.

"I didn't have my phone, but I think I got there somewhere around ten."

"The other three were already there?"

I felt like I might be doing something bad by telling him things, but it was a little late for that. He'd saved me. If nothing else, I owed him for that. "They must've been."

"Describe them," he said as he paced back toward the window.

"Will anything bad happen to them? Josh, my driver, he might work for Kevin, but he's a good guy. I don't want to him to get hurt. He's not an enforcer. He was probably just there to pick something up or give one of them a ride."

Reaper finally looked back at me, narrowing his eyes thoughtfully. "I won't do anything to them tonight. I just need to know what they were up to."

He looked at Grim and Az, then jerked his head toward the door. "Let's pull the footage in my office." He sketched an extravagant bow in the remaining woman's direction. "Styx, my love. Would you mind showing our guest around in the meantime? She's looking for some adventure this evening. Something of the more consensual variety than what she was going to experience with Thor. Please see that she finds it. I'll return your man as soon as we're finished. Shouldn't take long."

Without another glance at me, he pushed the door open and walked away.

I didn't know what I'd been hoping for, but it hadn't been that. He didn't care who I went out there and fucked, and I wasn't sure why I even wanted him to.

Styx kissed Az thoroughly, then slapped the giant man's ass when he followed Reaper out the door. As soon as it closed, all her sweetness vanished. "You dumb fucking cunt."

20

Styx rounded the table and advanced on me like she meant to fight. "Typical spoiled princess gets herself into trouble, yet other people have to bear the consequences."*

I'd put someone she cared about in danger, but I didn't have to accept her lashing out. "He chose to go."

She shook her head, still eyeing me like she was looking for weaknesses. "He doesn't think straight when it comes to you. And I bet your fiancé knows that and sent you to get close to him."

"King doesn't know I'm here, and my life depends on him not finding out."

She might've been smaller than me, but she looked fully ready to kick my ass.

"Do you have any idea what was at stake tonight? The—" She shook her head like it was taking all her self-control not to say more.

* GIRL WITH ONE EYE—Florence + the Machine

She was obviously angry. If I could just push her to snap, maybe she'd slip and tell me something useful. Just as I opened my mouth to goad her, I caught sight of the scars on her arms that her tank top revealed.

She saw me looking and glared. "Not all of us have lived a pampered existence," she practically growled.

I spread my fingers to show her the nearly identical burn marks on the skin in between a few of them. "Look familiar?" I snarled back. "Just because I grew up in an ivory tower doesn't mean I haven't suffered."

Her expression softened along with her voice. "King do that?"

I hugged Reaper's jacket closer. "No," I lied. "It was when I was younger."

She nodded, looking at me with eyes that saw too much. "Even if King doesn't hurt you, your fiancé does some really bad shit. You ignore that and you're complicit."

Like I didn't know that. If I had the power to stop him, I would've done it already.

I narrowed my eyes at her self-righteousness. "As though you're on the side of the angels? Your boss does some bad shit too."

She looked ready to fight again. "Never to innocents and only ever to protect people who can't protect themselves."

I snorted. "Bullshit. I was an innocent when he manipulated me into hooking up with him so he could have my father and King walk in and catch us. He was ready to humiliate me and ruin my life just because of a feud with my father."

She cocked her head, and her anger was replaced by amusement. "Oh, honey...is that really what you think happened?"

"I was there. And I heard Reaper and Grim talking about it. Grim was annoyed Reaper hadn't been *balls deep in Bryson's daughter* when my father walked in. Reaper admitted it when I called him on it, showed no remorse."

She grinned like I'd said something hilarious. "Grim? Grim damn near killed Reaper for going rogue that night. Whatever you heard was probably him still being pissed about it. Reaper hooking up with you had nothing to do with your father, and it wasn't their plan no matter what he let you believe. He told them some bullshit story afterward about seeing an opportunity for revenge, but they saw through it. Reaper is the villain in a lot of stories, but he'd never use sex against someone like that."

I put my hands on the back of a chair, trying to make sense of what she was saying. "Why did he do it, then?" I refused to believe he'd just been overcome with desire. He'd been calculated enough to let me think he was the man I was supposed to be marrying.

She studied me. "I like you, think we might be kindred spirits...but that's between you and the boss. I've already said more than I should've."

Before I could question it further, she gestured to the door. "Let's go turn your night of freedom around."

———

I'd heard people describe things as being a feast for the senses, but this party made those feasts look like a pauper's scraps.

Everything was sensual and soft: the lights, the music, the subtle scent of jasmine in the air. The people were uninhibited and joyful, appearing to lust for laughter and conversation as much as the sex that had caught my eye first. It felt like there was an invisible web connecting everyone, making us all a part of this bigger thing with infinite possibilities.

Styx watched me take it all in, and her face lit with wonder as she looked around like it was her first time here too. "Never gets old," she said wistfully. "You look like I bet I did when I first escaped, starved of experience and thirsting for *this*. All of it."

Her excitement was infectious, and I found myself genuinely smiling too. "I am...starved for experience, if you know what I mean. I've done...*it*. But not any of *that*. I think I'm in a little over my head here."

She grinned mischievously and leaned closer to my ear. "For what it's worth? If I only had one night and I weren't already madly in love with Az? I'd be looking for Reaper."

The excitement deflated from me like I was a sad balloon. "He made it clear he doesn't care who I spend the next few hours with, and I'm not going to beg if he's not interested."

She bit her lip like she was about to laugh. "Was this what he had to put up with when it was Az and me? This is painful. Sweets, you've gotten under his skin. That's why we're so worried."

My stomach swooped nervously. "What does that mean?"

The music had taken on a softer, sultrier tone, making it easier to talk. She pointed me toward a bar, and we ordered drinks. "Reaper has that whole *I-don't-give-a-fuck* energy about

him, right? But that man is terrifyingly calculated. He doesn't do anything without a strategic reason, and he *never* deviates from his plan unless a more strategic choice comes up."

I nodded as I took my drink from the bartender. That was all information I knew about him. "And you're saying it wasn't strategic for him to rush to save me tonight? I can see where you'd get the idea that he charged in heroically, but he had his reasons."

She led me over to a small elevated stage where someone gorgeous—sporting a neat beard and a well-fitted suit—was tracing fire along a blindfolded person's naked body. The sub wasn't tied up, merely grasping a bar above her head, leaving her vulnerable to him. She was gasping every time she felt the heat, but he was obviously being careful enough not to actually burn her.

The trust it must take to let someone do that to you!

Styx whispered, "You mean *reasons* like being able to blackmail you for info about King?"

I didn't need to answer, my wide-eyed expression must've told her everything.

She lowered her voice even more. "He made a move to intercept something of King's tonight. If we're right about what he's up to, the stakes couldn't be any higher. Did Reaper press you for information about it beforehand?"

"No, but I didn't know anything."

She looked at me like I was being naive. "You don't think he could've forced you to snoop? Forced you to put yourself at risk so he'd have better intel to keep his people safe?"

I was breathing faster just imagining how terrifying that could be. What if that was the price he planned to exact for saving

me tonight? "He's probably waiting until we're married. Doesn't want to risk King calling it off."

She smiled. "Oh...okay. And tonight? He had to have known the odds were one in a hundred that he'd walk out in one piece when he stormed in there alone, but he did it to get to you a little faster. I've seen him do some extreme shit to keep us all safe, but this was reckless. Minutes are all it would've taken to round up enough people for a show of force that would've given him better odds. Thor wasn't gonna kill you in those minutes, but the thought of him having that time to hurt you?" She paused, looking at me significantly. "Reaper put your safety before his. Before what he was trying to accomplish tonight, which he's spent months planning."

I turned my attention back to the stage, considering what she said. The Dom was on his knees in front of his partner now, pleasuring her with his mouth while still holding the fire stick so she could feel its warmth along the sides of her body. The sounds she was making were growing more frantic, and it was hard to tell if it was purely from pleasure or from the heat of the fire pushing her to a wilder place.

Styx was saying Reaper had feelings for me that went beyond my being an asset to him. I'd known he wasn't the complete monster I'd accused him of being, especially when he'd taken me at my word and protected me from Thor...but it seemed like she was saying more.

"Why are you telling me this?" I asked.

She lit up. "Because that meddling motherfucker once played cupid for me. He helped Az pull his head out of his ass. I'm trying to return the favor."

I gasped, suddenly connecting the dots. "You're the woman Reaper bruised! I was there the day Az almost killed him for it."

She grinned. "I knew what I wanted, and Az wouldn't give it to me even though he wanted it too."

I studied her. "Az was scared to hurt you, said you'd been through some shit. Reaper told him you just wanted to be treated normally, not like you're going to break."

She sobered and nodded. "He figured out that it wasn't the same kind of hurt." I squeezed her hands, and she instantly lightened again. "I don't dwell on it. I found my happily ever after. Reaper deserves that too."

I choked on an uncomfortable laugh. "I promise you he's not looking for happily ever after with me." I held up my left hand to flash my ring. "And even if he were, someone already claimed my ever after."

She grew serious. "I was married. *Before.*"

That one word spoke volumes. She'd been married in the cult, probably against her will. The tension between us was at odds with so much of what was happening at the party, but no one seemed to notice or care. Intimacy seemed to be the core thing people were seeking, and the emotional intimacy we were sharing had the same charge of trust as any of the BDSM happening around us.

She nodded once like she knew I'd understood. "You've got the same haunted look I had when I escaped."

I shuddered, wanting to deny it, but there was no point. "How did you stop your husband from coming after you?" I was petrified to even ask that question.

She smiled, but there was no joy in it. "I didn't. I killed him when he did."

I closed my eyes, trying not to think the dark thoughts that threatened to claim me. If I ever tried to run and Kevin had to hunt me down, he'd make sure everyone I cared about was collateral damage before he even caught me, which was a good reminder of why I needed to get home right away.

But I couldn't go yet, not until Reaper said it was safe.

Something about the energy of the party shifted, like there was a crackling collective awareness, and I knew without turning to look that Reaper was descending the staircase behind us.

I held my breath, waiting for him to come over, but when minutes passed and he didn't appear, I subtly turned to look. He'd taken his place on a throne that overlooked the dance floor. He sprawled carelessly with a leg draped over one of the arms of the chair, showing entirely too much of his thick thigh in the kilt he had on. He lounged there, tantalizing everyone with his unfathomable sex appeal, but I could tell he was tense from the set of his shoulders and the distant look on his face. He couldn't have been less interested in where I was or what I was doing.

But maybe I could change that.

"Dance with me?" I asked Styx.

She looked from me to Reaper to the dance floor and smiled knowingly. "Let's do it."

21

We made our way out onto the dance floor, and it was unlike anything I'd experienced before. Not everyone was conventionally attractive, and many were much older than the crowd usually found in a dance club, but they all seemed to be reveling in the music. There were plenty of sexy dancers who looked like they'd be at ease on a strip club stage, but just as many people were awkwardly flailing with enough vivaciousness that it was sexy too. Their confidence was infectious, and I found myself letting go of my uncertainty to flow with the music.*

It shifted into a sensual dubstep beat, and I rolled my body along with it, daring to steal glances over my shoulder at where Reaper still presided over the party from his throne. He was close enough that I could see the subtle line that creased his brow, but he hadn't looked at me.

* MOVEMENT (MAYA JANE COLES REMIX)—Hozier

The crowd parted as Azrael made his way across the dance floor to join Styx.

She grinned at something he said in her ear, then leaned closer to me. "Are you into women, Juliet? It would serve the meddling bastard right if Az and I took you upstairs to our place and gave him a taste of his own medicine."

I stopped moving for a second, breaking the flow of the dance. "I...don't even know. I've never really let myself consider it."

Her smile contained the kind of warmth and safety I'd never had in a friend. "If you ever want to unpack any of that trauma, I'm here for you. It seems we're sisters in suffering." She squeezed my hands. "But I'd rather be sisters in joy. Don't waste another chance." She jerked her head toward Reaper.

I shrugged out of his jacket and held it out to her. "If you're going upstairs, would you mind looking after this?"

She took it and squeezed my shoulder lightly, and then the two of them made their way back toward the staircase. I crossed the dance floor too until I stood not far from the base of Reaper's throne, directly in his line of sight. If he didn't want to look at me, that was fine, but it wasn't going to be because he couldn't see me.

A handsome man with dark brown skin, wearing only a pair of boxer briefs, held out his hand in offer. "Care to dance?"

Reaper still wasn't looking, so I nodded shyly. If he was determined to ignore me, I could savor my last night of freedom and live in the moment with someone else. Maybe Reaper was some kind of sex god, but at that point, I was happy just to be

touched with kindness. I sought any memory I could cling to in the months and years to come.

So, as the handsome stranger moved behind me and placed his hands on my hips, I closed my eyes and sank into the moment. He moved behind me, and I could feel he was aroused, but he wasn't deliberately rubbing it on me in a creepy way. In fact, he kept putting distance between us like he was making sure I was okay with it.

His fingertips barely brushed under the waistband of my shorts, and my eyes flew open in confused desire—only to find Reaper staring at me with such hunger, I thought I was going to ignite on the spot. I bit my lip, willing him to come down and claim me, but he looked away again, suddenly finding something across the ballroom much more interesting.

The man behind me chuckled against my neck. "Ah...I see the rumors are true. You're already spoken for this evening."

I turned my back to Reaper, draping my hands around the stranger's neck. "Hardly. He's ignoring me."

Mischief lit his face. "I can help with that if you'd like? It's clear that's where you'd rather be, and I can't blame you."

I nodded before I could lose my nerve, and we went back to dancing.

"He's watching you again," the man murmured.

I shivered with desire just knowing Reaper's eyes were on me. I needed to feel his hands on me again.

I pulled the man closer, letting one of his thighs slide between mine. I gasped when he put a hand on my lower back and encouraged me to rock my hips because it meant my clit rubbed against

his thigh. I didn't want this man the way I wanted Reaper, but I was surprised to find I still enjoyed his touch. He was so casual about it all, like we were on the same team and this was as amusing for him as it was desperate for me.

He turned me back around, and this time Reaper didn't look away. I felt wanton even though there were plenty of people literally having sex on the dance floor.

The pressure on my clit was gone, so I slipped my own hand into my shorts, holding eye contact with Reaper as I stroked myself and moaned.

"Do you want a taste?" I said slowly so Reaper could read my lips, like I was saying it to him. He raised an eyebrow but looked frozen, he was so still.

"Mmm, yes, please," the man behind me said.

He lifted my middle finger to his lips before sliding it into his mouth and dragging his tongue around it. It felt good, and I let Reaper see the way I reacted, parting my lips and arching my back.

Reaper cocked his head like he'd had enough and snapped his fingers. The man instantly released me and went to Reaper like he was in trouble. I followed close behind, already fuming.

If Reaper didn't want me, he had no right to intervene, and he certainly shouldn't be punishing the poor guy for it.

The man knelt at Reaper's feet, his head bowed obediently, but I charged to the side of his throne. "You said I could have anyone I wanted, and you made it clear you didn't care. He didn't do anything wrong."

His expression was furious, but his demeanor was still

perfectly calm. "You want something from me, Juliet? Stop being a brat and fucking ask for it."

I crossed my arms, too nervous to actually say the words to him.

He sighed with frustration and snapped his fingers again. This time the man rose to his feet and climbed onto the throne to straddle Reaper. My jaw dropped as they kissed, a slow, gentle touch of their lips that Reaper controlled by wrapping his fingers into the other man's braids. Reaper held eye contact with me until he closed his eyes in pleasure.

By the time he pulled the guy back, they were both panting, and I was ready to start touching myself again. But, hot as it was, I was frustrated and hurt that Reaper wasn't doing it to me. I had hours, maybe minutes, left before I had to go home. If I didn't speak up now, I'd be tortured by this moment forever.

"If you want to use jealousy as a weapon with me, darling, you'd better be sure you know how to handle it. It's sharp when someone throws it back at you." Reaper kissed the man on the cheek and whispered something in his ear that made the guy throw his head back and laugh. He climbed down and winked at me before he walked away.

We were at a party with hundreds of people around us, but in that moment, Reaper was the only one who existed for me.

He patted his lap, and I perched with my back against him, conscious of how many people were watching us. The barest brush of his lips at the back of my neck made me squirm. "Are you going to be a good girl now and do as you're told?"

I nodded eagerly, daring to slide my hand under his kilt and grip his hard cock.

"Prove it. Take off your top."

I stiffened but melted against him when he kissed my neck again.

"I've had a sneaking suspicion about you since those tabloid pictures from that club were first published...and you tempt me with it at every turn. I think it turns you on when people are watching and they shouldn't be."

"All these people will see my breasts." I should've sounded scared, but I was breathless at the idea of doing something so daring.

He rubbed between my thighs over my shorts, holding me back against him and thrusting so that we were basically dry humping in front of a crowd of people.

In one swift movement, I pulled my shirt off but clutched it in front of my chest. He sighed dramatically like I was being disobedient, so I slowly lowered it until it dropped from my fingers onto the floor.

I instantly started to breathe heavily, and my nipples turned to hard little pebbles.

Everyone can see!

I was topless in a crowd, grinding on a man who wasn't my fiancé...and it made me feel *bad*...the kind of bad I'd never let myself enjoy being before.

Reaper cupped my breasts in his big hands and lifted them a little like he was presenting them to the room. When his thumbs flicked over their sensitive peaks, I closed my eyes and whimpered. "I've never been so turned on in my life." I dropped my head back onto his shoulder. "What does that say about me?"

His teeth scraped against the spot where my neck met my shoulder. "That you were made for me, darling. Made to be shown off."

"You said if I wanted something, I should ask you for it?" Could he feel my heart thumping in my chest?

"Mmm?"

I got on my knees in front of him, looked up into his dark eyes, and said, "Fuck me."

He tugged me to my feet, and I thought he was going to pull me onto his lap, but he stood too and said, "Upstairs. Now."

I pouted at the very idea of having to wait. "Not here?"

He was already leading me toward the stairs when he said, "You haven't earned that yet."

———

"I was expecting a coffin," I said, as he kicked the bedroom door closed behind us. Everything was decorated in tasteful blacks and grays, but there was no leather to be seen and not a single BDSM implement hung from the wall.

He nodded to the window. "Stopped using it as soon as blackout curtains were invented."

I laughed at the unexpected humor, and he kissed my smile, pulling me into his arms, where it felt like I belonged. I was suddenly grateful for his aversion to shirts because it meant I could touch him without fabric getting in the way. As he slanted his mouth over mine, my hands roved over his shoulders and down to his chest, tracing the torque along his collarbone, then the line of his abs into the top of his kilt.

He put his hands on mine when I started to unfasten it. "Are you sure you want this?"

I was panting and ready to weep, I wanted him so badly. "You know I'm not a virgin anymore...I've had sex with Kevin. A lot of sex."

He closed his eyes for a second like he didn't want to hear it.

This time I was the one who made him look at me with a finger under his chin. "But that...*that* can't be it. Tell me there's something better than that."

His smile was actual magic, and I felt it all the way to my toes. "Fuck telling you. I'll show you."

22

Why are you torturing me?" I groaned moments later when all he'd done was strip me naked and kiss his way from my neck to my ankles, skimming down the front of my legs instead of straight down the middle where I needed him. *

He knelt in front of me, the muscles in his shoulders bunching as he kissed the inside of my left knee, a spot I hadn't been aware was so sensitive. I tried to tug his head up by weaving my fingers into his white-blond hair, but he nipped my inner thigh lightly with his teeth instead, and I yelped.

"I don't remember you being this greedy," he said with his lips against the skin of my inner thigh, so I felt every word. "That motherfucker definitely doesn't make you come enough."

I squirmed as he tickled my hip bone with a featherlight kiss. "He's never made me come." I couldn't look at him as I said it. I

* GLORY BOX—Portishead

was too embarrassed, but I could feel him watching me. "I think there might be something wrong with me."

Why don't you ever finish? You don't enjoy sex like other women do.

The sneer on Kevin's face when he said it remained branded into my memory. I'd started to fake an orgasm every time we had sex, and he hadn't complained again.

Without warning, Reaper planted an open-mouthed kiss on my clit, letting his tongue roll back and forth across it slowly as he sucked gently and held my hips in place. He moved faster but with precision, never letting the pleasure relent for even a second.

I thrashed and panted and fisted my hands in his hair so roughly, it probably hurt, but he kept going until my knees buckled. He had to push me onto the bed to stop me from tumbling to the floor as an orgasm crashed through me.

"There's nothing wrong with you, darling." With his hands on my waist, he slid me up the bed. "Grab the headboard." He tossed out the lazy command as his eyes swept down my naked body, alight with hunger and possessiveness.

I moved my fingers into gaps in the ornately carved wooden headboard and gripped it like it would somehow help me stay grounded.

But there was no staying grounded when he ever so slowly lowered himself over me, sliding down until his mouth hovered between my parted legs again. "Be a good girl, and don't let go until I tell you to."

Whatever word I'd been about to utter in agreement dissolved into a helpless moan when he licked up my seam and settled his

focus on my clit again. After my second orgasm, he pushed a finger inside me, then another one, making me come again as he curved them and stroked a spot that made my hips buck off the mattress.

When he tried to push a third finger in, I whimpered at the stretching pressure.

Reaper looked up at me, his expression focused. "If you're going to take my cock, baby, you're going to have to take another finger first. Just trust me and relax."

He put his tongue and his thumb over my clit at the same time while he worked the third finger in, and my vision splintered with pain that shattered into pleasure so intense, I was pretty sure I was screaming but felt like I was outside my body.

"Are you okay?" he murmured, thrusting gently, causing smaller waves of pleasure to keep radiating out through my limbs.

I nodded, not sure I remembered how to speak.

"Do you still want me to fuck you?"

I nodded again, spreading my knees wider and thrusting down onto his fingers to convince him I was ready. Instead of immediately pulling out, he flicked his tongue over my clit again, licking and working his fingers until I was about to come. Then he repositioned himself on the bed, replacing his fingers with the head of his cock. He'd taken his kilt off and put a condom on without me even noticing.

I hadn't thought Kevin was particularly small, but Reaper was thicker, stretching me open as he worked his way in with tiny strokes. He watched me closely, his eyes tender and attentive to my every reaction. When I winced, he lowered a hand to stroke my clit, and instantly all pain became pleasure.

In the mindless minutes that followed, he somehow managed to shove all the way in, groaning as he filled me completely.

Neither of us spoke, but we locked eyes as he began to thrust. The connection between us was palpable. I'd never felt so present and so completely lost at the same time. Only he was real, only the feel of him mattered. I forgot who I was and where I was as I came again, clenching around his cock.

His lips parted in awe. "Oh fuck, Juliet...I can feel you coming."

He groaned low in his throat and thrust deeper, holding himself there as he finished too.

I expected him to get up and go about his business, but he took care of the condom and looked down at me with an adoring smile. "You can let go of the headboard now, darling."

I pried my rigid fingers off the wood. I'd been gripping it so hard, I wondered if I'd left behind indentations. Without something to hold on to, I felt like I'd been untethered, and the force of what I'd just experienced threatened to swallow me whole. As I went to curl in on myself in embarrassment that I was so overwhelmed, Reaper climbed onto the bed and pulled me onto his lap, cradling me against his chest.

He planted a gentle kiss on my forehead. "Whatever you're feeling is okay."

"It scares me." I gripped his arm. He didn't question what scared me, and I was glad because I didn't think I could articulate it. He was probably used to people having an existential crisis after having sex with him.

"Just let me hold you, darling," he whispered. His arms

tightened around me. "It's about fucking time someone took care of you."

He scooted us back so he could lean against the headboard, making it clear he'd hold me as long as I needed. He'd just given me the most intense pleasure of my life. Now we were skin to skin, breaths entangled and hearts thumping against each other. He held me there until I relaxed, not saying a word, expecting nothing from me.

He was just *there*, holding space for my feelings.

23

When it finally felt safe to leave the cocoon of his body, I tilted my head up and kissed him lightly, feeling the soft brush of his lip ring. "Thank you."*

His lips quirked, and he kissed the tip of my nose before letting me slide down to the bed next to him.

He traced his fingers along my arm like he couldn't stop touching me. "Are you okay?"

I rolled onto my stomach so I could see him, wondering how to explain what I was feeling. I'd gone from *that's it?* to *that's the point of existing.* "Kevin supposedly '*took my virginity*'…" I put air quotes around the phrase. "But this felt like my first time. It's the first time I've understood why sex inspires art and poetry and wars."

He gave me one of his smiles I'd never seen before, a soft lift of his lips that was almost shy. "That might be the nicest thing anyone has ever said to me, darling."

* AS IT WAS—Hozier

Kevin hadn't *taken* anything from me when we had sex.

Reaper had.

He'd taken the part of me that could live without him and ground it to dust.

It wasn't just the sex.

He was patient and giving and called me on every ounce of my bullshit. All I wanted was to stay right here and figure out how to make him feel half as good as he'd made me feel.

"Are you normally into...kinkier sex than that?" I asked, pushing past my embarrassment.

"What do you mean?"

"I guess after *all that*"—I gestured vaguely in the direction of the ballroom party—"I expected to be tied up or spanked or something at the very least. You know, if that's what you're into, it's okay if we..." I trailed off, feeling foolish.

"If you want to be tied up, I'll gladly introduce you to bondage. And goddess knows you could use a good spanking sometimes." His big hand squeezed my ass gently. "But if you're asking what I'm into—what *my* kink is? It's pleasure. It's being the one to make you lose control more times than you thought was possible. It's making someone squirt after they didn't think they were capable of it or helping someone discover that an anal orgasm is a whole different beast from a regular one." My cheeks heated at the casual way he was able to talk about things I'd never even considered. He kissed my glowing cheeks like he could soak in the novelty of my inexperience. "I get off on finding every single way I can wring pleasure from my partner and then reveling in their experience like a goddamn emotional vampire."

"So that wasn't...boring for you?"

He huffed a laugh. "Juliet, I almost came in my kilt when you came on my fingers. For the rest of my life, I'll be beating off thinking about the sound you made when I first got three in there." He tilted his head back like he was savoring the memory. "I can't wait for you to attend another one of my parties."

I looked away. "That might be...challenging." If I'd gotten away with it tonight, maybe I could pull it off again with better planning. But was it worth the risk to everyone here?

He laced his fingers into mine like he could feel I was worried. "From what I'm told, you'll be at the Black Rose Auction this year. I host a play party on the third night. You'll come to me then."

I wasn't surprised he'd be attending the secretive auction. I'd only learned about it in recent months, when Kevin informed me I'd be accompanying him—our first major outing after the wedding and honeymoon. Everyone would be staying on the property together.

I bit my tongue, knowing that arguing with him right now was pointless. "Kevin will kill you."

He blew out a breath. "If he tries anything at the auction, he dies and no one ever finds the body. It's neutral ground on pain of death."

"And fucking someone's wife isn't viewed as violating that neutrality?"

He caught his lip ring between his teeth and released it. "So long as the lady consents, not in the least. He's too smart to try any kind of violence there, but it won't matter because I'll see to it that he doesn't find out."

He brushed his fingers down my spine, and it made me want to purr with contentment.

The sensation unlocked a memory from my childhood. "Have you ever played the game where you draw pictures on each other's backs and guess what the other person drew? We used to do it in boarding school."

"Your father should really get a refund for princess academy. They taught you all manner of nonsense."

I shoved his shoulder to roll him over. "Shut up. You just know I'm going to win."

He huffed but groaned with pleasure when I lightly traced a giant circle with rays coming out of it onto the skin of his back.

"It's a sun," he mumbled against the pillow.

"Your turn!" I said excitedly.

He rubbed his hands together like he was thinking. Then he drew a tiny circular shape in the center of my back. "This is your clitoris," he said, kissing the spot he'd drawn before tracing more lines in a crescent. "And these are the perfect plump lips of your tight little cunt."

I gasped when he traced his drawing with his tongue. I felt every lick between my thighs even though it was my back he was touching. I fisted my hands, already aroused again. "Mmm... you're not very good at this game. You're not supposed to tell me what it is."

He finished adding some anatomical details that made me blush. "Maybe I just like making you feel good." He kneaded his fingertips into my lower back, eliciting a low moan from my lips.

"Why does every way you touch me feel so damned good? I hope you charge an absolute fortune for your professional services because *good god...*"

He hesitated, then continued giving me the best massage of my life like it was nothing. "Does it bother you? That I fuck people for money."

He sounded so serious that I had to think about whether I was missing something. "No. I don't have any right to tell you who you should sleep with or why."

His hands worked up the sides of my spine, melting all the tension of the night away. "What if you did? What if you were mine and Kevin had gone to hell? Would it bother you then?"

I reached back to put a hand on his hip, needing to touch him. "A few years ago, I would've thought it would bother me. But that was before I'd had to find the place in my head where I can shut off my feelings and have sex with someone out of obligation. I'm guessing your work isn't always as...tedious as my marital duties can be. But it's shown me that not all sex is significant to the person having it."

It was odd to be having this conversation while I was still facing away from him, but in some ways it felt safer.

"What about outside work?" He pressed his thumbs into my lower back, and I made a groaning noise in my throat. "Not all sex is significant to the person having it, but it can be *in*significant in the best possible way. The guy you were dancing with tonight? Javier's primary partner will always have his heart. But in other circumstances, I might've liked to watch where things could've gone if I hadn't stopped you."

I bit my lip, so turned on that I was squirming against him now. "Are we negotiating the terms of a hypothetical relationship here?"

"Answer the question."

"Okay...I wouldn't mind you being with people outside work. It's who you are... And I think I might like finding out what *insignificant in a good way* looks like...and you watching me with someone else. Or maybe...fucking me in front of other people?"

He breathed a laugh against my neck. "I like it when you tell me what you want, darling."

I nodded and grinned, exhilarated to speak my desires aloud and have them met with enthusiasm. "What's the deal with your club? Styx mentioned going to their place upstairs. Do they live here too?"

"In a different wing of the house, but yeah. Grim lives in a guesthouse out back. Ophelia isn't always here, but she's got a suite for when she is. It just made sense for everyone to be on-site where I could make sure they were safe and we could all deal with the business."

They were more like a family than I'd realized. It was an enormous property like King's, but full of chaos and life instead of surveillance and hired help he treated like furniture.

"And the sex club?" The party had been happening in the ballroom, but I assumed hired escorts weren't just working out in the open during business operations.

"The lower level," he said in an exaggeratedly menacing voice. "I'll give you the full tour next time you're here."

Would there be a next time?

"Who does what in the business?" I asked, to distract from the despair I felt at the idea of leaving this place to get married.

His smile was tender. "Az and Grim are my partners. We started the club together. Az is our resident tech genius, and he oversees security, Ophelia is my head Mistress and general pain in my ass. Styx is a cam girl, but she's become a sort of personnel and recruitment manager on top of that. And Grim… is Grim."

I couldn't help laughing. "He's fucking terrifying."

"If you only knew the half of it. But I love him like a brother. There's nothing I wouldn't do to keep them all safe." When I was quiet for too long, wondering whether anyone cared about me like that, he nudged my shoulder. "We could use a business manager, someone whose accounting skills make my dick hard."

I cupped the dick in question. "Oh, it's my accounting that does this, huh?"

He bit his lip and nodded, mischief glowing in his eyes.

I laughed, feeling things for him that could put us all in danger. If he'd do anything to keep his people safe, that would have to include staying away from me.

"Why did you trick me that first night?" I looked into his eyes, saw him try to slide his indifferent mask into place only to drop it altogether.

The look on his face was achingly vulnerable. "I didn't mean to. I found out you were in that room alone, and I had to see you again. But you started acting weird, and I immediately knew that

you thought I was King. So I played along, knowing you'd kick me out if I corrected you."

He sighed heavily, dropping his head. "I caught a glimpse of how it would be for you. The mask you'd have to wear, the way you'd make yourself smaller to be who they wanted you to be. And I couldn't stand the thought of them erasing the woman I'd met in the boathouse. I don't know what I thought would happen. I'd make you come so hard, you'd want to run away with me? I'd never done anything so fucking selfish in my life, and I had to stop, or I'd never get another chance with you."

I kissed his stomach. "So you came to my room that night looking for another chance?"

He laughed. "I came to your room because I couldn't stay away, but by then your father had gotten to you, and I'd already made a mess of things. *Fuck*, I wanted you. And I knew you wanted me too. The fucked-up part of me knew if I pushed, you would've let me do whatever I wanted. But I didn't want you to regret it. I needed you to come to me willingly. And you never have."

My stomach clenched with shame. "I did tonight."

He blew out a breath. "You had no one else to call."

I looked into the dark depths of his eyes, struck by the spark in them I'd never felt this kind of connection with anyone. "Not then. On the dance floor. I came to you willingly and got on my knees in front of half of society. I came to you tonight. I'd stay with you if I could."

Styx had escaped and killed her husband when he'd come for

her. I had to find a way out that didn't involve running to Reaper and expecting him to risk everything to protect me.

A dozen emotions swam through the dark pools of his eyes before he said, "Call off the wedding." He didn't smile, didn't blink. "That's my price for saving you tonight."

"*Impossible.*"

He smirked. "So was getting us out of that clubhouse in one piece."

I dropped my head, wishing I could do as he said. "I have to marry him now. If I leave him two weeks before the wedding, he'd be a laughingstock no matter what story we spun. I can't do that to him."

Because he'd scorch the earth on a quest to destroy everything I love.

Reaper gripped my shoulders gently. "You had to sneak out in the trunk of a fucking car tonight, and you're telling me you care about his feelings?"

"He's controlling. But he doesn't deserve that." *He deserves worse.* "I'll marry him, then wait until the spotlight isn't shining quite so brightly on us to quietly separate. That way no one gets hurt."

"I can protect you, Juliet."

But who's going to protect you?

I could only shake my head.

He frowned. "A deal's a deal. That's my price." He was deadly serious about this.

"Why?"

He smiled sadly. "I told you...it's about fucking time someone took care of you."

I was so caught off guard, all I could do was blink at him in surprise. "I'll hate you if you force me into this. It makes you just as bad as them."

His thumb stroking down my jaw was gentle, but the look in his eyes couldn't have been harder. "I'm willing to live with that."

24

could just run. Reaper said he'd protect me.*

I stood in the shower back at King's house, letting the water cascade over my head like it might help me formulate a plan. I couldn't go through with the wedding, and I trusted Reaper to shield me, but I needed to find a way to shield the club from King's wrath.

"You're home early," I said, startled to find Kevin leaning in my bedroom doorway when I got out of the shower. I'd managed to sneak back in without getting caught, thanks to a diversion Reaper created, but it had been such a close call.

Worth it, I thought as I forced myself to kiss Kevin in greeting. Despite the corner Reaper had backed me into with his deal, it had still been the best night of my life.

Kevin's eyes sparkled with anticipation. "I have a gift to show you. An early wedding present..."

* CHERRY WINE (LIVE)—Hozier

Don't act nervous. He doesn't know anything. Don't give him a reason to be suspicious.

Once I'd pulled some clothes on, he led me to one of the downstairs drawing rooms that had been cleared out except for something in the center, enormous and covered by a sheet; some kind of art installation, it seemed like.

I braced myself to fawn over some modern art monstrosity, but when he pulled the sheet off with a flourish, it revealed a marble statue. For a moment, all I could do was stare.

"It's exquisite," I breathed, genuinely struck by the beauty of it.

A man and a woman were carved with such finesse that their bodies looked to be made of flesh rather than stone. The woman was in flight, mid-transformation. Her feathered arms stretched wide like wings, while her feet curved into delicate fins. A look of desperate anguish twisted her face as the bull of a man wrapped his arms around her, stopping her from fleeing.

The man was at ease, confident in his physical superiority. The look on his face was smug, like he was satisfied he'd captured her, perhaps amused by her attempts to flee. It was all a game to him.

I turned to look at Kevin in amazement. "It's incredible how much it looks like a Bernini. Who's the artist?"

His expression wasn't unlike the sculpted man's. "Bernini."

I blinked. "A descendant of Gian Lorenzo Bernini?"

He ran a hand along the woman's face, tracing a tear that looked real even though it was marble. I had the irrational urge to tell him not to touch her.

"Sculpted by Gian Lorenzo Bernini between 1625 and 1626. Commissioned by Cardinal Scipione Borghese."

It wasn't possible a piece of Bernini's this spectacular, on this scale, could've escaped the notice of art historians for centuries. But questioning Kevin was dangerous.

He wrapped his arms around me from behind, holding me to his chest as we admired it together. "You think it's a fake, and you're scared to tell me." I started to deny it, but his arms tightened. "Do you think I'm a fool, Juliet?"

"Of course not," I said quickly, trying to pull away.

He tightened his grip until it felt like he was crushing me.

I was scared.

"You must if you think I'd spend a king's ransom on a fake. It was a closely guarded secret, then made its way into a private collection. I purchased it at the Black Rose Auction last year. For you."

It was exactly the sort of thing that would be sold at the highly secretive auction we'd be attending a few months after the wedding. If that was where he'd gotten it, it was almost certainly not a fake.

"Thank you," I gasped, hoping he'd made his point.

"It's Zeus and Nemesis. He loved her, but she ran from him. She tried turning into all kinds of creatures to elude him, but he chased her to the ends of the earth and caught her."

Fear gripped my chest as tightly as he did.

"Where were you last night?" The gentle way he said it was more frightening than if he'd shouted.

"I was here…" I said, clinging to the hope that he was just testing me.

He released his hold on my chest. "I have another present for you."

He held out a velvet ring box, and I forced myself to smile when I took it from him.

As I opened it, he said, "You lied to me."

It took me a fraction of a second to realize what I was looking at, and I dropped the box in horror. Josh's pinky ring with its sapphire stone rolled onto the floor, still attached to part of a finger.

"I wasn't... He didn't!" I was hyperventilating too much to get a coherent thought out.

"Oh, I'm aware he didn't touch you. But he failed in his duty to keep you safe, and he'll pay the price."

I gasped like a fish out of water as the room spun around me. "I'm going to be sick."

He laughed softly. "But I've got another gift for you."

While I was in a foggy daze of guilt and terror, he dragged me out to the grounds and down to his menagerie, staffed by zoologists he'd stolen from the finest facilities in the world. He had a breeding pair of giraffes, an assortment of savanna animals, and smaller creatures like arctic foxes in enclosures.

But he didn't lead us to any of those areas. He steered us toward a new one he'd had built to accommodate a leopard.

When we stood just outside the enclosure, Eric handed him another, slightly bigger, velvet box. One side of his mouth turned up into a leering smile when he looked at me.

Kevin held out the box with a gleam in his eyes, and I shook my head, trying to yank my arm away from him. He jerked it so

hard, it felt like my shoulder was going to come out of the socket. "You'll only make this worse. *Open it!*"

My fingers were trembling so badly, I struggled to get it open. Inside was Lola's blue collar.

He spread his hands wide. "Your dog was suffering, waiting at home for you while you were out with someone else, so I put her out of her misery. She made a nice appetizer for my new huntress."

I choked on a sob, trying hard not to give him the tears he was obviously after.

He shrugged. "Better sport than Josh."

A sudden gut-wrenching scream made me actually look into the leopard enclosure. It took me a second to make sense of what I was seeing through the foliage, but the leopard had ravaged Josh's shoulder and was dragging him into the bushes. He was coming in and out of consciousness, probably from the blood loss, but he was fully awake and sobbing for mercy as she tore at the flesh of his arm.

"Leopards aren't usually this violent, but it's amazing what starvation and a little amphetamine concoction will do to a wild cat."

I puked onto the grass in front of me, then collapsed onto my own vomit, trying to drown out the sounds of his suffering with my hands over my ears.

This is my fault.

Kevin stood there and watched until the screaming stopped. It took so long, he made a phone call, discussing upcoming plans with someone; the bit of normalcy made me feel completely detached from reality.

Josh's screams went quiet, and all that was left in the enclosure were ripping noises that threatened to make me puke again.

Kevin snatched me by the arm and dragged me back up to the house. He took me into one of the downstairs guest bathrooms, turned the shower on, and shoved me into the stream of cold water. When he was content the worst of the filth had been washed away, he turned it off and mercifully left me sitting on the tile floor, hugging my knees and shivering so hard, my teeth felt like they were going to crack.

"You will be waiting here when I want you. You will never lie to me again. And if you try to run... Do you know the story of Bernini's first love?"

I shook my head, cowering against the wall.

"Bernini had an affair with a married woman named Constanza. He was hopelessly in love with her until she also had an affair with his brother, Luigo. When Bernini found out, he hired a man to hunt her down. Then he had the man cut her face with a razor blade so she'd never be able to trick another man into loving her again."

He snatched my jaw and forced me to look him in the eye. "He sliced her from her forehead..." He slashed his nails across my face. "All the way down to her chin, splitting her nose open and tearing her cheek so you could see her teeth through it. Defy me again, and you'll beg for a punishment so lenient."

I couldn't get words out around my sobs, so I tried to show him I understood by nodding, and he released me.

"Where were you?"

He doesn't know. He couldn't know, or he'd go after Reaper

and the others. What if Styx was next in that cage after everything she'd been through? I'd selfishly put them all at risk.

If he did know and I lied, I'd make this worse for myself, but it was worth it to protect them. If he knew I'd been with Josh, he already knew I'd been to Thor's bar.

"The biker b-bar off Forty-Seventh," I blurted, stuttering between sobs. "I...I didn't mean to go there. I just w-wanted to see my sister, and I knew you'd say no. I got stuck at the bar. I was scared they'd hurt me, and I hid in the woods overnight, then managed to get a cab home this morning."

He narrowed his eyes. "If I find out any of that is a lie..."

"It's the truth!" I pleaded desperately.

He pulled a towel down from the rack and wrapped it around my shoulders, urging me to stand. He pulled me into his arms and held me as I cried, and that was the thing that broke me. I had to accept the comfort of a monster as the tears consumed me.

I'd been a reckless fool, and others had paid the price. I'd never make that mistake again.

25

TWO WEEKS LATER...

Y ou look like a princess, sugar. A princess about to marry a
King," my father said with a wink.*

I managed to mask the hatred from my expression, but it was
asking too much to expect me to smile. He stood behind me in a
tux, inspecting my elegant wedding gown in the full-length mirror.

I'd wanted something simple and modern, but I'd been over-
ruled and hadn't cared enough to fight them about it. Did it really
matter what I wore to marry a monster?

"He's...not a good man, Daddy."

My father blinked, clearly caught off guard by the abrupt
shift, but he quickly regained his composure. "Neither am I,
sugar. Some of us don't have the luxury of being *good*." He
checked his phone, ready to end the conversation.

"No," I said firmly, turning to face him. "He's not good...
to me."

* BAD GUY—Billie Eilish

He shifted uncomfortably, refusing to meet my eyes, and I knew in an instant that I didn't need to elaborate.

"*You know*," I said with dawning horror. "You know exactly what a monster he is, and you still want me to marry him because it's strategic for you."

His doting-father mask slipped, and I caught a glimpse of the ruthless territory leader in him. "We all make sacrifices, Juliet. If you don't go out there and marry him—"

I held up my hand to cut him off. "You're finished threatening me. I'll do what needs to be done...*if* we strike a bargain. Jacque gets to make her own choices. She chooses her path in life and picks her partner when she decides she's ready for one. And you're going to send her on the yacht trip with my aunt and uncle."

Now he was suspicious. "Why the yacht?"

Because I need her safely out of the way, surrounded by Secret Service on a ship halfway across the world "Because she deserves to be young and have some fun."

From his scowl, it was apparent he didn't like being told what to do, but I could also tell he'd expected me to beg him not to make me marry King...so he was most likely pleased I was being compliant even if it came with conditions.

"Fine. You marry King, Jacque marries who she wants and makes her own choices, so long as they don't cause a scandal."

I shook my head. "I don't give a fuck if she causes a scandal." His sneer deepened at my use of profanity. It was the first time I'd ever cursed in front of him, and it felt good to stop making myself so polite to please him. It was time to find out what I was capable of if I pushed back. "It'll have nothing on the scandal I'll

cause if the film crews out there televise me jilting Kevin King at the altar. She gets to be a normal young adult. And I want it in writing, handled through a lawyer of my choosing."

He sighed heavily. "Fine. With you married to King, she doesn't matter anyway. Have your lawyer write it, and I'll sign." He glanced at his watch. "It's almost time."

He patted my shoulder as he left, but there was no affection in it. As soon as he closed the door, I let my composure slip and started to pace the room.

Minutes. I had only minutes left before the producer from the film crew came to retrieve me so we could start the wedding. I was ready to just get on with it. The longer we waited, the more afraid I was that Reaper was going to call in my debt since I hadn't called it off myself.

I hadn't heard anything from him and hadn't dared to reach out. If he punished me in some way for breaking our deal, it couldn't be worse than getting him killed.

A phone that wasn't mine went off on the end table by the window. I thought my father or one of the stylists had left theirs, but my heart raced nervously when I flipped it over and read the text.

Unknown: A deal's a deal, darling.

I sat in a puddle of wedding dress, losing all bravado with a single text. Would he dare to interrupt the actual ceremony? Surely, he wouldn't be able to storm in and object with security as tight as it was.

Was it possible he was here? Fear knotted anew in my stomach. If he was here, someone would spot him and King would start asking questions that could put everyone Reaper cared about in danger.

I deleted the message and hid the phone in a deep inner pocket of my suitcase. Having a phone King didn't know about removed a huge obstacle to my plan. I'd find a way to hide it better later, but there was no time now!

When I turned back around, I covered my mouth to stifle my scream of shock at finding Reaper sprawled on the couch I'd just been sitting on like it was the throne at his party.

"How did—what are—you can't be here!" I spluttered.

If anyone had seen him here, they'd immediately know he didn't belong. He hadn't even tried to blend in. He was wearing a white dress shirt with a lace collar and cuffs, but it was completely unbuttoned, leaving his bare stomach and chest on full display. A pair of skintight riding pants and brown leather riding boots matched his leather gloves. He looked like a Victorian gentleman who'd turned rogue.

He cocked an eyebrow. "You were just going to leave me on Read." He tutted like he was disappointed. "I see two weeks is too long to leave my brat undisciplined."

Two weeks of aching to call him, of lying awake thinking of him touching me.

"You have to go!"

"Why?" He extended a hand to summon me closer, and I obeyed without even realizing I was doing it. He put his hands on my waist, assessing my wedding dress with a look of distaste.

I frantically looked over my shoulder. "Because there's a film crew about to walk through that door!"

His slow grin was borderline feral. "And you're saying this wouldn't make for good TV?" He lifted one of my stockinged feet onto his thigh, running his hands up the sheer fabric that covered my calf, then stopping at the back of my knee. "You seem to be under the mistaken impression that you can break a deal with me, darling." He ran his hands up my thigh now, brushing his gloved fingertips over the white fabric of my panties before sliding back down to my knee.

He delivered his threat with the confidence of a man who had only to sit there to get what he wanted. If anyone caught him there, all hell was going to break loose and there'd be no wedding.

"You said you wanted me to come to you willingly. Give me that chance. Give *us* a chance. Don't make me do it like this."

He gave me a look so charged with frustration, I would've laughed if the stakes weren't so high.

I wove my fingers into his hair gently. "You're so used to being in control of everyone, making deals and guaranteeing outcomes with leverage. I'm asking you to trust me to choose you with no leverage and no deal on the table. Release me from this bargain, and I'll find a way to be yours."

Reaper pulled one of his gloves off and slipped two fingers into his mouth, then rolled his tongue around them. He dragged my panties to the side with his other hand and shoved the wet fingers inside me. "You're already mine." He crooked his fingers and stroked at an angle that took my breath away. "I'll tell you

what... I'll consider your debt repaid if you can make me come in this pretty pussy before someone comes through that door."

I gritted my teeth to stop myself from moaning as he stroked my clit with the leather of his glove and thrust his fingers deeper with his other hand.

I could've argued with him about the nuances of consent, but there was no point. We both knew I wanted to fuck him. We both knew I wanted him to leave before he got caught. Arguing about anything else was a pointless.

I glanced over my shoulder, torn between the temptation of letting him get us caught and the knowledge that the consequences would hurt people I loved.

"Better not waste time." He unbuttoned his pants, and his meaning couldn't have been plainer. "I'm not leaving until I've filled up your tight little cunt."

I pulled off my panties and hiked my skirt up, then pulled his cock out of his pants, and it sprung to attention. I sighed in frustration as the thick head nudged at my entrance only to slip forward without penetrating.

He spread his arms across the back of the couch, doing nothing to help me.

We both exhaled when I finally got the head in. I tried to sink onto it, but it was too thick to just ram in there. I whimpered, pushing against the stretching pressure that bordered on pain. I didn't mind the pain. I hoped I was sore later and it made me think of Reaper. He was the only one willing to fight everyone, even me, to keep me safe.

His smile curled into something feral. "You seem to be

struggling. Do you need my help, darling?" If he just thrust his hips up, he'd slide in deeper. "It would break our terms, but if that's what you need…"

"Don't need your help this time." We let out guttural groans when I thrust down and drove his cock deep inside me. If we didn't keep quiet, someone was going to hear.

The frantic need to feel this with him before I had to go ice-cold for the ceremony snapped something in me, and all at once, I was an animal thrashing against him, digging my nails into his chest as I rode his cock with abandon.

"Fuck…" Reaper breathed.

This wasn't what got him off, though. He'd told me as much. He wanted to feel me come.

I managed to tuck my skirt under one arm and lower a hand between my thighs, letting him see the way I was touching myself.

"You'd better get me off before that film crew comes in the door. Maybe you're stalling because you want to get caught. I know how much you like it when people watch."

He was talking shit, and it was turning me on, the threat of being caught, the scandal of it all. I was beyond thinking clearly enough to focus on the consequences. I couldn't tear my eyes from his as we thrust together. He lost control and snatched my hips, driving me over the edge of an orgasm just as he groaned and came.

I held my breath, fighting not to make the sounds that felt like they were going to explode out of me. It was cruel to ask me to endure such intensity in silence. I wanted to collapse against his chest and lie there until I stopped feeling like I was floating. But it was too risky.

"You have to go," I said, standing. As soon as he pulled out, the mess started to come out.

"You leave it there," Reaper growled. "Walk down that aisle and make whatever bullshit vows you want, but you're going to do it with my seed dripping down your thighs, reminding you that no matter what you say to him, you belong to me."

Someone knocked on the hallway door.

"Just a moment!" I called.

Reaper snatched me to his chest, claiming my mouth in a searing, possessive kiss. "This isn't over. I'll see you at the auction."

26

Eric knocked on my bedroom door the night after we got home from the wedding. "Mrs. King? I have a message from your husband."*

Mrs. King. I'd married him. Now I just had to survive it.

Eric had such an eager look on his face as he handed me the note that I immediately knew something horrible was about to happen.

Meet me down at the menagerie. I've got another wedding present for you.

My heart thundered in my chest, yet I had no choice but to go down there.

Who was he going to torture this time?

Reaper.

What was I going to do if he had Reaper in there?

Or Ophelia or Styx or Az or any of the other people from the club?

* THREE ROUNDS AND A SOUND—Blind Pilot

I dismissed Eric with a gesture to the door. "I'll be down in a moment."

He swung a set of car keys around his finger. "I'm heading to your sister's place. Mr. King likes me to keep an eye on her."

Shit! She wouldn't leave with my aunt and uncle until just before the auction, and King was making sure I knew Eric could hurt her in the meantime.

I lunged for his keys, but he snatched them away. "Don't you go near her!"

He shrugged as he strode from the room. "That depends on you. Now be a good girl and get down there, or you'll miss the best part."

I ran to the safe Kevin kept in his office, the one he didn't know I'd memorized the code to. I frantically spun the dial, opened it, and tucked one of the handguns into my jacket pocket after checking to see if it was loaded.

Then I ran for the menagerie.

I was too late! A man's incoherent screams tore through the quiet evening.

I stumbled as it happened again. My chest was being ripped open and my heart yanked out. I ran the last stretch to the enclosure, palming the gun in my pocket. Before I pulled it out, I caught sight of the man who was being ripped to shreds, and he wasn't anyone I recognized.

"Who is that?" I said urgently as I fought to catch my breath, trying not to puke.

King wrapped an arm around my shoulders. "That, my lovely wife, is the man who killed your brother." He held up his phone

and played a surveillance video that showed my brother talking to someone in an alley. Tears pricked my eyes at the sight of him alive. If Kevin was showing me this, were these the last moments of Geoff's life?

I cried out when the man next to him raised a gun and shot my brother in the chest. Geoff collapsed to the ground, and when the man turned to speak to someone off camera, I caught sight of the tattoo on his throat.

Die Free. I'd spoken to that guy at Thor's bar weeks ago. I looked back into the enclosure and recognized him now that I'd been reminded. His face was bloodied, but I could still make out the tattoo on his throat.

"He's part of the Serpents of Death MC, but it was a guy named Reaper who gave the order as part of a deal between them. I'll see to it he meets the same fate, little wife. Don't you worry."

My stomach dropped. *He couldn't have. He would've told me. Is this another one of King's head games to test me?*

The man in the enclosure screamed, begging for his life, offering to turn over information. He'd killed my brother in cold blood, but I still wasn't sure he deserved to die like this. No one deserved to die like this.

King moved closer, gripping the bars of the enclosure as he watched with eagerness rather than revulsion. "He gave her a good chase," he said wistfully. "Better than the others. She took her time hunting him, passing up chances to take him down, waiting until she was absolutely sure. It was a thing of beauty."

The leopard had ripped open the guy's stomach and dragged his entrails onto the ground. The stench was sickening.

He pulled himself up onto his forearms and looked at us, pleading desperately. There was a flash of recognition on his face when he saw me, and I wondered if he was mentally coherent enough to tell Kevin anything damning about that night. My story would unravel quickly if he said anything about me leaving with Thor. Would he think to barter his life with the information?

He'd be dead today no matter how this played out. It could be a slow, agonizing death, drawn out even longer if King questioned him. Or I could end this.

I yanked the gun from my pocket and fired a shot straight into the guy's head. King flinched and ducked, his eyes flying wide with rage at what I'd done. I could've shot Kevin in the back of the head where he was standing, and I watched the realization play out on his face: the flash of fear that was quickly replaced with anger. He was so shaken, he couldn't speak.

I put the gun back in my pocket, not letting him see how much my hand was shaking too. "My brother's murderer should be my kill. Not hers." I sounded icy calm, but the truth was that something feral had just been unleashed inside me. I wanted to rip King's entrails out like the big cat had done to the dead biker, but I had to wait. Eric was on his way to my sister.

King's mouth fell open in shock as he looked between me and the dead man like he still couldn't believe it.

"Are we finished here?" I asked dismissively.

When he didn't answer, I turned on my heel and headed back to the house.

Maybe I was a fool, but I didn't believe Reaper had ordered

my brother killed. The next time King took me down to that enclosure, it really could be Reaper or any of the others.

I had to stop King, and I already had the beginnings of a plan. For the three days of the Black Rose Auction, I'd be on neutral ground with all the players present and my sister would be safely away. Three days of protection to take him out at the knees. It only gave me a few months to figure out the rest of it, but that had to be enough.

Just like the leopard, I'd passed up a chance to kill him. I'd hunt him now. And wait until I could tear his throat out.

27

THREE MONTHS LATER...

D id he just take your phone?" Jacque whispered from across the drawing room, staring in shock at my husband's retreating back.*

The one he knows about...

"He likes to keep an eye on me," I said, like it was no big deal that he was currently snooping through my messages, emails, search history, and photos. He'd find nothing but evidence I was the perfect wife, obedient to him in every way.

"I can see that," she muttered, glancing at Eric, who'd been stationed in the corner throughout her visit.

He was staring at her instead of watching me. In a yellow dress that highlighted her blond hair and sun-kissed skin, she was the breathtaking picture of carefree youth. Had I ever been that young?

I was only ten years older than her, but it felt like a hundred

* NFWMB—Hozier

years separated us, even if I was dressed to look just as light
and untroubled. King hated it when I wore black, so I was in a
pink lacy sundress that matched my light-pink nails and the pink
ribbon my stylist had woven into my soft dark curls. My time for
black would come.

I wasn't going to let King's intrusion spoil the joy of seeing
my sister. It might be the last time I saw her if my plan went awry,
and I wasn't going to have her last memories of me be anything
but happy ones.

"I'm sorry... Is that a jaguar?" she asked incredulously, looking out the window at the cage they were transporting from the
vet outbuilding back to the menagerie.

"A leopard. One of Kevin's pets." I bugged my eyes at the
ridiculousness of it, and she choked back a laugh.

I shuddered anytime I saw the leopard now. It wasn't the
animal's fault. She was just another creature trapped in Kevin's
menagerie, subject to his brutal whims.

I tore my eyes from the window and focused on my sister.
"I'm going to miss you," I said, choking up and trying to hide
it with a beaming smile. "But I'm so excited for you to take this
trip." Three months on a yacht with my aunt and uncle. She'd
be far from Kevin's influence and aboard a ship with a Secret
Service detail. I could only light the proverbial fuse if I knew she
wouldn't be collateral damage.

She sighed in that world-weary way only teenagers had perfected, though she'd just left her teen years behind with her most
recent birthday, a celebration I'd missed because I'd been late to
dinner with Kevin the day before. He was drunk and accidentally

left the marks of his displeasure where people would see them. He didn't let me leave the house until the bruises faded and I was able to take the splint off my wrist.

It had been worth it. I was late for dinner in the first place because I'd taken a secret call with one of his enemies, one of the last things I needed. It was going to be the key to destruction. His or mine. Maybe both. I didn't fucking care anymore. I couldn't keep living like this.

"I'm excited for the trip too, but three months is such a long time to be on a boat with family and no one my age." She huffed.

I smiled gently. "Maybe you'll meet someone hot in Australia or Japan. A foreign dignitary's son…"

She frowned, but I could see the wheels turning in her mind.

"You'll find ways to have fun." I laughed.

"Did you?" She glanced at the interloper who wasn't even pretending not to listen. "Have fun before you got married?"

Reaper flashed through my mind. No matter how I tried to keep the memories of him shut away, they had a habit of spiraling into my thoughts: The way he'd held my wrist and smoked from my cigarette in the boathouse. The way his mouth curved slowly into that wicked smile. The wild abandon of what we'd done in the Kennedy Room and the sight of him tapping on my balcony window later that night. Kissing him. Touching him. Fearing him. Inexplicably trusting him with my life, my body… my heart. Being held in his arms.

I tried to keep my expression neutral, but it was Jacque's turn to smile. "I see," she said knowingly.

"There's something you need to know," I said quietly, even

though Eric could still hear me. "Daddy and I made a deal, and he promised you could pick who you marry, decide what you want to do with your life. It's been documented. Even if something were to happen to me, that deal holds."

She looked panicked. "What would happen to you?"

I moved to the couch she was sitting on and took her hands. "Hopefully nothing, but in our family, you never know. Mama made me a similar promise, and Daddy broke it after she was gone. I've made sure he can't do that to you. But I need you to make me a promise as well, sunshine."

She nodded intently.

"Promise me you'll pick someone kind. Someone who adores you just as you are."

If the cycle is broken with you, this will all have been worth it.

"I promise," she said as a tear streamed down her cheek.

She was young in so many ways but wise beyond her years in others. *She knew.* Not the specifics of any of it, but she knew I was miserable and that my misery had somehow bought her freedom.

"Thank you," she said, squeezing my hands. "You can be the maid of honor when I marry an Australian fisherman."

I laughed, fighting back tears. "Sophia's not going to appreciate that."

Brenner and Daddy better protect Sophia and her kids. I'd tried to find a way to shield her more securely from Kevin, but I was pretty sure she was safe.

"She'll be fine," Jacque said, like she was reading my mind.

"You should get going," I said, releasing her hands and standing to walk her out. "Kevin and I are leaving soon, and I know you need to get to the dock."

We said our goodbyes, and I watched her drive away, hoping she'd find the joy for herself that was missing in my life even if I wasn't there to see it.

I might not have had the traditional kind of happiness, but a grim, exhilarated kind of delight twisted inside me as I turned to go back inside. Jacque was safe, and I'd done everything I could to secure her future.

Time to go and end my marriage.

28

"Don't you think it's about time you stop taking those?" King asked, nodding toward the birth control pill I'd just swallowed. He stood at my bathroom doorway with an easy smile on his handsome face, a monster with classic good looks.[*]

"After the auction?" I suggested.

King wrapped his arms around me from behind, then kissed me on the cheek. "If one more week makes a difference to you, so be it."

He'd switched my pills out right after the wedding for placebos without telling me, but he didn't need to know that I knew. Just like he didn't need to know that I'd gotten an IUD in anticipation of him sabotaging them. It was done by the same doctor who patched me up every time Kevin smacked me around, and I'd played on his guilt to convince him to bring an IUD. It had been one of the acts of defiance that showed me I could still fight back.

[*] YOU SHOULD SEE ME IN A CROWN—Billie Eilish

If you spent enough time with a monster, you stopped expecting them to be anything but monstrous.

Once I was ready and packed for our trip, I lingered in my closet, running my fingers along the Bryson Blue Dress. My mother and grandmother hadn't been able to escape. One died in a mysterious car accident, and the other died in a tragic plane crash. I wondered now if either had truly been an accident. If my family was cursed, it was by men who craved power and were willing to crush anyone who didn't obey them.

One more week is *going to make all the difference...*

———

I stood in front of my Bernini an hour later, waiting for Kevin to come downstairs so we could leave for the auction. He'd taken everything from me, even my favorite artist. How was I supposed to feel the same way about Bernini's work now that I could relate more to the mistress he'd mutilated than the beauty of his art?

All I could see were the themes Bernini had chosen—the inherent violence of so many of his pieces, the entitlement of his male heroes, and the way his heroines suffered.

The Rape of Proserpina was so exquisite, it was easy to look past the subject matter. No one saw Nemesis's tears when they looked at the statue in front of me. Nobody cared that Daphne had turned herself into a fucking tree to escape Apollo's relentless pursuit. All we saw was art.

Similarly, my marriage was such a pleasing match to the press and the public and the territory leaders alike that no one cared

what really happened in this house. My pain meant nothing. No one cared that I would have to distort myself to escape him.

But I wouldn't become a tree or a bird or a fish like they had. I'd become a goddamned monster too.

I surreptitiously pulled out my secret phone, the one Reaper left me as a wedding present of sorts, and hit Schedule Send on the press release I'd drafted...then I walked away from that statue for the last time.

———

"I have a surprise for you," I said to Kevin, just as we were about to enter the ballroom for the pre-auction gala. "A belated wedding present of sorts..."

We walked into a ballroom filled with people posturing while they drank and socialized. A quick scan of the room, and I'd laid eyes on an actual prince, a mob princess, a cardinal, all manner of senators and judges, and eight of the top ten richest people in the world, including my husband, of course.

"Now isn't really the time for surprises," he said through gritted teeth, annoyed that I was doing anything but decorating his arm.

I handed him my phone with the news article up. *Kevin King Donates* The Lost Bernini *to Museum in Rome.*

"Isn't it a glowing piece?" I asked, watching his jaw muscle work as he stopped moving to read the article.

"Why would you do this?" he growled, knowing better than to show emotion in this crowd.

Because I hate looking at it, you sick fuck.

I blinked innocently. "I thought you'd be happy. It paints you as a champion of art for the people."

"Do you have any concept of what that sculpture cost? It's irreplaceable."

"It belongs in a museum," I said sweetly, steering him toward the bar. "Why don't you grab us some drinks? I'm going to say hi to my father."

I greeted my father coolly, giving him a brief hug. I wasn't going to pretend to be his perfect little daughter anymore.

With gleeful anticipation, I watched Peter Donahue stop Kevin as he crossed the ballroom so he could shake Kevin's hand and thank him profusely for the monumental campaign contribution. Never mind that Kevin knew nothing of the contribution and had handpicked Peter's opponent in the race.

I smiled, watching Kevin play his way through it like it had been intentional. He couldn't very well tell them his wife was running amok, funding his opponents to spite him.

He reached us and thrust a glass of champagne into my hand so violently, some of it spilled. "More of your handiwork, I suppose?"

I toasted him. "I just thought it might be strategic to support both sides, you know? Give the will of the people a chance."

He seized me under the arm roughly. "Why don't you stop with the theatrics and tell me what this is about?"

I looked down at where he held me in a grip that felt like it might snap my arm. "You know what it's about."

I winced, trying to dislodge Kevin's fingers from my arm without making a scene. If he kept this up, he'd get kicked out before

I was able to enact my plan. At that moment, I swore I could feel someone watching me, and I looked up to find Reaper standing on the other side of the room. He wore leather pants cut so low, I didn't know how his dick wasn't coming out. He was, of course, shirtless, but a long black cloak was fastened at his throat with silver jewelry dangling onto his chest. He was wearing black gloves again, and I shivered, remembering what they felt like when he touched me.

He looked at where Kevin held me and tilted his head. The ferocity in his expression made my heart skip a beat.

This was my battle to fight, and I didn't need anyone else getting hurt because of me.

This only works if I'm the only person at stake.

The Black Rose Auction was strictly enforced neutral ground for the entire three-day event, so as long as we were here, King couldn't seriously harm me. Most importantly, he couldn't kill me and get away with it. It would be tough to make it look like an accident where so many eyes were watching.

I had three days when I was protected from his wrath—three days to force him to let me go.

I shifted my focus back to Kevin, who'd managed to put his civilized mask back into place.

"Juliet?" my father said threateningly, looking between Kevin and me. "Do we need to discuss something?"

Kevin puffed his chest. "She's a King now, not a Bryson. We'll handle this privately."

He released my arm, and I fought to keep my hand steady as I took a sip of champagne. A headache was worth it if it steadied my nerves.

They carried on like nothing had happened because, in this room, it was a fatal mistake to show any kind of weakness. Everyone appeared absorbed in their own conversations, but they were all throwing glances over their shoulders, assessing allies and enemies. There was no chum in this room—only sharks.

Moments later, a proprietary hand slid across my lower back, and I stiffened. Reaper's long hair tickled my bare shoulder as he murmured in my ear, "We both know you don't drink champagne, darling."

My traitorous body wanted to melt against him. I hadn't known I was strong enough to fight back until I thought it was Reaper in that cage. He brought out the sides of me that I'd buried my whole life. For this man, I'd burn the fucking world down.

The horrified look on my father's face would've been funny if it weren't me living this nightmare. This wasn't part of my plan!

Reaper pried the champagne flute from my fingers and replaced it with the stem of a martini glass, handing the champagne to a passing server.

Then he brushed his gloved fingertips over the part of my arm Kevin had just bruised with his grip and looked straight at my husband. "Since it's not your first time at my auction, I know you're familiar with the rules. Give me a fucking reason to enforce them."

King's voice was ice-cold. "The rules are the only reason you're still standing after touching my wife. Touch her again and I'll have to inform the Concierge you were fondling what doesn't belong to you without permission."

Reaper's jaw clenched, but he schooled his expression into a

bored smile. "If you're planning to keep a pet, you should at least learn what she likes to drink. I hear wives can get restless if you don't keep them satisfied." He turned back to my father and said, "Isn't that right, Nathaniel?"

What the hell does that mean?

King tugged me away from Reaper, gripping the exact spot he'd already bruised. "I'll do as I damn well please with *my wife*. She likes it when I'm firm with her, don't you, babe?"

I sucked in a breath but managed to keep my face relaxed as I nodded. This wasn't the moment. He wasn't going to hurt me enough in front of others to face execution, but if he got us kicked out for making a scene, I'd never get another shot at this.

King all but dragged me back toward the elevators, and I let him because it served my ends.

I dared a quick glance over my shoulder and met Reaper's dark glare. He was simmering with rage. He tilted his chin in question, asking my permission to intervene.

I shook my head and followed King out of the ballroom.

29

As soon as King slammed the door to the suite shut, he exploded. "What the hell has gotten into you? You donate the Bernini. You give Donahue god knows how much money to make my life harder. Then you parade your infidelity for all the world to see!"*

His phone rang, but he ignored it and threw one of his suitcases from a chair onto the floor, scattering the contents everywhere. "Do you know what he does, Juliet? Is that what you want? You want to be a whore? Because that can be arranged!"

I laughed bitterly. "Now, that's an empty threat if ever I've heard one. Your fragile little ego wouldn't be able to handle letting me fuck other people."

He raised a hand to smack me but realized his mistake and dropped it again.

I lunged closer, getting in his face. "Do it! Hit me and make

* ANGEL OF SMALL DEATH AND THE CODEINE SCENE—Hozier

all this easier!" Any kind of serious violence between the auction attendees carried a potential death sentence, the kind where the body would never be found and no authorities would ever investigate.

He slammed a fist down on one of the dressers. "What the fuck do you want, Juliet? Another dog? A different priceless piece of art? I already buy you literally anything you desire. You're spoiled and ungrateful."

His phone kept going off, so he angrily picked it up and snapped, "*What?*"

He mostly listened, turning white with rage as the person on the other end of the phone spoke.

Then he exploded again, shattering his phone against the wall a few feet from me. "You had the government take my leopard? The Feds could prosecute me for that, Juliet."

I cocked my hip, needing him to think I was in control and unafraid even if I was really terrified. My tone was vicious. "Oh, this is just a taste, Kevin. Minor inconveniences that you'll sort through with enough money thrown at the problem. It only escalates from here if you don't let me go."

"Let you go *where*, for fuck's sake?"

He seriously didn't get it, hadn't even considered my leaving him.

I threw my hands in the air, no longer able to hide my anger under a mask of control. "I want a divorce, Kevin! I want to be free of you. And I'm not going to stop tearing things down until you let me go. I'll burn the fucking house down around me before I live one more day in it with you!" I didn't mean to

raise my voice, but I couldn't hold back the rage that bled into my tone.

"That can also be arranged," he said with seething menace.

I shuddered, taking a deep breath to make sure I was calm enough that he'd understand I'd planned for this. "If I die suddenly, a video will be sent to every major news outlet, not only detailing my belief that you intend to kill me but sharing every filthy secret of yours I've been privy to. And it's a lot, Kevin, because you've never really thought of me as a person, so you speak freely around me if I lurk in the right places. I have enough to crush your empire and send you to prison for the rest of your life."

"You think I don't have my own insurance policy?" His smug smile made my stomach turn. "That I don't have the skull of the biker you killed and the gun with your prints on it? It's really too bad your sister touched the knife I used to cut off his head. It's going to be hard to convince a jury the Bryson sisters weren't out for revenge."

Fuck.

I kept my back rigid, steady in the face of his threats. "I'll fucking destroy you." Divorce had never really been an option. He'd never let me go.

"Get out! I can't look at you without wanting to snap your neck." He yanked me by the shoulders and tossed me into the hall before slamming the door shut behind me. It was the most I'd seen him control his temper in all the time we'd been together.

I'd have to do better.

I could do this.

I had to do this.

The only mercy he'd given me since we'd gotten together was always wanting separate rooms, even when we traveled. He usually wanted me in a different part of the hotel, probably so he could party and fuck other people without the inconvenience of running into his wife. As though I cared.

With violently trembling hands, I opened the door to my suite and dumped my bag and keys on the table, heading straight for the fridge. I didn't bother making a proper drink. I just pulled out a mini bottle of gin out and took a few gulps, appreciating the warmth that crept into my stomach and loosened the tension in my shoulders.

"Did you fuck him?"

I jumped so violently, I spilled gin everywhere as I whipped around to find Reaper sitting in a dark corner. His hair was a mess, like he'd been dragging his fingers roughly through it, and there wasn't a hint of a smile on his face. He looked tormented.

I turned away so he wouldn't see how rattled I was from the conversation I'd just had.

"Answer the question, Juliet. Did he touch you?"

30

You're jealous?" Of all the reactions I would've anticipated from him, that one hadn't ranked among them.

"I don't get jealous," he said in a hollow voice.

"If you don't want my husband touching me, how is that not jealousy?"

He jumped up from the chair and paced like I'd seen him do on the hidden camera in his office that day. "I don't want him touching you because *you* don't want him touching you."

"What happened to insignificant sex not mattering? You want all your clients to touch you all the time?"

He stopped and pinned me with a stare. "This goes beyond that. You look like a ghost, Juliet."

Protectiveness might break me right now.

If I leaned on him, I was afraid I might just crumble.

He was quiet for a long moment. Then his hands were on my shoulders, his touch soft and reassuring like he was soothing

a spooked horse. "What's going on with you? Something isn't right."

I shrugged out of his touch and reached for another bottle of gin. "You just started shit with my husband in front of everyone."

"He was hurting you," he said in a voice that worried me. He sounded ready to murder King. If he found out the full extent of it, he might get reckless.

I needed to change the subject, and there were questions I needed him to answer. "That thing you said to my father...the hatred you have for him... What's the history between you?"

He swiped a hand over his mouth, looking uncharacteristically out of his element. "Years ago, when I was first starting my club, I arranged a liaison for your mother. A liaison that turned into something more. She fell in love with one of my escorts, and your father found out. He had them both killed and made it look like an accident. He's been on a mission to destroy my club ever since."

I waited for the outraged shock to set in, but it never came. Somehow, I'd known my father had been involved in my mother's death.

"Did you have my brother killed?" I said so softly, it was almost a whisper.

He blinked. "No."

His look of sympathy robbed me of breath. Suddenly, it all unraveled in my brain. "It was King. The three million dollars. The *TW* you wrote on the sticky note was Thor, wasn't it?"

Reaper jerked his chin in a nod. "I didn't know that's what it was for until later, when King picked up Thor's guy right after your wedding. Thor admitted to the whole thing."

King had paid Thor three million dollars, with the final installment being delivered immediately after my brother's death. I was disgusted with myself for not seeing it before.

I sat on the bed, not sure my knees would hold me up. "I married my brother's killer. I bet he did it to back my father into a corner so he could swoop in and save the day. He loves nothing more than a fucked-up game."

I didn't have time to spiral into grief again. There were only two days left of the auction, two days when I was safe. Then he'd find a way to make me pay for what I'd done.

I wanted to rip out his entrails like the leopard had done to the biker.

Reaper's hands returned gently to my shoulders. "I know that look, darling. Don't walk down that road alone."

"You have to go," I said, checking the locks on the door. "He'll have someone watching my door, and knowing him, someone will be patrolling outside at some point tonight."

"The guard on the grounds is…occupied at the moment." He paused. "Can I sleep here?"*

I wrapped my arms around him, resting my head on his bare chest. "I don't want you taking that risk for me."

He kissed my forehead. "You'd be doing me a favor, Juliet." He sighed heavily. "I'm tired. I'm tired, and I'm not in a head-space to fuck anyone, and if I sleep in my room, any number of people will come calling through the night."

"Can't you ignore them?"

He laughed, but there was no humor in it. "It's cute that you

* SUNLIGHT—Hozier

think they all knock. According to Grim, there's someone in my bed right now, someone whose needs I don't have the energy for. He'll take it personally if I kick him out, and I don't have the energy for the fallout of that either."

He looked genuinely exhausted.

It was so unlike him to be vulnerable that I wanted to snuggle him in the blankets and shield him from it all. "Stay with me then. I promise not to try to fuck you..."

Warmth flooded his eyes. "Mmm...definitely don't have the energy for greedy little brats tonight." He crossed to the sitting area and pulled the extra cushions to make a line down the middle of the bed. "Don't get any ideas."

He pulled his cloak off and tossed it over a chair along with his gloves and jewelry. I tried not to stare. I really did. But his every movement was an invitation. He caught me looking as he pulled his last ring off, and the corners of his mouth lifted. "I mean it. No sex."

He unbuckled his belt and tugged it out of the belt loops with a quick jerk. I flinched so violently, he froze.

I stood there for a second, mortified, then laughed shakily. "Sorry, you scared me. Thought you were about to get kinky with that belt."

He didn't laugh. He just stared at me like he was assembling a puzzle in his mind. He took a step toward me, then stopped himself and raked a hand through his hair. "Juliet, has he hit you?"

I turned around. I couldn't bear to look at him as I lied. "A few times. Not often."

He approached me slowly, giving me every chance to stop him before he hugged me from behind.

Two tears spilled from my eyes and dropped onto his arms. "I don't want you to look at me differently. Don't want you to think I'm a victim or be scared to touch me."

He nuzzled the side of my neck, then lowered himself to his knees in front of me, holding the backs of my thighs. "I won't look at you differently if you don't look at me differently once you know I was in an abusive relationship too. And no one pushed me into mine. I stayed because it's hard to leave, and it's hard to ask for help, and goddamn can trauma be like quicksand."

I studied him, trying to imagine how someone so strong and self-possessed could've ended up in a situation like mine.

As though he were reading my mind, he said, "It's not your fault, and being stronger wouldn't have helped. It can happen to anyone."

I gave him a watery laugh despite the tears that continued to tumble down my cheeks. "I expected you to lose your shit if you found out... Thank you...for understanding."

He smiled and squeezed my thighs gently. "Don't think for a second that my first impulse isn't to murder the bastard with my bare hands. But he can wait. Taking care of you comes first."

I put my hands on top of his on the backs of my thighs. "I got myself into this, and it's on me to get myself out of it. I won't have anyone else getting hurt because of me."

He rested his forehead on my stomach. "That's the trauma talking, Juliet. Let me in. Trust me to make that call for myself."

A new stream of tears rolled down my cheeks as I remembered

the sounds of the leopard tearing Josh apart because of me. "What if he hurts you?"

He stood and stroked his thumbs across my cheeks tenderly, like he could wipe the memories away. "Darling, he already has. Every mark on you, every flinch, every tear you've shed, every moment you've felt alone..." The expression on his face shifted from tender to fierce. "You're not alone."

"I saw his face tonight. He'll never let me go. I have to kill him."

"You don't have to do that, my darling. I'll do it. Or, hell, Grim will gladly do it."

"He's too well protected. Tell me you wouldn't have done it already if you could have. He's mine...and I have to do it before we leave the auction."

He shook his head sadly. "You can't harm another attendee. There are no exceptions. Not even for you."

"Unless he hurts me first."

He stepped away, and as the seconds stretched for an age, he just stared at me. Then he turned away and crouched like he needed to explode but didn't want to scare me. I stood silently as he processed, raking a hand through his hair again before he stood up and met my eyes. "You're going to deliberately provoke him, try to make him hurt you here so you can kill him without consequences." I was surprised his back teeth weren't ground to dust with the way his jaw muscle was working.

I inhaled deeply and released it. "Can you help me without putting anyone at the club at risk?"

He barked a laugh. "Styx about lost her mind that I let you go back the night of the party. She's barely spoken to me since.

Which means Az has been storming around because she's equally pissed at him. Ophelia muttered something that sounded an awful lot like *sniveling coward* the last time she saw me. Grim is the only one who hasn't said anything, but he left the newspaper wedding feature on my desk with a knife through Kevin's face... so I think his feelings are pretty clear."

He looked thoughtful. "I think we all knew instinctively that it wasn't right. I was trying not to force your hand. If I'd had any idea... I'm sorry I let you go back."

I made it to him in two steps and gave him the kiss I'd been dying for since my wedding day. He slanted his mouth over mine, reminding me that King hadn't taken this from me. I still ached for this man and what he could make me feel.

He tilted my chin up to deepen the kiss, parting my lips with his tongue. When he pulled away, I was breathless.

"You have nothing to be sorry for. I wasn't ready to tell you. I'm still not sure I want the others to know."

He wiped the last of the tears from under my eyes with his thumbs. "We're all close friends with trauma, darling. You've got nothing to be embarrassed about."

Reaper knocked the wall of pillows off the bed. "No funny business if you don't want it, but at least let me hold you."

He helped me to get my dress off. Then he finished taking his clothes off, and we both climbed under the covers naked. He tucked my back against his body, curling around me with his warmth. "You're safe now, Juliet. We'll talk about your plan in the morning, but you're never going back to him. Someone from Petite Mort will stay with you even when I have to be at the auction."

It was clear he wasn't happy about my plan to deal with King, but he wasn't pushing me. It could wait until the morning. I needed something else from him more.

"Hmmm, speaking of petite mort..." I said, rolling over and nudging at him to do the same. I drew a rectangular sort of shape on his back. "This is your throne at your next party. And this is me bent over the arm of your throne—naked, of course." The muscles on his back flexed as I touched him.

"And what was that?" he asked in a growly voice.

"My pussy dripping because you've fingered me while everyone watches. And now here's your cock, and here's me sucking on it, choking as I try to make you feel good."

He flipped me over so I was facing away from him again, and his hard cock pressed against my ass. He tucked it between my legs, not quite pushing it inside me, but nudging at my entrance.

Instead of fucking me, he traced a shape on my back. "This is you at my primal party the day after tomorrow. Will you be predator or prey?"

I squirmed as he tickled my back. "Definitely predator..." His cock was thick and hard between my legs, but he still hadn't put it inside me.

"In that case, this is you sitting on my face after hunting me down. And this is me licking that sweet cunt until you beg me to fill you up. And this..." He shoved inside me with one long, slow thrust. "This is you riding my cock until you scream my name, making sure everyone knows who you belong to."

I cried out, somewhere between a moan and a sob, when he gripped my hips and thrust into me faster. He lowered one hand

to the apex of my thighs and coaxed the sweetest release from me, like he managed to unravel all my fear and tension with his body. Then he sank deeper and held himself there as he came, growling, "*Mine.*"

I nuzzled my head into his shoulder, feeling so safe and content, but there was a thought I couldn't let go of. "I've spent the last few months scraping for dirt on King, looking for ways to sabotage him or hold leverage over him. I think I figured out what he does on his island...and it's awful shit. Like hunting people as big game. Should I just be giving the cops the evidence I have and letting them take him down?"

Reaper cursed against my neck. "He's too wealthy and too well protected. Even if it worked, it would leave you exposed. We need his allies to be afraid. And that piece of shit needs to die."

His phone went off, and he grabbed it. The deep breath he exhaled told me it wasn't good news. "King just added a last-minute item to the auction."

I tilted his phone so I could see.

The Bryson Blue Dress.

31

Reaper had convinced me to stay in a secure room with Az keeping watch during the auction viewing, where he confirmed King had put my most treasured possession on display. The catalog stated that I'd be modeling it during the auction, but Reaper said I didn't have to. To my disgust, King had implied the Bryson Curse might come along with the dress, an idea sure to titillate.[*]

The dress arguably belonged in the Smithsonian, but I hadn't been able to part with it. Mama had loved that dress.

King was selling it to a random stranger, and if he succeeded, I'd never see it again. It would be hoarded in some private collection where they'd do god knew what with it.

Reaper promised he wouldn't let it happen, but whatever solution he came up with to work around the auction rules, he'd be paying King for my dress. This was King's first move

* COME TOGETHER (LIVE)—AnnenMayKantereit

to retaliate against me for the things I'd done, and I couldn't let him get away with it. Now was the moment to strike back. Reaper would be in the middle of performing his duties as auctioneer, so there was no way to talk to him, but I couldn't let the thought go.

I rushed out the door of the suite. "I need to go to the auction," I told Az. Instead of telling me to stay put or saying he needed to check with Reaper, he studied me for a split second, then nodded once. He walked next to me without saying a word, but it felt like silent support.

I was allowed through the door to the backstage area because my name was on a list, and as soon as someone spotted me, they led me over to a holding area with seats.

"You're up soon," the busy-looking woman told me.

I tilted my fingers up to get the Concierge's attention.

The Concierge was an unassuming-looking older white person who spoke softly but wielded influence at the auction on par with Reaper's.

I gave them a polite smile. "Can I pull my item from the auction?"

They pursed their lips, looking thoughtful. "Only if you replace it with something of equal or greater interest."

Shit. Shit. I couldn't think what would be considered of greater interest than the dress. "Does the item have to physically be here?"

They spread their hands. "Yes."

"What about my ring?" I asked, holding up the giant rock on my finger.

They gave me the patient look of a person used to dealing with the excessively wealthy. "It's valuable, to be certain, but another like it could be acquired outside the auction. For an item to be of interest here, it must be...*unique*, unattainable elsewhere."

The low, playful rumble of Reaper's voice carried from the stage, where he was auctioning marriage to a pretty—though nervous-looking—young woman, pulling my attention to him, until a stunning woman in a beaded dress and a red necklace that looked like an elaborate collar walked past me backstage, obviously waiting for her turn.

Ruby Belmonte. Heir to the Belmonte territory, from a family as powerful as mine. She was so comfortable in her own skin, so confident despite all the chaos backstage.

"What's she selling?" I asked.

The Concierge looked in the direction I'd nodded. "Miss Ruby is selling three nights with her." They said it so matter-of-factly, like an heiress suddenly deciding to do a little sex work was no big deal.

I was thinking about this all wrong! "The night with me," I said, trying to sound like I knew what I was doing.

I held my breath, waiting for them to say they had to check with my husband. I didn't realize just how much I'd come to accept that phrase until they simply said, "I'll get you a contract."

I almost burst into relieved tears, then fought the impulse to laugh. I was relieved that I was considered a person with enough agency to...auction myself for sex.

They returned almost immediately with a thick document. I didn't bother reading it. I just filled it out, signed it, and handed it back to them.

They nodded. "I'll notify the auctioneer."

————

"What the fuck is this?" Reaper tossed the contract onto the table in front of me.

I took a deep breath, determined not to cave. "I'm going to be in the auction, and the winner can enjoy the pleasure of my company for the night."

He leaned closer, and his tone turned lethal. "Is he somehow forcing you into this?"

I kissed him hard and quick. "This is my *choice*. He tried to auction my most precious possession...so instead I'm selling his. He won't be able to stop it, or he'll look weak, like he can't control his own wife."

Reaper closed his eyes, pinching the bridge of his nose in frustration, muttering, "Devil save me from brats..." When he looked back up, seriousness stamped the chiseled planes of his face. "This isn't a game, darling. Do you know who's out there? Do you know what they'd do to Nathaniel Bryson's daughter if they had the chance? The depraved shit they'd do to Kevin King's wife just to make a point?"

"I don't care. Whatever humiliation I suffer, it'll be worth it to make him suffer too. He hates the idea of sharing me with anyone else. The thought of his torment for the night will get me through it. I can't think of anything more likely to make him

snap." I managed to sound sure, but I was trembling so violently, he must've been able to see it.

He put his hands flat on the table like he was keeping himself under control. "I don't have funds already cleared in an auction escrow account or a proxy able to cover what those assholes will bid for you."

King had shown too much control so far. If he was retaliating against me with the dress, then he thought he still had power. There was no telling what moves he was making in the background nor when he might leave the auction and blow my chance. I needed him to lose control, and there was no better way to trigger him, no matter the risks.

I laid my hands on top of Reaper's. "We don't have a better plan."

He gave me a look charged with intensity. "You remember when I told you I could protect you? I said it knowing perfectly well what kind of trouble you manage to get yourself into. If this is what you need to do...I'll just have to be true to my word."

Like it was settled, he nodded to a woman with a clipboard. "I'm ready for the next one, love."

With a hurried but thorough kiss on my lips, he pushed past the curtain and strode into the bright lights of the stage.

A frantic-looking woman appeared, holding up my grandmother's blue dress. "You're next up! Put this on quickly please."

I took the dress from her, clutching it to my chest and feeling irrationally emotional about it. I didn't want it anywhere near this sordid business with Kevin. "We changed the item. Please have the dress sent up to my room."

She shook her head. "That's the only approved outfit. You wear that or you wear nothing."

The nervous thrill that unfurled in my belly wasn't entirely coming from anger or fear. Did I dare walk out there naked in front of half of society? I'd been topless at Reaper's party, but then everyone had been participating in the debauchery. Here they'd all be watching from where they sat fully clothed. They wouldn't be able to say a word about it outside the auction, so I didn't need to worry about tabloids, but they'd all *see me*.

"Help me with this zipper please," I said, turning my back to her.

Her eyes widened, but she unzipped it and patiently gathered all my clothing into a neat pile as I removed it.

She ushered me over to the edge of the curtain, where I could hear Reaper bantering with the audience. I peered out, but the lights were too bright to identify anyone sitting out there.

They were all about to see me naked. I'd never known nervousness like this, trembling that seemed to ripple out from my lower back where knots of tension twisted and made it hard to breathe.

But this was *my* body. Mine to cover or expose. Mine to offer to another person.

"The next item will be different from what was shown in the viewing." Mutters and annoyed chatter broke out, but Reaper held up a hand. "I know...I know. Some of you were *so* eager to get your hands on that cursed dress. But I think you'll be delighted to learn you can get your hands on a more...intimate part of the Bryson family."

He held out a hand in my direction with a wicked smile on his face for the audience, but the reassurance in his eyes was all for me.

I slid my shaking hand into his steady one...and stepped out into the spotlight.

32

K evin King is going to kill me.*

It was the only coherent thought in my head as I found him in the front row and faltered midstep at the unmasked rage on his face. The muscles in his neck twitched, and his breathing made his chest pump aggressively, but he continued sitting there without saying a word.

Of course, he was in the front row like he'd wanted to be close enough to see the pain in my expression as I was forced to auction something precious to me. If Reaper hadn't intervened, King would've made me stand on this stage and model it. Now he had the best seat in the house to watch his former-virgin bride sully herself.

No one said a word. It had been quiet before, but this was different. It was the silence before an atomic bomb went off.

Soon enough, everyone started talking all at once, and Reaper

* CLOSER—Nine Inch Nails

used the noise to say against my ear, "You could've warned me
you were coming out naked, little brat." His gloved hand stroked
over my hip, and even amid my anxiety, my body responded.
"Now my dick is hard, and I've got a whole auction to get
through..."

"Would you like some assistance with that?" I murmured.

His chuckle burned away the knots of fear in my stomach
with tendrils of lust. "You'd like that, wouldn't you, darling? If I
fucked you right here on this stage while they all watched. We'll
save that for when we get home... Not everyone here deserves to
see."

Reaper had only to tilt his head to silence the crowd again.
Then he smiled at them indulgently. "I'd always heard Kevin
King was a philanthropist, but I never knew he was this generous, sharing his perfectly pure treasure with all of us. Well..." He
circled me slowly. "You can all look." He swept a hand up the
curve of my waist to cup my breast. "But only one gets to touch."

The room shifted again as people went from staring at me to
staring at King; they were watching for his reaction, wondering
why he'd allow this. Almost any way he played it would make
him look weak.

He crossed an ankle over his knee and smirked like this was
all planned, like he was treating them to something special from
his wine cellar. His posture was for all of them. The murderous rage in his eyes, an expression of undiluted hatred...that was
reserved for me.

All I felt was triumph that I'd landed a blow that upset him
this much. I'd expected to feel terror and humiliation, and to

be sure, those feelings simmered beneath the surface. But the feeling at the forefront, the one that thundered through me? It was power—vicious, burn-the-fucking-world-down-around-you power.

Someone a few rows back shot to their feet, and I realized with a start that it was my father. Shame licked at my insides, but I extinguished it with a hateful glare that rivaled the look of loathing on his face.

Does this make you uncomfortable, Daddy? It has nothing on the suffering you sent me to endure.

I leaned into Reaper's touch, parting my lips to gasp, arching my back and silently begging for more with every desperate inhale. My father stormed from the room.

I'd never felt such tension in a crowd before. The urgent whispers and impatient shuffling. It was a dam about to break as soon as he opened the bidding.

How was Reaper going to control this?

Reaper's mouth against my ear barely moved as he growled, "Tap me and all this stops." Loud enough for everyone to hear, he drawled, "Kneel, my darling."

I held his hand as I lowered myself into a kneeling position, tucking my feet under me on the wooden floor.

"Spread your knees," Reaper commanded. I blushed as he pushed my knees open with his boot, giving everyone in the room a view of my pussy. He rubbed it with the top of his boot, and my cheeks heated when it came away with an unmistakable shine. "Darling, you're *soaked*. Does letting all these people see your lush little pussy turn you on?"

They expected me to cower and blush, but I looked defiantly at King and loudly said, "Maybe it does…"

King nodded and said something to the man next to him, who grinned and nodded eagerly. Had they just made some kind of deal? Was King going to find a way to make sure I didn't go to someone else? Or that I went to someone horrifying?

Reaper watched the interaction as well and strolled casually over to the stool on King's side of the stage, leaving me in the center, exposed and alone.

Not truly alone. I trusted him.

"Shall we start the bidding?" he purred. Reaper tilted his head. "I'll open it by personally bidding. One dollar."

I blinked in surprise, wondering if it was a joke, but stunned murmurs filled the room.

He's serious.

King jumped up from his seat and called out, "*He* can't bid in the auction!"

There was some muttering, but no one backed him up.

"Do you really think you're in a position to tell me what I can or can't do, Kevin?"

King shut his mouth. He shut his fucking mouth and sat the fuck down like a scolded child.

Reaper's smile was slow torture. "One dollar. The prize of the Bryson family, the wife of Mr. Kevin King, going for the low, *low* price of one dollar. Do I hear two."

It wasn't a question. Not the way he said it. He was toying with everyone, showing them just how much power he had even in this room full of the world's most notorious people.

"Do I hear two?" he said again deliberately, without breaking eye contact with King.

The crowd shifted uncomfortably, clearly on the verge of mutiny, but it was obvious none of them were going to do a thing about it. No one was willing to defy him.

High in a back corner, a man partially obscured in shadow looked at Reaper defiantly. He fingered his paddle like he might raise it just to make a point. My heart raced nervously.

"The Mad Wolf is getting ideas." Reaper's voice still had its playful edge, but there was something viciously pointed in the way he reminded the man, "Too bad he plans to gobble up another tasty morsel."

Reaper looked around, daring someone to cross him. When no one said a word, he sauntered over to the podium to bang a gavel. "Sold to the handsome devil onstage! Looks like Kevin King's wife is mine for the night. Don't worry, Kevin...I'll *treat her right*. You can collect her tomorrow at my party, after the hunt."

It was the most erotic display of power I'd ever seen.

"You were fucking magnificent, darling," Reaper purred as soon as he'd walked me backstage. I tugged his head down for a kiss, savoring the feel of his tongue against my mouth, wondering if there was time for more before the next auction item.

Someone cleared their throat.

Ophelia and Styx stood there grinning.

Styx offered me Reaper's jacket, the one I'd left with her at the party. "You're my hero."

Ophelia bit her fist as I tugged the jacket on. "Your husband's face was...chef's kiss. I still have lady wood from it."

Reaper gave her a look of distaste, then focused on me even though someone was waving him back to the stage. "They'll take you to one of the auction rooms where winners can enjoy their spoils. You'll be safe there, but I'll be late. Don't wait up for me."

———

It turned out *late* meant *early*. Reaper staggered into the room the next morning, waking me from a fitful sleep.

"When a notorious sex club owner bought a night with me, this wasn't exactly how I envisioned spending it," I mumbled.

He gave me a tired smile. "I'm surprised you overcame your brat tendencies and didn't push the panic button just to get my attention."

"Thought about it."

He kissed me deeply, but when he pulled back, I realized with a jolt of fear that he had blood on his hands.

"Not mine," he said reassuringly, heading into the bathroom to start the shower. "Not King's either, unfortunately."

I gave him some space, and he reemerged from the bathroom minutes later, looking utterly drained. "You weren't the only brat running amok last night. A mob princess reneged on the sale of her virginity—decided to offer it up to her husband instead." His eye roll made his feelings on the rights of husbands abundantly clear. "There was an attack from people who hadn't been invited and shouldn't have been able to get past my security. An item was stolen from the fucking vault, and two of my security people were injured in the midst of this collective chaos."

I lifted the covers and patted the bed. "C'mere."

He climbed in with me and rested his head on my lap. "Styx, Ophelia, and Grim have gone to bed. Az will wake me if anything else comes up."

I ran my fingers through his damp hair, and his eyes started to close.

"Mmm…it was a bad night, but coming back to this makes it all better."

I kissed his forehead. "It's about fucking time you let someone take care of you too."

"You thinking of claiming that job?" he murmured sleepily.

"Already have, darling. You're as much mine as I'm yours. Now get some sleep. You promised to take me to a party later."

He huffed a laugh. Then his breathing deepened, and he fell asleep.

I stared down at him, overwhelmed by my feelings. Everything had been worth it if we got to be together. I'd do whatever it took to secure a future with him.

33

The hunt was about to begin.*

Reaper famously hosted a play party every year to close out the auction, and this year's theme was predator and prey. It was as though he'd chosen the theme specifically for me, even though it had been planned for almost a year.

Reaper was in his usual shirtless attire with leather pants and platform boots that made him even taller. He presided over his party with easy authority, but he was less at ease than I'd seen him at one of his regular parties. There was more posturing here.

I'd already watched him turn some of the most influential people in the world away at the door, and he'd made the Mad Wolf from the auction stand there while Ruby Belmonte sucked Reaper's dick before he let them into the party. She must've been the tasty morsel the Mad Wolf had been waiting to bid on.

She looked like trouble. The kind of trouble I liked watching

* ANIMAL I HAVE BECOME—Three Days Grace

with my man, even if the Mad Wolf looked like he was considering some murder of his own. I could tell Reaper was testing him, making him prove he could stay in control no matter what shit Ruby pulled in here.

Reaper had a remarkable ability to juggle so many people's needs and weaknesses and conflicts simultaneously, all while maintaining an air of godlike nonchalance. I was barely managing to handle my own turmoil.

I was wearing an outfit borrowed from Styx—a pair of black leather pants and a black tank top—plus Reaper's jacket. It felt practical but sexy in a way that none of my usual attire ever did.

King had been watching me for hours across the party. Every time I caught his eye, I cringed in fear and wrapped my arms around myself, careful to let him see only the old Juliet, the one who'd be terrified she was about to be returned to her husband. To be fair, I *was* terrified, but it wasn't because I was going back to him. No matter what happened, I was *never* going back to him.

He leaned against the wall and smirked, ever the patient hunter.

I was done being patient.

King watched as I cornered Reaper behind the bar and splayed my hands across his bare chest, savoring the feel of his arms wrapping around me.

"Promise you'll be the one to catch me in the maze," I said urgently, loud enough for King to hear.

"I'll always find you," Reaper promised with a scalding kiss on the side of my neck. He worked a hand under my top and cupped one of my breasts, rolling my nipple between his fingers

as he nibbled the spot right under my ear, making me shiver with need.

Even in those awful circumstances, with my husband standing there likely plotting my death, I wanted Reaper beyond reason. I wove my fingers into his long hair and pulled his head down for a kiss that made my stomach swoop. He groaned low in his throat like he felt it too.

I pulled back. "Maybe we should just fuck in front of everyone, let my husband know what it looks like when I don't have to fake it..."

King heard me, and so did the people around us. They laughed with delighted shock, glancing back and forth between King and me.

"Looks like you might've lost your wife, Kevin." One of the guys nudged him like this was all a game.

Another man in King's position might've exploded, but King only tucked his lips between his teeth and nodded like he'd made a decision. His eyes flashed with hatred, but he turned and made his way to the edge of the room closest to the patio doors.

Reaper laughed along with everyone else, but there was tension in his jaw. "He's about to snap. You lure him there and then get the fuck out of the way, Juliet. We'll do the rest."

A subtle glance across the room reminded me of exactly who the *we* encompassed. Grim's frightening blue eyes bored into me with zero show of emotion, and I was struck by gratitude that he was on our side.

"I love you," I blurted to Reaper, leaning my face against his chest and listening to his heart pounding.

He shook his head. "None of that shit like you think this will go wrong. Tell me that when it's over."

For all that he wanted to deny these might be our final moments together, the kiss he gave me was deep and fast, but marked with possessive intensity. With one last significant look, he released me and shifted back into his role as host of the party.

King's eyes never left me when I made my way to collect a red wristband that would mark me as prey for the hunt. I hugged the jacket around me tighter to check the gun in my pocket, letting King think I was afraid.

Reaper strode to the center of the room, pulling everyone's attention to him. God, he was sexy when he was in his element.

"Those who want to play will choose to be predator...or prey. Prey flees. Predators pursue. And if a predator catches their prey, they can have their filthy way with them. For this game, we'll follow the tried-and-true safe words: 'Red' means to stop. 'Yellow' is a pause. All our lovely prey will be wearing red wristbands. Understood?"

I allowed someone to put a red wristband on me—the last time I'd let anyone think of me as prey. There would be no safe words in my hunt.

Everyone had to stay on the grounds, but most would be too excited to stray far from the party. Reaper looked straight at me as he said, "It's time. Prey, your five-minute head start begins...now."

I sprinted with the rest of the prey into the manor house but quickly split off from the group and headed for the hedge maze. I had five minutes to lay my trap, five minutes before King would be allowed to come for me.

The maze was eerily quiet and well lit since it was surrounded by surveillance cameras, but the hedges themselves were a dark tangle of leaves where anyone could be lurking. I'd been brave until I was alone, but now I trembled with nervous anticipation. Grim was already in here ahead of me, and Reaper would be right behind King. I just had to get to Grim.

I stifled a scream when I turned a corner and found my father standing there, aiming a gun straight at me. "Juliet. Glad I found you."

We'd been trying to goad King, but clearly I'd underestimated my behavior's effect on my father.

"How did you know I'd be here?" I blurted when it became clear he wasn't going to lower the weapon.

He narrowed his eyes. "Your husband told me just before the hunt. Had a chat with him last night, and we came to realize we'd both be better off with you dead. We can play the pity of your tragic death to make him untouchable in an election." His face twisted with hatred. "You're a disgrace to the Bryson name. I should shoot you now, but I want you to watch your whore boyfriend die first."

Adrenaline surged through my body so rapidly, it drowned out the fear. I wouldn't let him hurt Reaper.

Could I draw my weapon faster than he'd pull the trigger? I had a gun in my pocket and a knife in each boot, yet I had still been fool enough to be caught off guard because I'd been focused on getting to Grim. I slid my hand into my pocket and palmed the gun.

"Toss it here," he barked in a voice he'd never used with me before.

I pulled it from my pocket but didn't throw it away yet.

I looked over his shoulder, hoping Grim would appear before King did. Surely he'd start working his way back soon if I didn't make it to the meeting point.

"Looking for the other one?" Terror squeezed my lungs when he blew a short whistle.

Grim walked around the corner behind my father with his hands up, and Eric followed with a knife against Grim's back.

No!

I thought I was going to puke, but Grim looked bored, like this was beneath him. As soon as my father turned back to me, Grim's eyes slowly tracked down to the gun that was still in my hand, then up and back, like he was indicating Eric behind him. He adjusted his wrist to show me he had a knife in his sleeve; then his eerily pale eyes flicked to my father. He wanted me to shoot Eric, and he'd take care of my father...which was good because I wasn't sure I could kill my own flesh and blood. Eric was another matter.

Grim made eye contact with me for an instant, making sure I understood, before he dropped the arm that held the knife so fast that for a split second, I couldn't even process what he'd done. But I raised my gun and shot Eric in the chest without a second thought.

My father fell to the ground with a knife protruding from between his shoulder blades. Eric dropped to his knees with blood leaking from the wound in his chest. He gasped twice, then collapsed.

I froze, trying to process how quickly it had happened. For all his faults, my father was a monumental figure in my life, and

now he lay dying before me. I waited for pain or grief to swallow me whole, but all I felt was relief. The puppet master would pull no more strings.

I exhaled slowly, steadying myself for the real fight ahead.

The world suddenly swung sideways, and the gun flew from my hand. Before I could make sense of what was happening, someone snatched me by the hair and fired two shots in Grim's direction. Grim disappeared, but I couldn't see if he was okay because the grip on my hair wrenched my neck in the other direction.

I cried out, and the grip tightened, shaking me roughly. "Shut up, bitch."

If I'd had any doubt it was King, I knew for certain once I heard his voice.

I tried to twist out of his grip, but he forced me to my knees just as Reaper turned a corner and strode toward us. His face contorted with rage when King aimed the gun at my head.

Terror consumed me as all my worst fears seemed to come to life. King was going to hurt the people I cared about and then kill me.

King looked back and forth between Reaper and Grim, the latter of whom was leaning around the turn on the other side of us. King had to know he wasn't getting out of this alive, which made him all the more dangerous.

He yanked on my hair again, jerking my body.

"Drop your weapons, or I blow her brains out."

"Don't!" I called out anxiously, earning me another rough jerk of my head.

Reaper and Grim ignored me, tossing their weapons to the ground.

Then Reaper edged toward us slowly and snarled, "You've only got time to kill one of us, you piece of shit. There's no way killing her would be as satisfying as killing the man who spent the night balls deep in your wife. Everyone saw me make you my bitch in that auction."

"Reaper, *no*!"

King laughed bitterly. "You're right." He released me and swung the gun toward Reaper. In a haze of frantic desperation, I lunged for the knife in my boot and drove it backward into King's stomach. He fired his weapon as he cried out in agony.

I screamed and ran for Reaper, reaching him just as his knees gave out. Shirtless as he was, it was easy to spot the bullet wound in his shoulder as blood ran from it. It had a clean exit wound and didn't appear to have hit anything major.

I glanced back to make sure King wasn't going to fire again. He had a knife embedded in his right hand as well as his stomach, and he'd dropped the gun. Grim must've thrown the knife at the same time as I stabbed King, throwing King's aim off enough to save Reaper from a fatal hit.

"He shot you!" I wept as I frantically pulled my shirt off and tried to staunch the wound.

Reaper's smile still took my breath away even when he was bleeding all over the ground. "You once asked me what could possibly be worth getting shot?" He put his hand on top of mine over the wound. "You. You're worth it."

"He could've killed you!" I tried to keep it together to

maintain pressure on his injury, but the horror of it all was catching up with me now that we were out of mortal peril. My whole body shook with shock.

He swiped a tear from my cheek. "Vampire, remember? Can't kill me with a regular bullet."

I choked out a laugh.

"You want to kill this motherfucker, or can I?" Grim said calmly from where he stood over King's pleading form. "I can keep pressure on that if you want to be the one to pull the trigger."

I'd imagined killing King too many times to count, had fantasized about the satisfaction it would give me. He sounded just like all his victims begging for mercy, but he'd find me no more merciful than he'd been. He didn't matter anymore. The real satisfaction was in knowing I'd survived him.

"You can," I said dismissively, and King started to weep. "He means nothing to me. The only man I've ever loved is right here."

Reaper pulled my head down to kiss me softly. "I love you too."

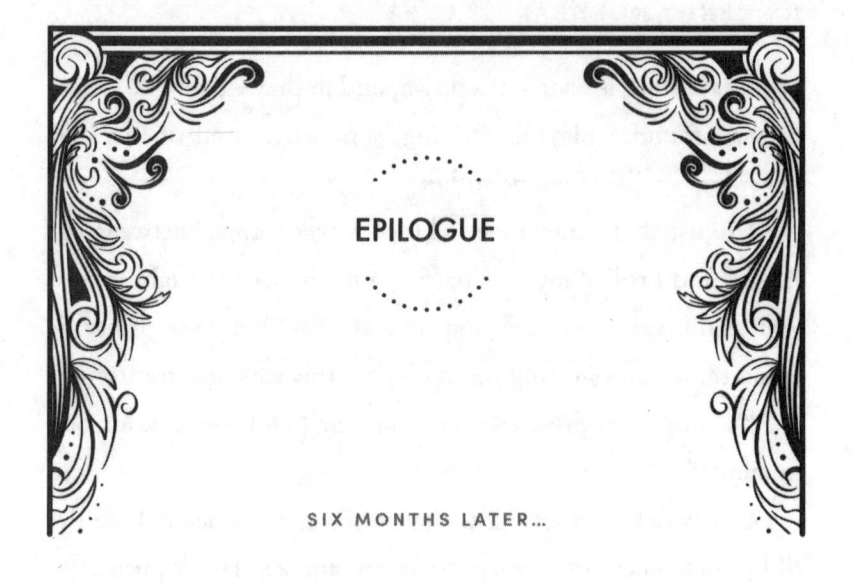

EPILOGUE

"What manner of depravity should we try tonight, darling?" Reaper tugged me onto his lap on his throne, and I melted against him. "Suspension bondage? A vac bed? Maybe some electroplay?"*

For tonight's monthly Petite Mort party, he looked like Thranduil, with his long hair down and a silver crown atop his head. A kilt made of white linen wrapped around his waist but made it delightfully easy to reach beneath it and tease him. I wore only a gold chain around my waist, which he loved to tug on to pull me closer. After a lifetime of being told to cover up, it was liberating to own my body and reject any shame.

In the months we'd been free of my marriage, I'd been hungry for experience, and my pleasure Dom had been all too happy to oblige. There had been nights I'd wept in ecstasy and others where I'd laughed until my stomach hurt at the joy of it all. We'd

* TOO SWEET—Hozier

both learned to let our walls down, and in that vulnerable space, we had found a playful, thrilling, supportive kind of love. I'd never known life could be so *fun*.

I adjusted him under me so his cock was trapped between my thighs, and I rolled my hips back against him. "I thought maybe you could watch me with someone else?" We'd done plenty of exhibitionist acts in front of others, but this was new territory.

"Mmm..." he growled against my ear. "Did you have anyone in mind?"

I surveyed the party, listening to his sultry voice tell me the filthy preferences of every guest in attendance. He skipped over a gorgeous blond woman in the crowd who was wearing a red corset and black lingerie with red platform heels. Her outfit fit the vibe, but something about her felt completely out of place. She was stiff and looked around the room with scorn.

"Who is that?" I nodded subtly in her direction.

"Joel Jeffries's daughter. Probably not a fun choice, darling."

I froze with alarm. "The ultraconservative billionaire?"

"The very same. Another one of his desperate attempts to infiltrate and destroy our club."

"*Then why did you let her in?*" The guy had been trying through means fair and foul to expose all the club members and shut us down.

Reaper nuzzled my neck. "Az is dealing with the lapse in door security, but facial recognition caught it within seconds of her being here."

I turned to face him. "She's going to out everyone now that she's seen them."

His villainous feline smile shouldn't have turned me on. "She'd like to. But to do that, she'd need to make it out of here. Grim is going to see to it that doesn't happen."

I narrowed my eyes, wondering what I needed to say to get him to spare her. He'd do anything to protect the club, and given the extremes his enemies were willing to go to, he sometimes had to retaliate with equal brutality. Yet I still wasn't used to it.

"Oh, don't look at me like that, darling. We're not going to kill her. Grim is going to make her comfortable in his guesthouse for a while, so she won't be able to tell anyone what she's seen."

Grim wouldn't touch her, but being trapped in a house alone with him was the stuff of nightmares.

"With a father like that, she may have had no more choice than I did."

His smile dropped. "She had a choice. It was her idea to come here, her idea to use deception to weasel her way in. She doesn't deserve your sympathy based on the things I've learned about her. She'd only use it against you."

Grim leaned against a column, watching her. I shuddered, wondering how she couldn't feel his deadly eyes on her. Like that was the very moment she felt them, she turned and flinched when she saw him lurking in the shadows. She all but ran into one of the side rooms but made the mistake of going into Grim's lounge.

It only had one exit. Grim stalked after her, pulling the doors to the lounge closed behind him.

She was cornered. And the embodiment of death himself was coming for her.